Slave Island

Simon Finch was born in Rio de Janeiro, where his father served in the Diplomatic Corps, and was educated abroad before attending university in England for studies in Classical History. Now making his home in Manila, he travels widely to lecture on Slavery and Ancient Customs. His first venture into novel writing was the ambitious and successful Voyager trilogy: *Golden Voyage*, *Pagan Voyager* and *Voyager in Bondage*, all available in Pan. Moving to the eighteenth century with *Slave Island*, he reveals the same talent for evoking the atmosphere of a bygone age in a story of epic proportions.

Also by Simon Finch
in Pan Books

Golden Voyager
Pagan Voyager
Voyager in Bondage

Simon Finch

Slave Island

Pan Books London and Sydney

First published 1983 by Souvenir Press Ltd
This edition published 1984 by Pan Books Ltd,
Cavaye Place, London SW10 9PG
9 8 7 6 5 4 3 2 1

ISBN 0 330 28244 1

Photoset by Parker Typesetting Service, Leicester
Printed and bound by
Richard Clay (The Chaucer Press) Ltd, Bungay, Suffolk

For Tony McCord

Historical note

In the Eighteenth Century, the sudden rise in slave traffic to the New World distracted the public's eye from the Ottoman Empire's enslavement of Europeans, and the selling of them in Arab bazaars or Turkish slaveports dotted around the Mediterranean and Indian Ocean. History still focuses little attention upon the fact that the currents of slavery also flowed from West to East, that there had been a centuries-old tradition for Muslim countries to capture and sell *N'zranis* – 'white infidel slaves'.

Simon Finch

Contents

Book One	***Vandal Witch***	9
Book Two	**Castle of a Thousand Wives**	79
Book Three	**Slave Island**	149
Book Four	**The Leather Triangle**	223
Book Five	**Pirate Masters**	269

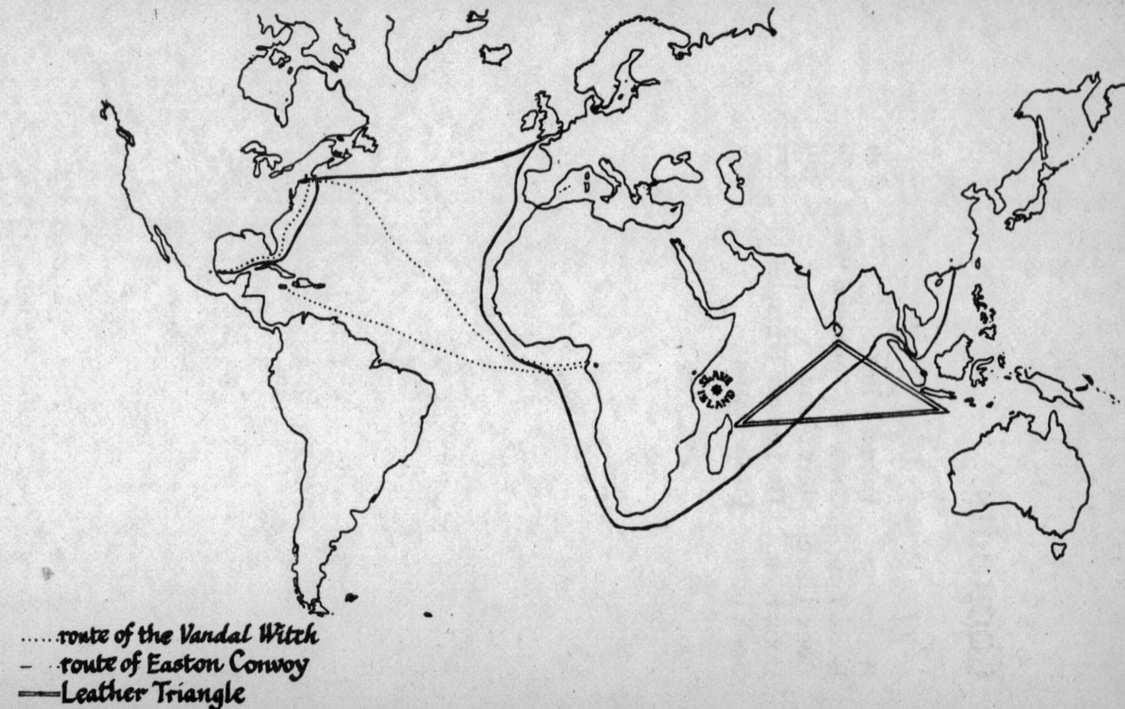
SLAVE ISLAND
route of the Vandal Witch
route of Easton Convoy
Leather Triangle

Book One
Vandal Witch

1

A heavy New England rain beat down on seven convoy ships tossing at anchor in Boston's wide-mouthed harbour on that foul April morning in 1761. Strong northerly winds crashed inky black waves over their bulwarks, washing white foam across careening decks, making the seven vessels rise and fall, tilt and dip, dance a hellish dance to the wild tune of the storm gale.

Violent and unexpected, the springtime tempest was the worst weather the seven convoy ships had encountered since departing five weeks earlier from the Mexican port of Vera Cruz, on the first leg of a merchant venture bound for China. The convoy had peacefully crossed the Gulf of Mexico, passed through the treacherous coral reefs dotting the Straits of Florida and climbed the eastern seaboard of North America, enjoying clement weather, clear skies, strong winds; until the first gulls began abandoning the convoy's wake off Nantucket Island, the disappearance of the scavenger birds being a harbinger of stormswept Massachusetts Bay.

Boston was a grim, grey Hades in comparison with Mexico's coral studded paradise. Forked lightning flashed across the northern sky. Thunder boomed beyond the peaked cedar roofs lining the colonial harbour. The Union Jack had been quickly pulleyed down the white flagpole fronting the harbourmaster's office. But roustabouts in oilskins continued their morning work, bending low against the howling wind as they carried bundles of animal pelts and tobacco leaves from warehouses to barges which would haul the freight across choppy waves to the newly-arrived convoy.

A small shore boat, rowed by two hunched oarsmen, transported a single passenger from the wharf to the cluster of convoy ships listing in the harbour. The oarsmen knowledgeably aimed the snub nose of the small wooden boat directly into the tallest waves, avoiding being capsized by their force; then applied muscle to the oars and continued carrying their lone passenger to a black schooner included in the ranks of the merchant convoy, a trim two-master named *Vandal Witch*.

As the shore boat bobbed and dived on its choppy course towards the black schooner, the wind flapped a rope ladder from the schooner's port entry. When the small boat finally drew alongside the schooner, one oarsman stood in the driving rain to help the passenger to his feet. But the passenger – a young man dressed in a long drill coat soaked to the athletic shape of his body, his blond hair plastered by rain to his skull – leaped unassisted from the stern and grasped eagerly in the wind for the rope ladder. He finally seized a wooden rung and, gripping a firm hold with the clench of both fists, he jumped from the shore boat and began a rapid climb up the hull of the schooner.

At the top of the ladder loomed the large, bulky outline of a man, a shapeless form of canvas and oilcloth and whiskers who bellowed down through the howling wind, 'Aye, mate! What business brings you aboard?'

The climbing passenger paused long enough on the wind-tossed ladder to see the whiskered creature blocking his entry, recognising that the large man showed no sign of allowing him aboard. The younger man, quick-witted and agile, began swinging from left to right on the rope ladder, swaying back and forth like a pendulum with the help of the gale and, in one quick leap, he hoisted both legs over the port railing and landed upright on the deck.

'You cheeky devil!' The whiskered man leaned closer to the newcomer's face, surprised with what he saw, 'And look! You're no more than a lad! A snot-nosed young lad come jumping aboard the *Witch*.'

The young man, brushing long, wet hanks of hair from his forehead, courteously extended his hand, while breathlessly introducing himself. 'The name's Billy Peake. I've got cargo stowed in the hold of this ship and I've come to take it ashore.'

The bellicose man glanced down at the proffered hand. 'You have, have you?'

The young man shouted through the deafening gale, 'I've got papers to show that we – my brother and me – are legal owners of cargo you loaded in Mexico.'

The big seaman grimaced. 'I don't care if you're King George himself and your brother's Louis of France. I'm Captain Kerr. Captain Stan Kerr, sonny. And nobody comes bouncing aboard my ship, swinging legs, shaking hands, shouting orders about removing no bloody ingots from my hold.'

'Ah! You say "ingots"! So you do carry our silver on the *Vandal Witch*!'

Captain Stan Kerr narrowed his porcine eyes and reappraised the rain-drenched young man calling himself Billy Peake; he judged him to be well fed and quick witted, probably the son of a gentleman, a privileged young Englishman who was most likely one of the many young adventurers travelling to England's farflung colonies, an outspoken, strong-minded youth who lived with and worked alongside more modestly born men out of choice rather than necessity. Captain Kerr considered such young men anathema compared to his own, struggling walk of life.

Turning away from Billy Peake, Captain Kerr grumbled, 'Go back ashore, laddie, and acquaint yourself with Mr Gabriel Easton. He's the guv'nor running this convoy. I've got a captain's work to do.'

Billy Peake tagged across the slippery planks behind Kerr. 'I plan to see Easton. But I heard your schooner arrived carrying silver ingots from Vera Cruz and I wanted to verify the rumour.'

Kerr scowled. 'You've done verified it, ain't you? Now away with you.'

Billy Peake began, 'But Mr Easton assured me the silver was to be shipped aboard a merchant gunner named the *Lion's Lair*.'

Kerr shouted over his shoulder, 'Well, it ain't, is it?

There's six other ships in Easton's convoy and the *Lair* ain't one of them.'

'Why not?'

'Because the *Lair*'s been laid up in Kingston, that's why not.'

Kerr continued walking towards the mizzenmast, wishing one of the high-washing waves would crash across the deck and sweep this meddling Billy Peake into the harbour.

Forked lightning flashed across Boston's stormy sky. Thunder boomed louder beyond the rows of cedar warehouses. The *Vandal Witch* continued tossing at anchor in the harbour.

Billy Peake moved alongside the mizzenmast to face Captain Kerr. 'You mentioned Kingston, sir. Did Mr Easton replace the *Lion's Lair* with your ship in Kingston? Did the *Lion's Lair* start out from Vera Cruz and sail only as far as Jamaica?'

Captain Kerr's single wish at that moment was to depart from Boston Harbour with no interference in his plans for the future, his own ambitions for the silver.

He replied with the most civil words he could muster. 'Mr Peake, it's clear to me you don't approve of my brig no more than I approve of you sticking to me like . . . some pup wanting tit.'

Billy wiped rain from his face. 'I don't mean to trouble you, sir. But I do think I deserve some kind of explanation why this schooner's carrying my silver to China instead of the ship promised.'

Kerr was weary and his temper thin. 'I know nothing about promises, laddie, except work needing to be done at hand, victualling and provisioning this ship for the next part of the voyage, the long haul across the Atlantic to England.'

Billy leaned forward to shout over the whistle of the wind. 'But it was agreed three years ago to ship our silver to China on a merchant gunner, Captain Kerr. No offence to you, but your schooner's too light, with too little defences.

It'll be July or August before you reach Africa. That's winter time down there. Your good ship will be nothing but shipwrecked lumber before you round the Cape.'

Captain Kerr leaned towards Billy, shouting, 'I don't have time to waste, youth, but let me tell you one thing. You don't have to teach Stan Kerr nothing about the sea and its seasons. No, laddie boy, no. By profession I ply what sailors call "The Slaver's Triangle". I sail from England to Africa to the Caribbean. I know about tropical storms and hemispheres and the differences of summers and winters topsy-turvy.'

Billy Peake stared at the pig-faced man chinned with red whiskers. 'You're a . . . slaver?'

'Aye, the *Vandal Witch* and me are slavers. And right proud of the fact we are, too. We've been slavers for more than ten years.'

'What's a slaver doing in a merchant convoy?'

'Gabriel Easton's making it worth my while to sell him a year of my life by joining this bleeding China convoy. It's Easton you'd best complain to, lad, and not me. Look up Easton, and leave me and my *Witch* to get on with our business. China's calling our name.'

'I also am going to China,' Billy shouted through the gale. 'I booked passage from Easton to sail on the ship carrying this silver.'

It was the scurrilous Captain Kerr's turn to be surprised. 'You have passage, boy? Passage to sail aboard the *Witch* all the way to bleeding China?'

Billy Peake nodded, explaining, 'To sail on the ship carrying the silver. My brother and I laid careful plans over the past three years. Our father died in '58, the Lord rest his soul and we're investing our inheritance in silver mined in Mexico. That was Andrew's idea – Andrew's my brother. He lives in the East Indies. On the island of Sumatra. It was Andrew's idea to ship the ingots of silver to China where silver's more precious than gold. Andrew's the clever one in the family. I've been beside myself the past six weeks worrying about the silver being loaded in Mexico. My nerves are a wreck. Mr Easton told me I should calm down and concentrate on settling my affairs here in Boston rather than sailing to Mexico to oversee the loading of the silver aboard the convoy. You see, Mr Easton and my brother worked out the details carefully between them, my brother being a sea captain himself and–'

Captain Kerr had not expected to hear a life story; he interrupted Billy's long-winded account, saying, 'Lad, I don't know and I don't care to know about your kin and their doings and what Easton told you to do. But let me tell you one thing. The *Witch* ain't outfitted to carry no passengers. If Easton took money to carry you and your cargo halfway round the world to bleeding China, that's his concern and yours. But if you sail aboard the *Witch* you fare no better than the crew. Maybe worse.'

Billy quickly reassured him. 'Oh, I'm not one to worry about comforts, sir. I've slept with nothing but a horse blanket and been grateful for it. I've gobbled stale biscuits for supper like they're roast beef with all the trimmings. No, I'm not worried about myself, Captain Kerr. But I do want to assure safe passage for the cargo. The silver represents a fortune to me and my brother. All our hopes and dreams ride in your ship.'

Billy Peake was innocent. Tall, muscular like a milk-fed farmboy; innocent as a lad fresh from Dorset. Captain Stan Kerr saw all those traits and he began to think how he might still be able to proceed with his own plans for the silver.

Kerr used a bluff. 'Unload your damned ingots, lad, if you have no trust in the *Witch*.'

Billy shook his head. 'No, I won't unload the silver. Not yet.'

'Then keep your mouth shut.'

Billy flashed a smile. 'They say such a thing's impossible for me to do, Captain Kerr. They say I'd talk back to the devil himself.'

Kerr was in no mood for humour. 'If the storm doesn't stick to the heavens, laddie, stand warned, I sail at tomorrow's dawn. Nobody needs you or your silver for this convoy. There's plenty cargo going begging in Boston.'

'I'll see Mr Easton at the trading company. Then I'll come back and give you my decision.'

Captain Kerr's estimation of Gabriel Easton was low. Knowing that Easton was a well-seasoned twister, he guessed that if the Boston trader had already prevented this talkative young lad from travelling to Mexico when the silver was being loaded aboard the *Vandal Witch*, then he could certainly be counted upon to make the young bumpkin shut his big mouth now.

'Aye, you go see Mr Easton, laddie. You go see Mr Gabriel Easton. He's your friend in this matter, not me.'

Billy Peake turned away from Captain Kerr, glancing at the few guns lining the deck as he moved towards the port entry. He realized his fears were true, that the *Vandal Witch* was virtually defenceless against buccaneers or preying Dutch or French brigs, that he was correct to want a larger, stronger ship to carry the ingots across the Atlantic and up the Indian Ocean.

Too absorbed in his thoughts, Billy did not notice a man climbing aboard from a second shore boat which had also braved the choppy waters from the wharf.

Quickly stepping aside for the boarding passenger, Billy saw a tall, broad-shouldered man passing through the entry port, a man who was handsome in an arrogant, nordic manner, and carrying a coil of leather bullwhips in his gloved fist.

Billy, gripping the rope ladder to descend the hull, wondered, 'Now if the *Vandal Witch* is no longer a slaver, why's a man boarding with so many . . . whips?'

2

A facial scar – shaped like the forked lightning flickering over the colonial town of Boston – disfigured the left cheek of the merchant, Gabriel Easton. Easton stood inside the snug warmth of his Fort Hill office, idly fingering the jagged scar as he looked through the rain pelting against a mullioned window and listened to Billy Peake complaining about the inadequacies of the *Vandal Witch*.

It was no secret to Easton that Billy Peake was an agreeable but talkative young man, generally even-tempered, interested like manly young men his age in grog, the companionship of females of easy virtue and entertaining hopes of adventure and riches.

There were two things, however, which separated the tow-headed young man from other colonials in the Massachusetts settlement, according to Easton's estimation. The first was the fact that Billy's older brother, Andrew, was betrothed to marry Easton's twenty-year-old daughter, Catherine. The second was that Billy and Andrew Peake had stumbled on the idea of buying silver in Mexico and reselling it in the Chinese market-place, an idea which promised to turn their modest inheritance into a vast fortune. Easton planned on profiting from the venture more than by shipping the ingots to Canton, more than either of the two Peake brothers suspected he would gain from the venture.

Easton stood at his office window, watching the ships' booms, masts and spars restlessly tilting below him in the wind-tossed harbour, patiently waiting until Billy paused in his complaints. Easton seized the moment to say casually, 'You do know, Billy, you no longer make decisions for yourself in matters concerning the silver.'

Billy, dripping a puddle of rain-water from his soaked clothing, promptly assured him, 'I will answer to my brother, Mr Easton. Oh, no worry about that. I'm prepared to accept full responsibility for any actions I take.'

Easton laughed at Billy's naïvety. 'Affairs have gone farther than you think, Billy. But even if it were just . . . family to consider, there's now more than you and Andrew involved in this venture. Catherine's future is also at stake. My beloved daughter's security depends on the profits derived from selling your silver to the Chinese.'

Billy began, 'Sir, if this convoy fails, your daughter . . .'

'Fails?' Easton turned from the window. 'Fails? My convoy will not fail. I failed once in life and I'm grabbing more heartily at this second chance I've made for myself here in the Colonies.'

Billy realized that Gabriel Easton was still haunted by the bankruptcy which had driven him and his daughter out of England, and he said generously, 'You are doing a good and fine job, sir, with the trading company.'

'I'm doing an excellent job, Billy Peake. A superlative job. When I came to New England to start afresh in life, I swore that nothing, absolutely nothing, would stand between me and riches this time around. Nothing. Now look at me. I'm the first merchant to send a convoy from the Americas to the Orient. I'm hop-scotching a fleet of seven ships from Mexico to Boston to England, sailing down past Cadiz, along the west coast of Africa, round the Cape, up the Indian Ocean to the China seas. I'm the first man to send minerals and sugar from Mexico and the West Indies. The first man to ship tobacco to the Orient from the Virginias; furs and lumber from New England and Canada; cotton and skullery from England. I will bring back teas, silks, nutmegs, pepper, all the precious spices of the East Indies, the Orient and China. Billy! China! Do you know how far away China is from –' Easton gestured to the grey harbour below him – 'Boston?'

'Sir, I know your venture is of vast compass and I commend you. I do truly commend you. But I also consider the dangers awaiting your fleet. Storms, foul seasons, French ships, pirates, buccaneers . . .'

'Pirates? Buccaneers?' Easton scoffed at the idea.

'Rubbish! There were more pirates plaguing the Caribbean than in any ocean still to be traversed.'

'Sir, I must argue with you on that point too. Andrew frequently writes to me about pirates, reporting there are more privateers, English as well as Turkish, Spanish and Dutch, sailing the Indian Ocean . . .'

Gabriel Easton was no longer listening to Billy; his attention had shifted to a man walking far below his window, a lone man braving the storm, a man leaving the harbour, the wind snapping his long cloak as he climbed an incline towards Easton's redbrick house sitting on the hill opposite the office.

'Damn that Dutch fornicator,' Easton cursed to himself and again began rubbing the jagged scar which marked his face.

Turning away from the window, Gabriel Easton tried to forget about the Dutchman approaching his house and decided to break the bad news to Billy Peake about the silver, but to broach the subject gently, indirectly.

Looking at the puddle of rain spreading on the floor under Billy's chair, Easton raised his eyes to study Billy's athletic body crushed into the small wooden chair and began, 'Lad, how old are you?'

Billy's eyes showed surprise. He did not understand why Easton would be asking such a question at this moment. He haltingly replied, 'Twenty-two, sir.'

'Have you a sweetheart? A lass you court?'

Billy shook his head; he considered the Welsh girl he had been sleeping with for the last months to be no different from other girls who surrendered their chastity to him with a shudder and a flash of blood on the sheeting.

'Do you visit Faith Wiley's brothel on Front Street?'

Billy furrowed his brow. 'Sir, I do not know what these questions have to do with our silver being shipped aboard the *Vandal Witch*.'

Easton realized that Billy was going to be deeply disturbed by his announcement, and he cautiously said,

'You keep talking about the *Witch*, Billy.'

Billy argued, 'But you promised Andrew and me that the silver would be carried aboard the *Lion's Lair.*'

'The *Lion's Lair* is no longer in the convoy.'

'So I discovered. Less than an hour ago. But how long have you known that the *Vandal Witch* was replacing the *Lair*? And why weren't we informed before now?'

Easton coolly asked, 'What makes you think Andrew did not instigate the change of ships himself?'

'Andrew? Change plans?' Billy laughed. 'No, Mr Easton. I have not heard from Andrew about any change of plans. In fact, I have not heard from Andrew in three months. That's one of the reasons I chose to remain here in Boston instead of going to Mexico. A post ship was due and I did not want to miss receiving any late despatch from Andrew. But I have received nothing, Mr Easton, and I'm afraid I have no choice but to tell you to –'

Taking a deep breath, knowing he was making an enormous decision, Billy bravely continued, 'I'm afraid I have no choice but to tell you to cancel our participation in your convoy. I cannot risk shipping our investment aboard a schooner. The voyage would be far too dangerous. It's not only the matter of distance. It's also the matter of defence. The *Witch* has only a few ten pounders on deck.'

Easton looked into the storm as he announced, 'I'm afraid it's too late even to contemplate removing the silver from the *Witch*.'

Billy sat to the edge of the chair. 'What do you mean, too late?'

Giving a deep sigh, Easton said, 'Billy, I thought you knew about the new contract. But obviously you don't or you wouldn't be speaking as you do.'

'Contract? What new contract?'

'The contract your brother signed with me, Billy. The contract witnessed in Sumatra by the Port Secretary at Fort Marlborough.'

Billy momentarily thought he was dreaming, that he

was fast asleep in his attic room on Spinnaker Lane and having a nightmare.

He asked, 'Andrew signed a . . . new contract with you? Without telling . . . me?'

Easton remained facing the window, both hands clasped behind the back of his frock coat. 'I thought you knew about it, Billy. But if your own brother didn't tell you, I'm afraid that matter rests between you two.'

'A new contract?' Billy repeated. 'What does it say?'

'Your brother sent me authorisation to transport your silver on the first ship leaving Vera Cruz. The *Lion's Lair* was unable to sail from Jamaica but, fortunately, I was able to entice Captain Kerr to join the convoy . . . at a considerable cost to my own pocket, I may add.'

Dazed, Billy asked, 'Andrew sent you a letter? A letter of authorization to change ships? Why did he send it to . . . you?'

'It is my convoy.'

'And part my silver!' boomed Billy.

'Andrew has very good reasons for his action. There is a new political upheaval in China. The group called the Red Lotus threatens to close all ports, including Canton. And Andrew, being close by on the island of Sumatra, knows these facts about the East and expressly wants the silver to arrive in China within the year. Those were his firm orders and, consequently, if I release so much as one ingot from the convoy, I would be liable to answer to your brother in a court of law.'

'What about . . . me?' Billy demanded. 'What about answering to me? My orders? The silver's half mine!'

Gabriel Easton had learnt many years ago to retain a calm, dignified voice when dealing with men who had lost their composure.

He began, 'Billy, did you or did you not entrust your brother to negotiate an original document with my company?'

'I did, but–'

'Billy, did you or did you not extend legal powers to your

brother to assign the bill of lading to my agents in Vera Cruz?'

'I did, true–'

'And were you not free to go to Mexico yourself, Billy?'

'Yes, but–'

'Billy, I respect that any correspondence which passes between you and Andrew is your own affair. I merely ask that my professional correspondence be my own affair.'

Billy stared at the back of Easton's frock coat. 'You are telling me you have a written contract in your possession, new papers signed by my brother, entitling you – and you alone – to ship our silver in whatever ship you choose? Even without my consent?'

Easton stared out of the mullioned window. 'I have such a document, yes, Billy.'

'You have it now? Here? In Boston?'

'I do, Billy. In this very office.'

Easton, foreseeing the next question, added, 'It's there, on my desk.'

Looking at the neat piles of paper on the birds-eye maple table placed against the wall, Billy asked, 'Can I see it? Examine it?'

'Of course. Private though it is, of course you may examine it. It's there, by the inkhorn. In fact I was just preparing to take it, along with the roll muster, out to Captain Kerr.'

Billy reached to the table, pushed aside a lead paperweight decorated with Easton's trading company insignia, a yellow snake on a green field, and lifted a long sheet of vellum covered with three variations of whorled script, neatly executed lines of indigo ink sealed at the bottom with an official red wax insignia and affixed with a blue ribbon.

The document was dated alongside the florid signature of Billy's brother: *Andrew Reynolds Peake, Esquire*.

Billy lowered the contract. 'How did Andrew have time to send you this when I haven't heard one word from him?'

'Your brother most probably sent you a letter explaining

his actions.' Easton's tone had softened; he again sounded concerned, avuncular.

Billy's voice rose. 'But I tell you, I received nothing. Nothing! If there was time for you to get this new contract from Sumatra, then certainly there was time for me to receive a letter informing me of such powers being given to you.'

'Your letter most probably got lost at sea.'

Billy clenched his fists in frustration. 'Damn it to hell! What can I do?'

'Nothing.'

'You knew about this all along yet I was told not a word. Not one word. Why didn't you tell me before today?'

'Have I nothing better to do than be a go-between for you and your brother?'

Billy shook his head in bewilderment, repeating, 'What can I do?'

Easton offered, 'If you don't approve of the *Vandal Witch*, you don't have to sail with the silver. That decision is still yours.'

Billy's laugh was empty. 'Oh, thank you, Mr Easton. Thank you very much indeed. But I'll sail on the *Vandal Witch*. I may hate every minute of the damned voyage, but I'll sail with the silver if for no other reason than to confront Andrew, and may Lord God be my witness –'

Easton interrupted Billy's acrimony, saying in a brighter voice, 'You keep asking me what you should do, Billy. I may be a fool to continue humouring your requests but I have one last suggestion.'

Billy glared at him.

'You mentioned Faith Wiley's house. The brothel in the harbour.'

Billy corrected, '*You* mentioned Faith Wiley's house, Mr Easton.'

'Did I? Perhaps I did. No matter. But as you are obviously tense and badly in need of some . . . calming pastime, perhaps you should consider visiting that woman's establishment. I give you that advice as one man to another.'

'And that may be the best blasted advice you've ever given me, Mr Easton.'

Billy Peake angrily left the Boston Trading Company, feeling betrayed, confused, not knowing what to do now or in the future.

3

Billy Peake slumped down Fort Hill from Gabriel Easton's office, thinking of his three closest friends in Boston: Dirk Kendrick, the stabler with whom he had frequently ridden through Massachusetts, Maryland and the Virginias, and to whom he had originally spoken about buying farmland to work and live on as a settler; Crab Lewis, the apple-cheeked Welshman who ran the grog shop on Beacon Alley and also dreamed of some day owning a Crown lease in the Colonies; Bennet Wylam, a young baronet from Essex who had shed his family title and was trying to make a success as a printer in Boston.

Billy had bade goodbye to these three good and true friends last night; today, they were at work, as were other people he knew in Boston, friends from all walks of life, colonials like himself making their homes in this brick-and-board community quickly growing from a religious settlement into one of the leading port towns of New England. Billy considered seeking out one or all of his friends, relating the story about Gabriel Easton, the *Vandal Witch*, his own brother trying to cheat him.

Remembering how he and his friends had all said their farewells, Billy did not want to return to them with a story of woe, and he decided against visiting any or all of them.

Next, he considered the idea of paying a visit to the office of Ned Barton, a solicitor involved in the underground movement of American Colonists seeking political independence from the mother country. Could Barton help him as a lawyer? Billy realized that he had no solid evidence to present to Barton that Easton – or his brother – was trying to swindle him. He also knew he had little or no time to seek an injunction to prevent Easton's convoy from sailing out of Boston with the silver.

Pausing in the driving rain, Billy weighed the idea planted like a poison seed in his brain by Gabriel Easton.

Should he go to the brothel? Narrow Street was nearby; he could find shelter and warmth there; also, he considered how long he would be at sea, how many days – months – he might have to wait until the next opportunity to satisfy his manly needs. And did not sailors and soldiers indulge their lust before leaving on a battleship or marching away in battalions?

Briefly, he considered visiting Ann Cricky, the young lady with whom he had spent the night. But he knew she was carding wool for her father and had no time to lift her skirts for him.

Billy stood at the foot of Fort Hill, huddled beneath a chandler's swing sign creaking back and forth in the storm; he thought how he was planning to sail halfway around the world, but, here he was, idling in the rain, not knowing what to do, where to go, how to spend his last few hours in Boston. It was too early to collect his belongings from his room on Spinnaker Lane. He had suddenly lost all sense of time, purpose, existence.

Oh, would he ever grow up and know his own mind? Truly be an adult man?

Faith Wiley, a hard-featured woman wearing a white cotton cap tied under her chin, eyed Billy suspiciously as he stood, drenched with rain, on the threshold of her unmarked bordello on Narrow Street, near Boston harbour.

Billy, stomping his boots, said, 'It's a hot drink I need and a companion to share it.'

Motioning for Billy to shed his dripping drill coat, Faith Wiley beckoned him into the cedar-shaked house and led him across a shadowy room to a small fire crackling on a field-stone hearth. She waved for a serving girl to bring a hot-buttered rum and, turning back to Billy, she said, 'You're just a lad. But I might have the recipe to dry you behind both ears, sonny boy.'

Billy, knowing that brothel keepers in Massachusetts Colony had to be cautious of the strict rules laid down by zealous Puritan leaders, respected the woman's careful manner with him. But the meeting with Gabriel Easton had left him in an irritable mood and he was tired of people always calling him a boy, of saying he was not 'dry behind the ears'.

He asked, 'Isn't shiny money from boys as good as coins from the linty pockets of old men, woman?'

'Oh, you've got a temper under that soggy clothing, have you?'

'A temper as well as a lot of randiness!'

'Mind you, I have to spit on my finger and hold it up to the wind. I must see which way a wind's blowing.'

'If you lowered your eyes, woman, you'd see a bigger weather vane sticking out from between my legs.'

Faith Wiley, grinning at Billy's rude remark, showed a mouthful of wooden pegs for teeth. 'I always question new visitors. I don't relish being sent to the Puritans' bloody gallows. And as I haven't seen you here before, why should I let you in without a question?'

Nodding her head with satisfaction, she said, 'But apart from seeing you're a spirited lad, you look too healthy to be the son of a mewling churchman. I'd guess you're a sailor who floated into Boston only this morning on the China-bound convoy.'

Billy took an earthenware mug of steaming rum from the serving girl and muttered, 'I'm sailing out on the China convoy and I say, may it be cursed and sink down to hell!'

Faith Wiley scolded, 'Lad, don't curse the fleet you sail on! And if you don't have respect for yourself, at least think about the good fortune the convoy will bring to this town.'

'You worry about Boston's elders clapping you in irons for running whores yet you still pray for their prosperity?'

'Prosperity brings gold to my door, insolent boy.'

'I'm no boy, understand, and I also say it's a sad town that prospers on the stench of hypocrisy – and there's no worse hypocrite in this damnable town than Gabriel Easton who organised the convoy.'

'Hear you now! You've the face of an angel but the tongue of a viper! For shame!'

Billy took a long drink from the earthen mug, licked his lips and muttered, 'I mean no offence to you, mother, but I've reason to curse the day I ever heard of Mr Easton and his seven ships bound for China.'

'Stop your cursing and swearing, sonny boy, and just wait here by the fire while your old mother sees what she can find for you upstairs in her pantry.'

Faith Wiley turned away from Billy Peake, chuckling to herself about his irritable mood as she mounted the narrow plank steps leading to the bordello's upper storey.

Billy, left alone by the fire, sank down onto a bench to enjoy the rum's warmth and try to calm his temper. Remembering he had not eaten one bite of food yet today, he realized he could easily and quickly become intoxicated. But, taking another long swallow of the sweet liquor, he reminded himself to enjoy a town's pleasures because he would be a long time at sea.

Mellowing with the rum's potency and the warmth from the crackling birch fire, Billy became aware that there were other men in the dimly lit room. One was a young man nodding asleep in a horsehair chair, and two sailors huddled together in a dark corner alongside the field-stone hearth.

One sailor, his red curls glistening in the dancing flames, leaned forward on a stool and said to his companion, 'I know a bloke who rounded Africa's Cape and he told me the Indian Ocean's as warm as a baby's bath but festering with pirates.'

'Pirates?' A long blond Glaswegian moustache drooped from the second sailor's ruddy face.

'Aye, pirates and flesh dealers,' explained the red-headed sailor. 'Dutch and Spanish and Portuguese swine mixed up in no-good business over there with Chinese and Arabs. Oh, they're a scurvy no-good lot of rotters in the East Indies and the worst of them operate out of that hellish prison called Slave Island.'

'Slave Island?'

'Near Mombasa Town, north of Madagascar.'

'I heard of that place – Mombasa.'

'Mombasa Town's a rich port on the east coast of Africa. But neighbouring Mombasa is Slave Island, a rock jutting up from the waves that's a prison for the worst Arabian, Turk and European scum, a Tower of Babel in the ocean for more sinners than saints, I be telling you. A seething pot of slave-running and prostitution and murder and drug-taking. Men say there's no sin bad nor depraved enough for Slave Island–'

'It's a prison, you say?'

'Aye, for criminals as well as Christian sailors like you and me, captured off ships or coshed over the heads in dark harbours – all men marked for some kind of slavery.'

'Who runs this Slave Island?'

'The Ottomans. Those Turks who have Caliphs instead of kings, bobs who wear jewelled turbans in place of gold crowns. All heathens from that part of the world, the whole bloody lot.'

The red-headed sailor proceeded to give an inventory of vice rampant inside a prison called Slave Island, crimes of rape, sodomy, pederasty, murder.

Billy stopped eavesdropping on the story; he knew he would only become more depressed if he listened to fireside yarns about dangers awaiting in the part of the world where he was sailing aboard the *Vandal Witch*.

*

Waving his hand for the serving girl to bring another hot rum, Billy soon settled back on the bench with the second earthen mug and brooded about his meeting with Gabriel Easton.

As hard as he tried not to become enraged with Easton or angry with his brother, for supposedly signing a second contract of lading with Easton and sending it from Sumatra without writing him a single word about some new decision or development, Billy could not help asking himself if it was true. Would Gabriel Easton lie to him? Would Easton forge Andrew's signature on a new contract? If he had, Billy would eventually find out that the signature was a fake. Oh, Easton was a scoundrel and desperate to assure his position in the world, but was he a fool? And what about Andrew? Would not Andrew eventually discover his signature had been forged, and then what would happen to his engagement with Catherine Easton?

Billy next wondered, 'But what if Andrew *did* sign the contract without telling me? Why would he do it? Is that story about the Chinese revolution only a hoax? Did Easton invent it? Or would my own brother side against me? But why? For money? For security in marriage? True, I don't approve of Andrew marrying Catherine Easton. I've never told him I think Catherine's a strumpet who had the good fortune not to be born on the streets. But by the same token, Andrew knows I have no fondness, not even respect, for Catherine Easton. Nevertheless, he also is aware that I wish him good luck with whomever he chooses to marry, even if it's a drab like Catherine Easton.'

Confused, vexed, and suddenly feeling discontent in a town which only a few hours ago he had considered to be his home, Billy again began slipping back into the melancholy from which the rum had begun to rescue him.

Trying to convince himself it would do him no good to worry about an action already completed, that it was useless to fret about a cargo loaded aboard a ship scheduled to sail in less than twenty-four hours' time, Billy gulped down the remainder of the rum and beckoned the serving girl to bring him a third mug. Taking the beverage from the smiling girl, he finally saw Faith Wiley come down the steps and wave him towards her.

Quickly rising to his feet, Billy felt the potent liquor already affecting his head; he moved slowly, slightly dizzy-headed as he crossed the plank floor to the narrow staircase.

Faith Wiley, leaning over the wooden banister, whispered, 'Lad, have you a liking for a tit-bird in each hand and two bushes for your willy-dick?'

'I might – if I knew what it meant.'

'A tit-bird in each hand, two bushes for your willy-dick, boy. That's not a puzzle for a man who's had two women in bed.'

'Two . . . women?' Billy had never before lain with more than one lover.

'If you ain't man enough to enjoy a pair of hussies, tell me right now and I'll rent them to one of those sea rats crouched over there by my fire.'

'Why can't I have one girl?' Billy suggested, 'and let somebody else have the other?'

Faith Wiley shook her head. 'Young hussies are hard to find and these two strumpets are something special. They ran away from Papist persecution up in Halifax and refuse to be parted from each other's company. The poor things still have nightmares about nuns flogging them with cat o'nine tails and pinching them hard on the arms, legs and bottom. So, if you don't have money for both of my frightened runaway wenches, or if you ain't man enough to handle two women in bed, lad, just say so and you can go back by the fire and wait till Old Polly is through.'

'And who, pray, is Old Polly?'

'Old Polly's the other wench I have working here today. Polly's not as young as the Halifax fillies but she tries hard to please a man and also has her own special little tricks.'

'Tricks?'

'If you've never had your willy-dick chewed by a wench with no teeth, then you just might enjoy spending a few bob on Old Polly – her mouth is as smooth as a new born babe's. See, Polly ain't had the pennies to buy herself none of these –' Faith opened her own mouth and pressed the flat of her thumb against the wooden teeth lining her gums.

Billy suspected that the brothel-keeper was lying to him, that she was embellishing on the origin of the two young prostitutes – as well as decrying the other wench – to dupe him into paying for two women instead of one. But he did not feel like arguing any more today, as well as suspecting that a diversification might be exactly what he needed to revive his flagging spirits, to give himself one last fling before leaving for sea.

Faith Wiley led Billy up the stairs, stopped in the low-ceilinged hallway, opened a small oak door and stood back for Billy to pass in front of her into a shadowy room. She whispered, 'I'll send up more rum.'

The glow from a fire glimmering in a small cast iron stove lit the milky white bodies of two naked young women intertwined on a pineboard bed. They ignored Billy and Faith Wiley standing in the doorway and continued to caress, to fondle, to kiss one another as they twisted and turned on the snowy white sheets.

Billy, moving past Faith Wiley, said, 'Forget about the rum, dear mother.'

Faith Wiley blocked him with an extended arm. 'Sonny, you pay me now for the girls as well as the rum – or your dear mother will show you the street, the storm, and the cold.'

Billy ignoring the brothel-keeper, stared at the two curvaceous prostitutes embracing one another on the bed. As his eyes became more accustomed to the room's faint lighting, he noticed that one girl had corn yellow hair and that the other had raven black curls. He saw that the darker girl had fuller breasts than the blonde, but that their nipples were both erect, rosy, like firm buds against the pink saucers forming their aureola.

Fumbling in his pocket for his chamois leather money pouch, Bill stuffed three coins into Faith Wiley's hand and said, 'Send the rum . . . do what you please . . . I'm staying here . . .'

He reached for the buckle on his deerskin belt.

Faith Wiley dropped the coins into the pocket of her long homespun apron. 'You're a game lad, ain't you, sonny boy? A very game lad who knows what he wants!'

Chuckling, she closed the oaken door behind her.

Hurriedly unbuttoning his cambric shirt, Billy dropped his wet trousers to the floor and moved towards the bed.

Billy's penis began to harden as he kept his eyes on the two prostitutes: the raven-haired girl was kneeling on the mattress, straddling the blonde who lay on her back; they were now both tonguing one another's vagina, hungrily eating and chewing the furry patches, working the feminine clefts with their fingers to expose more vaginal pinkness, endeavouring to inch their tongues deeper into warm moisture.

Next, the two young women moved their darting tongues over each other's trim bodies, licking in the opposite direction from one another, pressing their fingers still deeper into the womanly mounds.

The raven-haired prostitute, as if waiting for Billy to join them, removed her finger from the blonde's moist slit and held out the finger toward him, beckoning him toward their bed.

Billy, now completely naked, dropped to his knees alongside the bed, taking the prostitute's extended finger into his mouth, tasting the lingering flavour from the other prostitute's vagina.

The young woman made room for Billy to climb onto the bed with them; he quickly rose from his knees and snuggled between their naked bodies, feeling their bare legs enclose his thighs, becoming part of their tangle of warm flesh; each young woman wrapped one arm around Billy's shoulder, embracing him, and reached with the other hand toward his crotch: the raven-haired woman gripped Billy's scrotum; the blonde stretched her hand to encompass, to stroke, to squeeze his throbbing penis. And pressing their fleshy breasts against both side of his chest, their rosy nipples brushed his skin as their lips moved toward his mouth, to include him in their kisses.

The raven-haired girl whispered, 'Mmm, you feel . . . good.'

The blonde prostitute followed, 'We're farm girls and used to boys built like horses.'

The first young woman, darting her tongue from the blonde's mouth back to Billy's mouth, teased, 'So now you must be our own little pony.'

'Yes,' murmured the other young woman. 'Be a pony for both of us to ride, please, oh, please be our pony.'

'Can we ride you, little yellow pony?' The raven-haired prostitute pressed more tightly against Billy, asking, 'Can we stretch our legs across you and bounce up and down, up and down, up and down on that big . . . thing you've got poking up from your legs?'

The blonde, squeezing Billy's penis and making its crown turn dark purple with pressure, whispered, 'Such a big, fat, long willy our little pony has for the lasses to ride.'

The other wench pressed, 'Oh, let us ride you now, little pony. Let us start taking turns riding your big saddle.'

Across the dark room, Faith Wiley entered quietly from the hallway, carrying a steaming mug of rum and still chuckling to herself. She set down the mug and, lifting Billy's clothes from the floor, she began emptying his pockets, standing in shadows, watching the two prostitutes keeping Billy occupied on the bed.

She next reached into her apron pocket and, removing two small bits of verdigris, she dropped them into the mug, then moved toward the door, eager to report to Gabriel Easton that the downy-limbed lad would not be causing him any further trouble.

'Such a babe in the cruel woods,' thought Faith Wiley as she glanced back over her shoulder at Billy serving – and being served by – the two prostitutes.

Billy, groaning pleasurably from the sensation of one young woman sucking his penis whilst the other girl held his testicles in her mouth, began to toss his head back and forth on the pillow.

The raven-haired prostitute, fearing that Billy might see Faith Wiley leaving the room, quickly rose to her knees and moved over Billy's naked chest, placing her legs on either side of his head, preventing him from seeing the door.

She looked down at him, teasing, 'Time for pony to lick . . . time for the good pony to come lick . . .' She poked her opening vulva towards his mouth.

Billy was engulfed with physical sensations. The increasing movement of the warm mouth on his penis; the sweetness of a vagina smothering his mouth, his nose, all across his face; the press of two bodies against his nakedness; all this excitement convinced him that he had made the correct choice by coming to the harbour brothel.

4

Catherine Easton, twenty years old, with delicate features, graciously entertained her late morning guest, Paris Rhinelander, in the parlour of the Easton home – a cosy room decorated with floral prints, deep cushioned chairs, brightly polished andirons guarding a birch fire crackling on the hearth.

Despite the polite parlour talk passing between them, Catherine Easton knew the true purpose of Paris Rhinelander's visit to the house, and also what she desired from him. But, temporarily, she continued making idle conversation about the inclement weather, the imminent departure of her father's convoy, how bored she was with colonial life, and how she wished she were travelling to England.

Paris Rhinelander, born of Dutch parents but raised on the Caribbean island of Jamaica by English foster parents, spoke the King's English with only a slight accent, an occasional lilt which betrayed his true origins.

A broad-shouldered man, with a stern cast to his grey eyes and a firm set to his square jaw, Rhinelander sat across from Catherine Easton and announced, 'The Captain of the *Vandal Witch* informed me that Billy Peake's sailing all the way to China.'

Catherine Easton concentrated on making a posset, pouring hot milk from a yellow earthenware jug, Portuguese wine from a raffia-covered bottle, spooning brown sugar from a bowl.

She remarked as she worked, 'I understood all passengers were sailing abroad the *Prince George*.'

Rhinelander watched her slim hands delicately mix milk with wine for the warm beverage. 'I also believed the same fact. But last night your father sent word to my lodging about a change of plan. I went this morning to speak to the Captain aboard ship and I saw Billy Peake.'

Catherine raised her eyes; they had become deep emerald green and anxious.

'You saw Billy Peake? This morning?'

Rhinelander confirmed with a nod. 'Aboard the *Vandal Witch*.'

'He sails on the same ship as you?'

'I cannot tell you that.'

'Did he see you?'

'We passed.'

'Passed? But did he speak with you? Did he recognize you?'

Rhinelander was pleased to see Catherine Easton reacting nervously to his announcement. She was usually so much in command, conducting herself like a puppet-mistress, trying to control the lives and the passions of every man she met.

He replied, 'Why should Billy Peake recognize me? And what would be wrong if he did?'

Catherine, forgetting the posset and her lady-like pretensions to playing a hearthside hostess, angrily scolded,

'You know perfectly well, Mr Rhinelander, that I'm betrothed to marry Billy's elder brother.'

'After tomorrow, my presence in Boston will no longer place your betrothal in jeopardy.' Rhinelander did not smile.

'True, my name, my reputation would be ruined if word of our . . . friendship were exposed. Yet how I hate, how I truly hate seeing you leave Boston for England.'

Rhinelander decided he had suffered enough of this idle chatter. He rose from his chair and, gazing down at Catherine sitting demurely in her wing-backed chair, he ordered, 'Look at me, Catherine.'

Catherine raised her eyes, her gaze too beguiling to be the eyes of a proper hostess.

'I'm going to miss you,' she whispered as she raised one hand to grasp his large forefinger.

Ignoring her hand, Rhinelander demanded, 'Miss me? Or miss the diversion I provide for you on rainy afternoons in this town you hate passionately?'

The bluntly spoken question momentarily jolted Catherine. But she quickly replied, 'Are you reducing our friendship to a series of pastimes?'

'What else is it?'

She arched a thin eyebrow. 'Would you believe me if I termed them "lessons in addiction"?'

'I would believe that!'

She continued, 'And now that I've learnt to appreciate, to need the qualities you possess as a man, what shall I do after you leave?'

Rhinelander knew she was already teasing him, playing the coquette which it thrilled her to do.

He reached down to cup her pert chin and, lifting her head, ordered softly, 'Look at me.'

Catherine Easton gazed at Paris Rhinelander's finely sculptured nose, the trace of a blond moustache about his upper lip, the strong lantern jaw etched with a narrow beard.

Rhinelander regarded Catherine's finely-lashed eyes

studying him, enticing him; he admired the way her oval face remained inscrutable, passionless, even when she was teasing a man to seduce her.

'You're real little minx, aren't you, Miss Easton?'

Catherine was pleased with this evaluation.

Rhinelander smirked, adding, 'As well as being a true bitch.'

The vulgar word surprised her. 'Bitch?'

'A bitch. A she-dog. An avaricious little she-dog on heat. A doxy who can't decide if she prefers a husband with a fat purse or a lover with a fat–' Rhinelander groped the crotch of his tightly fitting breeches.

'Mr Rhinelander, is this farewell to be a mockery of me?'

'Would you enjoy that? A sound mockery? Or would you prefer playing the fine lady a while longer before you fall from your pedestal? Does a charade make your fall more delicious? Give you more satisfaction when you grovel on the floor, when you become some poor misused lady who's heartlessly punished?'

Catherine affected a pout. 'Now you do tease me.'

'No, I do not. I tell you what I think. How I believe you have been using me for your temporary pleasure the past months. But do not fear. After tomorrow you will hear no more from me.'

'Are you complaining?'

'No, merely stating facts.'

'Facts?' Catherine again reached for his hand. 'I loathe and detest facts. They confuse feelings. Feelings have nothing to do with facts. Feelings are appetites we must keep hidden, like fears. Most women find difficulty in speaking about what they desire. I am different, though. You, Mr Rhinelander, have told me as much. But you have also told me, sir, you enjoy being with me. That my desires match yours. That we make a good pair, a brace, yes, a perfect brace of lovers. But now after you've immersed me with entirely new passions, awakened desires in me, you're leaving me alone in this barren outpost, this backwater of bland manners, fierce weather, uncouth habits–'

All the time Catherine was speaking her small hand was inching around the large, paw-like hand of Paris Rhinelander.

Slapping away her pressing hand, Rhinelander demanded, 'What do you think you're doing, touching me?'

Catherine recoiled. 'Don't be angry.'

Rhinelander remembered scenes similar to this from past assignations with Catherine Easton, pastimes of teasing and enticement, games played, words parried, appetites whetted for illicit consummation.

But today Rhinelander was serious, angry with Catherine Easton, and he truly wanted to punish her.

He slapped her face, jeering, 'Disobedient slut!'

Catherine's eyes dilated with rage as she stared up at him, holding the side of her face.

Jerking Catherine from her chair, Rhinelander gripped her around the waist with one hand and reached under her dimity dress with the other hand; he worked his middle finger against her thin underclothing, pressing to prod deeper inside her, fingering to awaken her excitement.

'Don't,' she whispered in sudden subservience, 'please don't–'

The blunt tip of his finger worked more persistently between her legs as he whispered, 'You've been waiting for this and you know it's only the beginning.'

'Today there are servants–'

'Stop worrying about servants, spoilt wench. Be quiet!'

By custom, Catherine always pleaded in her games. 'But Father might return home.'

Slapping her again across the face, Rhinelander ordered, 'I said hold your tongue!'

A lock of auburn hair toppled from Catherine's coiffure to dangle over her temple.

Slapping her again, Rhinelander scoffed, 'You won't get this treatment from your fine English captain, will you, lily white bitch? Or do you think that fine English captains like to slap their bitches . . .?'

Rhinelander kept slapping her as he spoke. 'Do you think fine English captains slap around their wives . . . like this . . . and this?'

Catherine did not remember his strikes being so painful in past encounters. She tried to break away from him, crying, 'What are you doing to me?'

'Giving you what you need. What you want. I'm hurting you. Humiliating you. Punishing you for being naughty. Spoilt. Filling your store of fantasies so that no matter whom you marry, where you live, whose wife you become, you'll never be anything deep down inside you but *my* whore . . .*my* bitch . . . *my* slut.'

'You truly enjoy humiliating me like this, don't you?'

Rhinelander grabbed her by the neck and, bringing her closer towards him, ordered, 'Don't talk to me until I tell you to. And don't talk to me without calling me "sir". Understand? Now get out of that dress. I'm tired of seeing you in it.'

He shoved her away from him.

'Undress?' she gasped, holding her arms to her breasts.

He ripped at the bodice. 'Now!'

Catherine, trying to cover her creamy white breasts suddenly exposed through the torn garment, exclaimed, 'But it's daylight!'

'Don't argue!' He slapped her again, ordering, 'And call me "sir".'

Catherine Easton looked at Paris Rhinelander, remembering he would be leaving Boston tomorrow for London and that she might never see him again.

Quickly forgetting about her father arriving home, and about the servants in the kitchen, she yanked open the torn bodice of her dress, untied the sash and dropped the garment to the floor.

Paris Rhinelander had learnt many months ago that twenty-year-old Catherine Easton was not only a nymphomaniac but that she also enjoyed being treated as a servile love partner. He stood ready and eager to play her dominant lover for what he believed to be the last time.

Gabriel Easton, having walked through the morning storm from Faith Wiley's brothel in the harbour, stood dripping rain onto the oak floor outside the parlour doors, listening to his daughter and Paris Rhinelander speaking profane words to one another as they made love in a cruel, crude manner.

It was known to Easton that Rhinelander mistreated young Catherine in their love-making, slapping her, spanking her, occasionally binding and restricting her with leather thongs. But Easton knew that if Catherine did not receive such treatment from Rhinelander she would go out into the streets looking for a stranger to satisfy her unconventional appetites.

Indulgent of his daughter, Gabriel Easton knew about her unhappiness with dull colonial life, and he tried to humour her every whim, to fulfil her wants as the father of a chronically sick child sits at its beck and call.

Easton had arranged for Catherine's and Rhinelander's first meeting, for Rhinelander to travel from Jamaica and find work in Boston, for the afternoon hours they spent together undisturbed, pursuing Catherine's amusement. When the affair had gone as far as Easton could permit it to go without risking public scandal, he had also arranged for Rhinelander to be offered another job far away from Boston, for Rhinelander to sail from Boston aboard the *Vandal Witch*.

Easton, turning away from the parlour door, would now take a shore boat out to the *Vandal Witch* and receive assurance from Captain Kerr that his ship would not reach Canton with the other convoy ships, that the black schooner would sail its own course from Boston.

5

The storm tempered in the afternoon, passed during the night, and by morning the sky was cloudless and steely blue; the winds blew easterly gusts powerful enough to sail the China convoy across the wide Massachusetts Bay and out into the rolling Atlantic towards the next port of call – Gravesend, England.

Aphrodite, Duke of Cambridge, England's Rose, Prince George, The Royal Servant, Sea Castle, Vandal Witch. The seven convoy ships sailed in close formation, expanding their canvasses yard by yard, league by league, as they moved farther out into the open sea. The waves became stronger, stiffer, yet more familiar in their steady succession, curling into great sheets of water from the prows, plunging into the next wave, smashing downwards, intensifying the ocean's roar into loud rolls of thunder.

Forceful winds kept the jib, staysails, top gallants and topsails open and taut; at nightfall, lanterns were hung fore and aft, making the seven vessels look like giant insects blinking through the darkness, following slow paths across the silver-capped waves. Also at night, voices disappeared on deck except for the occasional command – or assent – from forecastle and poop, darkness quietening all activity at sea except for the churn, roll and crash of never-ending rollers.

Sea fog enclosed the convoy towards the end of the second day out of Boston. Lanterns were lit earlier than the previous evening; nothing else appeared different except when the second dawn broke: a greater distance stood between six ships in the convoy and the seventh ship – the *Vandal Witch* – had disappeared completely; the black schooner had vanished without a warning or distress signal from the wave-licked surface of earth.

Billy Peake awoke in darkness, not knowing his

whereabouts; his stomach felt as if it had been turned upside down inside him; his head racked with pain. He remembered visiting a bordello near the wharf, drinking successive hot rums, then being led by a woman wearing a white cap up narrow stairs to a dimly lit room where two young women made love on a narrow bed . . .

Remembering the two prostitutes, Billy reached alongside him on the narrow pallet where he lay to feel if he was still sandwiched between the pair of naked bodies. He felt rough cotton ticking, the thin pallet and a heaving motion beneath him.

Struggling to open his bleary eyes wider to see where he was, Billy saw nothing but murky darkness surrounding him.

Next, listening for familiar sounds, he heard the creak of rigging, the scream of plank decking, the rhythmic splash, splash, splash of waves beating against a wooden hull – all sounds of being at sea.

Realising through his torpor that he was either in a nightmare or the small cabin aboard a ship, Billy sat higher on the narrow pallet and tried to accustom his eyes to the darkness.

A man was sitting on the bed and rubbing oil into a long bullwhip.

Billy sat higher and blurted, 'Who are you?'

The man asked, 'Feeling better?'

'Who are you?'

'Paris Rhinelander.'

'Rhinelander?' Billy squinted his eyes to study the Nordic-looking man more closely in the darkness. 'Rhinelander? But you're . . . English.'

'I'm Dutch, but raised on the island of Jamaica by English foster parents.'

'Haven't I seen you before?'

Rhinelander nodded. 'In the harbour. You remember? This same ship? The *Vandal Witch*?'

Billy looked around him in sudden panic. 'We're aboard the . . . *Vandal Witch*?'

'Bound for Gravesend, England.' Rhinelander kept rubbing oil into the long leather whip.

'Bound for – how did I get here? Oh, Lord God, how long have I been sleeping?'

'You weren't so much asleep as drunk from a good long spree.'

'Drunk?'

'Stone drunk.' Rhinelander smiled. 'You couldn't even walk.'

'Couldn't walk? Then how did I get here?'

'Two sailors carried you aboard.'

'That's impossible,' Billy protested. 'I never get drunk. Not drunk enough to . . . pass out.'

Rhinelander did not argue, continuing to rub oil into the bullwhip, working the black leather into a long supple, pliable snake.

Billy lowered his legs from the bed, his voice still anxious as he asked, 'When did we leave Boston?'

'Two days ago.'

'Two days ago? I've been asleep for two days?' Billy felt dirty and itchy and sick to his stomach. 'And you say I was . . . carried aboard?'

Rhinelander nodded. 'By two sailors.'

'Did those sailors say where they . . . found me?'

'Near Narrow Street. By the wharf.'

'And we've been at sea ever since? Since they carried me aboard?'

'Ever since.'

'What happened to the storm? I remember a big storm. Heavy rain. Bolts of lightning. Wind so bad–'

'The storm passed down the coast.'

Billy felt the ship rocked with the motion of the sea and heard a large wave slap against the bulwark; he muttered, 'I thought that old hag, Faith Wiley, might be a rotter, but I never suspected she would lace anything–'

Suddenly remembering his money pouch, Billy felt in one pocket for it, then searched the other.

'Oh, no–'

Paris Rhinelander had been prepared to dislike Billy Peake, but, watching him awaken from a drunken bout and discovering he had been robbed, Rhinelander could not feel any contempt for this boyish-looking young man.

Remaining silent, Rhinelander watched Billy searching his pockets, his waistband, his shirt.

Finally, he asked, 'Something is wrong?'

Billy raised his eyes. 'Everything.'

'Were you robbed?'

Billy nodded. 'My money. My papers – oh, what a mess I've got myself into now.'

Rhinelander dropped one whip onto the pallet and picked up another.

Billy ran both hands through his tangle of blond hair. 'I've been packing, preparing, laying plans for this voyage for three long years. Three years! Then the day before I'm to leave, what do I do? I go to a whore-house and . . . get drunk!'

Rhinelander smiled. 'Perhaps you had good reason.'

'Self-pity is hardly good reason.'

'You mentioned a whore-house,' Rhinelander smiled. 'Was the visit worth your while?'

Thinking back to the brothel on Narrow Street, Billy remembered the two prostitutes, the delights and sensations he had never before experienced.

Nodding, he answered, 'Aye, I suppose it was worth it.'

'So you don't have a thing to complain about.'

'You're right. New experiences are not a total loss. Even if hindsight now tells me that two whores were used to distract my attention while an old woman robbed and drugged me. I've learnt to be more cautious in the future.'

'Or never go with more than one woman.'

Billy regarded Rhinelander more closely. He saw a handsome man, a man a few years older than himself, a man who was not trying to pry into his secrets, but someone whose eyes showed both humour and compassion.

Billy, feeling more relaxed in Rhinelander's company, said, 'If I'm going to burden you with my problems, sir, at least let me introduce myself. The name's Billy Peake.'

Rhinelander leant forward to grasp Billy's hand. 'Mr Peake, I hope things improve for you.'

Then, reaching alongside him on the pallet, Rhinelander picked up an orange from the tangled nest of leather bullwhips and tossed it to Billy. 'Eat one of these. Get some sustenance in your belly.'

Billy caught the orange and, beginning to peel it, he asked, 'Are we the only passengers aboard?'

'You, me, and a scruffy-looking crew. I should have insisted on sailing aboard the *Prince George.*'

'So you have a complaint, too?'

Rhinelander nodded.

Gesturing towards the bullwhips, Billy asked, 'Those all yours?'

'All mine.'

'Why do you have so many?'

'I make them. That's my trade. A tanner. And saddler. See, I rub oil into all the whips, quirts and riding crops I make to keep the leather more pliable, to last longer and better.'

'Whips and riding crops?' The idea intrigued Billy. 'Is that what you were doing in Boston? Making whips?'

'I learned my craft in Jamaica. I did work awhile in Boston, but now I'm headed for London.'

'London? Ah, so you'll not be sailing with me all the way to China?'

'No, I go ashore at Gravesend. I'm fortunate enough to have found a job in London.' Rhinelander added casually, 'The man who organized this convoy found me work at an outfitting house in St. James's.'

'Gabriel Easton?'

Rhinelander raised his eyes. 'You know him?'

'I've . . . I've met Mr Easton.' Billy slowly broke off the first segment of orange and remembered his parting meeting with Easton.

Silence hung inside the small cabin as Billy proceeded to eat the orange and Rhinelander oiled his whips; the only sounds came from the sea, the schooner's prow cutting through the waves, the creak of the rigging, the snap of the sails.

Suddenly, Billy jumped from the pallet.

Rhinelander jerked his head at the quick movement. 'What's the matter?'

Billy rushed to the door. 'I think I'm going to be ill.'

6

Billy stood starboard on the *Vandal Witch*, feeling a slight physical relief after leaning over the railing and disgorging the last of the sweet rum remaining in his stomach. He faced the open sea, enjoying the cool breeze, grateful for the fine pin-points of mist washing his face. As the dullness gradually lifted from his brain, he began piecing together details of his last morning in Boston.

The memory of Faith Wiley's brothel on Narrow Street seemed like a small fragment of a tortured nightmare. The bad dream had begun earlier, when two oarsmen had rowed him through the storm in their shore boat to meet Captain Kerr aboard the *Vandal Witch*, where Billy had learnt that the black schooner carried the silver ingots in its hold.

His brain becoming more lucid with the sea air, Billy listened to the steady rhythm of the waves and remembered his meeting with Gabriel Easton on Fort Hill, specifically recollecting Easton's argument why Billy could not remove cargo from the convoy; Andrew had signed a new contract with Easton, an agreement rendering Billy helpless, powerless, without a voice in any decisions regarding the silver. Easton's final words had been a recommendation for Billy to visit Faith Wiley's brothel.

The ocean spray beaded spoondrift through Billy's blond hair as he stood starboard, holding his eyes closed, facing the waves, considering how Easton had probably been in collusion with Faith Wiley and the two prostitutes, that the old hag with the wooden teeth had possibly stirred some stupefying elixir or powder into the hot rums, robbed him of his belongings, then allowed Easton's – or Kerr's – men to carry him from the house and out to the schooner. Easton had most probably arranged for Billy to be taken away quickly, quietly, from Boston to prevent him from causing any disagreeable problems concerning the *Vandal Witch*.

Billy felt no anger. His head was light; his limbs unsure of themselves on the tossing deck. His stomach was queasy; he was also still unnerved by the fact that he had been asleep for two entire days and nights aboard a ship bound for England. But it was not Billy's nature to indulge in anger, to harbour bitterness, allowing hatred to eat away at him like rot.

Frequently agonizing over disloyalties, however, Billy considered the fact that his brother might have betrayed him to Gabriel Easton for money, and his stomach churned with sudden nerves.

Was he going to retch again?

Taking a deep breath, filling his lungs with sea air, Billy looked around the deck of the narrow schooner and saw the morning sun attempting to emerge through a foggy white scrim.

Akin to a prayer, Billy told himself, 'Be thankful you're alive, old dog, and concentrate on chores you have to do.'

A question quickly followed: What *was* there to do?

He could not turn back to Massachusetts. That fact was certain. He was aboard an Atlantic vessel with the next port of call in England. He had no papers, no money, no change of clothing. Clothing did not matter. He could wash the togs he was wearing. They would dry quickly in the wind. He was also fortunate to have been wearing good horseleather boots with sound soles. As for money, what was there to spend money on? His passage had already been paid. Also he did not consider himself to be a complete imbecile and suspected he would somehow be able to solve the problem of money before the convoy touched land at Gravesend.

There was only one logical thing for him to do at the moment, he decided, and that was to go below deck and look at his silver. Yes, go down into the hold and see what the Mexican ingots looked like.

Billy, feeling better after prodding himself to revive his spirits, turned away from the starboard railing to expedite his new resolution.

Yes, he told himself, he would go to the hold and inspect the ingots. Hold one of the damned things. Feel it. Sniff it. See how heavy they were. Inspect how they were stored. Perhaps even gauge the total number of the load, begin forming some sort of tally.

Glad he had decided to spend his time being constructive rather than indulging in self-pity, to gather knowledge, perhaps even collecting evidence to serve him later in the voyage if he needed it to call upon, Billy moved towards the hatch with a slight bounce returning to his step.

What was life if not to be enjoyed?

He suddenly stopped. His optimism momentarily wavered. He looked back over his shoulder, glancing again at the blur of sunlight breaking through the morning fog. Billy realized that if the *Vandal Witch* was sailing eastwards – to England – the sun should be rising above the ship's bowsprit and not off the quarterdeck.

'Odd,' he thought, scratching his head. 'Very odd . . . isn't it?'

Next, Billy looked across the uneven expanse of silver-capped waves and saw an empty horizon, no signs of sails, masts; the rest of the convoy was gone.

'Extremely odd, old dog.'

He made another complete turn on deck – like a slowly moving dervish – and still he saw no sign of other ships.

Spotting a sailor nearby the yardarm, he shouted, 'Aye,

there! Good morning to you! Have we changed course?'

The sailor, his cheeks bushy with greying mutton-chop whiskers, looked blankly at Billy.

Billy pointed to the bright smudge of the sun rising in the east. 'We sail south. Why?'

The sailor did not respond.

'Where are the other ships?' called Billy, gesturing at the empty horizon, at the waves lapping the earth's curvature.

The sailor shrugged his shoulders.

Billy shouted, 'Do we chart a different course from the rest of the convoy?'

'Talk to the captain,' answered the sailor and turned to walk away from Billy.

'Where do I find him at this hour? The stern?' Billy was still not becoming angry, trying to remain calm with his recently decided serenity.

The sailor called over his shoulder, 'Pilot's in the stern.'

'So where's Captain Kerr? His cabin?'

'Captain Kerr left orders not to be disturbed.' The sailor walked away from Billy, calling, 'You've got to talk to him later.'

Billy decided that a bit of sternness might aid him. He announced in a more forceful voice, 'I'm owner of cargo aboard this ship.'

'Captain's orders are not to be disturbed.'

Billy, deciding to speak to Captain Kerr, moved toward the quarterdeck, descended three steps and rapped on a small teakwood door with one fist.

He called, 'Captain Kerr! You in there, Captain Kerr?'

A gruff voice shouted from inside the cabin, 'God damn you to hell! Leave me in peace!'

Billy hesitated, asking himself if he should go away and return later. But realizing that nobody had shown any courtesy to him, he called, 'It's me, Captain Kerr, Billy Peake.'

'Go away, Peake.'

Billy, leaning closer to the door, heard the sound of a

scuffle inside the cabin; he raised his voice, 'Captain Kerr, I have to talk to you. I truly do.'

The sound of a muffled cry rose inside the cabin; there was more scuffling; Billy kicked on the door and Kerr bellowed, 'I said go away, Peake.'

Billy guessed that Kerr had someone with him inside the cabin. But having set out to learn a few answers, he wanted them.

He pursued, 'We're sailing the wrong course, Captain Kerr. I want to know why we're sailing the wrong course.'

'God damn you to hell, Peake!'

The curse angered Billy and he shouted back, 'I'm not leaving until I get an answer from you, Captain Kerr! I'm going to stay right here and be a . . . pest!'

Iron bolts suddenly slid inside the door; a chain rattled; the cabin door opened and Billy stood facing Captain Kerr.

'What do you want?' slurred Kerr, his breath foul with whisky, his clothing ripped, his unshaven face bleeding from what appeared to be fresh scratches from raking fingernails.

Billy, politely but firmly, began, 'My pardon for disturbing you, sir, but we are sailing south instead of east. There's no sight of the other convoy ships–'

Kerr sneered, 'You warned me you wanked your cock by thinking you're a sailor.'

Billy stared at Kerr's ragged face, taken aback by the profanity. He calmly asked, 'We sail south. Why?'

'Who says south is off course, God damn it, you snot-nosed young brat?'

Billy again lost his temper, demanding, 'If we're on course, where are the other six convoy ships? We were supposed to be seven when we left Boston.'

'How do you know what we were when we left Boston? You were pissed drunk and had to be lugged aboard. I was a fool even to let them carry you onto my ship.' Kerr moved to slam the door in Billy's face.

Blocking the door with his booted foot, Billy said, 'I

was foolish in Boston, true. But that's over, so forget about it. Just tell me what's happening now.'

Leaning closer to Billy, Kerr raised his clenched fist, warning, 'Get your foot away from my door or I'll slice off the bloody thing at the ankle and hang you – bleeding stump and all – over the stern as shark bait!'

Billy held his foot firm. 'I'm not leaving till I get some answers.'

'Peake, I'm telling you one last time. Get your foot away from this door or–'

'Threats aren't going to get rid of me, Captain Kerr. I'm not leaving till you tell me what's happening. It's my silver you carry in your hold. I've got a right to know what's going on.'

'It *was* your silver. But not any more. Not even Gabriel Easton can claim those ingots now. They're mine,' he said, thumbing his chest, 'mine!'

Billy, forgetting about his resolution to be level-headed, flared, 'Yours! You've got nothing, you stinking old goat, but a slave ship! And damned little you know about sailing it if you can't tell south from east–'

'Curse your cheeky tongue –' Kerr's fist flew toward Billy's face.

Ducking the blow, Billy hit Kerr on the chin with his own fist, sending him tumbling backwards into the cabin; Billy followed him down to the deck, his clenched fingers choking Kerr's neck, demanding, 'Tell me . . . what's happening . . .'

Kerr, jolting upwards, knocked Billy sideways and, jumping to his feet with the agility of a much younger man, began driving his fist against Billy's face.

Blood spurted from Billy's lower lip. But, angered as well as being frustrated, Billy broke Kerr's hold and slugged toward his chin, his jaw, his eyes . . .

As Billy and Captain Kerr rolled fighting across the deck, a woman dashed from the darkness of Kerr's cabin, a young woman with long red hair and a ripped cotton dress.

Running past Billy and Kerr, the young woman quickly

moved up the steps, but she was abruptly stopped by members of Kerr's crew rushing towards the fight.

One man grabbed the red-headed woman while two other men pulled Billy off Captain Kerr.

Kerr, stumbling to his feet, held his bleeding face with one hand and ordered the man holding the woman, 'Get that bitch back to my cabin!'

'Aye, sir,' said the sailor and shoved the red-headed woman down the steps.

Kerr next looked at Billy pinioned by two sailors to the deck. 'Take him to the helm and tie him to the deck rings. Tell Scully to fetch one of the Dutchman's bullwhips.'

Turning towards the cabin, Kerr slammed the door and shot the iron bolts.

The sound of a woman's painful cries rose inside the cabin as the crew members dragged Billy towards the helm.

Two sailors pressed Billy Peake to the deck as two more secured his wrists and ankles to iron rings with leather thongs. The crew gathered amidship, scarcely more than a dozen men crowding together to watch the first mate, Tim Scully, administer the first flogging of the voyage.

Tim Scully, a barrel-chested man, wore a brimless felt hat and had a mouthful of black teeth. He positioned his boots on deck and snapped the tip of a long leather bullwhip over his shoulder, acquainting himself with the feel of the whip, finding the proper distance to stand away from Billy's half-naked body held in a spread-eagle position in front of him by the deck irons.

Cries were already rising from the crew.

'Look at the lily-assed English kid!'

'He ain't English,' shouted another man. 'He's Colonial scum. He's what they're calling "American" these days.'

'Is he the kid Burke and Hardy had to carry like a babe from the harbour?'

The first snap of the whip cut through the air; Billy flinched, his back burning from pain when another stroke cut across his bare skin, then a third, fourth, a fifth lash of the black leather whip.

Trying to hold back his screams, Billy was deaf to the sailors' cheers, listening instead to the whip slicing through the air, hearing the tip whistle towards him, feeling it cut across his skin, feeling as if his skin had been set afire by a torch.

Tim Scully, striking in steadily timed strokes, did not keep his aim centred on Billy's upper torso; he struck Billy's waist, caught him across the biceps, hit his naked shoulders, tore skin from his lateral muscles.

Billy, determined not to cry for mercy, dug his fingernails into the flesh of his palms as he twisted and writhed in the bondage constricting him to the deck irons.

The crew, pleased at the first sight of blood smearing down Billy's welts, shouted and taunted louder.

'Make him beg for mercy!'

'Come on, Scully! Show the American kid what a good Englishman can dish out to Colonials!'

'Give the American a taste of what's waiting for him where Captain Kerr's taking him!'

Tim Scully continued to crack the bullwhip, making Billy's back a ladder of red wounds.

As the pain became more severe, Billy felt his mind begin to slip into blankness, his body becoming limp against the deck.

The sun was finally breaking through the foggy white scrim to the east as Billy fainted in a pool of blood.

7

Billy lay in damp, sweltering darkness aboard the *Vandal Witch.* His body was weak, his back numb as he awakened to the ship's sounds: the monotonous splash and rock of the prow cutting through thudding waves, the hiss of the spray; the above-deck accompaniment of canvas flap, boom swing, clatter of block, pulley, top sail, the muffled shouts of sailors.

Rhinelander's voice came from nearby in the hot, stuffy darkness. 'You feeling better?'

Billy groaned, emerging from a feverish sleep.

Rhinelander crouched alongside a bed improvised from folded tarpaulins. 'I've been putting salve on your back. Your welts are already forming a crust. That's good, yes?'

Billy's voice was no louder than a whisper. 'How long have I been asleep . . . this time?'

'Three, four days. It doesn't matter. Rest.'

'I feel dreadful.'

'Do you think you could keep something in your stomach?'

'Have I been eating anything?'

Rhinelander nodded. 'A little. Don't you remember?'

Billy's forehead burned with the fever but his mind was beginning to regain some clarity; he could barely open his eyes; his lips felt thick with sores and his tongue made of cotton.

He whispered, 'Can I please have some water?'

A trickle of water sounded in the darkness. Rhinelander held out a tin cup, softly ordering. 'Drink this . . . slowly. Don't gulp it.'

Billy, raising himself on one elbow, groped for the tin cup, but it was too heavy for his weak grip and he dropped it. He fell back onto the bed and began to moan, whimpering from sheer weakness.

'No, lad! Don't cry. We've got more water.' Rhinelander refilled the tin cup from a skin water-bag and offered it to Billy, suggesting, 'Let me hold it this time. You just sip . . . but drink slowly, yes?'

Billy moved his cracked lips towards the cup. 'I've got to get stronger . . . I've got to . . .'

Taking the cup from Rhinelander's hand, Billy grasped it

more firmly, slowly moving the water toward his mouth. He gulped it and held out the cup to be refilled from the water-bag.

'Too much will make you sick,' Rhinelander poured only half a cup. 'We've got to get some food in your belly.'

Billy drank the second cup more slowly, feeling its coolness flow down his throat, pass through his chest into his stomach, making him feel as if he were gaining at least a modicum of strength.

Rhinelander squatted alongside him in the darkness. 'I've got oranges.'

Billy shook his head. 'No oranges.'

'Why not? What do you think's been keeping you alive, my friend?'

'I've been eating oranges?'

'Mostly drinking the juice. Now you must eat the pulp. You must also start eating bread soaked in water. I know it doesn't sound too appetizing. But you'll be able to digest soggy bread and rebuild your strength.'

Billy did not want to talk about food; he asked, 'Have you been able to find out where we're going?'

Rhinelander, ignoring the question, took a piece of coarse white bread from a cloth sack and began breaking it into small pieces.

Billy repeated, 'Have you been able to find out where we're going? Did you see where the sun rises and sets? Are we back on course for England?'

Rhinelander, still not answering Billy's questions, dipped a small chunk of bread into half a cup of water and handed it to him, ordering, 'Eat this.'

Billy ignored the food. 'Do we still sail alone or with the convoy?'

'I don't know. Take this. Chew it, chew it very well. Then swallow.'

'You don't know?'

'How can I know any more than you? I'm locked down here, too.'

Billy raised his eyes, seeing faint shafts of daylight

filtering around the edges of an overhead door. He realised for the first time they were not in the cabin. 'Where are we?'

'In the hold,' Rhinelander held out the bread chunk. 'Now eat this.'

Billy took the soggy bread, forcing himself to swallow it. He took the second piece quickly offered by Rhinelander, but held up his hand, refusing the third piece as he still chewed the second soggy crust.

Rhinelander watched Billy's mouth moving slowly. He apologised, 'I'm sorry. I'm spurring you.'

Swallowing the bread with a difficult gulp, Billy took the third piece, but before putting it into his mouth asked, 'Why are we locked in the hold?'

'Open your mouth. I'm not a very patient nurse.'

'Why did they lock you down here?'

'Eat.'

'How long have you been here?'

'Same as you. From the day they tied you to the deck and took one of my whips . . .' Rhinelander softened his voice, apologising, 'I'm sorry about the whip. But there was no way I could stop them from taking it from me.'

'It wasn't your fault.' Billy chewed, again swallowed.

Rhinelander shook his head. 'It was my whip and if–'

'You had no control over those wretches. They outnumber you, ten, fifteen to one.'

Billy studied the Dutchman; he realized how different the hulking big blond man was from the first impression he had had of him in Boston harbour. Paris Rhinelander appeared to be a rugged, insensitive, self-centred adventurer; but, in actual fact, he was proving to be a very considerate and warm-hearted person. Billy was grateful to have such a man for a companion.

Despite his gratitude, Billy wanted to know all the facts and he pressed, 'So how long have we been locked here?'

'Four days, five. Maybe a week.' Rhinelander shrugged and explained, 'I thought Captain Kerr was sending me down to tend your wounds. But before I knew what was happening, he had thrown my clothes down behind me and slammed the hatch shut. Now a sailor lowers food and water once a day for us.'

'We're prisoners?'

Rhinelander nodded. 'Captain Kerr's prisoners.'

Billy looked overhead at the battened hatch, then studied the darkness of the hold. It was small and he remembered that the *Vandal Witch* was a slave ship, that the economical design of the hold was necessary because speed was important for a ship carrying a perishable cargo such as slaves.

Glancing around him in the darkness Billy saw sheets of tarpaulin hanging like heavy curtains, canvas suspended everywhere except for a wall of dark, dullish grey in front of him.

Raising himself higher on one elbow, Billy studied the grey wall.

He whispered, 'There it is! There's all the . . . silver.'

The silver ingots were large, but smaller than the red bricks used in English masonry, and instead of being made of clay they had been cast from precious molten metal, smoothed, formed with squared edges, becoming smooth rectangular blocks bearing no stamp, no hallmark, no insignia proclaiming their origin, no mine nor ore company, no country nor owner.

Billy studied the heavy ingot which Rhinelander had laid in front of him for inspection. He finally slumped back on his elbow atop his makeshift bed to study the stacked ingots forming the wall.

Rhinelander returned the ingot to its place amongst the other metal blocks. 'I found them when I was gathering the canvas to fold for your bed.'

Billy glanced at the other dark lengths of tarpaulin surrounding them. 'Are there ingots behind all the canvasses?'

Rhinelander nodded. 'Behind every one. Piled into deep wooden shelves built in the ship.'

'The shelves must be where Kerr usually carries slaves.'

'But now carries your silver.'

Billy looked back to the dullish grey expanse of metal ingots. 'Do you think that's why I'm locked down here? Because of those ingots?'

'Why do you ask that? Do you think Kerr plans on keeping the silver as his own?'

'I'm not saying anything for certain. I'm only asking. Guessing. Trying to think of reasons why all this is happening.'

Rhinelander rested one hand on Billy's shoulder. 'My friend, if you start thinking too much you'll lose what little energy you're gaining.'

'No, I must force myself. I must know what's going on. We don't have much time.'

'Time?' Rhinelander laughed. 'One thing we do have plenty of is time.'

Billy's feverish brain tried to work. He again remembered Boston, the last meeting with Gabriel Easton, the announcement of the new contract with his brother.

He said, 'Maybe I should tell you about Andrew –' Pausing, Billy looked at Rhinelander, explaining, 'Andrew's my brother.'

'You told me.' Rhinelander also remembered Catherine Easton speaking to him about Captain Andrew Peake, and he asked, 'What's he like, this brother of yours?'

'Older than me. More worldly wise.'

'Are you friends with each other, you and your brother?'

'I used to think so. But I'm not certain any more.'

'Did you grow up as friends?'

Billy thought back to his childhood in the village of Richmond. 'Our mother died when we were young. But somehow her death brought Andrew and me closer together. Our Pa was a shipbuilder. He apprenticed both of us at an early age to an old shipbuilder in Greenwich, Tommy Poole.'

'So you stayed together even when you left home?'

'Until Andrew went to sea. The East India Company was

hiring cabin boys and Andrew received one of the plum jobs at the age of thirteen. Now he's twenty-seven and has a commission as Commander out of Fort Marlborough on the island of Sumatra. Andrew's a success in everything he does.'

'Do you resent his success?'

Billy looked at Rhinelander. 'Do you want a very honest answer?'

'Honest as you can give.' Rhinelander dabbed perspiration from Billy's forehead.

'I don't resent Andrew's success. I'm proud of him. I suppose I even take advantage of him. His good qualities reflect on me. Many people say I'm irresponsible. That I play the fool. And who knows? Maybe I do. Pa was always more proud of Andrew than me. But to give Pa his due, he was fair to both of us.'

'If your father was a shipbuilder, he must have been a very rich man.'

'Oh, richer than either Andrew or I ever dreamed he was. But Pa raised us to be sensible. We were brought up to respect work – and to do a lot of it. When Pa died he left a larger fortune than either Andrew or I ever thought he had accumulated. But Andrew was worried the money might change our lives. That's when he suggested we take a gamble – what the jack? – and invest our inheritance in something big. Andrew came up with the idea of buying silver ingots in Mexico and shipping them to China to sell.'

'Why China?'

'Silver is dearer there than gold . . .'

Billy's blue eyes glazed at the idea of Andrew perhaps now covertly plotting with Easton to get a larger share of the money.

'You look tired,' Rhinelander said. 'Enough stories. Get some rest.'

Falling back into his makeshift bed, Billy admitted, 'I feel tired. I never felt like this before. Tired like an . . . old dog.'

Pausing, Billy smiled and explained, 'Andrew gave me

that nickname, "old dog", when we were boys.'

'Rest.' Rhinelander saw Billy looked weak.

Billy, his blond hair pasted with feverish perspiration to his pale forehead, laid his head on the end of the tarpaulin rolled into a pillow and gazed at the dull sheen of the silver.

Weakly he reminisced, '. . . old dog. I used to tag behind Andrew like a faithful . . . old dog.'

As his blue eyes moistened with tears, he continued, 'Andrew had his nickname, too, you know.'

Rhinelander urged, 'Save your strength, lad.'

'You'll never guess what Andrew's nickname was.'

'What was Andrew's nickname?'

'Andrew used to come jumping out from behind bushes and darting out from around corners. He loved giving me a fright and grabbing anything I had . . . Raspberry sweets . . . A little green pouch of marbles I used to have . . . Seeds I picked from a sunflower . . . Pieces of Madeira cake I got from Mrs Kendall in the kitchen . . . Oh, yes, Andrew always used to scare me and take things away from me.'

Rhinelander, seeing tears welling in Billy's eyes, urged, 'My friend, shouldn't you try to sleep?'

Billy was not listening to Paris Rhinelander; his mind was far away, wandering back to his childhood in Richmond, to a boyhood spent in a big brick house surrounded by plane trees, to hideouts built in leafy copses of lilac bushes; to boyhood friendships with kindly servants in the kitchen; to his devotion to an older brother.

'I was Old Dog and Andrew was . . . Robin Hood.'

Tears began to stream down Billy's face. 'Andrew was Robin Hood because . . . because he said there were poor people in the world who deserved my sweeties, my cakes, my marbles more than I did. He took them away from me to give to poor people. But you know what I think? Do you know what I still think after all these years?'

Rhinelander quietly asked, 'What do you still think, my young friend?'

'I . . . I. . . I think Andrew hid in some secret place and

ate my cakes and little sweeties and buried my marbles without sharing them with anybody. That's what I think. No, Andrew's not Robin Hood at all. Andrew's just bad . . . Andrew's just selfish . . . Andrew's always been a thief who . . .'

Stopping, pressing his eyes shut, Billy sobbed, 'Oh, I don't know what I think any more.'

'Rest,' Rhinelander consoled. 'Try to rest.'

8

Despite the discomfort of the increasingly hot temperature in the dark, stuffy hold deep within the *Vandal Witch*, the heat quickened Billy's recovery; perspiration washed the fever from his body and healthy scabs formed on the whip welts laddered across his back.

Due to Paris Rhinelander's patient companionship, Billy eventually began to stand, sit, perform physical exercises in the small space of their prison. Every day a crew member unbattened the hatch to lower food, buckets of fresh water and hoist up their buckets of waste. Rhinelander stopped shaving his whiskers and cutting his corn yellow hair; he gave his shaving equipment – razor, strop, soap and brush – to Billy, who shaved daily and kept his hair neatly washed and barbered. They also performed daily exercises, doing sit-ups, stomach bends, a variety of leg movements, keeping their muscles and tendons in good, firm condition, optimistic that they would soon be released.

At the beginning of the *Vandal Witch*'s fourth week out of Boston, the heat grew worse rather than abating, and the destination still remained a mystery.

After finishing a midday meal of salted beef and hard

biscuits, Billy asked, 'Do you think we sail for the West Indies?'

Rhinelander, his beard now bushy and red, replied, 'We would have reached the first islands by now, sailed through the Bahamas or Antilles and heard the crew hail land.'

Billy considered the few alternatives. 'Captain Kerr bragged to me about being the captain of a slave ship. Do you think we're heading south-east towards Africa? Making our way down the Slave Coast or one of the Guineas?'

'Africa would be more logical than the Caribbean. But what would Kerr do with us if we do sail for Africa? And what about that wench you saw trying to escape from his cabin?'

Rhinelander, as well as having been concerned about Billy's physical recovery, had also worried about Billy's mental stability. But he was satisfied now that Billy was out of danger, both physically and mentally.

Although Rhinelander had learned that Billy was concerned about Andrew Peake truying to cheat him out of his share of silver ingots, he was still convinced that it was best to keep Billy from thinking of, or speaking about his brother at all, not to dwell on the past but to concentrate instead on the present, to pass their hours discussing the *Vandal Witch* and its crew, to guess at their destination, making survival a game, a diversion to retain their sanity. And it had been in these remedial conversations that Billy told Rhinelander about seeing a young woman fighting with Captain Kerr, a lively, red-headed woman who had dashed from Kerr's cabin on the day when Billy had been whipped.

Rhinelander, still wondering why Captain Kerr had not thrown the girl down into the hold said, 'Who knows? Maybe Kerr's given the poor wench to those baboons and jackals who serve as his crew.'

Billy disagreed. 'No, I'd guess Kerr's too selfish to share anything, especially a woman, with another man.'

'Who can she be? And how do you think she got aboard

the ship? Drugged? Press-ganged like you?'

'There are many English bond servants working out their time in the American colonies,' Billy told Rhinelander. 'Men and women who sell themselves into bondage for passage to the New World and a new chance in life.'

Rhinelander knew the classification of servitude and he asked, 'Do you think the young woman's working out her term aboard this ship?'

Billy added another theory. 'Possibly. Or she might have purchased passage to England. As innocently as you or I did.'

'I'm not so innocent.' Rhinelander sat on a tarpaulin rolled into a small log and studied his large hands as he admitted, 'There are a few things I have not told you.'

'About what?'

'About me and Gabriel Easton.'

'You told me how Gabriel Easton helped you find the job in Boston.'

'Yes, but I knew Easton before I arrived in Boston,' Rhinelander admitted. 'It was Easton who persuaded me to move from Jamaica to Boston.'

'Easton is a friend of yours?'

'Not a friend,' Rhinelander quickly clarified. 'I first met him in Kingston. He had come to Jamaica making early preparations for his convoy. That's when I first met him and learned what he wanted from me.'

'Wanted? From you?'

'My story is difficult to tell. Especially to someone I now consider a friend.'

'Why would our friendship hinder you speaking?'

'Because of your brother.'

'Andrew? You also know Andrew?'

'No, I know not your brother. But I do know . . . Catherine Easton.'

'Easton's daughter?'

Rhinelander did not raise his eyes. 'Catherine is, or I should say was, my lover in Boston.'

The ocean pounded against the ship's hull; its steady

crash and wash, rise and drop, accompanied by the masts creaking in the lee of the wind, filled the silence following Rhinelander's announcement.

Not raising his head to look at Billy, Rhinelander explained in a low voice, 'Gabriel Easton procured me in Jamaica to be the lover for his daughter.'

The statement stunned Billy. He felt dizzy and wondered if he were suffering a sudden relapse.

Rhinelander elaborated. 'Gabriel Easton procured me, enticed me to move to Boston by telling me about a job available at a tannery on Parsonage Green.'

Billy stammered, 'I cannot believe what I'm hearing. I cannot fathom Gabriel Easton – respectable, self-satisfied Gabriel Easton – procuring a lover for his own flesh and blood.'

'Ah, the world is not what it seems, my young friend. Not are we humans. Oh, Catherine Easton has the outward appearance of being a genteel young lady. But would you be surprised if I told you that beneath her elegant, Mayfair façade boil the hot-blooded desires of a voluptuary. That Catherine indulges in love-making which her father fears will become known and condemn her as a harlot?'

'Desires? What kind of desires?'

'I prefer not to elaborate too specifically. But you are my friend and I will say this. I do not believe Catherine Easton would make the best spouse for your brother.'

'I am not fond of Catherine Easton but never did I–'

Billy stopped, looking in bewilderment at Rhinelander. He was still uncertain about the story and he asked, 'But why would Gabriel Easton try to induce you to travel all the way from the West Indies to Boston to become Catherine's lover? Are there not enough men in Boston?'

'I told you, Catherine possesses unique tastes. She has desires and appetites which are not easily satisfied by many men.'

'And you are capable of satisfying these special tastes?'

'I am.'

'Excuse me for prying, but how did Gabriel Easton learn of you as a potential lover for Catherine?'

'He asked the right questions at the appropriate public houses in Kingston and the answers he received led him to where I was working.'

'And what were those questions?'

'Ah, now, I will not be too specific, my young friend. Allow me only to say that there are certain men in this world who enjoy dominating women in the act of love-making. To dominate women more than in the ordinary masculine role of sexual aggression, even to participate in physical punishment of their lovers.'

Billy believed he understood. 'You dominate women.'

'Totally.'

'And hurt them?'

'When the fair ladies enjoy such sensations, yes, I do.'

'You inflict pain?'

'Often.'

'But –' Billy shook his head. 'Your manner. Your personality. It's so gentle, so contrary to . . .'

Rhinelander smiled at Billy's naïve evaluation of sexual phenomena and quirks; he said, 'Billy, a man's social manner has little to do with his more private indulgences.'

'And you enjoy this power you exert over lovers? This role of a master?'

'I must enjoy it, must I not? I participate in it. But please, do not ask me *why* I enjoy it. In past conversations with other men, I have been told that I hate women, that I'm an egoist. That only a self-centred man needs adoration, adulation, homage from a woman. Perhaps I do. Who knows? But what I do know and believe is that it is best not to question the enjoyments we pursue in this life. Not to question needs, appetites, pastimes.'

Billy stared disbelievingly at the Dutchman. 'Have I lived so innocently up to now? I considered myself to know something of the world but I do not! I have been duped by a man who's the father of my brother's betrothed. I have invested my inheritance and might lose it. And now I learn a man panders to his daughter, produces lovers who will beat his own flesh and blood. Have I been so innocent up to now?'

Before Paris Rhinelander had time to reply, the hatch opened and both young men raised their eyes, squinting at the sudden sunlight pouring into the hold; they discerned the brawny outline of Tim Scully, followed by four crewmen, climbing down the wooden ladder into the hold.

9

Tim Scully ordered his men to drag Billy up the ladder and then battened the hatch to keep Paris Rhinelander prisoner in the ship's hold as his men shoved Billy from the coaming to the larboard.

Billy, not having been in daylight for a month, tried to shield his eyes from the bright, blinding sun; despite his daily exercise his legs were still wobbly and he lurched, tripping across the tilting, slippery deck.

Taking deep gulps of fresh air as he moved, he filled his lungs with the salty breeze and squinted to look beyond the wooden railing. He saw land in the distance, a bar of white sand, the jagged outline of palm trees slanting sideways, a row of squat buildings edging the lapping blue ocean.

Stumbling closer towards the larboard, Billy groped for the railing and wondered what port they might be approaching.

A coarse voice called behind him, 'Don't get no clever idea, laddie.'

Billy turned and saw Captain Kerr glaring at him.

Kerr, dressed in a soiled shirt, breeches and worn boots, slurred in a rum-soaked voice, 'Don't be fool enough to jump overboard and try to escape.'

'Where are we?'

'A long ways from home, laddie boy! A long ways from home!'

Kerr's smugness angered Billy and, losing his temper, he lunged forward with both hands ready to grip Kerr's throat.

Crew members quickly surrounded Billy; they grabbed his arms and pushed him down to the deck. Kerr stood above him, shouting, 'Damn you and the likes of all you toffee-nosed brats to eternal hell and damnation! Nothing's going to give me more pleasure than knowing you're a slave.'

Billy lay pinioned to the deck by four sailors, shouting, 'Where are you taking me? Where are we going?'

'Razor Cove, laddie. That's where. The land you see out there is Africa. Those buildings are Razor Cove, the fort where I will be selling you as a slave.'

'A slave? Me? You can't do that!'

Kerr laughed.

'I'm English!' Billy protested. 'You can't sell an Englishman into slavery!'

'Why? Is there a law stating only a man with black skin can be sold into slavery?' Kerr laughed again, and louder.

Billy, struggling, kicking, pulling his arms against the tight hold of the crew pressing him to the deck, demanded, 'Is this Gabriel Easton's idea?'

'Aye, the fine and mighty Gabriel Easton told me to get rid of you. One way or another. But it was me who decided I might as well make a few bob off your hide. Jack Razor can probably get a fine price from you from some slave trader.'

'Jack Razor? Who in damnation is Jack Razor? Where are you taking me?'

'Razor Cove, laddie boy. Jack Razor's Cove.'

Jerking his arms, thrashing against the sailors' strong grip, Billy shouted, 'What about my silver? Who gets my silver?'

A loud blast from a conch shell sounded from below the railing. Captain Kerr moved towards the larboard, hailing the first natives paddling wooden canoes out to greet the *Vandal Witch.* Beyond the small boats, the tangled forests of Africa rose darkly above the shore line, a jagged white line of sand serrated like shark's teeth by the continuous wash of the Atlantic Ocean.

10

Far across the Atlantic Ocean the weather remained unseasonably chilly, and Boston looked little brighter than the dour days of winter.

Young Catherine Easton had been confined to her bed during the last week of April by illness, a sniffle which had developed into a severe cold. As April changed into May her condition became more of an aggravation than a complaint, but she nevertheless remained tucked in her bed as the grey, gloomy, interminable spring days dragged on and on.

Gabriel Easton spent little time at his office on Harbour Hill during these bleak springtime days; instead he chose to sit at home with Catherine and peruse his ledgers, receipts, waybills, accomplishing work in the company of his daughter who was still confined to her sick room.

Catherine, cushioned by three lace-bordered pillows, studied her father sitting alongside her in a wing-backed chair, his brow furrowed as he peered through a pair of wire spectacles perched on the bridge of his aquiline nose. He was inspecting a sheaf of lading bills which his clerk had prepared for him.

Catherine interrupted his concentration. 'Excuse me, Father, but are you worried about the convoy?'

Easton looked up from the papers and answered, 'I fear the convoy's out of my hands, Catherine. My English agents – and the good Lord Almighty – have control over what happens at the next juncture of my enterprise.' He smiled at his daughter wrapped in a pastel bedjacket.

'Father, I know so little about commerce and trade. But should you not have gone to England with the convoy? Supervised the loading and unloading of the ships before they continue to Canton?'

'I can't return to England until certain outstanding debts are completely settled, so I must trust those duties to Messrs Harbottle and Wiggins.'

'Father, does the bankruptcy still cloud our life?'

'Do not worry your pretty head about money problems, dear heart. I have everything in hand. I'm not a man to be thwarted by one mere failure and, I assure you, we'll both be returning soon to London, moving once again in best society.'

'Plans, plans, plans,' Catherine shook her head wearily and asked, 'will we ever be rich again? Be able to escape this narrow-minded place? Leave the provincial life of Boston and move back to London? Buy back our old house in Charles Street?'

'Have confidence, dear heart,' Easton urged, laying down his sheaf of papers. 'We'll regain it all. Our home in Mayfair. A coach and four. The private box at the opera. Your daily shopping trips to Bond Street. Catherine, I promise we will soon be richer than ever before.'

Sitting forward in bed, Catherine's eyes glistened for the first time in days as she asked with new excitement, 'Is this China convoy going to make us truly rich?'

'Not only the China convoy, my dear,' Easton assured her, 'but other ventures as well. I've learnt not to trust one enterprise any more. I've learnt to sow seeds in alternative gardens.'

'Father, you're keeping a secret from me. Oh, what is it? What's your other secret plan?'

Easton was not yet ready to confide in Catherine the plans he had laid to profit from the idea conceived by her fiancé, Andrew Peake, and his brother, Billy.

He replied, 'I have only one request to make of you, Catherine.'

'Name your request, Father, and it is yours.'

'To trust in whatever I do.'

'Trust?! Oh, ho, Father! You are the one and only person I do trust on the entire face of this merciless earth.'

Cautiously Easton asked, 'What about Andrew? Do you believe your husband-to-be not to be worthy of your trust?'

'Andrew Peake?' Catherine idly picked the embroidered edge of the linen sheet. 'I haven't seen Andrew Peake in three years, have I, Father? Andrew could well be a different man from the suitor I fell in love with when I saw him on his one and only trip to this wretched place.'

Suspecting that his daughter meant that she – and not Andrew Peake – had changed in recent years, Easton replied, 'Everybody changes, dear, and who knows? Perhaps you'll surprise yourself by breaking the betrothal yourself. Has the prospect ever occurred to you?'

'Would such a decision upset you? Distress you, even dishonour you? If I broke my engagement?'

Easton replied without hesitation. 'I would only be distressed knowing you were to enter an unhappy marriage.'

Catherine reached for her father's hand; she pulled it gently towards her breast, pledging, 'For the moment, I do not want to think of any man but you.'

Easton smiled; he had showered Catherine with love since her mother had died in the girl's infancy. He knew he was too often guilty of spoiling his daughter, indulging her with favours and gifts; but now, sitting alongside her bed, he forgot about any anxiety she had caused him in the past and looked proudly at her.

Catherine, warmly clasping her father's hand in both of hers, reminisced, 'Remember when I was a girl in London, Father? Remember Nurse Bingey? And when I was naughty, Nurse Bingey could not cope with my impudent ways and you would have to scold me?'

Easton, smiling at Catherine recalling her childhood in

Charles Street, Mayfair, thought about the sharp contrast of those past, happy days in England with the unsavoury times now when Catherine hungered for men to dominate her in crude sexual acts.

Thinking about his daughter's adult attitudes, Easton also thought about Paris Rhinelander, how the big Dutchman had been easy to get rid of and was at this very moment possibly sailing aboard the *Vandal Witch*, perhaps had even reached Africa.

Easton considered too, how Paris Rhinelander and Billy Peake had undoubtedly spoken by now, had compared stories, more than likely had even discussed the fact that Catherine was little better than a drab, a strumpet, certainly not worthy to be the wife of Billy's brother, a respected commander and stockholder in the East India Company.

Catherine's voice interrupted Easton's thoughts. She asked, 'Do you remember, Father?'

The question jolted Easton. He glanced back to Catherine propped up by the lacy pillows on the bed and asked, 'Remember what, my dear?'

'How you used to pinch me? To punish me with your razor strop?'

He immediately protested. 'I never stropped you, Catherine!'

'You did! You did punish me! You were a very stern taskmaster, Father. But I am grateful for it.'

Easton reconsidered the matter, 'Perhaps you needed discipline as a child, Catherine, and I made you toe the line. But I most certainly did nothing more severe than to send you to your room without supper.'

'Father, please! Don't apologise! I'm not complaining. If anything, I'm . . . thanking you! When I needed punishment you certainly administered it to me with the necessary authority and sternness.'

Shaking his head, Easton insisted, 'No, no, I never punished you, Catherine.'

'Father, to punish me doesn't mean you didn't love

me. Punishment is often a form of affection.'

'But I have more than affection for you, Catherine. I'm your father. I love you.'

'And I love you, Father.' Catherine pressed her father's hand to her breasts.

Easton began, 'I try to provide you with the best –' Stopping, he suddenly realised that Catherine was pressing his hand to her nipples, that she was making herself taut with his fingertips. He quickly pulled away his hand and stared at her with astonishment.

Catherine smiled sweetly. 'I'm a woman now, Father, am I not? With womanly attributes and tastes.'

To Easton's mind the innocent-looking smile only increased the horror of her actions.

'I'm a woman, Father, but sometimes I do act like a naughty little girl, do I not?'

Easton began to shake his head in horror.

Catherine assured him, 'I promise you I won't be naughty, Father, if you give me what I want.'

Easton's throat was dry as he asked, 'What . . . do . . . you . . . want . . . Catherine?'

Catherine Easton was cunning; she recognised she had shocked her father into obedience. She quickly proceeded with her plan, explaining, 'I saw a man, Father.'

'A . . . man?' Easton's mind was still stunned by her prurient overture to him.

Catherine nodded. 'A man working down the street from our house. I want you to send him to me.'

Easton spoke without emotion, neither with approval nor disapproval, only shock; he faltered, 'Have I not always produced the young . . . gentlemen you desired to meet in the past, Catherine?'

'That's the problem, Father. They've all been "gentlemen". So well bred and nicely mannered. I want to try something new, somebody with his feet in the soil.'

'Soil?'

'A workman. A day labourer.'

'And where did you see this particular . . . workman you now desire?'

'There's a road gang cobbling the street down from our house, close to Squire Haney's house.'

Easton remembered the road gang, coarse-faced and roughly clothed men; he believed they were Irish, convicts sent to the colonies after being released from British penal institutions. Rowdy and disreputable dregs of society.

Catherine went on, 'One of the workmen has dark curly hair, Father. He doesn't wear a cap like the other men in the gang.'

Easton, beginning to regain his wits, asked, 'You now want a . . . labourer? A day labourer, Catherine?'

She nodded, 'I do, Father.'

'After I educated you? Dressed you in fine clothes? Paid for spinet, dance and elocution lessons. You want a . . . labourer?'

'But he is so handsome, Father! Not too young. In fact I'd wager only a few years younger than you.'

Easton's forehead was beaded with perspiration; he thought how he had been sitting here and foolishly lost himself in past memories, how he had been thinking of Catherine as being an innocent young girl in Charles Street in Mayfair and had gullibly, stupidly allowed her to lead him into a trap.

She proceeded, 'I'd like you to get the workman for me, Father. That is, unless *you* want to be my new friend this time.' She paused before sweetly asking, 'Do you?'

He recoiled, 'Catherine!'

Lowering the sheets from her breasts, she shamelessly teased, 'I've grown into a very big girl, Father. Perhaps you would like to see how I've developed . . .'

Easton stood quickly from the chair, turning his head and ordering, 'Stop this!'

Catherine's mocking laughter filled the bedroom.

'Stop this, I say! Stop!'

Laughing at him, she challenged, 'Perhaps you should

punish me, Father? If so, do you choose a rod or your razor strop?'

'Be still!'

'Or a cane?' she persisted, like a demon. 'A cane would make welts on my little pink bottom.'

'Be still!'

Easton stormed from Catherine's bedroom, sickened that his daughter was using the most heinous sin on earth to blackmail him to secure her new lovers, men off the street.

He told himself, 'I must get this girl married off to Andrew Peake before nobody will take her. But how? Is it too late to achieve? Does the goal of one ambition cancel another?'

The tall Irishman with curly black hair and heavily lashed eyes was named Brendan Keenan, and he appeared at the back door of the Easton home the following afternoon. He was shown to the cellar where he was greeted by Catherine Easton, who asked him to help her mend a piece of old furniture, a wooden chair.

Bidding Keenan to sit down in the chair, Catherine knelt down on the cellar's dirt floor in front of him to explain what she wanted done to the chair, but she accidentally slipped forward, her face landing in the Irishman's lap.

In an attempt to raise herself from the awkward position, Catherine's hand fell onto the Irishman's crotch, discovering there were no buttons on the fly of his twill work trousers and that his penis readily became erect with the pressure of her hand.

Catherine, pretending to fumble in raising herself from his lap, discovered that the Irishman's penis was not only large in length but also in width. She brazenly leaned forward for a closer inspection.

'Fine lady, please,' pleaded the Irish labourer, moving to cover his instant reaction to her prodding.

'Sir, you are my guest.' Catherine did not look at his face as she spoke. She knelt on the floor, pushing away his hand, trying to peer more closely at his penis.

'"Sir"?' he asked, his voice touched with a brogue. 'I am no gentleman to be called "sir", fine lady.'

'You are far better than a gentleman.' Catherine then lowered her mouth, stretching her lips to begin satisfying him and her own salacious desires.

The brawny Irishman, soon forgetting about the social barriers separating him from such a well-spoken and fashionably dressed young lady, watched Catherine's head bob up and down in his lap. He finally commented, 'You be a surprising young lady to know how to make a man feel so content.'

Pleased with his compliment, Catherine kept moving her head back and forth, positioning her hands on his muscular thighs to balance herself on her haunches.

'You certainly do know how to serve a man proper.' The Irishman soon grew bolder, praising, 'I feel not one bite of a tooth against me and it's a good sized piece of meat you be sucking with your mouth, miss!'

Enjoying the taste of the erect organ, Catherine removed it from her mouth, savoured the flavour, and proceeded to rub it across her lips, over her eyes, back and forth across both cheeks; then began kissing its full length, from the crown down to the scrotum.

'Enough of your kissing and cooing now, mind you.' Brendan Keenan grabbed his penis and pushed it towards her lips, ordering, 'Put my prick back in your mouth and let's be feeling you pulling on it again with that fine pair of rosy sweet lips.'

Catherine again resumed providing pleasure for the Irish labourer, moving her head back and forth, being careful not to cut his tenderness with the undercut of her teeth.

Brendan Keenan, now totally at ease, feeling in complete control of the situation, announced, 'I might allow you to continue all afternoon down on your knees in front of me, lass.'

The next afternoon, Brendan Keenan appeared at the back door of the Easton house and again met Catherine in the cellar. He reappeared at the back door on three more visits and, finally, on his fifth visit to the Easton house, Keenan became more aggressive, calling at the front door, demanding to be taken into the parlour for a glass of spirits and a pipe of tobacco before he allowed Catherine Easton the privilege of sucking his penis.

Across Boston harbour Gabriel Easton stood behind the mullioned window in his office and watched the Irish labourer being admitted through the front door of his home.

Nervously fingering the jagged scar on his cheek, Easton decided, 'I've got to do something with that girl before it's too late, before she's locked in the public stocks and persecuted for being the wanton sinner that she is.'

Easton's solution was not resolved. But he knew he must begin making plans for guarding Catherine as if she suffered from some rare form of dementia, was diseased in the mind. And was she?

Book Two

Castle of a Thousand Wives

11

'A white man? Travelling on foot? Across mucky Africa? You must be crazy, Jack Razor, crazy as a bed-bug in a hot kettle!'

'Africa's no more dangerous than the Atlantic bloody Ocean, you old bugger, Stan Kerr, and how many times have you crossed the Atlantic bloody Ocean in that walnut shell you call a ship?'

'At least the Atlantic bloody Ocean's not full of nignogs and woolly heads fixing to eat my ass for their breakfast!'

'But you don't understand!' argued the slave trader, Jack Razor, a pot-bellied Englishman with sun-baked skin, a thick grown moustache and piercing blue eyes. 'There's trouble brewing hereabouts between the Dahomey and the Fanti. I've got to leave this mosquito-swarming hell-hole for two, maybe three bloody months while they go to war.'

It was late afternoon. The African sun was sinking towards the Atlantic's rippling horizon, colouring the raggedy cocoa palms lining the slave station, Razor Cove, located on the stretch of West African coastline called the Slave Coast. A short distance off-shore the *Vandal Witch* lay at anchor, motionless in calm waters after her transatlantic voyage. The slave galley rested low in the bay, heavy with the ingots stored in its hold, basking in the rich colouring from the brilliant orange disc of the sun, surrounded by white foam collecting in the surf in circles around its hull.

Beyond the scaly palm trees lining the driftwood-littered shore, Captain Kerr and Jack Razor sat under a grass-roofed pavilion built in the middle of a complex of small wooden shacks and straw huts. Kerr and Razor were sharing a bottle of coarse rum while a black woman, her prune-coloured cheeks gashed with tribal marks, squatted on the dirt floor next to Razor's cane chair.

The mood at Razor Cove, compared to the last weeks

aboard the *Vandal Witch*, was relaxing, even tranquil for Kerr; he ignored the stench of faeces pervading the dirt compound, slapping at the buzz of flies and mosquitoes, and enjoying exchanging stories with his conniving old friend, Jack Razor.

Kerr's and Razor's reunions were simple: they drank rum, they exchanged stories about their pasts, they discussed plans for the future and they both tried to cheat one another, in small or large ways, while they both secretly studied one another's face to gauge how time, the tropics, the lonely business of slave-trading, were taking their toll; if the other man showed signs yet of syphilis or the flux, or a hint of fever in the whites of his eyes, if he was perhaps getting a little closer to madness.

Kerr and Razor discussed the Africans whom Razor agreed to sell to Kerr, the white people Kerr would be leaving at Razor Cove, and Razor's plan to evacuate the slave station temporarily and travel across Africa with a foot caravan of slaves, supplies and native porters.

After listening to Razor's scheme for leaving his slave station, Kerr aske, 'Why don't you sail around Africa instead of walking across it? Ships pass your front door and would sail you for a small take of your cargo. Dangers are one thing, mate, but, good Lord Almighty, do you know how bloody long your trek will take?'

Razor was confident, even stubborn about the success of his foot expedition. He leaned back on the back legs of his chair, saying, 'I figure four weeks, no more than five, will see me across Africa. Let me show you why I'm thinking four or five weeks.'

Razor grabbed a riding crop from the table and grunted as he leaned forward in the chair to draw an inverted triangle in the dirt.

Pointing to the left side of the triangle, he said, 'Here. Let's say this is where we are now . . . Razor Cove. And across the other side . . . is . . . Mombasa Town. So the shortest, most sensible way to travel from here to

Mombasa Town is across . . .' Razor drew a diagonal line across the middle of the dirt triangle.

'The turds of a hundred bullocks, Jack Razor!' Kerr shook his head as he stared at the crudely drawn map. 'You'll never live to see Mombasa or any other town. Some Johnny Nignog will eat you for breakfast and shit you out by supper.'

Kerr's opinion did not deter Razor; he refilled both cups from the rum bottle, saying, 'Maybe a few tribes are cannibals and have their strange rites. But I've been warned about them tribes. I won't pass through their countries or little patches of power.'

'Warned? You'd be best "warned" not to go at all!'

Razor still insisted, 'I've got good friends, friends of long standing who'll be helping me. Don't forget, mate, I've been trading with the three most powerful tribes in all Africa for the last dozen years. Don't forget that, mate. Jack Razor's their friend. Those chieftains and warriors come down from the mountains to bring me their prisoners.'

Again pointing his riding crop at the roughly drawn map on the dirt floor, Razor explained, 'The Dahomeys will lead me to here, to the border of the Oubangi kingdom. The Oubangi will lead me to here, the Humari. And the Humari will take me over the last big mountains, down to the plains of Mombasa.'

'You sit there telling me, Jack Razor, that three nit-picking tribes control all Africa?'

Razor waved his hand over the dirt map. 'I'm only talking about the route I'll be walking. The three *big* tribes. Take the Humari, they control the lives of seven whole nations. Maybe more. Their main place is called Humari Umbtari. Captain Kidd was there himself, what, seventy-five, eighty years ago? Kidd dubbed the place "Castle of a Thousand Wives". Its queer ways even confused Kidd.'

Kerr was impressed. 'Kidd? The pirate? He made this trip?'

'Kidd ventured on foot into Africa from the other side. I

got the story from a bloke who said farewell to him down in Dar es Salaam. But no white man I know of ever crossed Africa from shore to shore. I'll be the first.'

Kerr was not interested in a man setting a precedent; he was still thinking about Captain Kidd, the story of one ruler possessing so many spouses. He asked, 'And there's a city Kidd called the "Castle of a Thousand Wives"? One king with a thousand women all his own?'

'A thousand's a bit of an exaggeration. There's probably no more than two or three hundred wives in any one place for any one African ruler. They're like those Ottomans with their harems up in Turkey.'

'Two or three hundred women! Imagine that much pudding!'

Razor's voice affected a lofty tone now that he was aware he possessed facts unknown by Stan Kerr. He said airily, 'Of course, the number does not include the king's courtesans and prostitutes.'

Kerr was ogle-eyed. 'Prostitutes as well as wives?'

Razor nodded. 'Women to be touched by no other man but the king.'

Shaking his head in wonderment, Kerr said, 'I tell you this much, Jack Razor. Those kings got more pudding than you've got brains.'

Jack Razor had discovered in the years of trading with Stan Kerr that the sea captain knew little – and cared less – about the dark-skinned people he transported in his slave galley to flesh markets in the New World. Jack Razor was no scholar or expert on cultures; he spoke no tribal dialects, nor African tongues; but he was familiar with native customs and practices as well as traditions which meant life, death and prosperity to him.

Splashing more rum into Kerr's cup, Razor said, 'I do not have many choices, Stan. I can head across Africa or stay right here in the Cove and get slaughtered. When the Dahomey nation goes to war, it's a big war, a blood-hungry war and any white man who gets in the way will lose everything he's got – including the head on his shoulders, the nuts between his legs and the heart beating in his chest. But if I make myself scarce, show a bit of respect for their power, the Dahomey will bring their prisoners to me for peaceful trading when I come back.'

'What if they lose this war?'

Razor nodded his head towards the foothills, the forests climbing into shadowy mountains in the fading sunlight behind him. 'I know how the card deck is stacked out there in the bushes, and the Dahomey won't lose. They're strong, powerful, smart people.'

'Dahomeys? They're the niggers who've been selling you prime slaves all these years?'

Razor nodded. 'The Dahomeys are a rich, proud nation. They take many prisoners in raids on mountain villages. And they are good traders. They learned long ago not to be dazzled by trinkets and gaudy rags most white men try to flog off onto them.'

'Any Dahomeys for me on this trip? I get a good price for a sound nigger in Jamaica. I could pack a hundred and twenty, hundred and fifty with those ingots down in my hold.'

Razor shook his head. 'No, I told you, Kerr, I'll sell you fifty and that's all for this trip. I've got to keep a hundred or so for myself to trade along the way. Don't forget, Africans get as greedy for slaves as the white men. I want to see, too, what kind of price I can get in those slave markets over there on the east coast.'

'What market's going to be east that's not here?'

'Mombasa. Madagascar. The Turk's prison, Slave Island. Who knows where I'm going to end up? Could even make Khartoum. White slaves go for a good price in Khartoum. This war brewing here is giving me both a chance and good reason to spread my wings.'

'Jack, you ain't got no wings. You've got feet. Two big, clodhopping feet. And they're going to be a right sore pair of bloody stumps before you can say Johnny Pirate. Now, I ain't blaming you for wanting to go places like Khartoum or Mombasa. But taking niggers across Africa to sell, well

Jack, you don't know what you'll be running into along the way, do you? Those heathens out there in the jungle will make one big meat pie out of you, Jack Razor.'

Razor calmly replied, 'I've got porters from every tribe to see me safely across the mountains. Dahomey. Oubangi. Umbtari. All the best men. They work peacefully together, those tribesmen. Believe me, mate, I know what I'm doing.'

'You're making a big mistake, Jackie Razor, that's what you're doing. Making one big mistake. You've built yourself up a grand reputation for yourself here in this cove. No tribe's going to harm you if you stay put right here at home. I say sell all the slaves you can spare to me and stay here to build up a good little stock of prize niggers. I'll be back in four, five months. The nignogs' big war will be over. You'll be here to cream off the prisoners, then you and me, Jack, can be partners. In business all ourselves.'

Kerr leaned forward in his chair, leering at Razor as he confided, 'I've got my shipful of ingots out there in the cove, don't you forget. I'll be selling them for gold and have money to invest. Start our own slave market in the West Indies, Brazil, maybe in America. You and me, we can be partners. Forget about auction houses and clearing docks owned by other greedy geezers. We'll do the clearing and the profiting ourselves. What you say to that, Jackie boy? What you say?'

Razor did not immediately respond; he appeared to be considering Kerr's proposal for partnership. He knew Kerr had consumed a great deal of rum in the few hours since coming ashore. He also knew the wily, whiskered captain was trying to get as many slaves as he could and that Kerr did not want to scour the west coast of Africa for more slaves. Also, Razor remembered the story about the Mexican ingots stowed aboard the *Vandal Witch* and Kerr's plan to cheat the Englishman in Boston from his share of the shipment.

Razor finally answered, 'You don't need a new partner like me, Kerr. What you need is help dealing with the partner you've already got. It doesn't sound to me like this Gabriel Easton fella is a man who's going to take too sweetly to being cheated out of his silver.'

'Cheated? It ain't Easton's silver in the first place! It belongs to that Peake kid and his brother. That tow-headed brat you've got locked up back there in a hut!'

Jack Razor had not yet had time to examine Billy Peake. But he liked the idea of selling white slaves to African and Arab dealers in Umbtari or Khartoum. The prospect added to the lure of his expedition. Considering the profits of selling robust young Europeans in Africa, he asked, 'Why don't you give me that big blond Dutchman you've still got aboard the *Witch*? Let me sell the Dutchman along with the English kid and your red-headed wench.'

'You call me greedy! Listen to you!' Kerr slumped back in his chair, insisting, 'No, you get the English kid plus the Brett wench. You go sell those two to the Arabs. But you don't get my Dutchman. He's locked on the *Witch* and he stays there – all the way back to Jamaica! I can get more ransom from his stepfolks than you could get from any Arab slaver wanting white infidels for the auction block.'

'Tell me about your redheaded wench,' Razor asked, 'She knocked up?'

'Not by me, she ain't,' Kerr snorted. 'Devilish-eyed young bitch. Why do you think I'm dumping her here? I ain't for raping a woman. A bit of a fight ain't bad, but a hurricane? Not for me!'

Kerr glanced at Jack Razor's African concubine squatting on the dirt floor of the pavilion. He lowered his voice, confiding, 'The white bitch almost sliced off my pecker with her fingernails, she did. The hussy's a tiger. Got claws like a bloody tiger. The jungle's a good place for the likes of those claws.'

Razor considered the young red-headed woman now being brought ashore in a skiff. 'I'll probably mate her with the English kid. Africans and Turks are no different from white men. They like to buy a wench with a sucker planted in her belly. Makes them think they're getting a bargain.'

'Talking about buying, Jack, let me see what you've got in your pens before it gets too dark. I plan to start loading tomorrow and weigh anchor in two, three days time. I've got a close schedule to keep on this crossing, a schedule that'll make the difference between being a pauper or a . . . bloody king myself!'

Downing the cup of rum, Kerr rose from the table and said with resignation, 'So, if you ain't letting me have more than seventy-five niggers, I might as well start picking them now.'

'Seventy-five?' Razor laughed as he also rose from the chair. 'No, Kerr. You old bugger, I said fifty and not a head more. That includes the price for the two white skins you're leaving here.'

Razor shoved the bottle of rum towards the edge of the table and nodded to the black woman. 'Here, Hai Tai. Bring drink for our friend. He's going to need it.'

The black woman, Hai Tai, sullenly rose to her feet and lifted the rum bottle from the table. She followed the two white men from the pavilion, her generous hips lazily swaying beneath the folds of the red cloth wrapped around her midsection.

The slave pens at Razor Cove – a large dirt compound surrounded by a palisade of bamboo poles – were located down-wind from the pavilion and small house which Jack Razor used as his living quarters.

More than two hundred people, mostly Fanti males taken prisoner from mountain villages, sat cross-legged on the dirt inside the compound. Green flies buzzed in the fading light of the day. A yellow dog stood barking as the pole gate creaked open; two dark-skinned porters began shouting in Fon at the prisoners, poking them with sticks, hurrying them to their feet as Captain Kerr, Jack Razor and Hai Tai entered the compound.

Kerr studied the collection of impassive black faces, many of them with war mud still caking their heads, a few with white paint slashed across their foreheads; he was displeased and muttered, 'Sickly looking bunch ain't they?'

Razor shrugged. 'What the hell do you expect? There's drought in the lowlands. Not much food this year. I've been fattening them up on dab-a-dab. You take decent care of them in the crossing and they'll be in good shape by Jamaica. I'll throw in a big jar of palm oil. You shine up the bad ones with cheat.'

Kerr knew the many ruses of selling sick and infirm slaves to buyers in the New World. He looked around the fetid compound, asking, 'Where's the wenches?'

'Wenches are down there,' Razor nodded towards a group of women squatting on the dirt. 'Not too many wenches this year.'

Kerr ordered, 'Mix them wenches with the bucks. I want to look at them together.'

Razor passed the order in Fon to his guards and then nodded for Hai Tai to hand the rum bottle to Kerr.

Fortified with more liquor, Kerr approached the first male African and reached to finger his mouth, feeling for teeth, looking at the condition of his gums for any sign of disease. Shaking his head with disapproval, Kerr stepped back to study the man's spindly arms, a stomach sunk into his rib cage.

'Poor, poor. I'll take him but he won't last a month on a sugar plantation.'

Kerr passed down the line. The next prisoner was taller, a man with a muscular frame, his high cheekbones decorated with a curling design of needle welts. Kerr stared into the man's bloodshot eyes and then, for no apparent reason, punched him in the stomach.

The African, gasping for breath, bent forward, both hands gripping his stomach.

Kerr stepped behind him and shouted to the two black guards, 'Sammy! Komo! Hold open his fat arse!'

The guards, Sammy and Komo, having worked with Kerr on previous visits, understood what he wanted and they moved to either side of the prisoner, holding back the fleshy black cheeks of his buttocks.

Kerr wrinkled his nose as he leaned forward to inspect the man's anus. Nodding with approval at what he saw, Kerr rose to announce, 'No worms. One nigger with worms crawling out his arse, the whole ship's got worms crawling out its arse.'

He passed down the line, stopping next in front of a woman who balanced a small child on her hip.

'Razor!' he called. 'This wench and the sucker count for one, right?'

'Damn you, Kerr. Stop trying to cheat me. The kid's big enough to stand. They count for two!'

Kerr was not listening. He ignored the child, examining the woman more closely, feeling the sag of her breasts, pushing her, turning her so he could see the size of her buttocks, the condition of her skin, the clutch of her vagina.

Appraising her, he explained across the compound, 'That damned white wench cheated me out of my fun so I need a good woman for the way back.'

He moved to the next person, but looked over his shoulder at the black woman balancing the child on her hip. He called to Razor, 'Much obliged, Jack, to see more of her tonight in my bed.'

The west coast of Africa had become a second home to Captain Stanley Kerr in passing years; he always got a reception, if not happiness. The Grain Coast, the Ivory Coast, the Gold Coast, the Slave Coast. From the yellow plantation forests of Senegambia, down to the dusty grey settlement of Cabinda at the wide mouth of the Congo River, Kerr had paid calls to filthy slave stations built along brackish inlets and sailed into fine stone harbours of cliff-top fortresses guarded by shiny black cannons.

Kerr had dealt with the Portuguese, French and Spanish, as well as the English, since he had first begun working the slave trade. Kerr had seen pomp wither and disappear, the demise of bewigged gentlemen dressed in lace jabots and brocade frock-coats; he had watched the proliferation of coarse men like his friend, Jack Razor, bare-headed traders who struggled for two things; to make a shilling and to survive in the tropics, men who forgot about pomp and gilded ideals

Kerr knew that royal charters from European courts had long ago disappeared from West Africa, were now gone with flowery permission granted to companies 'to buy and sell slaves for the express purpose of developing the resources of the New World.' Greed and muscle ruled the slave trade; Kerr suspected those values had always been king and, like other men profiting from slavery, kept up his energy with rum, brandy, liquors from Europe, coarse wines from tribesmen – any concoction to dull his brain against the miseries he saw, smelt, heard, as well as to forget the diseases he constantly feared.

As on past visits to Africa, tonight's heat was stifling for Kerr and he lay awake, sweating, irritable, on the small cot inside the wooden shack which Jack Razor had allocated to him at Razor Cove. Again tonight Kerr thought about getting out of the slave trade. He had wanted to escape long ago after his first crossing, but there had never been the chance, never the money to leave, never the opportunity to retire.

Believing that his opportunity to escape had finally come, Kerr lay on the cot and thought about the fortune stowed in the hold of the *Vandal Witch*. The night outside the shack was dark, thick with blackness, alive with mysterious noises, crawling, chewing, twisting, buzzing sounds. But Kerr turned a deaf ear to the night's mysterious noises and concentrated instead on his plan for sailing back across the Atlantic to Jamaica.

Gabriel Easton had given Kerr orders to break from the China convoy, to follow a separately charted course around Africa, north through the East Indies up to China and the port of Canton, where the silver was to be sold at the price received for gold in Europe. But Kerr did not know the East Indies and China. Nor the Indian Ocean and the Orient. He told himself that the Atlantic had always been his haunt. The Caribbean waters, the west coast of Africa.

So why profit but get lost in the process and be unable to enjoy his money? Also, why not reap the profit by selling *all* the silver instead of just half of it? Would not the hog share outweigh the difference in the selling price?

The clicking of a tongue disturbed Kerr's plots for the future; he knew it must be the visitor he was expecting, the woman he had seen in the slave compound.

Kerr, without rising, grunted for the African woman to come into the hut.

The tongue clicking subsided but the woman did not appear in the doorway.

Kerr raised himself on the cot and shouted, 'Here! Inside, dummy!'

Finally, seeing the woman in the doorway, Kerr also saw the child still riding high on her hip. He shouted, 'Leave your brat outside.'

The woman spoke no English.

Kerr, motioning towards his own hip, shook his head and said, 'The kid – leave the kid outside. Understand?'

The woman understood. She set the infant on the dirt before sheepishly entering the doorway.

Kerr motioned her to step closer towards his narrow cot. He said, 'Let's get a good look at you, Blackie.'

The woman was hesitant, her eyes large and flickering with fear.

'Get over here!' Kerr shouted and reached for the leather quirt lying alongside the cot.

The woman had been a captive long enough in Razor Cove to understand the threat of a quirt; she obediently scuffled her bare feet towards the cot.

As she stood in front of the cot, Kerr sat on the edge of the thin mattress, his legs open so the woman could step closer to him. He rubbed his hands over the fabric tied around her curvaceous hips and in circular movements over her fulsome buttocks. 'Hmmm. Put together preety good, ain't you, Blackie?'

The woman stood stiffly, awkward in front of him.

Kerr raised his eyes as he reached towards her large

breasts, freeing them from their cloth wrapping.

'Look at them titties!'

Placing both hands on the woman's breast, Kerr moved his mouth forward, parting his lips to taste one brown nipple spreading from the tip of her bosom.

He nibbled, chewed, sucked on the nipple, moving his mouth to the other breast, groaning pleasurably, murmuring 'Tit . . . hmmm . . . nice, good, tittie . . .'

Kerr, sucking like a babe on the other nipple, began to free his penis from his trousers when he heard the child start to cry outside the shack.

Pulling back his head, Kerr bellowed towards the doorway, 'Shut your face, brat!'

Outside the shack the child's cry became louder.

Kerr shouted, 'Shut your face, God damn you to hell, you little nigger brat!'

The child's wails grew more desperate.

'Shut your face, kid or–'

The woman stepped backwards; she motioned to herself, then to the doorway, miming that she would go outside to quiet her child.

Kerr understood the message she conveyed with her hands, but he did not approve what she proposed.

'No, God damn it to hell! You stay here, I'll shut the little bastard up myself!'

Kerr, rising from the bed, pushed the woman aside and again grabbed for his quirt.

The young mother, seeing Kerr taking the quirt to punish her child, instantly grabbed at the short leather lash.

Kerr pushed her down to the dirt floor. 'Don't fight . . . *me*!'

The woman clung to Kerr's leg, snatching for the quirt, pulling him down with her in a sudden surge of strength.

'Goddamn you, black nigger molly!'

Kerr floundered on top of her, lying astride her spread legs, trapping her beneath his body.

Kerr, beginning to laugh, said, 'Look what's happened!

I got you trapped, Blackie! I got you trapped exactly where I want you!'

Kerr, now ignoring the child's cries outside the shack, concentrated on amusing himself with the young woman, freeing his penis from his trousers, feeling for the slit of her womanhood, laughing at her terror.

The first jab of his penis brought a cry from the woman. Kerr laughed louder, pushing his erect penis faster, harder, deeper between her legs.

The mother continued resisting Kerr as his hips drove against her, his saliva dripping down over her face.

Laughing at her struggling, Kerr taunted, 'That's a girl, you wiggle, Blackie. You wiggle and make yourself hot. Heat up your pudding. Toss around and wiggle!'

The woman, gripping her hands into fists, began to beat against Kerr's shoulders, to tear at the long greasy hanks of hair, to grip at his chin whiskers.

'Slut!' Kerr roared, slapping away her hand. 'I told you I had enough of you wenches fighting me!' He struck her again, ordering, 'Stop your fighting me!'

The young African woman clawed at Kerr's face, trying to thrust up her stomach and throw him from her.

Kerr, heavy and insistent to enjoy sex, hit the woman with a harder blow, his penis beginning to reach a tingling sensation inside the warmth of her clutch. Her resistance had tightened, heating her vaginal hold on him, and he drove faster, suddenly laughing again, his saliva drooling over her face.

'Damn women!' he grunted, driving his hips faster and faster on top of her. 'Damn women! No matter what colour you are, all you want is to fight old Stan Kerr, don't you, slut? Don't you? Don't you?'

Kerr's breath came faster; he panted, 'But I'm getting you . . . I'm getting you . . . oh, am I getting you!'

His shouts of sexual ecstasy soon filled the shack; his body jerked with the orgasm, his hips driving harder, faster against her.

Outside the shack the child continued to cry but now a

brown sticky fluid poured from the child's tiny mouth, the first visible sign of disease, the tropical contagion called the flux, a carrier of death.

12

Billy Peake was awakened by the sound of loud hollering outside the palm hut where he had been taken from the *Vandal Witch* and spent his first night in Africa.

Springing from the dirt floor, Billy pulled back the doeskin hanging over the low doorway and saw two sentries, dressed in breech clothes, still guarding the hut.

'I am English,' he said, gesturing to himself. 'I come from that ship –' He pointed to where the *Vandal Witch* was anchored in the cove.

Billy, seeing two rafts transporting black-skinned people shouting and wailing as they were carried from the shore to the slave ship, realized that the hollering came from them, that the *Vandal Witch* had begun loading prisoners to take away as slaves. But why? Where would Kerr take them? To China? Was Kerr going to unload the silver here and take on slaves? What was happening?

The two sentries pushed Billy back inside the hut; the doeskin fell into position and again the hut became dark, lit only by a small hole in the centre of the conical roof.

Pacing the dirt floor of the hut, Billy remembered the thought which had nagged him when he had been trying to sleep last night: Kerr had told him yesterday he was going to sell him as a slave.

'A slave?' Billy slowed his pacing. 'Me? A white man? Sold into slavery? Is such a thing possible?'

Looking around him at the tightly woven walls, Billy thought about the many helpless people in the world who were slaves. 'Is this how an African feels when he's chained and shackled aboard a slave ship? Does a Negro, chopping sugar cane on a West Indian plantation, think it's impossible for him to spend the rest of his life as a . . . slave?'

Billy's heartbeat quickened; he felt dizzy; the palms of his hands broke out in a cold, nervous sweat. Hoping he would not get hysterical, Billy told himself it was important to remain calm, level-headed, in control of all his senses, if he hoped to survive.

Then he heard voices outside the hut again. Moving quickly back towards the low doorway covered by the doeskin, Billy stopped abruptly when he saw the skin move and Captain Kerr enter the hut.

Kerr, looking tired and even more slovenly than when Billy had last seen him, was followed into the hut by another white man, a portly man with a thick moustache who Billy guessed must be the slave trader, Jack Razor.

Two African guards followed Razor into the hut; one guard moved alongside Billy and the other led the red-headed woman whom Billy had seen once before – four weeks earlier aboard the *Vandal Witch*.

Kerr, standing directly in front of Billy, spoke to Jack Razor, 'This here is the lad who don't know how to keep his mouth shut.'

Razor's eyes became small, black and beady as he appraised Billy's athletic body through the ragged, soiled clothing.

Nodding his head, Razor admitted, 'Not bad-looking. Strong too, is he?'

'Strong? Strong as a mule. Takes a whipping like a nigger. Don't be afraid to treat him rough when he starts making too much noise.'

Razor paced around Billy. 'Looks healthy. Could travel straight away.'

'Travel where?' Billy asked.

'Hear that, Jack?' said Kerr. 'I warned you. The problem is he can't keep his mouth shut. Always getting himself into trouble with that big mouth.'

'What trip?' Billy, unconcerned with Kerr's opinion of him, asked, 'Where are you taking me?'

Kerr chuckled. 'The lad just can't keep that bloody mouth shut.'

Turning away from Billy, Kerr added, 'He's your problem now, Jack. Him and this little piece of baggage here –' Kerr took the young woman by the arm, shoved her towards Billy and departed from the small hut.

Jack Razor appraised Billy and the red-headed girl standing side-by-side and then he too left the small hut, beckoning the guard to follow him.

'You must be Billy Peake.'

'How do you know that?'

'Captain Kerr was always complaining about you.'

'Good.' Billy studied the young woman; she was smaller than he had remembered her to be, almost petite, with a dainty nose, small chin, hair the colour of bright, burnished copper, and large liquid green eyes. He asked, 'What's your name?'

'Jennifer . . . Jenny Brett.'

'Jenny, do you know any more than I know why we are here?'

Shaking her head, she murmured, 'No, but I –' Stopping, Jenny's upper lip began to quiver and she choked back sudden tears. 'I promised myself,' she sobbed, 'I promised myself I would not shed one tear–'

'Go ahead. A cry might do you some good.' Billy noticed the creamy skin on her forehead was slightly freckled.

Jenny Brett shook her head. 'No, I don't want to cry. I haven't cried once since we left Boston. I am strong. I fought that pig, Kerr, day and night. I won, too. I did! I fought and I kept that man from having his way with me.'

Billy detected a Cockney rhythm to her voice and said, 'You're English.'

Sniffing, Jenny nodded and answered, 'From London, I am.'

'Me, too. At least near London. I was born and raised in Richmond. Do you know where that is?'

'Richmond!' Jenny's wet eyes suddenly brightened and, wiping away her tears with a knuckle, she said happily, 'I've never been to Richmond but I know where it is. Oh, home, home, home!'

'How did you end up in Boston, Jenny? How did Captain Kerr get you on that ship?'

'Captain Kerr!' Jenny's small face tightened with anger. 'I'll have Kerr's life for doing this to me. I'll get out of here somehow. I don't know how I'll do it. I don't even know where I am! But I'll get out of here. And I'll report Kerr, that's what I'll do! I'll report him to friends of Squire Philpott and he'll report him to the Harbourmaster, and the Harbourmaster will arrest him the next time he sails into Boston. I know the Harbourmaster myself, I do. Least I saw him with my own eyes, I did. He and his missus came to supper at the home of Squire and Mrs Philpott in Boston one night when . . .'

'Wait! Wait! Hold your words a minute now, Jenny Brett. I asked you how you came to be aboard the *Vandal Witch* and you're telling me about a supper party in Boston.'

'I am, ain't I?' Jenny sheepishly lowered her head, mumbling, 'Kind of daft, ain't I?'

Sniffing, she added, 'Daft, but look . . . Billy Peake, you're making me smile. You've brought a smile to my lips for being so blooming . . . daft!'

'That's more than I can do for myself.'

'Let me answer your questions, Billy Peake. You asked how I came to be aboard the rotten ship.' Jenny took a deep sigh and began, 'I came to America on a penal ship. No use hiding that fact. Not no more. But I want to make one thing clear here and now: I didn't do nothing bad like murder to get thrown in gaol and sentenced to the penal ship. I pinched some goods in Lantern Lane, a length of flowered muslin from a haberdasher's shop.

'The Philpott family bought me off the penal ship in

Boston harbour. I was their bond servant. But then Squire Philpott up and died and Mrs Philpott got sweet on a pedlar, a no good pedlar man who was after her money. Botts, that was the pedlar's name. Charlie Botts.

'Charlie Botts liked to have his hand up more than one skirt. He had a go at me but I gave him what for and slapped his face, didn't I? My temper gets me into trouble many a time. So Botts, he sold the rest of my bond term to a tavern keeper, Robert Hoolihan, who skipped out of Boston on a bad debt and I was the one who got thrown in the slammer. And that's where Captain Kerr found me, back in the slammer again.'

Billy eyed the spirited young girl, her green eyes now lively with fire and fight. He asked, 'If Kerr paid money to get you out of prison, why is he leaving you here?'

'Paid money? Captain Kerr didn't pay one penny to get me out of prison! The warden let Kerr *take* me away! It saved the warden a crust or two of bread. Kerr's leaving me here because I was more than he'd bargained for, that's what. And I thank God for that blessing, too. Who wants to sail back across the Atlantic? Least of all to the West Indies with Captain Kerr? Who wants to sail off again in that rocking, creaking, tossing bucket of guts back across the Atlantic?'

Billy leaned his head closer. 'Did you say sail *back* across the Atlantic?'

'Ain't that daft? Captain Kerr is out of his blooming head.'

Billy still did not believe his ears. 'Kerr told you he's . . . sailing *back* across the Atlantic Ocean?'

'With a boat load of poor souls he's taking aboard here, slaves to sell to those West Indian plantations. I don't know exactly where we are but I tell you the truth. Kerr plans to sail from here with slaves as well as that gold he's got locked down in the belly of the ship.'

'Silver, not gold.'

'Gold, silver, what's the difference?' Jenny shrugged. 'All I know is there's something valuable locked down inside that bleeding tub of his.'

'It's silver and it belongs to me.'

'You?' Jenny studied Billy. Fair complexion, blond hair, a young man who looked like he might be carrying an apple in his pocket, a happy tune whistling on his lips, maybe even a teller of fibs.

She suspiciously asked, 'That silver is . . . yours?'

Billy nodded. 'Kerr's stealing it from me. That's why I'm being held here.'

'Stealing? From you?'

'From me and my brother.'

'Is your brother here, too?'

'I don't know where my brother is now.'

She believed him and said, 'And I thought Kerr done *me* raw!'

Then, again appraising Billy's innocent-looking face, Jenny thought that he looked harmless, a bit helpless, even lost; she offered, 'I guess I should've paid more attention to what Kerr said. I could've told you his plans and helped you.'

'Nothing could help me much now. But thank you for the offer.'

'You never know.' Jenny looked more closely at Billy. 'Believe me, I'm sorry.'

'Don't apologise. Please. How were you supposed to know?'

'You're nice, ain't you, Billy Peake?'

'You are, too.'

'Can I call you Billy?'

'Why not?'

Eyeing him, she said, 'If you own all that silver and talk like a gentleman, as you do, you must be somebody important or somebody–'

'Important? No, I wouldn't be here, would I?'

Jenny, holding her head at an angle, said, 'Billy, do you mind if I put a question to you?'

Billy shook his head, saying, 'Go ahead. Ask your question.'

'Are you certain?'

Billy nodded. 'Positive.'

'I know it's only morning. I know we only just met. That we're no more than strangers. So don't misunderstand me. I'm not getting cheeky. But well, I feel I can be honest with you and can say I feel . . . frightened . . . lost . . . don't know where I am . . . what's going to happen to me . . . and, Billy, would you mind ever so much if you put your arm around me, to hold me for just a minute or two? Like a brother?'

Billy looked down at the slim, pixyish Cockney girl delicately dusted with freckles. He saw a look of desperation in her liquid green eyes.

Gently, but firmly, Billy pulled Jenny towards his chest, wrapping both arms tightly around her, asking 'Now does this please you?'

Jenny snuggled into Billy's protective arms. 'Hmmmm. Ever so nicely.'

On and off throughout the remainder of the morning Jenny laid her head against Billy's strong shoulder. Shortly after midday they ate the spicy stew brought to them in wooden bowls and drank some water from a calabash. They talked a great deal. They did not discuss the future, speaking only about the past, where they had come from. Jenny was an orphan raised in Whitechapel; Billy told her about his brother living on an island called Sumatra, and they laughed at a few silly but welcome jokes.

They did not kiss until late afternoon. The sky was dark with night above the centre hole in the hut's conical roof when their laughter had turned to soft smiles, the smiles sweetened into kisses and, soon, they were making love on the dirt floor.

Jenny's mouth, sweet tasting from one of the mangoes brought to them to eat, welcomed Billy's tongue. She did not speak to him as he held her against his reclining body.

Billy brushed Jenny's face with kisses, feeling through her clothing that her slim body was firm and very feminine.

Jenny sighed when Billy touched her breasts; she did

not resist the explorations of his hands; she did not pull away when he freed his erect phallus from the confines of his breeches.

Billy was not suprised that an orphan from Whitechapel no longer possessed her virginity, but he was surprised she accepted him with such tenderness and warmth, even a hint of love. Jenny's gentle conduct meant more to Billy than the fact that she might have done this with other men in the past.

When her small hands felt the muscle capping Billy's shoulders, she asked, 'Why can't all men be like you, Billy?'

'Because you'd be with them and not me.'

'Here?' Jenny lay on the hut floor, cradling Billy between her legs, laughing. 'Africa or wherever we are?'

'I don't wish you any ill fortune but I am pleased you're here with me.'

'I don't know what I'd do if I was here alone.'

Jenny soon began tossing her head from side to side, feeling Billy filling her with his power, awakening another crest of ecstasy deep within her.

Billy, watching pleasure spread on Jenny's face, ivory as a cameo, praised, 'You're little but like an ocean, you know that? You sweep me with waves, warm, warm waves deep inside you . . .'

Jenny spread her legs wider, opened a deeper path for Billy to chart, to sail deeper into her waves of excitement, to feel a tidal wetness surrounding him.

Billy was soon unable to hold back his own explosion; the crown of his penis throbbed with an excitement he had never before enjoyed; he felt a closeness with this red-headed girl called Jenny, a fulfilment he already suspected was not merely passion, not only the appetites of an animal.

Jenny, clinging onto Billy, held him in her arms, feeling him shuddering, gripping the muscles in his body contracting as he shook with his orgasm.

When Billy had spent himself inside Jenny, they sat on the floor of the hut, Jenny crouching over his lap, Billy's penis still in the moist clutch of her femininity.

Jenny saw the contentment twinkling in his eyes; she leaned forward to kiss him lightly and they wrapped their arms around one another. They pressed their lips together in a passionate kiss.

Jenny whispered, 'Are we really here? Are we really here in the jungles of Africa or is this some wild . . . dream?'

'Let's not fall asleep to find out.'

Jenny complimented in a voice which tickled Billy's ear, 'You're nice, Billy Peake.'

'Jennifer Brett,' he said, as if making certain he would not forget the name. 'Jennifer . . . also known as Jenny . . . little Jenny Brett.'

'A bit daft some times, you are,' she added, cosily, 'but ever so nice.'

'Jenny Brett . . . hmm. So are you . . . very nice.'

13

A horn blast disturbed Billy's dream, a golden-tinted dream about himself and Jenny. Jenny had been dressed in a ruffled white dress, visiting him in Richmond; a dream in which they were carefree as children – perhaps they even were children – but they made love with each other, both having adult knowledge of love-making, both being endowed with full sexual maturity. A boy with a man's penis, a girl with fully developed breasts, a magical dream and the first restful sleep Billy had enjoyed in well over a month.

Becoming aware of Jenny's elfin body still cradled in his arms, Billy pulled her towards him, remembering where they were, and he quickly told himself to enjoy this moment of pleasure.

The horn blasted again.

Jenny stirred in his arms. 'What was that?'

Billy buried his nose in her hair. 'Shhh . . . go back to sleep.'

Jenny, snuggling lazily in the protection of Billy's strong arms, whispered, 'Aren't there wild animals, tigers and lions in Africa? And those people with sharp pointed teeth called Hottentots?'

'I'll protect you.' Billy chewed the lobe of her ear.

Suddenly above them in the darkness, two lanterns appeared and a man's voice ordered, 'On your feet!'

Billy, sitting bolt upright on the dirt floor to shield Jenny's body, saw Jack Razor's face in the yellow glow from the lanterns.

Razor stood inside the low door flanked by the two African sentries holding the lanterns and long sabres. Razor looked from Billy to Jenny, saw thay had been sleeping curled together and wondered if they had already begun their love-making as he had hoped and expected they would.

'What do you want?' demanded Billy, blinking his eyes at the harsh yellow glow of the lanterns.

Razor threw two woollen blankets and a pair of small lumpy cloth sacks onto the dirt floor. 'Wear those blankets for warmth. There's food in the sacks but don't eat it all like pigs. It's got to last you.' He turned towards the low doorway.

Billy called after him, 'Where are we going?'

Razor disappeared under the doeskin and the sentries hurried Billy and Jenny to their feet.

The morning sky outside the palm hut was dark and glittering with stars; the air was cold and Billy and Jenny gratefully wrapped the grey woollen blankets around their shoulders as they hurried from the hut to a long line of people forming in the early morning darkness across the compound.

The people, all Africans, formed a foot caravan: men,

women, children old enough to walk, porters balancing large bundles on their heads, slaves carrying baskets tied to poles resting on their naked shoulders, guards dressed in village weave, moving up and down the long line, prodding the prisoners with long wooden staffs, shouting in shrill dialects, whistling as if they were herding cattle or sheep.

The fresh air and the excitement of the caravan jolted Billy and Jenny from their drowsiness; Jenny looked nervously at the long column and whispered, 'Where are they taking us now?'

A conch horn sounded; the guards ran more frantically back and forth along the column waving their wooden staffs.

Jenny whispered, 'Are we the only white people?'

'Remember that Dutchman I told you about? Paris Rhinelander? The man who kept me alive on the *Witch*. He could be here.'

Billy stepped out of line, looking up and down the lengthening column of black-skinned people, but a sentry shoved him back into place.

The conch shell blasted again; the guards waved their staffs and slowly the long column began to move, crossing the slave compound, passing from the small settlement of board shacks, palm and mud huts, long grass-roofed pavilions, keeping to a narrow dirt trail which soon skirted a marshland of reeds.

The sky was lightening to a faint blue when the column reached the head of the marshland; the terrain began to climb into gentle foothills and the distant dark mountains took tall, soft shapes in the clinging morning mist.

The steady pace warmed Billy; he soon dropped the woollen blanket from his shoulder and rolled it into the back pack he had made by knotting the sleeves of his drill coat.

'You hungry, Jenny?' He felt the food sacks, suspecting they contained dried biscuits, fruit, perhaps some salted meat or strung fish.

'I'm starving,' answered Jenny as she hurried alongside

Billy on the path. 'But let's not eat yet. Remember what Jack Razor said. We don't know when we'll be getting our next food.'

Billy smiled at how Jenny had hitched up her long skirt and had tied her copper hair into a knot on top of her head. She looked like a jaunty young English woman out for a stroll across a moorland, or perhaps on a trek through the Lake District. Why did it feel as if he had known her for longer than twelve short hours?

'You're quite a sport, aren't you?' he said.

Jenny kept the steady pace of the column, climbing the stony incline, not losing her balance in a roll of small rocks; she replied, 'I learned a long time ago, Billy Peake, that complaining gets you nowhere.'

'We're of the same heart, Jenny Brett. Cut from the same cloth.'

'I don't pretend to be what I'm not. I am a fighter and I fight hard to protect what I am, what I got and what I want.'

'You're gold through and through.'

'Listen to your line, Billy Peak! You've got a tongue in your mouth to charm all the ladies, I wager.'

Billy climbed the rocky incline, answering, 'I don't know many ladies, Miss Brett. Save yourself.'

'I heard once that a woman's only so much a lady as the way a gent treats her. And I must admit you treat me like a duchess dressed head to foot in silks and all the fine feathers a lady wears to meet the king of the realm.'

Billy, smiling to himself as he listened to Jenny's melodic voice, felt strangely light-hearted for being so far away from home; here he was, part of a slave column, headed into a wild, uncharted world. He was alone, except for Jenny Brett, the slave trader Jack Razor and a caravan of African tribesmen headed for slavery. So why, why did he feel so happy? He had not felt this happy before in his life. What was the feeling? Madness? Lunacy?

By late morning, Jack Razor's slave column had climbed the first foothills of West Africa and begun the ascent of the land mass rising from the Atlantic. The expedition had passed through a thick forest of trees, lush with ferns, verdant, coiled with vines and flowering vegetation, noisy with the caw-caw-caw of orange-beaked birds perched in the bark trees, buzzing with crickets grinding a see-saw from pearly grey bushes, humming with flies with green bodies and transparent wings.

The guards shouted, waved their wooden staffs and the slave column halted on a rocky plateau from which could be seen the speck of Razor Cove far below in the distance and the cobalt blue Atlantic Ocean tonguing miles of white tropical wilderness like a benign monster at a salt lick.

Billy put his arm around Jenny. 'Beautiful, isn't it?'

Jenny gazed at the green vista sloping down to the turquoise sea backed by a blue sky downy with cotton white clouds.

'Who'd ever have thought I'd be standing here at the top of the world?'

'Better than being locked in a hut.'

'Like they say – what good is life if you don't have a little variety?' She laughed.

'How do your feet feel? Tired yet?'

'Mistress Philpott gave me these boots before she ran off with Mr Botts. They're quality, these boots are, but I don't know how long they will hold up to all this climbing and hiking and walking through jungles.'

Razor's voice disturbed them. 'You two better eat something.'

Billy got his first good look at the slave-trader. An Englishman, he guessed him to be in his mid-forties, a strong frame, good face, but his eyes showed disillusionment, probably from living so long in the isolation of a slave station, from being involved in the inhumane business of selling humans as cattle.

Billy asked, 'Mr Razor, are you going to tell us where you're taking us?'

'You know my name.' Razor glanced at Jenny and said, 'There's no need to tell you two anything.'

'Where are you taking us?' repeated Billy.

Razor pointed eastwards. 'See those hills in front of us? We're headed beyond them.'

'How far beyond, Mr Razor?' Billy asked. 'Africa's a big land.'

'Do you know where we are now?' asked Razor, amusement glowing in his eyes.

Billy considered, then replied, 'I'd guess we're some place near the Ivory Coast. Near the Equatorial Line. What sailors call the Equinoctial. Some place near the mouth of the River Niger.'

'Not bad, not bad at all. This is the Slave Coast. Part of what's known as the Leeward Coast, nearing the Bight of Biafra.'

'Judging from all the equipment you're packing, Mr Razor, we're setting out on a long journey. But where? Why?'

Razor asked, 'You ever heard of Mombasa Town?'

Billy narrowed his eyes. 'Mombasa? Is that where we're going?'

'If we're lucky,' answered Razor. 'So you see, you two better eat something because you're going to need it if you ever hope to get there.'

Jenny, emboldened by Billy's questions, asked, 'What happened to Captain Kerr? Has the swine already packed himself back across the Atlantic like he planned?'

Razor lifted one eyebrow and nodded. 'You *do* know everything. Little use me telling you two anything.'

'What did Kerr tell you to do with us? Why are we here with –' Jenny pointed to the tribespeople lined in front of them. 'What's to become of all of us?'

'And my silver?' Billy added. 'What did Kerr do with that? He didn't have time to empty the hold. Did he buy a few slaves from you and crowd them down with the silver?'

Razor, nodding his head, said, 'You two have all the answers.'

'And what about Paris Rhinelander?' Billy asked. 'A big Dutchman Kerr had in the hold?'

'Rhinelander?' Razor shook his head and walked back towards the head of the column.

'What'd he say?' Jenny whispered eagerly to Billy after Razor had departed. 'Where we going?'

'Mombasa.'

'Is that far away? This . . . what did he call it? Mombasa?'

Billy shook his head. He saw no reason to frighten Jenny to tell her that Mombasa was on the other side of Africa.

His heart sank. *Mombasa*!

14

Mombasa! City of white cubical houses set with star-shaped windows latticed in brass to reflect the glow of Allah's brilliant sun. *In sha Allah!*

Mombasa! A maze of narrow, winding backstreets redolent with spices and the sweet smoke of fish charcoaling on blinking braziers.

Mombasa! A harbour crowded with red-sailed dhows and caïques garishly painted like determined old prostitutes.

Mombasa! A haven for beggars and thieves and sailors hawking potent Indian love amulets, deadly African curses, precious Arabian jewels.

Mombasa! An underground of dens for smoking kif, the narghileh and papaver tar distilled from the resin of poppy.

Mombasa! A stepping stone from the continent of Africa to Arabia, the East, the Orient, the balmy waters of the Indian Ocean said to be filled with tears – salty and warm – flowing from lovers buried under the sands of . . . Mombasa!

Hospodar, Grand Master of the Slave Island, was

sending his Turkish deputy, Mustafa Zabin, to the city of Mombasa – as well as to other slave markets farther inland on the African continent – to find field workers, labourers, weavers, a variety of slaves to sell on Slave Island. Zabin was ecstatic in anticipation of the journey, praising Allah, *In sha Allah*, for a vist to his most cherished city.

The monsoon had passed, the hot days already begun, and there was much work to do before Zabin could leave for the mainland.

Although a busy centre for the buying and selling of slaves, the Ottoman fortress was also a hive of industry, of slaves quarrying stone, building new walls, repairing old walls, enlarging the harbour, as well as working at practical crafts.

Overseeing this work fell upon Zabin's shoulders when the Grand Master was away on his ship, the *Cessina*, to capture sailors from enemy vessels; the last foray had yielded sixty-six slaves – Circassians, Abyssinians, Sudanese – all fine specimens of manhood who would fetch a fine price at the next auction.

Zabin was again left in charge of Slave Island and, apart from overseeing work duties, he also had to satisfy the demands of the Grand Master's wife.

Slave Island was a tedious outpost for Lady Iona. She had little to do but watch new prisoners being unloaded from ships, see them exercising in yards far below her latticed windows, then return to diversions provided by her slave girls.

When Hospodar left on an excursion, Lady Iona always sent a message to Zabin, ordering him to supply her with a lover from the men's dormitory deep in the bowels of the stone fortress.

Zabin, eager to leave for Mombasa on his own voyage, already had a lover waiting to take to Lady Iona when he received her expected message.

Zabin led a dark-skinned Sudanese slave up, up, up the spiralling steps which led from the deep chasms to Lady

Iona's private apartments, preparing the dark giant for tonight's visit.

He warned, 'The Grand Master's away on his ship. So I personally will yank out your tongue from its roots if you speak about this meeting.'

The Sudanese, both hands bound behind his back, silently climbed the steps.

As Zabin's backless yellow leather slippers slapped against stone worn by centuries of use, he cautioned, 'Do not be surprised when Lady Iona tells you to perform certain acts with her, slave. Lady Iona's an aristocrat. She's descended from the ancient kings of Ioxa and has the purest Othmanlis blood. So do not question her tastes!'

Zabin thought of the payment with which Lady Iona would reward him for bringing her a night's companion, precious coins he could use to buy *papaver tar*, the resin of the poppy to which he was addicted.

Beckoning the Sudanese to hurry behind him, Zabin climbed the dark winding stairs as he spoke explicitly – in crude terms – so that the slave could not fail to understand him.

He spoke in the argot of the Sudan, advising, 'Do not be ashamed of your pizzle. You've a good specimen of manhood. One of the largest I've seen. So be proud of it. I chose you from many prisoners because of your size. Flaunt your meat when the time's ripe. Display it like a trusty weapon. Let it catch the candle's glow. Show her you're proud of your manhood.'

The slave kept following Zabin.

'You are not circumcised but do worry about those rumours you might have heard about gold rings being put through a man's foreskin here on Slave Island. If you please Lady Iona she will protect you from being pierced. The act's called infibulation. But if you disappoint her, slave–'

Woefully shaking his head, Zabin said, 'The Grand Master's wife is a woman with curious demands. She possesses a collection of special phalluses, of penises cut from men, packed tightly with sand, and mounted on carved ivory sticks . . .'

Zabin began to unroll a cloak he had been carrying under one arm, saying, 'You have a fine prick. What happens to it depends on your performance. But, also, you have pride to your manner. That will please Her Ladyship. You will not grovel in front of her like some common peasant.'

Stopping in front of a pair of tall wooden doors flanked by two smouldering torches, Zabin pushed the Sudanese into the shadows, threw the hooded cloak over him, and turned to pound on the doors with both fists.

He called, 'It is Mustafa Zabin! Deputy to the Grand Master of Slave Island, His Greatness, Hospodar Pasha, and humble servant to Your Ladyship, Iona, Princess of Ioxa.'

Waiting, Zabin soon heard iron bolts pulled inside the thick wooden doors; the doors slowly creaked open and two veiled slave girls appeared, beckoning Zabin and the covered slave across the threshold.

The slave girls, padding softly in silken slippers, led Zabin and the slave down a long hallway redolent with patchouli, and emerged in an alcove where brass lamps hung by silken cords from the carved cedar ceiling, a reception area banked with Kashmiri cushions, layered with silken carpets, dotted with tripods wafting incense, and a claw-footed divan draped in leopard skins, heaped with richly embroidered pillows.

Lady Iona, a short, statuesque woman dressed in a lavender silk pelisse embroidered with golden thread and edged with jangling Venetian sequins, appeared from behind swags of velvet draperies. She halted when she saw the cloaked figure standing alongside Zabin in the centre of the alcove.

Zabin bowed low, greeting, 'Lady Iona . . .'

He touched his chest, chin, and forehead in a deep salutation, and, then, with a flourishing sweep, he pulled off the cloak from the slave, slit the leather thongs from his wrists, and shoved him forward for Iona to see.

Iona stared at the tall, totally naked Sudanese, his sculptured body oiled and glistening in the lamp's glow. His black shoulders were wide, strained with tendons, and his chest moulded like an obsidian statue; his stomach was flat, furrowed with muscle, and his legs bulging with strength; his calves, straight and sturdy.

Iona said, 'Slave, I hope you perform as well as you look.'

Zabin stepped forward. 'Your Ladyship, the slave does not speak the *lingua franca* of the agora–'

The slave surprised Zabin, interrupting, a rich voice rising from deep inside his chest, saying, 'I do understand the language you speak.'

Iona waved for Zabin to hold his tongue as she studied the slave's arrogant face, his hooded eyes, flared nostrils, broad chin. She lowered her eyes down his chest, passing his sinewy stomach, slowing by the patch of wiry black crotch hair, lingering on his penis – a thick, long organ fully crowned and wrapped with a neat forskin.

She said, 'If you speak our language, slave, you will understand me when I ask, does that . . . grow?' She pointed a carmined fingernail towards the limp phallus.

The Sudanese, nodding, held his black eyes on her face.

'It grows . . . larger?'

The proud slave repeated his nod.

'Do you not speak to me?'

The Sudanese kept his silence, his black eyes shining like water at night.

Iona, annoyed by a slave refusing to speak to her, irritably asked, 'You spoke to my servant, yet you do not answer me. Why? Is this a practice in your homeland? Not to answer . . . authority?'

The Sudanese slowly shook his head.

'Impertinent wretch!' She demanded, 'Do you mock me?'

He smiled. 'No, I do not mock you, Your Ladyship.'

'Ah! So you *do* speak to females. I was asking myself if

you might be a man who neither speaks – nor makes love – to a woman.'

The slave held his smile, a row of perfect white teeth flashing through his full lips.

'Now you laugh at me, slave?'

Zabin listened nervously to this exchange between Lady Iona and the Sudanese, beginning to perspire, to visualize coins trickling through his fingers. Why was this slave acting like he himself was royal?

The slave replied, 'Your ladyship is a most handsome woman. If I enjoyed the pleasure of women, I would be honoured to be your partner in bed.'

'So you *are* a creature who lies only with boys. You are a pederast, a pervert, a deviate.'

'Mistress, there are many names for many pleasures.'

'But you would rather have a boy than me,' insisted Iona, allowing her breasts to lift beneath the diaphanous pelisse.

The slave held his eyes on Iona's painted face and replied with dignity, 'Your Ladyship does herself a great disservice by requesting comparisons.'

Iona was no longer listening; her Othmanli pride had already been injured.

She turned to Zabin, ordering, 'Go to the cellars. Bring me a boy. Bring me the prettiest slave boy you can find.'

Zabin, his forehead now dripping with nervous perspiration, knew well enough not to argue with Lady Iona. He quickly moved to cover the naked Sudanese with the voluminous hooded cloak.

'No! Leave the wretch here!' commanded Iona. 'Leave him exactly as he is. You go and find me the boy. Now!'

Zabin, touching his chest, chin, and forehead, hurriedly departed from Iona's apartments, asking himself why life had to become so difficult when he had so little time remaining before he left for Mombasa.

Zabin returned to Iona's apartments within the hour, bringing a young Persian boy no older than sixteen years, a pretty, delicately featured youth whom Zabin had been saving to sell to one of the pederasts from Europe who frequented the auctions on Slave Island.

Lady Iona, hating effeminacy in males as much as youth in pretty females, eyed the exotic young Persian and said, 'Boy, I will give you your freedom if you arouse this man.'

The young Persian, his eyes lashed like a girl's, nervously glanced from Iona to the giant black slave still standing naked in the lamplight of the richly appointed alcove.

'Do not be frightened,' coaxed Iona. 'Use charms which I, a mere woman, obviously do not possess.'

The Sudanese interrupted, his voice beseeching as he insisted, 'Your Ladyship does herself a great injustice–'

'Silence!' screamed Iona.

She walked towards the boy, grabbed him by his thin shoulder, shoved him down onto the silk carpets, commanding, 'Get down on your knees, little flower! Get down on your knees and take that pizzle like a . . . whore!'

The boy, trembling with fright, obediently knelt in front of the brawny Sudanese, pressing his eyes shut, appearing to be praying.

'Your freedom!' Iona reminded him with a shriek. 'Make this man's phallus hard and I'll give you your freedom!'

The big Sudanese slave tried one more time. 'Your Ladyship, I was wrong to be so disrespectful to you. But I am a prince in my land–'

'Silence!' shrilled Iona. 'Silence or you rob this boy of his one chance for freedom.'

The Sudanese looked from Iona back to the boy: he saw him trembling on the carpet; he took a deep breath, determined to make himself erect.

Blackish-brown and smoothly sheathed, the Sudanese's penis hung long, straight, and limp in front of his generously sized scrotum. The organ's crown was large, but not too large in proportion to the rest of the genitalia, a phallus and testicles beyond measure of most men.

The thickness began to expand, first indiscernably, then became increasingly rounder, fatter, larger until the crown slowly began to poke through the foreskin like a tree's bud blossoming, expanding, preparing to open through its brown sheath.

Iona, spying the first hint of the erection, immediately turned to Zabin, saying, 'Fine! Take them both down to the dungeon. And bring me back *that*!' She pointed to the Sudanese's penis.

Her voice became more derisive as she pointed to the Persian boy's small penis, ordering, 'And being me *that* little acorn as well.'

The Sudanese boomed, 'But Your Ladyship! You gave your word! You promised this boy his freedom if he aroused me.'

'Freedom? He'll get freedom! As will you! The freedom you both deserve!'

Iona, Princess of Ioxa, Exalted Spouse of Hospodar, Grand Master of Slave Island, turned and departed from the alcove, as her slave girls hurried behind her in the wake of the fluttering silk pelisse.

Lady Iona received the two penises, one cut from the Sudanese slave and the other sliced from the Persian boy. Both organs had been dried in the sun and packed tightly with sand, then mounted on carved ivory sticks, making two more phalluses to add to Iona's collection.

Both the Sudanese and Persian had died during their sexual defilement; their masculinity was further profaned by Iona ordering their corpses to be sewn into bags, like the bodies of unfaithful Arab wives, then dumped in the sea.

When Zabin sailed from Slave Island to Mombasa he dropped the corpses in the Indian Ocean. He swore to himself that somehow, someway, somewhere, he would find a suitable man on this journey to bring back to Slave Island for Lady Iona. He knew his own future depended on it.

15

The African countryside became more mountainous as Jack Razor's slave column pushed eastwards from the Atlantic to the Indian Ocean, moving over a high range flattened into a topical plateau. There were fields of dwarf plantain trees; flocks of small, spotted eagles that glided, dipped and soared against a cloudless blue sky; herds of antelope – bubale, gazelle, waterbuck – leaping, racing on fragile legs across golden plains dotted with trees twisted into strange shapes by the wind called the harmattan.

Deeper into Dahomey's exotic kingdom they passed villages composed of white mud huts where men and women wore white *dhotis* knotted around their middles. Humped-backed bullocks pulled wooden ploughs in small plots of rich land.

Jack Razor used cowrie shells to purchase fruit and root vegetables, and to pay for the right to refill waterskins at a stream. Dahomey escorts used sharp crescent-shaped knives to hack a path through tangled undergrowth as the mountains grew steeper; slicing willowy cane brakes, resilient branches, fallen logs, even snakes, nesting birds and fawns, if the small creatures did not escape the sharp singing cut of the blade.

The nights became chilly at the higher altitude; porters ran ahead of the column to prepare camp, using flint chips to start fires and arrange stones in magic circles to ward off evil spirits.

A separate fire was built for Billy and Jenny apart from the rest of the prisoners. They happily kept to themselves, enjoying their privacy, eating specially prepared food, dried meats, cured roots, to prevent them from contracting diseases from which native Africans possessed inherent immunities.

Jack Razor stayed away from Billy and Jenny during the daylight hours when the column was on the march, but at night he occasionally paid visits to their camp fire, replying vaguely to questions about the future, doling out scraps of information, now and then giving them useful items of clothing – breeches for Jenny to wear instead of her long, cumbersome dress, a shirt for Billy as a replacement for his ragged garment – and some netting to sleep under at night. But Razor never imparted anything of true value to Billy or Jenny. He always returned quickly to his own fire, to his rum bottle, to the African woman, Hai Tai, who kept him warm throughout the chilly nights.

Billy and Jenny accepted their transient existence with few complaints. They enjoyed one another's company as well as the sights of white mud villages, rain forests abloom with red, yellow and blue flowers, valleys cut with steep waterfalls, natives standing in the far distance to watch the slave column move through the land of the Dahomey, inching towards the next great African empire, the forests of the Oubangi.

The morning sun glinted through a cool dark forest of teak trees as Billy trudged behind Jenny in the foot caravan, watching her trim figure agilely moving in front of him along a narrow path tangled with vines and alive with the chatter of flying monkeys.

Billy called, 'If Jack Razor and I aren't the first white men to cross Africa, Jenny, you're certainly the first white woman.'

'You think so?' Jenny had barbered her long copper hair with a bamboo-handled knife she had found at an encampment. She washed her hair nightly when she bathed in chilly mountain pools, or splashed in icy streams cascading over mossy stones.

Billy enjoyed how quickly, how easily Jenny had adapted to new ways, how she wore men's breeches and her shorn hair, but seemed to be more feminine than ever.

He called, 'When you get back to England, clubs and societies will invite you to give speeches. You'll probably be asked to write articles for *The London Journal*.'

'You truly believe we're getting out of here, don't you?'

'I get my faith from watching you.'

Jenny carried a tall walking stick these days, swinging it at bushes and watching butterflies take flight. She paused to look at a flurry of butterflies fluttering with enormous orange and pink wings, then hurried to keep apace on the path.

She called back over her shoulder, 'Life would be easier if I knew where we were going. I know the town's called Mombasa. But I do wish I could picture what it looked like.'

'Why?' Billy still had not told her Mombasa was across Africa.

'I've never been to Brighton or Edinburgh or Liverpool. But I've seen drawings and watercolours of them, so I know what they look like. But Mombasa. It's a mystery, a big mystery to me.'

'We're not stopping in Mombasa. At least I hope not. I don't want to spend the rest of my life in Africa.'

'Where do *you* want to go?'

Billy and Jenny spent many hours discussing plans, making choices, some viable, some no more than games, pastimes.

'China.'

'Billy Peake, are you still secretly fretting about silver? For shame!'

'No, I'm not fretting. But I still want to go to China. I like to see places I was meant to visit. And the East Indies, I want to go to the East Indies, too.'

'To quarrel with your brother? Shame on you!'

Billy had told Jenny his fears about Andrew in detail, how his older brother might have signed a secret contract with Gabriel Easton to cheat him out of his share of the silver.

Billy answered, 'No, I do not look for a quarrel with my brother, but I do want to learn the truth.'

Swinging her walking stick at the bushes, Jenny gaily called, 'I thought I might be able to tempt you to stay with me in this place called Mombasa. To help me run the inn I plan to open there.'

'Inn? What inn?'

'A road house. A nice little place with tables, benches and beamed oak ceilings, where I'll serve ale and game pie to slave-traders and pirates.'

Jenny laughed at the idea, adding, 'Don't you think that sounds like a good plan?'

'You make light, Jenny Brett, but I wager you're half serious.'

'And why not? I like making a farthing or two. It comes from having to survive in the world all my life.'

'I'll follow behind you and gather your crumbs.'

'When I stop hearing you behind me, singing like a blue jay, Billy Peake, I will worry.'

Billy laughed at the idea of singing like a blue jay. It was better than 'old dog'. He felt complimented, happier than ever before.

He did not know exactly the true feelings he had for Jenny. Friendship? Infatuation? He did not know for certain, though, that he felt more than mere lust. Day by day he was becoming increasingly fond of her, treasuring the friendship they shared, the high spirits they kindled in one another, the way they slept intertwined by their fire, protected only by a swag of white netting, a flimsy but useful shield against flies, mosquitos and, they hoped, scorpions, snakes and poisonous lizards.

They made love too. Jenny made Billy feel like a man, complete and powerful as he had never felt before. But, also, Jenny kept him from brooding about his future, from pondering about his brother trying to cheat him, from agitating about Gabriel Easton, cursing Captain Kerr, groaning about losing the Mexican ingots.

Changes were indeed taking place in Billy Peake. He sensed a hardening in his already athletic body but he was also aware of the changes in his mind, in his attitudes, his visions of life and the ways to survive life's problems. Billy felt he had been granted armour against shocks, or at least a new way to accept them.

He had always been what men called 'easy-going', but he had secretly vexed about his problems, his future, his loneliness, a place to call home. But now he felt no problem was big or bad enough to ruin one entire day of his life. Was this new feeling maturity? Was he becoming a man? Finally shedding the self-pity and frivolity of youth? Or was he becoming even more removed from the course of other men?

Whatever the answers were to Billy's many questions, he attributed them to his present situation – to the daily surprises of Africa and to the pixyish Cockney girl he held every night in his arms.

Was he in love?

Nor did Jenny Brett know her true feelings these days. Africa. Destined to be sold as a slave. Travelling on foot across a wild, foreign land.

Being realistic about her lot in life, Jenny suspected the future held no great comforts, nor genteel privileges in store for her wherever, however she lived. Jenny had been born and orphaned in the working class district of Whitechapel in the slums of London, a slave in every respect but name.

When Billy spoke to Jenny, made love to her, was her friend, she did secretly entertain visions of the some day being married, of them settling down in a pretty little thatched cottage back home in England, or perhaps in a new saltbox house in one of the American colonies. Of having a family with Billy, telling their children fireside stories about how their pa got those lash welts on his back, of how they had walked like two mules across Africa. But then their African memories would grow dim, the recollections of these days would be replaced by new stories, by chores, by the delicious aroma of a lamb stew boiling in a kettle on a jack in a stone hearth, by problems such as a milk cow drying up, neighbours calling on them for help to put up their hay, watching their own cheeky, spirited, and probably freckled children growing older and acquiring their own dreams, collecting their own memories.

Like a blinding morning light, though, realism always jolted Jenny back to harsh reality; she reminded herself that Billy Peake belonged to a different world, to a different class, that even to *consider* marriage was silly, stupid, a daft thing to do. She must enjoy Billy's company for the moment; she must keep these days of captivity, of wandering, of imprisonment, as days of happiness, tenderness and warmth.

Jenny also realized that although Billy was a fully grown man, in many ways he was still a lad. He was playful, soft-hearted, dreamy, thoughtful. All the qualities a woman finds scarce in a grown man and thrills over in a son.

Jenny, thrifty and maternal, yearning for a home, was accepting rugged life in Africa as the closest thing she had known to happiness. She knew that there was only one reason – her blue jay called Billy Peake.

Their happiness did not escape the attention of the black people in the slave caravan. The African men watched Jenny and Billy from a distance, admiring their playfulness, unlike the few other white-skinned people they had ever seen. The African women and children surrounded them at every opportunity, little boys and girls laughing as Billy spun them round and round in the air, women and girls giggling at the touch of Jenny's soft red hair.

Jack Razor's concubine, Hai Tai, was the last woman from Razor Cove to approach them. Both Jenny and Billy were surprised to hear Hai Tai speak a few words of English.

Hai Tai brought two calabashes of fresh water to their fireside. She set down the gourds but, before returning through the camp to Jack Razor's fire, she paused, holding out a clenched fist from her waist.

'Gift,' she said. 'You.'

'A gift? For us?' Billy looked down at Hai Tai's clenched black fist and then to her broad face gashed with tribal marks.

'You.' Hai Tai nodded at Jenny, going on, 'You, take.' She opened her fist.

Jenny, looking down at the pink palm of the black woman's hand, saw two leather thongs, each strung through a small piece of obsidian, a black bead.

Hai Tai impatiently motioned for Jenny to put one thong over Billy's head and for Billy to place the other thong over Jenny's head.

Jenny looked from Hai Tai to Billy. She suspiciously asked, 'Is this . . . right?'

Billy was also wary. 'You don't think it's some kind of magic spell or . . . voodoo?'

Hai Tai quickly grabbed their hands, joining them together and motioned again at the thongs. She nodded her head and smiled, the first time Jenny and Billy had ever seen the normally sullen African woman smile.

Billy suddenly understood. He blurted out, 'It's like getting married, or betrothed!'

Jenny had suspected the same thing but had not dared mention it. Nothing would make her happier than to be married, or even betrothed to Billy.

Looking at her, Billy asked, 'Does it . . . bother you?'

'Bother me?'

It was an awkward moment for Jenny. She looked from Billy to the two thongs and back to Hai Tai's smiling face.

'It doesn't bother *me*!' Billy said. 'We don't want to hurt this woman's feelings either.'

He held out his hand, coaxing, 'Come on. At least put one on me.'

Jenny, lifting a thong, carefully slipped it over Billy's head letting the black bead hang in the middle of his chest. Then she held out her own head, allowing Billy to slip the cord over her neck.

Looking at one another, Billy and Jenny sheepishly grinned, then turned to Hai Tai. But she had disappeared.

Neither Billy nor Jenny mentioned the black beads, nor their possible meaning, for the rest of the evening. But that night their love-making took on a new, deeper passion.

Billy held Jenny protectively to his chest, kissing her eyes, butting his strong chin over her pert little chin, pressing his moist lips firmly against her mouth, holding the kiss, pressing his tongue deep into her mouth.

Jenny accepted Billy's silent pressures; she strained her mouth to hold his pressing tongue, stretching her small thighs around his firm body, eager to take his prodding penis. Her anticipation had moistened her womanhood: the full head of Billy's penis slid easily into her cleft. Jenny moved one leg, then the other, contracting the wall of her vagina, making a love nest for Billy's penis, a home.

Billy, holding Jenny's lips close to his mouth, driving his penis deeper into her clutching warmth, began to rub her naked back with one hand, feeling her thin shoulders, her slim waist, her round buttocks, as if assuring himself that it was her.

'Is it you? Is this you?' Billy's whisper was soft, almost begging. 'Is this really . . . you?'

Jenny understood the questioning. Billy was asking her if she was a person who loved him. He was asking for permission to love her. But Jenny could not answer him with words, could not answer, yes, it was her and he could love her because she also loved him. That would be unwise. What did they know about the future? They were joined in body and in spirit, as well as by a crude African charm.

Also, Jenny was pleased that Billy wanted to love her because she believed she was carrying the seed of his baby in her womb. Nevertheless, she was too practical, too realistic, too uncertain about the future to say, 'Yes, I love you and we will be, perhaps already are, married to one another, my lovely Billy boy.'

16

Then Africa turned cruel.

The forests became barren, growing red thorns and prickly burrs which caused pustules on the skin if touched; worms appeared unexpectedly on hair and clothing, in blankets, inside eating utensils; the harmattan blew humid air which brought black flies; the paths became dangerous with hard-shelled reptiles which flicked long red tongues, tusked warthogs charging on short legs through the undergrowth, yapping jackals on the prowl for carrion.

This was the Land of Dead Warriors, the mountains where lost souls were said to wander, a desolate zone in the east of the Oubangi region. The caravan porters carried spears ready as protection against renegade tribesmen and Jack Razor kept a firelock pistol primed in his belt.

Jack Razor also made Billy and Jenny cover their faces with cloths and keep their sleeves rolled down to their wrists when they passed near villages, cautious because of the superstition that evil spirits had white skin, that Billy and Jenny – even Razor himself – might be devils bringing drought, famine, death.

Villages became sparse in this land of red thorns and white spiders. Human skulls appeared on stakes driven into the ground. Huts were made of oozing mud decorated with sunbleached human skulls and bones.

Brief but torrential deluges occurred throughout the day and night, the rain often falling so hard that Razor had to order the caravan to take temporary refuge, waiting under trees, inside caves, beneath rocky overhangs, until the burning sun reappeared.

Billy and Jenny, standing side by side under the lip of a shallow mountain cave during a late morning downpour, looked in fascination through the rain at distant storm clouds gathering momentum, clouds moving and constantly changing shape as they eddied across the turbulent African sky beyond the curtain of heavy silver rain.

Thunder sounded beyond the far storm clouds.

Jenny, wrapping her arm around Billy's waist, looked at the rolling, changing clouds and shuddered.

'This reminds me of the day before we sailed out of Boston. The bad storm we had.'

Billy distinctly recalled that fateful morning; he remembered the small shore boat which had taken him to the *Vandal Witch* tossing at anchor. He remembered his meeting with Gabriel Easton and his visit to Faith Wiley's bordello in the harbour.

Pulling Jenny closer to him, he said, 'That day seems like an eternity ago.'

'Innocent, I was,' murmured Jenny. 'I believed myself to be sailing home to England and Captain Kerr was going to give me my papers at Gravesend.'

Billy sighed. 'We both were a bit innocent back then.'

A streak of lightning suddenly forked across the stormy sky; voices spread through the slave column. The lightning streaked again, an African screamed a short distance away from where Billy and Jenny stood. Men, women and children began running from the cave, charging out into the downpour of rain.

'What's happening?' cried Jenny. 'Where are they going? What's the matter?'

The Africans' cries became more hysterical; a scream rose above the din of the others; more Africans ran out into the rain.

Billy, seeing a small group of porters gathering under the slate overhang, grabbed Jenny by the arm to run and see what what happening.

Suddenly he stopped, pressing Jenny towards his chest to keep her from witnessing the hideous spectacle.

A large serpent inside the cave had wrapped itself around one of the African prisoners, pressing out blood from his nostrils, making his eyes pop from their sockets.

Thud, thud, thud went the knives of the porters as they hacked at the large brown-spotted snake, trying to break its hold on the man. But the man was already dead from the snake's coiling grip.

The men gathered around huge bonfires that night, beginning the burial rites for their fellow tribesman. The women cooked at a separate fire, preparing the carcass of the cave snake.

Jack Razor squatted near the sputtering glow of Billy and Jenny's small fire, explaining that the people would eat the serpent which had killed their brother.

He said, 'Snake meat is good and the wenches cook it for a burial feast. They remove all the poison and what they think to be the evil spirit. Now all there is left to do is free the evil spirit from the dead man. That's what the men are doing now, listen to them.'

The Africans had quickened their beat on small drums which they had improvised from logs. The tops of their tall bark masks jerked up and down in a circle. There was a rustling sound of dried grass, the shake of hand rattles, all crude, hurriedly prepared decorations and instruments.

'Can we see?' Jenny asked, sitting next to Billy on a log.

Razor shook his head. 'Women are not allowed to witness a death ceremony. Not even the lad here or myself. We have white skin.'

Billy asked, 'How long does this take? How long will we stay here?'

Razor listened to the persistent sound of the musicians, the cries, groans, shouts rising from the dancers.

'We'll make a fresh start in the morning.'

Jenny said, 'We heard a woman screaming all afternoon. Who was that?'

Razor took a swig from his brandy bottle and wiped his thick moustache on his shirt sleeve. 'That was the man's widow. She's young and blames herself for what happened.'

'Why?' Jenny was fascinated by the mystery of the ceremony.

'The girl believes she brought down evil spirits on her husband.'

'How?'

'By carrying a piece of carved wood inside her.'

'A piece of . . . carved wood?'

Jenny looked at Billy.

'A sort of charm,' explained Razor. 'A crude carving.'

Billy asked, 'A carving of what?'

Razor hesitated before answering, 'Her husband's prick.'

'*Inside* her?' Jenny asked.

Razor pointed towards his groin. 'Inside her, right down here, between her legs. She's been carrying it inside her every day since we left The Cove.'

Billy pulled Jenny closer to him.

Razor took another swig of brandy, continuing, 'See, the young fellow was built just too damned big. He was painful for her. So she was stretching herself for him. Now she says the gods are punishing her for not being able to serve her husband.'

Billy watched Jenny staring at the dancers, their tall masks weaving, encircling the large fire. He wondered what she was thinking; he worried when the novelty of new sights, strange ways would become a burden for her mind.

'These Africans,' said Razor, 'they've got beliefs we don't even begin to understand. Like a snake. To Africans a snake symbolises both hate and love. Some tribes use snakes as weapons.'

Billy turned his eyes back to Razor. 'Weapons? How do men fight with snakes?'

'Like sabres. Swords in a duel. Oh, it's not as difficult as you think. Not if you get a good firm grip on the butt of the snake.'

'But wouldn't a snake turn on you?'

'The secret is to get a randy bull snake.' Razor chuckled, 'A snake fighting mad to protect his lady snake.'

A momentary silence hung over the small fire. Jenny kept staring into the distance. Razor smiled emptily into the glimmering coals while Billy looked at Jenny and listened to the sound of dried grass, gourd rattles, the quickening drum beat continuing beyond them.

Jenny, turning back her head, broke the eerie silence.

'Mr Razor?'

Razor did not raise his eyes from the coals.

'Mr Razor?' Jenny said, louder. 'What are you going to do with Billy and me, Mr Razor?'

'Do?'

Jenny continued, 'People all have their traditions, their ways, Mr Razor. And it's not the ways of white people to sell each other as slaves . . . is it?'

Razor still did not raise his eyes from the fire as he asked, 'So you think you're better than some nigger, do you?'

'I didn't say that, Mr Razor, I asked–'

Billy interrupted, 'Don't, Jenny.'

'No, let the little lady say her piece,' said Razor. 'It's time the truth be out.'

He turned back to Jenny, saying, 'Yea, I'm going to sell you, missy. And I'm going to get a right good price for you, too. You may not be much from where you come from back in England. But out here in Africa, where every wench has coal black skin and kinky wool for hair, you're more valuable than you ever dreamed.'

Razor's bushy moustache lifted into a smile, exposing his yellowed teeth, as he added, 'Especially now that you're knocked up.'

Jenny sat upright on the log, her fingers instantly curling into claws.

Razor nodded. 'A right smart piece of baggage you be, lassie, now that you're carrying his kid in your belly!'

Billy pulled Jenny back alongside him. 'Don't listen, Jenny. Don't listen to him. He's had too much to drink.'

'Damn you to hell!' Razor cursed. 'Drink's got nothing to do with it. I talk the truth. Why do you think you two have been having it so good? Your own fire every night, food, privacy. A bloody damned holiday? Is that what you think you've been having? A bloody damned holiday?'

Billy demanded, 'Is that why you haven't been bothering us? Because you wanted us to . . . make love?'

'Damned right, laddie!' Razor laughed, adding, 'And if you know anything about cattle, young Master Peake, you know a cow's more valuable with a calf in her belly, now ain't she?'

Billy lunged forward, cursing, 'You damned son of a whore–'

Razor pulled his firelock from his belt, pointing the barrel at Billy, threatening, 'Don't make me put a hole through your head, because I will. You ain't nothing to me. Not like she is. This molly here is worth a right fortune.'

Jenny, her face set more with horror than anger, sprang from the log and ran into the night.

Billy moved to follow.

'Stay where you are,' Razor ordered, prodding the pistol forward. 'She can't run far. Porters guard camp. They'll stop her.'

Billy stared into the darkness, his fists tight with anger at his side, cursing, 'You bastard, you no good bastard!'

'Go ahead, curse me all you want. But your good times are over. From now on you and your floosie sleep apart.'

Holding the barrel of the pistol on Billy, Razor said, 'Sit down and start thinking about yourself, laddie. From here you go it alone.'

Hai Tai had watched Jack Razor go to the young white couple's campfire, kept an eye on them from the distance, heard their shouts above the singing of the tribesmen, and then seen Jenny run into the night.

Having consoled Jenny and left her under the watchful care of a Fanti woman by the cookfire, Hai Tai again returned to her hiding spot in the forest, the place from which she had overheard the argument, the location where the black porter named Pra was stationed tonight as a guard against prisoners trying to escape.

Hai Tai and Pra were lovers; they had been secretly

meeting to make love for more than two years, since the time that Jack Razor had taken Pra from the Dahomey tribe and elevated him to be a guard at Razor's Cove.

Pra, a slim man with great physical strength, never spoke to Hai Tai about Jack Razor when they met, nor did Hai Tai speak to him about the white man who kept her as his concubine. There was no way for her to escape being Razor's mistress without being killed – or by murdering him. And Hai Tai respected human life too much to take away a man's life, even a white man who enslaved black people and sold them to be taken away on great boats across the water.

Tonight, beyond the roaring cookfire, Hai Tai welcomed Pra's body; she needed him to make love to her more than ever tonight, to remind herself that she was not totally possessed by the evil white man, Jack Razor, to let herself know she was an African woman, could satisfy a good African man.

All white people were not evil. Hai Tai had learned that from the young lovers, Jenny with the red hair and Billy with the yellow hair. She saw that Razor also took advantage of them. He was as evil as the other white man, Captain Kerr, who too often visited the Cove.

Hai Tai, losing herself in her need for Pra, lay on the soft bed of leaves he had prepared for them in the darkness, cradling his body against her nakedness, hungrily chewing his chin, his ear, even his nose as he knelt between her spread thighs and rapidly drove his penis into her womanhood, a penis long like an arm, a penis that tingled and touched every point of her vagina.

There was no lover like Pra, thought Hai Tai as she felt him plunge, stir, them plunge deeper into the moist channel he made inside her. Jack Razor used her as a mere instrument to satisfy his own sexual needs, but Pra made love to her, satisfied her needs as well as his own masculine demands.

Feeling herself breathing faster, her entire body shivering to the sensation Pra awakened inside her, Hai Tai pressed her mouth shut, trying not to cry out in ecstasy, not to scream the excitement running from the tips of her toes, up through her body, even turning her brain into a whirlpool of thrilling emotion.

The sensation again centred on Hai Tai's midsection as Pra pulled away from her, kneeling on the ground between her legs, but still keeping the rhythm of his penis driving into her slit, now adding the pressure of his fingertips around her vagina, prodding the wet orifice, tickling it, poking and probing and enhancing the sensation of his driving, armlike penis.

Biting back another shout of ecstasy, Hai Tai opened her eyes when she felt Pra's hands enclosing her breasts, working her nipples, teasing them, snapping them like insects, pulling them like animal teats, pressing them between his fore- and middle-fingers, and now sinking the thick head of his penis even more deeply inside her, with greater strength than before, the sign that he was going to join her in a fulfilment of love-making, that he also was going to explode his sexual excitement.

Hai Tai, gripping the calves of her legs around his naked buttocks, worked her vagina against him, pulling his penis deeply inside her, closing the gap between them so that not one inch of the penis showed outside the black hairs curling in her patch, never wanting to let him go from her – yet still keeping one ear open for a prowler in the night.

Forbidden love affairs were never complete, Hai Tai knew, but feeling Pra's penis jerk its sperm inside her womanhood, she thought about the black woman who could not accommodate her husband's great penis, and had to stretch her orifice for him with a piece of wood. Now that woman had no husband. He was dead. Had the gods truly been displeased? Hai Tai did not know.

Hai Tai had much to be thankful for. She might not be able to marry Pra, but they always managed to meet one another, to share a few moments every day. He was a strong man, built longer than any man she had ever seen, and she was also grateful to accommodate every inch of his manhood, to take it all into her vagina as well as to open her throat and take the head of the great penis down deep until her lips touched his scrotum.

Despite sexual powers and abilities, Hai Tai knew she also had other things to be thankful for. She thought about the white girl with red hair and knew that her love affair with the white boy with yellow hair was now over, finished.

Hai Tai felt sad for them. The white girl was as much a slave of Jack Razor as she was. Perhaps even more so. At least Hai Tai could keep meeting Pra. But the white girl would now have nothing except the black amulet to remind her of her lover. Hai Tai hoped the powers of the amulet would work and that the white girl would at least have a baby to remember the white boy by.

Silently, carefully, Hai Tai moved back through the night to the cookfire as the sound of the dancers still filled the night like a wind pounding dried, scaly trees. She was thankful this part of the foot journey would soon be over, that they were nearing Humari Umbtari.

17

Umbtari warriors, tall men with iron black skin and foreheads stippled with needle pricks, took command of Jack Razor's slave column at the eastern border of the Ougbangi kingdom and led it to Humari Umbtari, the mountain capital surrounded by a red clay wall.

Foot and wagon traffic passed into Humari Umbtari – the Castle of a Thousand Wives – through a wooden portcullis raised and lowered by grinding iron chains.

The main square, also serving as a market-place, was alive with activity; vendors squatted on grass mats selling small grass cages of lizards, parrots, water snakes; stall keepers stood under brightly coloured umbrellas hawking nuts, dried fruits and brown pods stuffed with spices which filled the air with a sweet redolence; veiled women and children with shaved heads carried trays of colourful feathers, tufts of fur, painted beads; cattle, goats, fowl moved freely among the people, and few people noticed the slave column arriving in their city.

A tall man, wearing a red loincloth and shells dangling from his ears, removed Billy from the slave column at the edge of the main square and led him down an alleyway between yellow clay buildings, through a wooden door and along a hallway illuminated by the sunlight filtering through a ceiling of woven palm leaves.

The tall Umbtari man stopped in front of a bamboo door, unlocked an iron chain and stood aside for Billy to pass in front of him. The door closed behind Billy and was locked.

Billy, alone in the room, looked around him in the near darkness. He saw that the walls and floor were covered with small green leaves and that there was a window latticed with bamboo. There was a tiled pool in the centre of the room and a divan covered with cushions.

Tired and despondent, Billy had little curiosity about his whereabouts and collapsed onto the divan to think, yet again, about Jenny.

Billy had not seen Jenny, nor spoken to her, since the night she had run from the camp fire. Razor had kept them apart, keeping Billy under armed guard at one end of the slave column, refusing to answer any more questions.

Billy's head was a jumble of anger and worry. Where was Jenny? Was she safe? Was she here in some part of this clay castle called Umbtari? How could he see her? Would he ever see her again?

The door opened and two women entered the room, young African girls dressed in long blue robes with white *tarhahs* wrapped around their heads.

They brought trays with small bowls of food and leather bottles of wine. They emptied cisterns of fresh water into the pool.

Waiting for the women to depart, Billy forced himself to shed his dusty clothes for a bath and, soon, leaning back in the shallow pool, he gave a deep sigh, welcoming the cool water soothing his naked, aching body. Again his thoughts turned to Jenny.

A voice suddenly came from behind him.

'Ah! So you are the infidel slave from the Americas!'

Billy jerked his head and saw a swarthy man wearing a white turban, gold earrings and a long hemp robe, standing alongside the pool.

The man bowed, touching his chest, mouth and turban in salutation.

'Who are you?'

'I am Mustafa Zabin. Deputy to the Grand Master, Hospodar Pasha, Governor of Slave Island, possession colony of the Ottoman Empire.'

'Slave Island?'

'Slave Island is a rock in the Indian Ocean off the east coast of Africa, north of Madagascar. I will escort you there.'

'Me?'

Zabin nodded. 'You and the other slaves I buy here in Umbtari.'

Billy jumped to his feet in the pool, angrily shouting, 'I am not a *slave*! I was *not* taken in war! I am *not* a political prisoner. I am a free man. You hear me? Free!'

Zabin ignored Billy's tirade, quietly appraising his naked body, suspecting he might have found a man suitable to be Lady Iona's lover.

Grabbing a cloth to cover himself, Billy insisted, 'I am a subject of King George the Third. He's a very powerful man and does not look kindly upon his subjects being enslaved.'

'Ah, we in the Great Empire of the East know all about you English and your King George . . . the Third!'

'If you know so much, then tell me about an English girl called Jennifer Brett.'

'The girl with the red hair?' Zabin woefully shook his head. 'It is too bad about her.'

'What's "too bad" about her?'

'The slave trader, Jack Razor, refused to sell her to me.'

'Sell? *Sell*? God damn it to hell! Jenny's not a slave either.'

Zabin chuckled. 'She thinks as you! She put those tiger claws on both cheeks of the English slave trader.'

'Jenny scratched Jack Razor? Good! She still has her old fight.'

'Fighting will do her no good.'

'Can you take me to see her?'

'Even if I had the privilege to wander King Torit's castle, it would be impossible for me to take you to see the young woman with hair like a flame.'

'Why?'

Zabin raised the palms of both hands. 'She's gone.'

'Gone? Where? We only just arrived here.'

'She has left in a caravan leaving for the Sudan. The English trader was fortunate to arrive when one was departing. He might have had to wait another three, possibly four months.'

'A caravan?'

Mustafa Zabin nodded. 'To the great city of Khartoum. The English trader believes he can get a fine price for the wench in Khartoum. You see, Sudan is both African and Arabian. Many powerful chiefs and rich desert sheikhs go to Khartoum. But then –' Zabin smiled, adding, 'the same people – and more – come to Slave Island.'

'Slave Island – where is Slave Island?'

There was a scratching noise on the door.

Mustafa Zabin clapped his hands. A slave girl entered. Zabin bowed to Billy, then moved towards the door.

Billy, clutching the long cloth in front of his naked body, shouted, 'Is that where you're taking me? Slave Island?'

Mustafa Zabin ignored the question, lingering in the doorway to point at the window latticed with bamboo. 'If you hear a noise outside later this afternoon, do not be alarmed. It is the execution ceremony.'

'Execution? Of whom?'

'The adulterer. King Torit commands it.'

Zabin narrowed his beady black eyes, warning, 'Do not try to cry out to King Torit when you see him. Do not try to shout that you are mistakenly held prisoner. His Highness, King Torit, tried to buy you himself for ten golden lopes. He would gladly kill you rather than see you leave Umbtari with me.'

Mustaf Zabin closed the door gently behind him, leaving Billy alone with the slave girl.

Billy drank the bittersweet palm wine from the leather bottles as he lay on the divan, watching the slave girl remove yellow leaves from the walls and replace them with fresh green ones she carried in a covered basket.

The slave girl dipped the tip of each leaf into a bowl of resin and then pressed it onto the wall, busily working, ignoring Billy's presence in the room.

Billy soon lost interest in watching the girl's silent activity. He returned to his thoughts about Jenny and the information he had learned from Mustafa Zabin.

Khartoum. How long would it take a caravan to reach the capital of Sudan? Would Jenny have to walk? Was she able to ride? Would it be a caravan of camels? Horses? Donkeys? How long would it take her to get there? When had she left this odd place where men hung shells from their ears and women pasted small leaves onto walls?

Billy suddenly jumped at the touch of a hand on his bare leg. He saw the slave girl kneeling on the floor alongside the divan, gazing towards his crotch.

The slave girl, staring hypnotically at Billy's crotch, began darting her tongue in and out of her mouth like one of the hard-shelled reptiles in the Land of the Dead Warriors.

Billy was tired, he wanted to sleep, he did not want to make love. But the slave girl was persistent, moving both hands forward, using one hand to lift Billy's limp penis from his thigh and, using the other to lift his scrotum, she leaned forward and began to lick him.

Billy lay motionless on the divan as the slave girl soon

began to work her mouth on his penis and, instead of resisting her, he thought about Jenny, the nights and days they had spent together after leaving Razor Cove.

Billy remembered holding Jenny's hand. Tasting her mango-sweetened mouth in long, passionate kisses. Holding her protectively in his arms. He remembered the love charm which Hai Tai had given them and, reaching towards his chest, he gripped the black bead in his fist, thinking about Jenny, thinking how much he loved her, wondering if she might be carrying his child in her womb, wishing they were indeed man and wife.

Billy exploded his seed with thoughts of love for Jenny; he lay whispering her name as the slave girl licked the sperm from his penis. She then rose from the floor to bathe him with a moist cloth.

It was not until Billy saw the slave girl washing herself, that he saw a long penis dangling between her brown legs: the slave who had just sucked his penis was not a girl, but a boy, a slave boy dressed as a girl.

18

The realisation that a young boy dressed in feminine clothing had just made love to him did not alarm Billy as much as it would have done a few short months ago. But he had not been in love a few short months ago. He had not known the desolation of being separated from a sweetheart, someone so dear and important to him as Jenny.

Thinking about love, and about the many recent changes in his life, Billy stood alone in the window of the leaf-covered room and looked down at the cobbled courtyard below him. He had been awakened by loud blasts of a conch shell and now watched the beginning of the ceremonial execution which the King of Umbtari was inflicting upon the man accused of adultery.

Billy saw a tall, black-skinned man with a large head and a fat belly, wearing a zebra skin cape, enter the courtyard and sit on a garish throne made from red velvet and elephant tusks. A brightly dressed crowd had assembled in the courtyard and applauded the fat man who Billy guessed must be King Torit.

Next, two Umbtari guards wearing cheetah pelts tied around their oily black groins led in a man who Billy realised was the adulterer – an African as tall as King Torit, but younger and slimmer.

The guards pressed the adulterer to the dirt and two more guards brought a sobbing woman to stand in front of the king.

Billy, guessing that the woman must be the King's unfaithful wife, watched the guards shove her down to the dirt alongside the man.

The crowd hissed and snapped their fingers.

King Torit nodded; a guard ripped away the woman's clothing, shoved her prostrate on the ground, and rolled her over onto her back. The other guard pushed the adulterer on top of her and yanked off his breech cloth.

The King nodded again and one guard removed a sword from his leather scabbard, while the other guard pulled a quirt from his belt.

Loud sharp thuds of the quirt filled the crowded courtyard as the guard beat the adulterer's bare buttocks and back.

Slowly, the naked man began moving his hips, in a semblance of fornicating the woman pressed beneath him on the ground.

The crowd stomped their bare feet, snapping their fingers, their shell necklaces and grass headdresses clanking, rustling, swaying as they moved.

The King shouted. The guard raised his sword in both hands and, swinging it down to the ground, cut off one of the adulterer's feet: blood gushed fron the severed ankle;

two guards held the screaming man on top of the hysterical woman; the third guard used his foot to hold his midsection in the position of fornication.

A guard brought his sword down onto the adulterer's hand which still grasped the woman's hand, cutting through both their hands with one strong slice.

Billy turned his head away when blood coloured the cobblestones. He saw the Turk, Mustafa Zabin, standing alongside him in the leaf-covered room.

'You are shocked?' asked Zabin.

'Is the crime of adultery always punished like this in Umbtari?'

'Adultery?' Zabin shook his head. 'That man did not commit adultery.'

'What did he do?'

'Nothing.'

'Then why does the King punish him like this?'

'The King does not want the world to think nobody desires his wives.'

'The King is killing an innocent man?'

Zabin nodded.

'For appearance's sake?'

'Torit is king,' Zabin answered. 'He has power over life and death.'

Billy shook his head. 'Africa is a very strange land.'

'Probably no stranger than your place called The Americas.'

Then, brightening, Zabin added, 'Tell me, did you enjoy Jeddo?' He motioned to the divan in the corner. 'The slave I sent you?'

'You sent him?'

Zabin nodded.

'You knew he was a boy?'

'Did that trouble you, infidel?'

'I do not go to bed with boys.'

'But you were pleased.' Zabin's words were not a question.

'Why did you send me a boy? Why did you even send me a slave?'

Zabin smiled, lowering his eyes to appraise Billy's athletic body. 'You have lust needing satisfaction.'

'But not with boys.'

'Now I know. And I am pleased to learn it. Your preference for women may serve you.'

'Who are you?' asked Billy. 'Where is this place called Slave Island you're taking me?'

Not replying, Zabin lowered his eyes from Billy's face and saw the thin leather thong and black bead hanging from his neck. He reached forward and pulled it off in one quick tug.

Billy grabbed for Zabin's hand. But Zabin quickly produced a dagger, warning, 'Slaves do not raise a hand against their masters. Remember that, infidel.'

'That charm is mine!' Billy protested.

Zabin shook his head. 'Slaves possess nothing but honour for their masters.'

He then clapped his hands and two guards, wearing skullcaps and voluminous pantaloons, entered the room carrying iron manacles and chains to prepare Billy for the journey to Slave Island.

19

Ezekiel Henley, a wiry and meticulously dressed man with ginger side-whiskers, was the captain of the fifty-ton frigate, *Lady Charlene*. Henley had only recently arrived in Boston on this early summer morning.

He stood in Gabriel Easton's office above the harbour, reporting, 'I saw the *Vandal Witch* when I rested a few days in Port Royal on my voyage north from Maracaibo to Jamaica. I knew the *Witch* had sailed in your convoy, sir, and should be rounding the Cape of Africa at that time. So I asked questions in port, hearing that the *Witch* had sailed from the Slave Coast to Port Royal, that Captain Stanley Kerr had brought a handful of Fanti slaves as well as a cargo of silver to Jamaica.'

Gabriel Easton was stunned by the news which Captain Ezekiel Henley was telling him but he forced himself to contain his anger and hear the rest of this curious report.

'The silver's said to be Mexican ingots,' explained the immaculately groomed captain. 'There's port rumour, too, that Stanley Kerr's also telling stories about carrying a kidnapped Dutchman in the hold of the *Witch*.'

Easton wondered if Kerr had taken leave of his senses. But he still controlled any show of anger and asked with concern, 'Did you hear mention of . . . names?'

'Rhinelander. But I also hear Rhinelander's only a given name. The Dutchman supposedly has foster people who are rich masters of a sugar plantation down there in Jamaica. There's gossip that Kerr is demanding a ransome for him.'

'Scurrilous,' muttered Easton. 'Criminal and scurrilous and – oh, do excuse my disgust – proceed, Captain Henley, proceed with your story.'

Captain Henley nodded. 'Aye, I thought you would want to know about this matter, Mr Easton, about a captain meant to be part of your China convoy.'

Easton guardedly asked, 'Was there harbour rumour about other . . . passengers aboard the *Vandal Witch*?'

'No other passengers, sir. Only the crew, the Dutchman and, of course, the heathen slaves. Those wretches who had not died of flux and had to be thrown into the sea. But that talk was all hushed. Most of the gossip was about Kerr's silver. The Mexican ingots, its asking price being so attractive.'

Easton could no longer hold his tongue. 'That swine! That silver's not his!'

'I doubted it was, sir.'

Controlling his fury, Easton added, 'That precious metal is the property of two brothers, one of whom is betrothed to my own daughter.'

'Sir! I suspected Kerr was up to no good. But I had no idea he was thieving from your friends as well as your kin!'

Easton turned his head, saying, 'You can imagine, my good man, how this news devastates me.'

'Sir, accept my apologies.'

'Captain Henley, you did right in coming to me.' Haltingly, Easton asked, 'Did Captain Kerr sell any of these contraband ingots in Port Royal?'

'No, sir. Not whilst I was there on the island. And I doubt if he will find a buyer before end of harvest.'

'Which is when? Next month?'

'Aye, Mr Easton. Nobody has a shilling or a farthing to spare in all the West Indies till harvest and distilling.'

Easton, pleased with this news, turned back to face the sea captain. 'I appreciate you coming to see me immediately on your arrival in Boston.'

'Sir, I know you're a man of many concerns as well as knowing you're a gentleman who forgets no man who serves you.'

'I never forget a good deed. You can count on my gratitude.'

'Sir, also do not forget *Lady Charlene* is free at this time if you find yourself in need of a ship.'

'Then I urge you not to leave Boston without informing me.'

'Mr Easton, it would be an honour to serve you.'

'You will be hearing from me, Captain Henley,' Easton assured him. 'You will most definitely be hearing from me.'

Left alone in his office, Easton stood in front of his mullioned window and fingered the scar on his cheek as he reconsidered the report which the captain had brought him.

He had no doubts about the story's veracity. Nobody could invent a story about Mexican silver as well as the name and details about Paris Rhinelander.

Easton cursed Kerr's greed and stupidity. Not only was Kerr a thief, but also a fool. Why sail back from Africa to the West Indies with the cargo of silver? Why not continue sailing to China as they had both originally planned? A fortune was to be made by selling the silver in the rich port of Canton. Who but a fool would come back to Jamaica with the silver and – Easton laughed bitterly – a handful of sickly slaves? Who but a greedy, damned fool!

The idea was so absurd, so preposterous that Easton had not even considered it, not even in his wildest, most convoluted dreams.

Thinking about Paris Rhinelander still being aboard the *Vandal Witch*, Easton wondered what Kerr had done with Billy Peake. Where was Billy now? Left at Razor Cove as they had planned? Sold to an African chieftain somewhere along the Slave or Gold Coast?

Easton, having answers to none of these questions, knew he must act at once or risk losing the silver as well as probably becoming implicated as a criminal partner in Kerr's stupid actions. How did he know that Kerr was not divulging everything he knew in the grog shops of Port Royal? Prattling away vital secrets?

Grabbing his three-corned hat from a wooden peg by the door, Easton left his office, convinced he must somehow try to seize the silver himself and, at the same time, perhaps solve a problem presently threatening him and his daughter.

The problem was Brendan Keenan.

The Irish labourer, Brendan Keenan, had grown bolder and excessively cruel in the months since he had moved into Easton's home.

Catherine Easton no longer considered Keenan to be handsome or even sexually attractive. But she could not get rid of him. Keenan had quit his job on the road crew, refused to leave the Easton home, assumed the airs of a gentleman and threatened to expose Catherine's sexual habits if the Eastons threw him back out onto the street.

Apart from being a blackmailer, Keenan hated women. Catherine Easton was certain of the fact. Why else would a man want to make a woman suffer so much?

Catherine's buttocks were red, her nipples ached from being pinched and tortured, her skin was black and blue from being belted, beaten, pounded, slapped and pummelled.

Again today, a fair New England afternoon, Keenan lounged in the Eastons' parlour, dressed in breeches, a ruffled lawn shirt open to his hairy navel, and a cat-o'-nine-tails tucked into one tall leather boot as if it were a riding crop.

Drunk from Easton's brandy, Keenan wanted Catherine to teach him the ways of educated, sophisticated society.

Catherine, sitting disgusted in a far corner of the parlour, scolded, 'First you have to learn to conduct yourself properly in front of servants. And since you've pushed your way in here, all our servants have left.'

'Then *you* wait on me, hussy!' Keenan's curly black hair tumbled over his forehead and his square jaw was black with stubble.

Catherine icily answered, 'That's all I've been doing.'

'So get down on this floor, bitch, and . . . crawl to me.'

'Please . . .' Catherine was tired and exhausted; she knew that when Keenan's lessons in etiquette failed he always returned to the subject of sex, but she no longer desired him.

'Please *who*?' he demanded.

'Please, *sir*,' she quickly corrected. But then she wearily added, 'Brendan, please. I have no patience for any more charades.'

'Charades? What kind of fancy talk is that, bitch? *Charades*? Don't get smart with me, wench.'

Catherine frowned.

Keenan, angrily springing from the chair, steadied himself at the mantelpiece and then pulled down the front of his breeches. His penis fell into view, the thick fat penis which

Catherine had once craved, spent nights adoring, talking to as if it were a person, but which was now an object she could no longer bear to look at.

Keenan slurred, 'Come say hello to my prick.'

Catherine could not resist answering, 'I would rather say "good-bye" to it.'

'Too good for me, are you?'

'Brendan, you're drunk–'

'Drunk? I'll show you how drunk I am.' He pulled up his breeches with one hand and grabbed with the other hand for the cat-o'-nine-tails in his boot.

Catherine, recognizing too well the look on his face, dashed for the parlour doors.

Keenan, lunging to block her escape, grabbed her by the shoulder and bellowed, 'Where do you think you're going, missy?'

'Leave me . . . alone!'

'Alone?' He laughed and ripped at her bodice, tearing the fabric to her waist, exposing her bruised breasts.

'Look what you've done to me! Look! Isn't that enough?' Catherine's voice was pleading, serious. Her eyes were wide with fright, touched with the look of madness.

Grinning, Keenan said, 'Let's see what's back here–'

Spinning her around, he yanked at her skirt, ripping it by the seams, then yanked at her pantaloons to expose her bare buttocks.

Catherine tried to fight him, to beat him with her fists. But he shoved her face forward onto a chair, ripped the rest of the skirt from her body, and slurred, 'I need some satisfying, bitch.'

Catherine's voice now reached the pitch of hysteria. 'Brendan! I can't take any more! *I can't take any more!*'

'You'll take a lot more.' He slashed the cat-o'-nine-tails across her already bruised buttocks.

'I beg you–'

'You'll beg me, all right. You'll beg me to beat you harder and harder. That's what I want. I want you begging me. Telling me I'm a gentleman. A dandy. A fine man who's better than you. You're nothing. You're scum. But me, I'm your lord. Your master. And I give nothing but . . . this!'

The cat-o'-nine-tails again slashed through the air.

The excitement of punishing Catherine, of hearing her cry, of seeing her lose complete control of herself, excited Brendan Keenan; he again pulled down his breeches, but his penis now was hard, firm, sprung forward from his groin, the crown purple with blood.

He jerked Catherine from the chair, pushed her down to her knees in front of him with one hand and slapped the fat penis against her face.

'Adore that big prick, whore. Adore it like your . . . god.'

Catherine hysterically screamed, 'Leave me alone! Leave me alone!'

'What's the matter? Is your man playing too rough? Is your master too hard on you, bitch?'

He slapped her face and his penis bobbed higher from the thrill of dominating her.

Screaming, Catherine fell to the carpet.

Keenan, determined to exert his total authority over her, fell on top of her quaking body, saying, 'You're really going to get it now, little bitch.'

Catherine shook her head back and forth, too frightened to speak.

'You're really going to get it now but I ain't going to screw you. Oh, no. I ain't going to screw you. Least, not like a lady. I'm going to screw you like . . . trash!'

He spat on her face.

She opened her eyes, glaring at him.

He spat on her again, then, laughing, he slapped her across the face, repeating, 'Trash!'

Catherine began to take deep gulps of air, whimpering.

Keenan nodded. 'That's right. Cry . . .'

He pulled back, and rolling Catherine over onto her stomach in one quick movement, he kneed open her legs and rammed his penis towards her buttocks.

Catherine screamed.

'That's right. Cry . . . scream . . . let me hear you . . . cry . . .'

Occupied with the seduction, Brendan Keenan did not hear the parlour door slowly open behind him, nor did he see Gabriel Easton enter the room.

The long knife sank once, then a second and third time into Keenan's back. The steel blade pierced tissue, broke muscle, crunched bone.

As Catherine's cries filled the room, Gabriel Easton kept stabbing Keenan, splattering the carpet with blood, driving the knife up and down until all life was gone from the Irishman's corpse.

Easton, taking deep gulps of breath, sat on the floor alongside the dead body.

Catherine, blood smeared on her face, in her hair, across her body and ripped clothing, sobbed against her father's heaving chest.

'Shhh, baby,' Easton soothed. 'Shhh, now.'

'Thank you. Oh, thank you, thank you, thank you.'

Easton continued soothing, patting his daughter. But his mind was quickly working about what he should do now. He looked at the mutilated corpse, the blood-stained carpet, and he thought how the corpse could be wrapped in the carpet. He next thought of weights, of heavy iron chains, of dumping the carpet-wrapped corpse in the harbour.

'Oh, thank you, Daddy. Oh, thank you for saving me.'

'Shhh, baby. Shhh. I'm going to take you away from all this. I'm going to take you far, far away. You won't even remember it. Shhh.'

Easton was now thinking about Captain Henley, the *Lady Charlene*, the island of Jamaica, and the silver.

Book Three

Slave Island

20

The sound of approaching footsteps grew louder; the echo of leather-heeled boots pounding a tattoo against a marble floor became sharper; the resonant sound punctuated by the slamming of doors reverberated through a series of interconnecting halls to the vaulted chamber where Billy Peake stood naked, like an alabaster statue, on a stone dais.

Mustafa Zabin nervously paced around the dais as he listened to the heavy footfalls approaching the chamber. 'The Grand Master is angry, listen to his footsteps.'

Billy remained motionless, silent, uncaring.

Glancing at the carved door, Zabin warned, 'Do not be fool enough to address the Grand Master when he enters this room, infidel, or your tongue will be yanked out by its roots.'

Billy had spoken little since leaving Humari Umbtari and had no intention of speaking now. Having arrived at Slave Island only a few hours ago with more than two hundred other captives, Billy knew little about the stone fortress rising like a black spectre out of the Indian Ocean, except for the bits of information he had gleaned from the few English-speaking prisoners packed in with him on the dhow sailing from Mombasa to Slave Island.

With a crash the carved door suddenly flew open and a short barrel-chested man stormed into the room. He was ruggedly handsome and wore a scarlet turban, a brown leather jerkin dotted with brass studs, a pair of brown woollen pantaloons and tall black leather boots.

Zabin bowed obsequiously, touching his chest, chin and turban. 'Greetings, Hospodar Pasha. Praise be to Allah for directing you safely home.'

'Home!' Hospodar crossed the tessellated floor, slapping a short cane bastinado against the palm of one hand. 'I've been without a home since the Sultan sent me to this miserable rock seven years ago!'

'But Grand Master,' Zabin eagerly followed Hospodar towards a long wooden table heaped with books, silver globes, rolled leather maps, 'the Sultan honours your wisdom and friendship.'

'The Sultan!' Hospodar's face flushed with anger and the veins stood out in his neck. 'Padisha Abdul Mohammed sits in the Sublime Porte and forgets I'm alive. There are men of The Exalted Gate who poison the Sultan against me. Men who call me a pirate and say I jeopardize the Sultan's name when I seize prisoners from foreign ships to sell from the auction block. But do those same men scorn the revenue I send to the coffers in Constantinople? No, those sycophants grow fat on my labour. And they are not the only danger to my life – the English pigs shoot cannonballs of fire at my ship. The accursed Chinese are fighting amongst themselves and closing their ports to foreign trade. The Indians refuse to buy or sell slaves. The French want to control traffic in the Leather Triangle. I do not know what's happening to the world–'

Hospodar stopped. He spied Billy standing on the short dais in the far corner of the chamber.

Pointing his bastinado at Billy, Hospodar asked. 'Who's that?'

Bowing, Zabin answered. 'A new infidel, Grand Master.'

'What's he doing here in my *selem*?'

'Because of this particular infidel's worth, Grand Master Pasha, I brought him directly from the dhow for you to inspect.'

Turning to Zabin, Hodspodar demanded, 'How many slaves did you find in Africa?'

'By the grace of Allah, Grand Master Pasha, I brought back more than twenty score male slaves, and two score female slaves, many of the girls being virgin, a few beauties of the highest order, as well as fifteen good weavers from the village of Umbtari.'

Looking back to Billy, Hospodar asked, 'And so who is this infidel you bring to me like some pale *houri*?'

'He is English, Grand Master.'

'English, eh? A sailor? If so, where are the other sailors from his ship? Was it a ship of that troublesome East India Company? Was it one of those monstrous vessels called an Indiaman? Where is the big ship? Why does this sailor look more healthy than the last batch of English sailors we had, men with sickly white skin, ginger hair and caved-in chests?'

Zabin tried to keep track of Hospodar's rapid barrage of questions. He followed behind him, finally interjecting, 'This infidel is not a sailor, Grand Master, I purchased him from an English slave dealer in Umbtari where I went to find weavers.'

'How much did you pay for him?'

'Two gold weights plus one lopes, illustrious Pasha.'

Hospodar slapped the bastinado against the palm of his hand. 'Not cheap.'

'He is young, Master. But he is no puny boy. Look, see how the muscles bulge in his arms and legs. Prod his shoulders and feel strength of iron. If you examine his teeth–'

'His hair,' Hospodar tilted his turbanned head to one side as he studied Billy's luxuriant yellow hair flowing back from his forehead, 'his hair is like the mane of some fine Arabian stallion.'

'If my Master observes the infidel more closely, he will see he resembles a stallion in other ways, too.'

Hospodar ignored Zabin's gesture towards Billy's naked groin, still looking at his head. 'He has an empty look to his eyes. There's no life in those eyes. His eyes are blue but vacant. Void of life. Like the eyes of a dead man. Most infidels believe they cannot be enslaved and they fight us. Why is this man not shouting and babbling like other Christian infidels?'

Zabin shrugged. 'He is a wretch of few words, Master Pasha. He spoke when I first brought him and spewed profanities like infidels do. But then he stopped.'

'Perhaps he is ill.' Hospodar asked in a sharper voice, 'Zabin, do you bring back sick slaves to my island? I have a fortune here in slaves. Illness on Slave Island is like fire in a granary. My enemies will say "Fool, Hospodar bought one sick slave and lost an entire island!".'

'No, no, Grand Master,' Zabin quickly assured him, 'this infidel, he is not ill. He is as sound as a Greek peasant.'

'Eh? So what are these?' Hospodar pointed the tip of his bastinado at Billy's back. 'What are these welts on the infidel's pale skin?'

Zabin explained, 'Those are lash marks invisible to most eyes because they have healed so well. But you, my noble lord, you instantly see them. Ah, Hospodar Pasha still has the best eye in the market-place.'

Unmoved by Zabin's flattery, Hospodar asked, 'Why was he lashed? Was he punished for bad behaviour? Speak! Tell me the dog's history!'

Bowing, Zabin said, 'The infidel told me he was lashed by sailors on a ship crossing the Atlantic Ocean to Africa.'

'Lashed by sailors? Crossing the Atlantic Ocean? I do not understand, Zabin. I thought you told me he was *not* a sailor!'

'He lived in the American colonies and travelled by ship to Africa.'

'Ah, he's from the Americas. The Americas! I see.' Hospodar studied Billy with renewed interest. 'Perhaps he will be able to tell me a little something about the Americas.'

Zabin, reassured that he had been correct to bring Billy to Hospodar's chambers, believed he must proceed quickly with his plan.

'Grand Master, it is my humble opinion that we will get a fine and most generous price for this infidel at the forthcoming auction. As you see, the infidel is in good health. A few days exercising in the training yard will add the necessary tug to his muscle, will enrich the colour of his skin like a dove roasted in honey.'

'No,' Hospodar shook his head. 'We do not sell this infidel at the auction.'

'Not sell him? But Grand Master, the auction is less than three weeks away. Many rich and powerful men travel great distances to come to the auctions at Slave Island.'

'No, Zabin. We do not sell this infidel at the auction. He goes to work building walls.'

'Building . . . walls?'

'The new wall being built in the harbour, Zabin.'

'But wall-building is dangerous, Grand Master. I heard only a few hours ago that a slave fainted in the sun and plunged to his death. He has already been sealed into the wall with other poor wretches who met the same fate.'

Hospodar was unmoved. 'Bones strengthen a wall.'

'But do we waste such a fine man as this for mortaring stone?'

'The wall, Zabin. The infidel builds the wall and works in the quarry.'

Zabin obediently bowed, intoning, '*In Sha Allah*.'

Hospodar turned to the table as Zabin threw a *dhellabah* at Billy and beckoned him to step down from the dais. Zabin was secretly pleased that Billy would not be sold at the slave auction and that his devious plan was already working. All he had to do now was somehow allow Lady Iona to hear there was a new slave in the men's prison, a slave who might please her as a paramour.

Hospodar, standing alongside the cluttered table, called, 'Zabin?'

Zabin paused with Billy by the tall carved doors. 'Yes, Grand Master?'

'Tell the jeweller to infibulate this American infidel.'

'Infibulate . . . him?'

'Put a ring through his foreskin. We have too many dark-skinned wenches who would gladly surrender their virginity to such a man. We don't want to gamble the price difference between a virgin and a ruined woman.'

Zabin, thinking how infibulation would destroy all plans for the slave with Lady Iona, gently asked, 'The weather,

Hospodar Pasha. Is it not too hot, too unhealthy for–'

'You have my orders. Now leave.'

Zabin again bowed, wondering how he was going to solve this problem.

'And, Zabin?'

'Yes, Grand Master–' Zabin stopped in front of the door, bracing himself for another disappointment.

'Send word to my wife that I have returned from my voyage and will dine with her tonight in her apartments.'

'I am your obedient servant, Grand Master,' Zabin replied, 'but I am certain her Ladyship, the Princess of Ioxa, already knows of her beloved husband's arrival and that she, the nightingale of your heart, eagerly awaits your visit to her apartments.'

Hospodar's sea-weathered face creased as he smiled with contentment. His voice warmed as he said, 'I suppose I am a lucky man.'

'And a wise one, Hospodar Pasha.' Zabin again bowed, then impatiently shoved Billy through the door, muttering, 'Get along, you troublesome wretch, or I'll have a dog bite off that foreskin with his teeth!'

Billy stumbled forward.

21

The low dining tables in Lady Iona's apartments were elegantly draped with squares of Burmese brocade for Hospodar's supper and crowded with a glittering array of Damascene platters, gilt bowls, Chinese glazed porcelain cups, chased silver goblets. A steady parade of serving girls brought honeyed fowl, lamb delicately turned on a spit, spicy condiments, sugary compotes, fruits and vegetables grown in the island's herbages or brought by *mahone* from the neighbouring islands of Comoro and Aldabra.

Iona and Hospodar lounged on richly stitched cushions flanking the low tables. Hospodar commanded the conversation, complaining about spotting no foreign ships on his recent voyage north to the Arabian Sea, describing the squabbles between the English and Dutch trading companies in the nearby Spice Islands, speaking about the guests soon to be arriving for the auction sale on Slave Island.

Iona dutifully listened to her husband's monologue, asking questions and giving praise at the appropriate moments whilst also unobtrusively ordering her slave girls to bring or remove dishes of sweetmeats, decanters of wines, to decrease or lengthen wicks inside the pierced brass oil lamps hanging from the tented ceiling.

A single golden salver of almonds and two small ruby red glasses of a digestive liqueur were left on the table. Hospodar sipped at the potent brown drink, complimenting, 'Ah, delicious.'

Iona smiled. The soft glow of the flickering lamps enhanced her exotic features, making the strands of black pearls shimmer in her hair, catching the iridescent blue and green of peacock feathers stitched onto her purple robe.

Demurely she replied, 'The drink is distilled from wild berries and nuts on the island of Pemba, husband Pasha.'

Hospodar took another sip. 'I like its sharpness.'

'I shall have a cask loaded aboard the *Cessina* for your next voyage.'

Hospodar patted Iona's hand. 'You are a good wife.'

Lowering her eyes, Iona idly studied the ring Hospodar had brought her from Ceylon, a ruby set in golden prongs fashioned like an eagle's talon, the gem hanging topheavy on her forefinger.

Hospodar, seeing her regarding the precious gift, said, 'You deserve better, brighter attention than rubies.'

'Your safe return is my reward.'

Hospodar sighed pleasurably, studying the myriads of small trembling stars thrown across the tented room by the flickering flames inside the pierced brass lamps. He confessed, 'I have done nothing but complain of my problems since I've arrived. You must tell me how you have been filling your days in my absence.'

'The Sultan has nine wives and a harem of four hundred *houris*. Does he listen to their problems?' Iona shook her head, adding, 'No, a man does not have time to hear the tedious chores of women.'

Hospodar politely argued, 'All the beauties in Padisha Abdul Mohammed's harem and the nine *khadines* who call themselves his wives cannot compare in beauty or intelligence to my beloved.'

Again patting Iona's wrist, Hospodar insisted, 'Tell me about the entertainments you've arranged for our guests. The amusements to be presented before the auction.'

Iona's sudden smile was playful, touched with coquetry. 'The entertainments are meant to be a surprise – even for you, Hospodar Pasha.'

'Not even a hint?'

Iona hesitated. 'I can tell you there will be a duel, that some blood will be spilt.'

Hospodar shrugged. 'Men who are bored and idle enjoy seeing blood. But no man – or woman – need know my wife arranged the duel . . . whatever it may be.'

Hospodar took another sip of his liqueur, continuing, 'Yes, it was very clever of you, Iona, to suggest we provide entertainments before this auctioning of slaves. I think you are correct when you say that some excitement will put everybody in a more expansive mood, will relax and move them to bid higher prices on the work slaves.'

'Men do not buy slaves only for labour,' Iona reminded her husband. 'Apart from work slaves, you also sell pleasure slaves at your auctions. I am therefore providing some erotic titillation to whet the guests' appetites for pleasure slaves. Does that bother you, Hospodar Pasha?'

'No. But we must be cautious whom we invite to those particular entertainments. I understand the Sultan's mother, the Sultana Valideh, will attend this auction on

Slave Island. I do not know the woman but we dare not allow the Sultan's aged mother to witness anything ribald or lewd. I understand Abdul Mohammed is most protective to her.'

Iona agreed, adding. 'We must also be cautious of the Englishman who wrote to you from Khartoum – what was his name? Sir Oliver Bull?'

Hospodar nodded. 'Yes, we will be wary of this mysterious Englishman. The English are prudish and censorious so we will wait to see what breed of slaves interest him before we extend more intimate hospitality.'

Raising his eyes to the starry dots dancing on the tented ceiling, Hospodar went on, 'And we will definitely not invite the Dey of Algiers to anything too provocative. The Spanish Pirate, yes. Oh yes, Don Julio do Castenaldo is a degenerate and nothing could shock him. But the Dey of Algiers, no, he is one of my sharpest critics in Constantinople and he would go straight back to the Sublime Porte to give bad reports to the Sultan.'

Iona said, 'Have no fears about gossip, Hospodar. The one report which will impress the Sultan is the amount of gold you send him from the auction. That is all that matters and I adamantly believe that these little entertainments, insignificant though they may be, will relax the visitors and loosen the strings of their purses.'

Hospodar said, 'Then my success will be due to your genius, dear Iona, and I am indebted to you–' his eyes lowered, '–even . . . enslaved.'

Iona gazed at Hospodar, considering how handsome, how virile he looked in the scarlet turban, his brown dining robes the same colour as his face. She knew he was ferocious in battle, brave in stalking ships or being pursued himself. But she also knew his virility was only a façade: in the privacy of her apartments, with her, Hospodar enjoyed being passive, subjected.

Preparing herself for the evening's next phase, Iona held one hand out to her husband, assuming a more authoritative voice. 'Come. It is getting late. I think the hour is approaching for us to learn how good a spouse you have been in your absence.'

Hospodar did not reply.

Iona, rising from her cushions, announced, 'I am retiring to my alcove.'

Hospodar followed her into the adjoining chamber, disrobing as he moved.

Soon, Iona held Hospodar's cane bastinado in her hand and stood dominantly over him lying naked on the cushions.

Iona, her face stern and her voice like that of a tutor speaking to a recalcitrant student, began, 'You did not visit me immediately on your return? Why did you avoid me?'

Hospodar was shuddering with excitement as he lay face down on the cushions. 'I was . . . frightened.'

'Frightened? Why would you be frightened? Unless you had reason to be frightened . . .' Iona rubbed the tip of the cane bastinado over Hospodar's hirsute buttocks, going on, 'Did you sleep with a wench when you were away from me? Did you fear I would learn of your unfaithfulness and punish you?'

'Yes, your ladyship,' Hospodar replied and, then, dropping his head into the cushions, he muttered the rest of his words.

Iona struck him sharply with the stick, ordering, 'Speak up!'

Hospodar answered in a louder voice, 'I was frightened to see you because . . . because . . . I bedded a wench on the voyage . . .'

Iona struck the bastinado more soundly against Hospodar's bared buttocks. 'Is that what you do when you leave Slave Island? Entertain . . . *whores* on your ship?'

Hospodar pleaded, 'But a husband has privileges! Rights and–'

'Privileges! Do not talk to me about manly rights and privileges! It is a privilege for you to have an understanding wife like me!'

Iona hit him again, repeating the strike, making the cane bite into his flesh.

Hospodar, flinching with each cane stroke across his naked buttocks, begged, 'But, your ladyship, she was only a common whore!'

'A whore? Do you allow whores to beat you? Tell me! Confess! Do you allow whores to beat and punish you?'

'Not like you, your ladyship, not like–'

She hit him again, demanding, 'Do you or do you not allow whores to beat you?'

'Yes, your ladyship, I do allow whores to beat me. But I do not enjoy–'

'Is this how your whore hit you?' Iona stepped back from the bank of cushions and put her slippered feet on the silken carpet to take fuller, longer strokes with the cane bastinado.

'Harder, your ladyship,' Hospodar confessed, 'she struck me harder.'

'Like this?' Iona beat him with rapid strokes of the thin cane.

Hospodar, grasping the pillows as Iona punished him for being unfaithful to her, pleaded, 'I told the whore about you. I told the whore what a good wife I had. The whore said I was not worthy of such a good wife. The whore beat me for being such a piece of . . . shit.'

'Shit? Ha! For once a whore speaks the truth!' ridiculed Iona. 'For once a whore is correct! You are nothing but a piece of shit, Hospodar. Nothing but a piece of dried camel shit.'

Iona made welts on Hospodar's buttocks, listening to him groan with a mixture of pain and satisfaction, hearing him confess his unfaithfulness to her, begging her for her forgiveness.

Iona knew that this punishment was more satisfying to Hospodar than his adultery with some insignificant prostitute. Iona suspected that her husband might even be fabricating stories to make her beat him, but whatever his fantasies were, Iona did not care. Her mind was lost in her own images, in her own reasons for striking him. Iona struck Hospodar for failing to be a husband who could satisfy her, punished him for not being the strong man she wanted and needed in love-making.

Hospodar was a passive lover, always making Iona play the dominant role. His appetite had transformed her into a frustrated, lonely woman with a voracious appetite for love-making and cruelty, always needing new and different ways to vent the bitterness building inside her.

Love – romance and devotion from men – had not always been unrewarding for Iona, Princess of Ioxa.

By the age of fourteen, Iona had received five formal proposals of marriage; by the age of seventeen she was beautiful, proud, arrogant and still unmarried; by the age of twenty she was contemptuous of all suitors asking for her hand as a wife.

Iona was raised as the ward of her uncle, Prince Achmet bin Achmet, in Kari Palace on the Levantine island of Kypros; Iona knew her ageing relative was eager to marry her to anyone and the latest in the succession of influential young men to appear at Kari Palace was an Algerian named Hassan serving the Ottoman Empire by dispensing the privilege of the *usanza del mari* – the Sultan's permission to be involved in piracy.

Hassan, a dark man with a thick black moustache and heavily lashed eyes, was instantly intrigued by young Iona when she appeared at a small gathering on the rooftop of Kari Palace. He asked Prince Achmet's permission to allow her to show him the sights from the nearby balustrade; the old man quickly consented.

Iona, bored with the overly attentive Algerian, stood alongside him on the marble balcony and drily announced, 'You can hire a cicerone from the marketplace to show you the sights.'

Hassan answered in a rich voice, 'I require no ordinary guide.'

Iona held her eyes towards the orange sunset colouring

the city's curved and cubical skyline. 'A man of your importance can have anything he wishes.'

He asked, 'And anyone?'

Before Iona replied, she felt his hand gently caressing the inside of her thigh.

'Stop,' she hissed in the fading light. 'My uncle will have you beheaded for touching me!'

'Ah, but you will not tell your uncle, will you? You will continue pointing out minarets and walls to me and I assure you that neither your uncle, nor any of his distinguished guests, will be the wiser of what we are doing.'

The Algerian's audacity surprised but thrilled Iona; she soon felt his hand stroking her softly, petting her thigh as if she were a cat.

'Now drop your left hand to your side,' he instructed.

She obeyed but whispered protestation.

'Shhh.' He took her hand and, putting it between the folds of his own robe, he asked, 'You feel what hangs between my legs? How would you like to have that poking between *your* legs?'

Iona had never before seen or touched a penis; her thumb and fingers encompassed a long thickness, a soft bulky organ which quickly hardened against the palm of her hand.

He asked, 'How would you like to give a home to that between your legs?'

She whispered, 'How would you like me to scream?'

'Oh, no. You will not scream. I can tell by your voice you will not betray me.' Hassan prodded her tender cleft, adding, 'My finger also assures me you won't betray us with a scream.'

'What can your finger possibly tell you?'

'My finger feels moisture between your legs. My finger tells me you are as pure as a girl but moist like a woman. So I will treat you as a woman.'

The promise excited Iona.

Hassan, still pretending to be viewing the sights of the ancient harbour from the terrace, curled his finger into

Iona's vaginal lips, saying, 'I must be cautious, though. I must not crack with my finger what I can break with my prick.'

'You are crude as well as bold, sir.'

Hassan's voice remained confident as he informed Iona, 'I stay in a house on the Street of the Bird-Sellers, I shall be there alone tomorrow at midday.'

She whispered, 'I dare not visit you inside a house.'

'Then it is your loss.' He removed his hand from her robe, rearranged his own robe and bowed, saying, 'But I suspect I will see you tomorrow.'

The next day, Iona made a pretence to visit a silversmith across the city and ordered her litter-bearers to carry her to the narrow hillside street echoing with the twitter of caged bulbuls.

Hassan was waiting for Iona in the centre garden of a sienna-washed house. He led her to an adjoining room, cool with blue, yellow and white tiles, and lined with large cushions; he began kissing her, feeling the curves, the mounds, the firmness of her body as they embraced, nibbling at her ear, cheek and neck, rubbing her breasts, nipples, her feminine mound.

Quivering, Iona asked, 'Why do you tease me?'

'Tease you?' A brilliant line of white teeth flashed beneath his black moustache as he smiled.

'And you laugh at me!'

'Laughter should always be part of love-making. Is not love a fulfilment of joy?'

And it was joy for young Iona to learn about love-making from Hassan in the house on the Street of the Bird-Sellers. The loss of her virginity was only one part of her education. Hassan showed her miniature Indian paintings of lovers in a variety of sexual positions. He promised her they themselves would explore all the mysteries of their bodies; he taught her how to use her mouth, both by sucking him and by him tonguing her vagina to reach moments of physical ecstasy. He laid her on cushions in a position in which he could easily stroke what the Chinese called the 'flower of the back garden'.

Hassan used the Indian, and Chinese, miniature love paintings, as well as ancient Arabic engravings, as lessons for Iona, tablets to give her guidance in a variety of sexual acts to perform, and as proof for her that she was not the first female ever to indulge in exotic acts.

The mouth was as important as a vagina, Hassan showed her, and he filled Iona's mouth with warm tea, not enough to make her choke, just enough to increase the sensation for his erect penis driving between her working lips.

Hassan also duplicated the large beads attached to a long string which was pictured in one Oriental work, pushing the string of beads up Iona's vagina and giving her excitement by pulling down the string at various speeds, making the beads create a sensation against her vulva.

He said, 'These beads are also very useful when women make love to one another.'

Iona did not pursue Hassan's remarks about women making love to one another but the idea did not repel her and she made secret note of the pictures showing women tweaking one other's pink nipples, fingering another woman's furry delta, kissing like lovers.

Iona returned daily to Hassan in the hillside house, quickly passing from being a sexual initiate to a skilled partner of love. Canes, sticks, rods, silken cords to bind her hands and legs in bondage – the Algerian introduced her to the many mysteries of Eastern love-making, both playful and tinged with pain.

It was Hassan, too, who taught Iona about substitutes for an erect penis. He eased a dildo in and out of her vagina. Then he next pushed a stretched leather phallus into her mouth, telling her to imagine that she was sucking the penis of a third man, teaching her that an imagination was as important – as exciting – as the body in sexual pursuits.

Then one day Iona arrived at the house and Hassan was not there. Thinking he had been called away on business, she returned to her uncle's palace and went back the next day. But Hassan was still not there, nor was there a message for her.

After five consecutive visits, Iona stopped going to the Street of the Bird-Sellers. Then, in the following week, she received a visit from a stern-faced young man wearing blue leather boots, a long moustache, a red plumed turban: she immediately recognised him as a Janissary, one of the Sultan's elite guards.

The young Janissary, arrogant and officious, informed her, 'Hassan Pasha has left the city island of Kypros and does not want you to pursue him.'

'Left . . . Kypros?'

The guard explained, 'He sailed at dawn and does not want you to follow him.'

'What is the meaning of this?' The announcement had stunned Iona.

'Hassan Pasha knows many ladies. But he is soon to be married and is also a very busy man in the services of the Sultan.'

'Married? You come here and talk to me about married men? I have never before been so insulted.'

Iona's heart was pounding. She was tempted to call for her uncle, to demand that the young Janissary be punished for dishonouring her. But, quickly regaining her wits, she realised punishment would involve an investigation, that the truth about her assignations with Hassan might be discovered and she would risk being humiliated. She could lose all chance of ever being received at the Sublime Porte in Constantinople.

'Do not come here any more,' she haughtily ordered. 'I am recently betrothed to–' quickly thinking of the last young man who had discussed marriage with her uncle, Iona stammered, '– I am soon to wed,' she grasped for a name, any name, finally visualising the strong face of the young man called Hospodar.

Now, seven years later, Iona had almost forgotten about Hassan the Algerian; she was married to Hospodar and had discovered his sexual perversions. She indulged in illicit sexual partnerships during Hospodar's absences from Slave Island but always kept him believing she was a devoted wife. Unfortunately, though, few men satisfied Iona and she kept looking, waiting, longing for a satisfactory lover who could indulge in the mysteries of Eastern love-making, would practise love as a fulfilment of joy, as Hassan had taught her on the Street of the Bird-Sellers.

Seventeen nights had passed since Hospodar had visited Iona in her apartments and the auction was only five days away; it was morning and Iona lay in the coolness of her porphyry tub, her nerves lulled by the gentle plucking of a lute. She had spent another sleepless night, tossing, turning on her divan, her loins aching for a lover, any kind of lover.

Dreading the arrival of guests in the fortress, loathing the attention they always required during their visits, Iona lay in the deep tub, watching her nipples bob in the perfumed water, the aureola making small rosy islands.

Shrill laughter suddenly broke from a small group of slave girls gossiping in the adjoining alcove. Iona's jealousy arose as she listened to the girls discussing their lovers, confiding about the men's sexual preferences.

Falahalla, an Abyssinian girl, said, 'He likes to do nothing. He lies there and I squat up and down, up and down on that great pole of his. That's what makes him happy.'

'Stupid girl,' thought Iona. 'Tell your man's desires to your best girlfriends and they will try their own luck with him as soon as you aren't there!'

A Sudanese, Siri, said, 'My Torco just lies there, too. But all he wants me to do is suck him. Sometimes he just lies there looking at the stars, staring at the sky for hours, making me suck, suck, suck.'

Falahalla made an unpleasant noise, asking, 'Do you like to do . . . that?'

Siri answered, 'It makes him happy so–'

The slave girl, Karaba, interrupted, 'Admit it. When a woman gets a taste for sucking a man she forgets she's got a hole between her legs. Don't tell me you do it if you don't enjoy it.'

The girls all laughed; Iona lay in the tub, listening to them teasing Siri; shortly, the Abyssinian girl, Falahalla, announced, 'Do you imagine, it is yellow! Hair like gold!'

Iona, although frustrated by their talk about making love, was secretly upset that they had now changed their conversation to what she believed was the subject of other slave girls.

'Oh, how I would love golden hair instead of this black wool I've got!' complained the African girl named Karaba.

The Burmese girl, Mari, asked, 'What does water do to silky fine hair? Make it curl?'

Iona, irritated by the senseless prattle, called from her bath, 'Silence! Do not gossip about other slave wenches.'

There was a momentary silence beyond the saffron dyed curtains separating the two chambers; Falahalla answered, 'Your ladyship, forgive us, but we do not speak about other women.'

The sound of giggling followed Falahalla's announcement and then Karaba explained, 'No, your ladyship, we speak of a new male slave.'

'A male?' Iona's curiosity was instantly piqued. 'A new male slave with . . . yellow hair?'

'Yes, your ladyship,' answered Karaba. 'He has a body like a god. Mari saw him yesterday when she went to the rocks to gather snails.'

Mari added, 'It is true, your ladyship. The young slave is English. But he is not like other English sailors we have seen.'

'No, you are wrong,' interrupted Falahalla. 'The blond sailor comes from a land called the Americas. I heard the guards speaking about him.'

'The Americas?' asked Karaba. 'Where are the Americas?'

Iona was no longer listening to the girls' gossip.

She had risen from the tub, calling to the girls, 'Bring me my robes . . . Send for Zabin . . . Stop your gossiping and tell Zabin to come to my apartments . . . Quickly, move quickly, you wenches . . .'

22

The bright orb of the sun blazed down on a ragged gang of prisoners swinging pickaxes on the granite promontory which formed the eastern tip of Slave Island. The steady clank, clank, clank of axes kept a rhythm with a second group of prisoners working nearby, wielding heavy iron hammers to break large boulders into smaller pieces of rock.

More than two hundred and fifty men toiled in the sun beyond the walls of the stone fortress; the colour of their skin ranged from blue-black, deep brown and dusky amber, to the lighter complexions of the countries of northern Europe. Brawny Turkish overseers moved amongst them, ready to flail short knotted ropes against the naked back of any man who idled at his job or spoke to the man working alongside him.

Billy Peake had begun his first day of work on Slave Island by quarrying stone with a pickaxe. He had kept a protective cloth knotted over his head and his hands tied with rags, but his fair skin had quickly become scorched by the sun and his hands blistered from the axe handle.

After his first week quarrying stone, Billy was sent to work on top of the wall being built alongside the island's harbour. Billy emptied baskets of stone hoisted from the ground by long hemp ropes and then spread the stones onto a wet mixture of lime and straw.

By the end of his second week on Slave Island Billy's skin had toughened against the sun's scorching heat and his aching body had become accustomed to the strain; he had also gleaned a few words of Turkish and Arabic from the other slaves, as well as learning phrases from their *lingua franca*, a mixture of Arabic and African dialects, combined with a smattering of French, Spanish, Dutch and English.

Amongst the slaves Billy met during those first weeks on Slave Island was Brian Macpherson, a talkative Scotsman captured from an English merchant ship out of Glasgow. At night Macpherson slept on a bed of rags close by Billy in the subterranean cavern which the male slaves used for their dormitory. The slave's work began before dawn, when the men shuffled from the torch-lit cavern through a seepage pool of brackish water, to a cavern where they collected their rations of food for the day.

Brian Macpherson, always fresh after a few hours of sleep, stood in line behind Billy with a calabash to scoop gruel from a deep wooden tub, and imparted an endless stream of facts about Slave Island, Hospodar and the far-reaching domain called the Ottoman Empire.

His speech touched with a Scottish burr, Macpherson said, 'This castle is cursed for its bad luck, laddie. They say it was built eight hundred years ago by a king running from Mohammed's holy war and he met his death down here in a pit of vipers. The Good Lord only knows how many poor souls died down in these inky black bowels since the Ottomans seized control of this accursed ocean and the pagan lands surrounding it.'

Billy, his eyes heavy with morning sleep, stumbled along in the food line, asking questions more to awaken his brain than to hear details from Macpherson's seemingly endless store of information. He asked, 'Who are the Ottomans?'

Macpherson gently pushed Billy along in the line as he replied, 'The Ottomans are Turks, laddie, and have been in power around the Eastern Mediterranean for the last five hundred years. Their religion is Muslim and they now hold power over other Muslims across North Africa. The cities of Tunis, Tripoli and Algiers are 'regencies' and have governors known as 'Dey'. The Ottoman king is called Sultan and he rules from Constantinople in a palace known as the Sublime Porte.'

'That's where Hospodar gets his orders?' asked Billy, dipping his calabash into a tub of coarse brown gruel. 'From this place called the Sublime Porte in Constantinople?'

Macpherson warned, 'You live on Slave Island, laddie, and you call Hospodar "Pasha". As we address important men "sir" and "my lord" back in our countries, the Ottomans call their leading citizens "pasha".'

Billy moved with the other ragged, half-asleep men waiting to take a piece of salted fish from a wooden puncheon. The gruel and cold fish had to satisfy the slaves' hunger until sundown.

Macpherson, following Billy, said, 'There are stories that Hospodar Pasha was exiled here to Slave Island because he fell out of favour with the Sultan, that Hospodar's wife disgraced him and they were sent in bad odour to this outpost.'

'Hospodar's wife lives here too?'

'Aye, like a grand queen. Mind you, laddie, I've never caught one wee glimpse of the lassie and I've been here for three long years.'

Billy looked back over his shoulder at Macpherson, 'You've been here . . . three years?'

'Aye,' answered Macpherson, motioning for Billy to move with the line. 'My ship was taken in the Bay of Bengal in the spring of '58. I'll never forget the fine morning when we spotted a square sail moving down on us with the wind and, before we knew what was happening, an unholy horde of Arabs and Turks, armed with scimitars and pikes, came screaming across from their ship, murdering some of the crew and bringing the rest here to Slave Island.'

'Three years is a long time to be kept prisoner,' Billy said. 'Why haven't you been auctioned by now?'

Macpherson's laugh was empty. 'They talk a lot about

auctions here on Slave Island, laddie. But don't you believe everything you hear. Hospodar Pasha, he needs workers to quarry stone, build walls, make boats, weave cloth, bake pots. This may be a slave station but it's also a factory. Sometimes there's near enough a thousand slaves working here.'

'One thousand slaves? How many of them are white men?'

'Two, maybe three hundred. The number varies. But I've noticed very few – if any – white slaves being sold at the auction sales. I don't know where white slaves go, men called "infidels". Maybe they're sold secretly, to private buyers. But somehow they disappear and new white slaves arrive . . . like yourself.'

Billy asked, 'Why isn't the outside world told more about white men being sold into slavery?'

'Because politicians back home like to talk about African slavery, that's why. The African slave trade is their favourite subject. It's closer to home. Us infidel slaves are too embarrassing to England, to the King, to Parliament. Why, we're their own people being enslaved by heathen countries. It's said that a quarter of Algiers' entire population is made up of white men in slavery. That means almost fifteen thousand European slaves in Tunis and Tripoli and Sallee. And that number is just one small amount of all the European slaves owned by the Ottomans. You visit any city from Benghazi to Baghdad and you'll see white men dressed in those collarless shirts, baggy trousers and caps.'

'Is that a uniform, baggy trousers, and shirts with no collars?'

'Aye, it's against the law for infidel slaves to wear robes and turbans in Islam. All the bare-headed slaves you see in a city are probably Christians.'

'So the Ottomans must have at least one hundred thousand white slaves from Europe?'

'More like a quarter of a million, laddie. Scots, Irish, English, French, dagos from those countries bordering the Mediterranean, and colonials from the Americas. Some men are kept in slavery for ten, twenty years. Others die in their chains. So you see, my three years on Slave Island are nothing. I just hope they don't decide to make me a beylik slave. Then I *am* lost.'

'What's a beylik slave?'

'A beylik is a slave owned by the state. A man is seldom freed then.'

Macpherson pointed at Billy's soiled feet, saying, 'As for you, laddie, you haven't even got your big toe wet yet. Two weeks on Slave Island isn't a drop in the bleeding ocean.'

The Scotsman, seeing a Turkish guard approaching them, fell silent and nodded for Billy to move forward in the line.

On the night of Billy's eighteenth day in captivity, he lay on his bed of rags in the subterranean dormitory, mulling over Brian Macpherson's story about the number of Europeans being held as slaves in the Ottoman Empire. He wondered how long he himself could survive as a prisoner, a slave, another man's property, little better than a horse or donkey.

Thoughts of Jenny also plagued Billy tonight; he had long ago passed from merely missing her companionship, and her love-making, worrying instead about her safety. This change of concern told him he truly loved her, that Jenny had been more to him than a convenient lover. He lay on his bed of rags, thinking how he had lost all desire to live when they had been parted, after Jack Razor had told them why he had allowed them so much privacy in the encampments.

Had Jenny been taken to Khartoum? Was she pregnant? Had Jack Razor got a fine price for her as he had hoped? If so, from whom? And would Jenny be put into a harem? Used as a concubine? What would happen to the child if she had one?

Billy tried to fight his jealousy and possessiveness. His better judgment told him that it was senseless to be jealously enraged for sexual reasons. It was not as if Jenny had a choice between him and a man who bought her from a slave block.

Billy, lying in the darkness of the underground dormitory, realized that he also was as powerless as Jenny, that he no longer had a choice either about a lover. He must perform sexual acts if forced into those actions by a new owner.

Although exhausted from work every night, Billy nevertheless was beginning to regain a desire for love-making. He thought of Jenny and his penis immediately sprang into hardness. But he refused to masturbate in the secrecy of darkness. Other prisoners talked about wives, mistresses, women back home. Billy even heard noises in the cavern at night which told him that some male prisoners had sex amongst themselves, or that guards chose prisoners who appealed to them and had the prisoners serve them as women.

'Sex? What are all these thoughts about sex?' Billy asked himself, and tried to find a comfortable position on the rags to sleep. The time for a new work day would arrive in a few hours.

Rolling over on the rags, Billy began drifting off to sleep, feeling a bit happier, realizing he still had desires, that slavery had not completely robbed him of everything, and that he was slowly, gradually recovering from being the sad, lonely dejected person he had been after Jack Razor had parted him and Jenny.

His brain was wavering between thoughts of recovering his heartiness and the oblivion of sleep when he heard a noise in the cavern's darkness.

Thinking the sound came from prisoners buggering in the black dormitory, Billy pulled the rags over his head, telling himself to mind his own business and try to enjoy at least a few hours of sleep.

A foot suddenly kicked him.

Sitting bolt upright in the darkness, Billy saw a torch sputtering above him and the faces of two men staring down at him in the flickering yellow light. One was a guard and Billy immediately thought how the Turkish guards were said to take prisoners to their own beds.

The other man standing above Billy was Mustafa Zabin. He kicked at Billy, ordering, 'On your feet, infidel!'

Billy blinked in the torch's light. 'What's . . . happening?'

The surly guard grabbed for Billy's arm, grunting an inaudible command.

Billy protested, 'It will soon be morning. I still have a few hours sleep.'

Zabin repeated, 'On your feet, infidel!'

Before Billy realized what was happening, the guard grabbed him by the arm and was shoving him across the sprawled bodies of sleeping men to follow Zabin.

Billy, remembering Hospodar's order to Zabin about having him infibulated, called, 'Where are you taking me? Are you taking me to have a ring put through my foreskin? Is that's what's happening?'

The guard raised his club above Billy's head.

Zabin waved his hand, ordering, 'Do not mark the infidel. Not yet.'

They continued across the dormitory, following the sputtering torch toward a stairway cut into stone.

23

By late morning Billy had been scrubbed by two Kurdistani slaves in a small windowless room where Zabin had taken him from the dormitory. The quick-moving Kurdistanis washed his hair, rubbed the calluses from his hands and feet with a pumice stone, pared his finger and toe nails, and shined palm olive oil into his dry skin.

Dressed in a clean white linen loincloth Billy felt

revitalized, even surprisingly relaxed as he followed Zabin up a circular stairway lit by sputtering torches.

Zabin's yellow leather slippers slapped against the worn stone stairs as he warned, 'Infidel, you are a lucky slave. So keep your mouth shut when you learn where I'm taking you. One word about this visit and you die.'

Billy silently followed.

Zabin continued, 'I have kept you from having a gold ring pierced through your foreskin. So I expect you to be grateful to me, slave. Understand?'

Billy grunted his assent, suspecting that Zabin did nothing that did not benefit himself.

'Infidel, I want you to show the utmost respect to the person I am taking you to meet.'

Billy was unable to calm his nerves. He could not imagine why Zabin was suddenly showing him so much attention, bathing and grooming him, giving him instructions on how to conduct himself. Why? Where were they going? Who was this person he was to meet?

Stopping in front of a pair of tall wooden doors, Zabin caught his breath before knocking on the doors, knocking again until the sound of chains rattled on the far side of the doors.

The doors slowly creaked open and two veiled slave girls beckoned Zabin and Billy to enter a small candlelit foyer. The girls pushed shut the doors, then led Zabin and Billy through a series of curtained archways, padding over a succession of plush carpets, and emerging in a tall vaulted chamber flooded with bright morning sunlight.

Billy hesitated in the splendour of the room, his nerves momentarily disappearing as he gaped at intricately carved cedar tables, banks of silk cushions, diaphanous curtains billowing in the breeze.

A woman – dark-skinned and statuesque – her black hair twisted with pearls, richly attired in lavender robes, emerged from behind a tall ivory-inlaid screen.

Zabin bowed, touching his chest, chin and turban, murmuring, 'Greetings, Lady Iona.'

Billy immediately recognised the name; his heart began to pound, realising where Zabin had brought him.

Iona, ignoring Zabin, appraised Billy's physique with a cold calculating eye.

Zabin said, 'This is the American infidel, your ladyship.'

Encircling Billy, Iona did not speak as she studied his face, shoulders, his naked chest tapering to a flat stomach hardened by work on the harbour wall.

Obsequiously, Zabin continued, 'Your ladyship, you can judge for yourself why I have not brought you this miserable wretch. See, his skin is burnt by the sun. His nose is peeled like a pomegranate. His hair grows every which way like a mule.'

Iona remained silent, her eyes scrutinising Billy's body.

Zabin went on, 'The Grand Master sent the wretch to work on the harbour wall and rightly so, your ladyship. What kind of price would such a dog fetch at the auction?'

'He looks healthy to me.' Iona's words were clipped.

'Healthy? Oh yes, you are indeed correct, your ladyship. You are always correct in your astute observations. But–'

Zabin recognized Iona's interest; he knew she wanted Billy, but prolonged his theatrics, wringing his hands as he whined, 'Was I not correct, Your Ladyship, to think this cur isn't worthy of your attention? Look, see this sad specimen is not even a man.'

Iona did not face Zabin as she ordered, 'Leave us alone, Zabin.'

'Alone?' blurted Zabin. 'Unprotected with this . . . savage beast?'

Iona laughed. 'Beast? He's barely older than a boy!'

Then, lifting a gold chain from around her neck, she handed it to Zabin, repeating, 'Go, Zabin. Leave us alone.'

Zabin, accepting the gold chain, quickly stuffed the precious links into the folds of his hempen robe as he began backing towards the archway.

'Zabin,' Iona called as she held her eyes on Billy. 'Keep my husband away from my apartments for the rest of the day. Do you understand?'

Zabin bowed, touching his chest, chin and forehead, replying, 'I know for a fact, your ladyship, that your beloved and distinguished husband has many important duties to occupy him until sundown when the *muezzin* calls him to prayer.'

'Good.'

Iona waved for the two slave girls, Falahalla and Mari, to escort Zabin from the chamber.

Billy had no idea how starved he was for attention and affection.

In the past weeks on Slave Island, he had seen no cleanliness, no physical comforts. He had been eating scraps for sustenance, toiling like a beast of burden, sleeping on a bed of lice-infested rags. He had not realized how much he had been missing comforts until Iona pressed her body against him, came close to him with the seduction of perfumes, the soft feeling of silk, the touch of appraising, eager, exploring hands.

Iona's appetite unlocked desires locked for too long inside Billy; he pulled her against him, held her, fondled her breasts, explored her body, fell with her onto the bank of waiting cushions.

Dropping her robes, Iona tore the loincloth from Billy and his penis sprang into a firm erection. He groaned as she insisted on exploring his naked body, to work her mouth over skin tightly hugging his muscle.

They made love on the cushions. They knelt face to face on the carpets. They stood together in front of long polished mirrors, looking at the reflections of the joined bodies, Billy taller and dominating her; Iona, short, and more curvaceous, eager to be passive to his youthful virility.

Billy assumed total control, leading Iona into many positions, spreading her thighs to sink his tongue into her vaginal lips, mounting her from behind like a dog, driving into her vagina from behind her thighs, laughing with joy, pumping harder as Iona embarked on a series of orgasms making her cry, shudder, break out in perspiration, exploding into more rushes of ecstacy, insisting that Billy, too, enjoy an orgasm.

Billy shook his head; his masculinity had been pent-up for too long and he still did not want to break the excitement growing from the roots of his testicles.

Standing above Iona, he watched her chew on his scrotum, again suck his penis, running the tip of her tongue around and around the edge of the organ's full crown.

He thrilled at the touch of cooling grease, a pine-scented ointment, she rubbed onto his penis, slowly caressing his throbbing maleness with her hands, gently working the grease into the penis, making it tingle, deliciously burn.

He held her down to the cushions on her back, lifting up her legs high in the air, standing between her spread legs as he drove deeper and harder into her wet delta, smiling as he listened to her groan – then scream – with pleasure.

He held her in the crook of one arm as he reached with his other hand to finger her vagina, stretching it with his fingers, exciting her vulva, gently snapping his fingers, feeling her become tense, then feeling her loosening herself, gushing forth more wetness.

And, finally, unable to hold back his own excitement, he pushed her down onto the carpets and began steady strong strokes into her, developing his deep drives into long, slick plunges, making her cry out for him to explode, to fill her women's hole with the hot explosion from his penis.

It came, the seed which had been locked inside Billy for weeks, tormenting him at night and building with frustration and hunger and pain. It came, and Billy's shouts filled the room as he pounded his hips against her, pressing his eyes shut, pumping, pushing the last drop of sperm from his penis shooting deep inside her contracting, expanding, welcoming vagina.

Sunlight was fading over the far horizon of the Indian

Ocean, a golden light spreading over their spent bodies when Iona finally spoke to Billy lying alongside her.

Speaking in English, she said, 'How long have you been on Slave Island?'

'Two weeks.' Billy lay stroking her hair. 'Maybe more.'

'Two weeks.' She sighed, saying, 'Oh, how I wish I had heard of you before today.'

Billy, feeling warmed, satisfied by providing pleasure for another person, snuggled against her breasts.

'Look, you blush. You make love like a man but – yes – you blush like a boy.'

Billy raised his head, nibbling on her lobe. Yes, he felt more like his old self again.

Iona pulled back her head, suddenly asking, 'Do you think I'm desirable?'

Billy laughed. 'Have I not already answered that question?'

'You are younger than me.'

'You are a very beautiful woman.' The words did not make him feel disloyal to Jenny. Did not Jenny only laugh when he called her beautiful, even when he said she was pretty?

'You mean it, don't you? That I'm beautiful.'

'You are the most beautiful woman I have ever seen.' Billy added, 'And the most accomplished.'

Again, he felt no guilt. He had not said she was the 'most desirable', that he would rather be with someone else.

Iona brushed the hair from Billy's eyes, asking, 'Do you know who I am?'

'Would I be frightened if I knew more than I do?'

'There could be reason for you to be frightened of me. But, no, I doubt if you'd fear me.'

She reached for his penis, squeezing its limpness, saying, 'You are not circumcised.'

'No. But I hear there's a practice here to put a gold ring through the foreskins of men.'

'It's called infibulation. But have no worries about that. You have me to protect you.'

Iona lowered her head, kissing the tip of Billy's penis, then moved to rise from the cushions, reaching for her robe.

Billy's penis hardened from her kiss. He held out his hand to stop her from leaving. He felt sexual excitement returning to him.

Iona pushed away his hand. 'I'm loath to leave you, beautiful infidel. But I must. My slave girls will lead you downstairs to a room where you shall find food, a couch to rest on for few hours, a bath. Zabin will then lead you back to the dormitory. I do not know when we can meet again. But neither of us must lose our senses. Today's visit is very dangerous. For both of us.'

She disappeared through the archway.

24

Billy returned to work the next morning atop the harbour wall, pulling heavy baskets from the ground and spreading rock over fresh layers of wet lime and straw. Somehow the work seemed easier than on other days. Billy felt more like his old, happy-go-lucky self than he had done in weeks.

Brian Macpherson, working alongside Billy in the sun, pulling baskets from the ground and spreading rocks on the wall, said, 'So the heathens took you into the castle yesterday and tried to convert you to Islam, did they, laddie?'

Billy had told no one, not even Macpherson, about yesterday's visit to Iona. Iona's warning about danger had made an impression on him, and he decided it was wise to keep his silence about their meeting.

Macpherson, straining on a hemp rope, continued, 'I understand, laddie, if you don't want to talk about your session with the Muslims. But don't be ashamed of it..

Heathens always try to get Christians to convert to their religion.'

Billy realised with amusement that Macpherson had arrived at another conclusion about his disappearance yesterday and he decided to allow him to continue believing it.

Macpherson, pushing with Billy to empty the basket of rock onto the layer of lumpy straw and lime, continued, 'Men say there are only two ways of escaping from Slave Island. One is by ransom. The other is by converting to Islam.'

Billy knew Macpherson liked to talk so he enquired, 'Ransom? Ransom by whom?'

'There are professional men hired by families of friends back home to make deals with the Turks. Most Europeans can be ransomed for thirty-five or forty pounds. But some prices go as high as one thousand pounds.'

'One thousand pounds? For a man?' The amount was astronomical to Billy.

'Aye. And women fetch more. Especially well-born ladies. There's a daughter of some fancy duke down in Cornwall who got kidnapped from a ship sailing home from a Spanish convent and she got ransomed for three thousand pounds.'

Yesterday's visit to Iona's apartment had only increased Billy's desire to be with Jenny, thinking how time spent with Iona had been no different than being with a prostitute, satisfying physical needs, easing frustrations, but certainly not fulfilling emotional desires or providing any love. He wondered if he might some day ransom Jenny from slavery.

Macpherson continued, 'Then there's a London merchant who got five thousand pounds for his freedom. Now that's a pretty bit of money, ain't it, laddie? But old sailors like me go for less, a lot less, if we're lucky enough to get ransomed at all.'

'A man must never give up hope.'

'No, laddie, and there's a saying in Islam "A Christian

for a musket''. I've always figured that's what I'd go for. A musket. Maybe a bit of powder and a wee bag of shot thrown into the bargain. But take a fine set-up laddie like you. You would make some Turk a fine *garzon* – or so they would think – and so you could go for a great deal more.'

'And what's a *garzon*?'

Pushing the basket toward the pulley hanging from poles, Macpherson replied, 'You ever hear talk of buggery, laddie?'

Billy thought of the noises he heard at night in the underground dormitory. He nodded, answering, 'Aye, Macpherson.'

'Well, Turks wallow in buggery and they have special men slaves whom they spoil and pamper and call their *garzons*. So a fine set-up laddie like you must be on his guard.'

Billy, next thinking how he had explored every conceivable sexual activity with Iona less than twenty-four hours ago, answered, 'I suppose these Turks indulge in everything. Both the men *and* the ladies.'

Macpherson was not listening; he was looking down to the slaves working far below them, pointing towards the rocky field, asking, 'See those two Turks pointing up here?'

Billy stepped near the edge of the wall to look down and saw two men wildly gesturing, beckoning to them.

'Isn't that Hospodar Pasha's deputy?' asked Macpherson. 'The slimy Turk bastard named Zabin waving up here at us?'

Billy recognised Zabin. 'I think you're right, Macpherson.'

'Laddie, is it you they're waving at? Do you think they want to take you away again today for more questioning? Try to get you to convert to their religion?'

'You might indeed be right, Macpherson.' Billy wondered if Iona had awakened this morning as hungry for sex as he had done? He answered, 'If they do want me, how do I get down from here? The guards took away the ladders for the day.'

Macpherson laughed. 'Oh, I'll help you, laddie. Even if I may be helping you to renounce the true Christian faith, giving you a hand to slide down to hell. You're a grown man and know your own mind.'

He pulled back a rope, pointing for Billy to step into one of the baskets. Billy quickly hopped inside and, laughing at the idea, grabbed tightly onto the sides of the basket.

Macpherson, slowly lowering Billy in the basket, called, 'If they make your swear to the Crescent, laddie, keep your fingers crossed and the good Lord's bound to forgive ye!'

'Aye, Macpherson!' Billy shouted as he descended toward the ground. 'And if I get free, I'll come back and ransom you with a musket!'

'A promise, laddie boy. A promise.'

Billy scrambled from the basket when it landed with a thud on the rocky ground; Zabin hurried forward, grabbing Billy by the arm to lead him away from the guard, whispering, 'You're going to be auctioned, infidel.'

Billy's joviality disappeared. 'Auctioned?'

'The Grand Master orders it.' Zabin tugged at Billy's arm to walk faster.

Billy lagged, arguing, 'But Hospodar ordered you *not* to sell me. I heard him tell you that with my own ears. On the day I arrived here.'

'That was three weeks ago.' Zabin tugged harder at Billy, adding, 'Something made him suddenly change his mind.'

'Did he find out about yesterday? About you taking me to meet his wife?'

Zabin's eyes narrowed and his fingernails dug sharply into Billy's bicep as he warned, 'Hold your tongue about yesterday, infidel, or you may find you're not . . . alive to be auctioned.'

Billy reluctantly followed Zabin from the base of the

harbour wall, wondering why Hospodar had changed his mind, why he was going to be sold.

25

The Sultan of Oman was a delicately featured man, his flashing hazel eyes and thin nose enhanced by fine golden cloth wrapped into a towering turban, ornamented with an egret feather clipped by a pearl-encrusted crescent above his forehead.

The Sultan sat in the shade of a silken fringed umbrella in the walled gardens of one of his many palaces dotted along the coastline of Africa, the Palace of the Frangipani, situated on the outskirts of Mombasa. The heady scent of the waxy white flowers perfumed the garden's air as the Sultan listened to the girl with red hair speaking to a visitor called 'the Spanish Pirate'.

The Sultan of Oman did not know how many slaves he possessed; he purchased men, women, and children from auction blocks like other people bought singing birds and trained monkeys in a bazaar; he was also as kind to his pet slaves as people were to their birds and tame monkeys – even more kind.

The girl with red hair, the young English woman named Jennifer Brett, particularly appealed to the Sultan of Oman. He did not want her for one of his harems. He seldom visited the women he owned, anyway, who lived behind the latticed walls in his palaces. The Sultan liked Jenny because she reminded him of a flower. She had skin the colour of his beloved frangipani, and hair like a poppy. She also intrigued him because she was heavy with child, the pregnancy enhancing her own particular beauty, making her skin even whiter than usual, and the freckles on her forehead look like the exotic spots colouring the inside of an orchid.

The Sultan had brought Jenny south in a caravan travelling from Khartoum. He knew she was still exhausted from the trip. She had ridden most of the way in a *houdah* atop a camel, but its sway, and the desert heat, had taken its toll on her condition.

Despite her fatigue, though, Jenny insisted on telling her story to the Spanish visitor at the Palace of the Frangipani, Don Julio de Castenaldo, the man whom the Sultan knew frequently helped enslaved Europeans become reunited with their families and friends. Don Julio charged a fee for his services but the Sultan of Oman was rich as well as considerate, and he had no concern for money when he could make his own slaves happy; and there was a young man whom Jenny desperately wanted.

Jenny, wearing a white pelisse tenting down from her narrow shoulders as she sat on cushions in the garden, toyed with a black bead hanging on a string around her neck as she spoke about the young Englishman who was the father of the child she carried in her womb.

She said, 'Billy and I were separated in a place called the Castle of a Thousand Wives. Jack Razor took me to Khartoum where this good man, here, the Sultan, bought me for–' She shrugged, saying, 'I don't know how much money and I don't want to know.'

The Sultan shook his head.

'And Billy, I think, was brought here to Mombasa. That's where the rat, Razor, first said we were coming. So, oh, do try to find him for me. Do.'

The Spaniard was a tall, sharply featured man, dressed in a heavily-embroidered frock coat and ruffled shirt, clothes too heavy for the climate.

He dabbed a lace handkerchief at his face and neck, saying, 'I've searched the bazaars and marketplaces of Mombasa, but there is not a trace of a man fitting the description of your . . . lover.'

The Sultan said, 'He could have already been taken from Mombasa.'

Don Julio de Castenaldo nodded. 'That is the most likely possibility, your Highness. But taken where? To the south? To Madagascar? To the far East? To China? North to India? Even to Khartoum?'

The Sultan shook his head. 'No, I know the slave traffic moving across the desert and through the forests. I would have heard if any infidel slaves had been taken there from Mombasa. But there is the possibility, too, he was taken to Prasada Kali.'

The name meant nothing to Don Julio. He wrinkled his perspiration-beaded brow.

The Sultan explained, 'Slave Island. The Ottoman fortress which is a slave marketplace for the Sultan of Constantinople.'

'Ah, yes! Slave Island! Of course! The castle where slaves from all over the world are sold at those auctions!'

'Have you been there?'

Don Julio smiled. 'I sail there from Mombasa.'

Jenny blurted, 'Is that where you think Billy is? Is that where he was taken?'

Don Julio looked from Jenny to the Sultan. 'Let us hope not.'

'Why not?' she cried. 'What do they do to men there?'

Don Julio explained, 'The Grand Master is named Hospodar, and he sells slaves for great prices. Those are African, Indian, Oriental slaves. I know white slaves are sometimes sold there, too, but never at auction. And their prices–' He shook his head.

'How would they be sold?' Jenny demanded.

'Private entreaties. The Sultan of Constantinople can not risk war with European nations. He can not openly sell citizens of England and France and Spain, at least not in the official government marketplace at Slave Island.'

'But you must look there for Billy!'

'Even if he is there, young lady, and if Hospodar

would sell him, the cost would be astronomical, beyond reason, beyond–'

The Sultan waved his thin hand. 'You speak of money when you see the tears in this pale young girl's eyes? When you know there is life growing inside this frail body?'

Jenny, although weak and extremely eager to be reunited with Billy, was nonetheless distrustful of this Spaniard called Don Julio. The Sultan had showed kindness to her and she blurted to him, 'Your Highness, do you never worry about men taking advantage of you? Just listen to this Spaniard! He's putting cheese out for a mouse!'

The accusation stunned Don Julio. But the Sultan laughed at Jenny's explosion.

Jenny, turning to Don Julio, warned, 'I do not want you paying one price for Billy and coming back here and saying you paid another. Let us get that understood right now!'

Don Julio shook his head. 'You English women never fail to amaze me. One moment you are crying for your lovers and, then the next moment, you are haggling like a fishwife!'

'Don't say nothing bad about fishwives!' Jenny warned. 'I could have been one myself! That's why I understand your type. You're a businessman. You ransom white folks for a profit. This good man, the Sultan here–'

The Sultan interrupted. 'If it makes you feel any better, my flower, we will set a price of – what do you say?'

Don Julio said, 'The prices at an auction on Slave Island are always conducted in the marketplace currency of gold weight.'

The Sultan asked, 'And how many gold weight would a Englishman fitting the description as this young lady told us receive at an auction?'

'Fifty. A hundred at most.'

'Then you have my permission to pay two hundred gold weight for the young Englishman if you find him.'

'Two hundred,' Don Julio repeated, his mind quickly working. 'And does that include my commission? I naturally will need to attach a small charge for my services.'

Jenny, forgetting her delicate condition, shrieked, 'You talk about me haggling! Listen to you! I thought you were supposed to be a man who helped poor, captured Christians!'

The Sultan raised both hands for silence; he nodded as Jenny sank back on her cushions, then said, 'Don Julio, you may bid two hundred gold weight on this infidel, Billy Peake, an amount which does not include the charge for your services. And may you sail in good health.'

Don Julio nodded, careful to avoid Jenny's penetrating stare, as he confirmed, 'A price of two hundred gold weight, plus the charge of my services. And what did you say his name is?'

'Peake,' Jenny said. 'Billy Peake.'

Don Julio again nodded; he thought he had heard the name correctly. He recognized the name, Peake. And he was already forming another plan, how he could make more than a commission from two hundred gold weight if he found the young man on Slave Island.

26

The first ships began to arrive for the auction.

The billowing white sails of the *Roxanne* appeared like a large cumulus cloud on the distant horizon of the Indian Ocean, its top gallants puffed in the breeze. The wind carried the frigate forward on a southeastern course, the stay sails slackening as she approached the grey-black walls of the fortress rising from the bedrock of Slave Island.

Luffing, parading a full complement of three sturdy masts, the *Roxanne* appeared sleek and powerful, flying the red white and blue British flag from the mizzen peak and a small red triangle snapping from the foremast, a pennant to identify the ship as a guest arriving for the slave auction.

Sir Oliver Bull, a robust Englishman dressed in a short white jacket with snug scarlet breeches, stood on the quarterdeck, holding a brass spyglass to his eye to study the crenellated walls of the fortress.

When a British flag briskly rose up a spire on Slave Island – a signal that safe harbour was being granted to the *Roxanne* – Sir Oliver Bull shouted for the deckmaster to make towards the harbour. The deckmaster in turn called to the first mate, who passed the order on to the crew.

Soon the frigate was alive with activity, the masts and rigging busy as the frigate prepared to drop anchor in the bay of blue water off the harbour of Slave Island.

Less than half an hour after the *Roxanne*'s arrival at Slave Island, the sails of a second ship fluttered against the windswept sky, a cumbersome Spanish galleon approaching from the northwest.

Flying the flag of Spain, the *Empress of Cadiz* also showed the red triangle of good intent requested by Hospodar of all visitors to the auction, as well as flying the coat of arms of Don Julio de Castenaldo, the colours identifying him as Count of Farago.

Don Julio remained sequestered inside his cabin as the galleon drew closer towards anchorage fronting the harbour, still not stepping onto deck as a Spanish flag of welcome rose alongside the Union Jack on the fortress.

The galleon's crew worked to drop anchor while servants hurried to stretch canvas above the taffrail, preparing a sunshade on the quarterdeck for a small luncheon party to be hosted by Don Julio for his fellow travellers as they waited in the bay aboard the ornate *Empress of Cadiz*.

Two Eastern ships next arrived at Slave Island, travelling in a small convoy with four sharply-prowed escort ships fitted with battering rams and cannons. The *Famagusta*, a sleek galliot, flew the Star and Crescent and carried Hamit

Nizzan, the Dey of Algiers. The second ship was the *Hamadan*, a felucca with a black hull pierced with a bank of oars, a floating *seraglio* for Tyla Karazin, the Sultana Valideh Pradashana, the mother of Sultan Abdul Mohammed of Constantinople, ruler of all the Ottoman Empire.

Like the *Roxanne* and the *Empress of Cadiz*, the two Eastern ships remained in the bay, their passengers not disembarking for the fortress but standing at anchor in the bay as the next ships arrived.

Indian dhows, Chinese sampans, Persian praus – vessels large and small appeared throughout the day and early evening, dropping anchor in the bay, their passengers and crews remaining aboard to await tomorrow's slave auction before entering the fortress.

A colourful line of flags soon fluttered along the front of the fortress, welcoming visitors from Algiers, Anatolia, China, England, Egypt, the Kingdom of Naples, Persia, Spain, from slave-owning lands as well as countries which had outlawed slavery but still profited from the trade of human bondage practised between other nations.

Shore boats moved back and forth between the fortress and the ships, carrying greetings, letters of credentials, requests from the visitors for an early viewing of slaves before the commencement of the auction sale.

Night-time approached and the rippling water was suddenly enveloped in blackness. Lanterns were lit aboard the ships, festooned on their decks, making the collection of vessels look like a swarm of phosphorescent insects gathered around the dark, ominous bulk of Slave Island.

Smells of cooking and the pungent whiffs from charcoal braziers wafted over the water, carrying the scent of spices and herbs, aromas and odours indigenous to the countries from which the visitors had travelled. The perfume of abalone, lamb, turtle, oysters seasoned with anise, cinnamon, cloves, coriander, mint, nutmeg. A mixture of sounds, too, filled the night, delicate oriental chimes ringing from a sampan; heavy sea shanties booming from the English frigate; lusty ballads plucked on a guitar and floating from the Spanish galleon; a mournful song from inside the felucca where slave oarsmen lay chained to their hammocks.

Lady Iona sat in a mullioned window of her apartments high inside the stone fortress, gazing down into the darkness at the ships dotted around the bay. Despite the beauty of their lights flickering below her window, the lanterns twinkling like stars in the sky, Iona still remained preoccupied, obsessed with the report she had received three days ago from Mustafa Zabin.

The American infidel was to be sold at tomorrow's auction. Iona had been and still was devastated by the news. When Zabin had first told her she had flared up, 'What do you mean, sold?'

Three days ago Zabin had already begun showing signs of strain, his eyes dulled by the demands made on him by Hospodar. The usual guile and syrupy manner was missing from his voice as he replied, 'The Grand Master has decided to sell the infidel slave.'

'But did not Hospodar demand that the infidel remain on Slave Island? To work on the wall? Did you not tell me so yourself, Zabin?'

'That is true, your ladyship. But your husband changed his plans. I can only follow the Grand Master's instructions and am obediently preparing the infidel to be sold.'

Iona had begun to speak, to ask Zabin if he knew whether or not Hospodar suspected her adultery with Billy Peake. But recognising Zabin's frayed nerves, suspecting he had little control over himself during these pressing times in the fortress, she checked her question and irritably waved him to leave her chamber.

Now, sitting in the darkness of the secluded apartments on the night before the auction, Iona was unable to concentrate on her duties as the Grand Master's wife. The Sultana Valideh, the Dey of Algiers, the Caliph of Kura, General Yannina – these were only a few of the rich and powerful people who dallied aboard their ships below her window at this very moment, visitors waiting to come ashore with bags of gold to spend at the auction. All Iona could think about was a slave she desired for her lover!

Curses! Iona loathed her stupidity, her feminine weakness, her lack of control. Had she connived, plotted, come this far in life only to choose a love affair with a slave, risk being exposed as an adulterous wife, rather than conduct herself with dignity and cunning in the presence of powerful visitors?

Despite Iona's desire to gain control of herself, she was as helpless as a lovesick young girl. She wondered if a woman's need for a man, for love-making, was truly more consuming than her appetite for riches and influence.

She asked herself, 'What did that infidel do to me to turn me into such a simpering maiden?'

A firm body, an authority in his muscular grasp, a honeyed sweetness in his kisses, a boyish smile as he performed like a man, the inquisitive probe of his tongue, fingers, a penis never losing its firmness – those were the reasons why she needed him. She began to pace her room, cursing her feminine appetite for a man, asking herself why she was so desirous of men, thinking how much more simple life would be without men, the trouble this lust for men caused women.

Stopping alongside a brass footed table, Iona saw her collection of stuffed phalluses and with one sweep of her hand she sent the sand-packed knobs clattering to the floor.

Hospodar lay naked on a narrow cot in his *selem*, cupping his penis with his fist, moving his fist back and forth, up and down, in a quickening motion, masturbating as he indulged in a fantasy, a plan, a new idea for an activity he soon hoped to indulge in with Iona, perhaps even tomorrow night after the first day of the slave auction.

In the past Hospodar had enjoyed confessing sexual infidelities to Iona, but he had learned from Zabin that Iona had recently been unfaithful to him, and so Hospodar was plotting a new pleasure, a different sexual release with his wife. He only hoped he could keep his jealousy at bay until that moment when he would obtain the ultimate pain from Iona.

In the secrey of his room on the night before the auction sale, Zabin hunched over a brazier's faint glow and heated a copper bowl of water, crumbling two small black chunks of the poppy resin onto a perforated disc placed on top of the bowl.

When the water finally began to bubble in the copper bowl, Zabin took a cloth, draped it over his head and leaned towards the brazier. He closed his eyes and took deep breaths, allowing the fumes from the resin to travel down his throat into his lungs, through his sinuses, behind his eyes, making his heart pound and his mind explode like the million stars dotting the sky . . . one, two, three exhilarating moments, the total quiescence . . .

27

Tall, iron-bossed gates opened from the rocky yard fronting the harbour of Slave Island, leading to a bricked courtyard inside the fortress. An arched colonnade with twisted Moorish columns encircled the courtyard with multi-coloured striped silk curtains hanging from the succession of arches. There were chairs, divans, small tables placed behind the curtains to provide comfort as well as privacy for the guests. The small alcoves were separated from the main courtyard.

By late morning on the day of the slave auction, brightly painted caïques began carrying the guests from their ships to the fortress; Hospodar and Iona waited inside the courtyard, progressing from archway to archway, visiting important guests behind the drawn curtains. They finally took their own places on carved cedar thrones placed under a baldachin erected at the head of the courtyard.

Female slaves passed through the colonnade, carrying urns of Muscat wine and trays of honey cakes as the first entertainers appeared at the far end of the courtyard, a progression of Javanese dancers dressed in glittering costumes of embroidered gold.

Iona, her face veiled with almond-dyed silk, wore a lilac *kufiyeh* draped over her head and around the shoulders of her elegant clothing, light gowns layered in colours ranging from deep purple to palest pink. A long strand of grey pearls hung around her neck, interspersed with pendants and chains. Her eyes were painted with kohl and remained cold and dramatic above her veil as she watched the Javanese dancers move to the sound of tinkling bells.

Hospodar, wearing a red turban, a brocade robe, white cotton pantaloons and kid-skin court slippers, sat cross-legged on his throne as he watched the dancers. He did not take his eyes from them as he spoke to Iona, saying, 'The Sultan's mother is younger than I expected her to be.'

Iona did not avert her eyes from the dancers as she agreed, 'Young as well as beautiful.'

Hospodar continued, 'The Mother Valideh spoke to you for quite a long time. She is obviously very taken with you.'

Iona did not want to divulge the nature of her conversation with the Sultana Valideh and so replied, 'She knows my uncle in Kypros and was gracious enough to enquire about his health.'

As Hospodar watched the lithesome dancers bending sideways, pointing their petite hands in unison as they dipped, he asked, 'Is not the Dey of Algiers also friendly with your uncle?'

'Husband Pasha, you are still worried about the Dey carrying false rumours about you back to Constantinople.' Iona softly but firmly urged, 'I keep telling you, Husband Pasha, you have no reason to fear. The Sultan only hears good things about your auctions on Slave Island. He wants the gold.'

Hospodar did not immediately respond, finally complimenting, 'You have worked hard, Iona, assembling entertainment for the guests.'

'No harder than you have been working, Husband Pasha, preparing slaves. I have not seen you in many days.'

Before the Javanese dancers left the courtyard the next entertainers appeared, two half-naked young men with huge pythons wrapped around their bare chests. The men moved rhythmically to the jangle of temple bells, intermixed with the sound of a flute. They lifted their bare feet in a stylised manner, holding their backs erect as the pythons coiled, twisted and writhed around their backs, their extended arms, their straight necks.

Iona smiled behind her veil as she watched both gargantuan snakes coil in unison under the men's thighs, rising like arched penises from their midsections.

She said, 'This dance has been performed for years on the small island of Bali.'

Hospodar, recognising the phallic signficance of the ancient dance, smiled and said, 'After today it will be performed in all the palaces of Arabia.'

Suddenly one python sprang forward, darting towards the other dancer. Both men immediately produced short daggers from their loincloths and the entertainment abruptly changed from a dance into a duel.

Iona, keeping her eyes on the duel between the two men with sharply honed blades and phallic pythons, returned to speaking about other matters.

She asked, 'Husband Pasha, you have studied the credentials of the guests. Are you satisfied with everyone?'

Hospodar's tone was non-committal, almost bored. 'It is always difficult, even imprudent, to ask a man or woman too many questions about their wealth or importance. I must often rely on intuition, working on instinct, occasionally even making decisions on hearsay.'

His voice lightened as he added, 'But then, Iona, I must

also do that in other matters too, mustn't I?'

Iona had listened carefully to Hospodar's words and she wondered if he was trying to employ a double meaning, to say one thing and mean another, if he was insinuating that he knew about her unfaithfulness with the infidel slave and was waiting to take steps to punish her.

Trying to avoid any trap he might be setting for her, and trying to sound innocent, she replied, 'Certainly your work is easy in that some men are more notorious than others, Husband Pasha. For example, I have heard one guest here today is openly referred to as a brigand and a pirate.'

'Don Julio de Castenaldo? The Spanish Pirate?' Hospodar laughed. 'Oh, Don Julio has a dishonourable reputation. But I suspect he is not as dangerous – nor as rich – as he pretends to be. But we will at least have a chance to judge the extent of his riches for ourselves today.'

'How so, Husband Pasha?'

Hospodar enjoyed breaking the news. 'I have asked for a certain slave to be put on the block, a young man who will certainly tempt Don Julio. The slave will raise a high price.'

Iona held her eyes on the duel, watching both young men slashing their daggers at the pythons, hacking to free themselves from the strongholds in which the snakes had constricted them.

She tried to sound unconcerned. 'Because I have not seen you in the past days, Husband Pasha, I do not know the order of the sales. Do you sell men or women today?'

Speaking like this with Iona excited Hospodar, talking about one subject and implying another. It teased his perverse appetite for the love-making he hoped to enjoy tonight with her. As his penis hardened inside his pantaloons, he explained, 'I am mixing both men and women together in these sales.'

'Clever,' complimented Iona. 'And you also answer another question for me, Husband Pasha.'

'What is that?' Hospodar longed to reach inside his

robe, to fondle himself as he thought about Iona's adultery with the infidel slave, about making her uneasy as he discussed the young man.

She explained, 'I wondered why so many people arrived this morning for the first sale. Guests often stay aboard their boats waiting only for the slaves in which they have interest.'

Disappointed in her astute but sexually innocuous reply, Hospodar decided to tease, to try to torment her a little bit more about the American infidel.

He said, 'Today I am also changing another tradition from past auctions, Iona. Rather than reserving special slaves for private sales. I am putting them in the public auction on the same block with common work slaves.'

'And what, Husband Pasha, deems a "special slave"?'

She had fallen for the bait and Hospodar felt his penis harden. He knew Iona was definitely interested in learning more about her lover. He reached under his robe and slowly, carefully, rubbed his hand over the crown of his erect phallus, letting his eyes glide over the arches where guests were sitting.

He explained, 'Special slaves are men captured from European ships, Iona. Prisoners who are usually sold to private buyers rather than auctioned publicly, so risking a war with their countries.'

Iona suddenly turned her eyes towards Hospodar, asking in a sharp voice, 'You have the Sultan's permission to make such a move? You can risk . . . war?'

Hospodar stopped his hand. His mind became a blank. He expected her to strike out at him, like one of the pythons, with a sudden question.

Quickly controlling himself, he answered, 'You assured me, dear wife, that the Sultan is only concerned with the money I send him.'

'But today his mother is here,' Iona hissed. 'Surely to take such a chance is too risky, even folly–?'

Hospodar, regaining his confidence, began to fondle himself again, saying, 'Fortunately, Iona, you are now friendly with the Sultana Valideh.'

Iona sat staring at the two men in the courtyard. The duel was over, their bodies were mangled and covered in blood. Turkish guards were dragging them across the brick courtyard and the pythons – dead, cut into slashes – trailed behind them like two long bloody tails.

A loud fanfare of drums suddenly filled the courtyard; Hospodar turned his head to see the new commotion, asking in a brighter voice, 'Now what have you prepared?'

Iona did not reply as she watched two burly athletes run into the courtyard. Each athlete was snapping a rhinoceros hide whip, one arm was bound with hemp, coated with pitch, and the pitch in turn had been dabbed with shards of sharp glass to enable the athlete to use his forearm – as well as the whip – as a weapon in battle.

The first snap of the whip echoed in the arched courtyard.

'Enchanting,' praised Hospodar, like an excited child, unfolding his legs from under him and sitting on the edge of the cedarwood throne.

Iona's voice was quietly defiant. 'I prepared this especially with you in mind, Husband Pasha.'

Hospodar looked attentively at the two athletes flailing whips, jabbing their jagged forearms at one another's face. He said, 'I have the feeling you will find more ways to please me, dear wife.'

The three pens of male slaves to be auctioned at today's sale were separated by iron gates from the courtyard. Billy squatted with the group of men in the first pen, telling himself to keep his pride, not to feel humiliated because he was waiting to be sold like an animal.

Unable to see the entertainers performing in the courtyard, Billy heard the tinkle of bells, followed by the song of a flute, a loud fanfare of drums, then the lashes, shouts, grunts and cries of men fighting one another with whips.

Now listening to a voice he recognised as that of Mustafa Zabin, Billy heard a formal salutation addressed to Hospodar Pasha, Lady Iona, the Sultan's mother and a list of illustrious guests spoken in Arabic, Indian, Turkish and Swahili.

Zabin, next speaking in the *lingua franca* of Slave Island, described the physical attributes of an African woman, the first slave to be auctioned. Billy sat on the floor of the pen wondering if the black woman might be one of the slaves who had crossed Africa with him and Jenny from Razor Cove.

'Oh, how long ago that seems now,' Billy thought, closing his eyes, remembering Jenny, their campfires, the way she had bobbed her red hair, how she had carried a walking stick, had laughed about giving lectures on Africa back home in England, about opening a roadhouse for pirates and slave-dealers in Mombasa. Billy now did not know anything about Jenny, if she was laughing, crying, a slave, even alive. He again considered how much had happened to him in that time. Half-listening to Zabin's call for bids on the black woman, he wondered what would have happened to him if he had not made love to Iona and remained working on the harbour wall.

But had there been a choice? Could he had resisted? Refused? Not gone with Zabin and the guard from the dormitory when they had awakened him from his sleep on the rag bed? Considering these questions Billy knew that a man did what he was told to do on Slave Island or was whipped for being disobedient, perhaps even killed.

The rattle of chains sounded outside the pens; the men moved restlessly on the floor; whispers spread amongst them. Before Billy turned his head he felt a hand rest on his shoulder.

The nerves tightening in his stomach, Billy rose to his feet, straightened the cloth knotted around his midsection and followed two Turkish guards from the pen across a forecourt, out between two twisted columns and into the bright sunlight of the courtyard.

Zabin, dressed in a fresh white cotton robe and turban, stood behind a podium placed alongside a large wooden block in the middle of the courtyard.

He called in English as the two guards marched Billy towards him, 'The first male slave is a prisoner of war–'

Murmurs spread around the courtyard as Billy walked stiffly, awkwardly, terrified, to the auction block.

'–a slave for any household, a pity to chain to an oar, or put to work in a rice paddy–'

Billy stepped up on the block, holding both arms to his side, keeping his eyes straight ahead of him. He saw Hospodar and Iona seated side by side at the far end of the courtyard and, fleetingly, he remembered Iona's promise, 'Don't worry, you now have me watching out for you.'

Zabin beat a wooden gavel against the top of his stand and the opening bid came from a woman for ten gold weight. Her bid was quickly topped by a man for twenty gold weight, third bidder called in Spanish, raising the amount to fifty gold weight.

The woman, speaking in heavily accented English, bid sixty.

'Sixty-five,' offered the Spaniard.

'One hundred gold weight!' boomed the Englishman.

Fear slowly gave way to curiosity and Billy began wondering who these three people were who were bidding for him.

The woman called, 'I pay one hundred-twenty for the slave.'

The Spaniard raised his bid to one hundred and thirty gold weight.

'I pay one hundred-*fifty*!' called the woman.

A silence followed her offer; Zabin beat his gavel, proclaiming, 'I have been offered one hundred and fifty gold weight for this infidel slave. Is he not worth more than that? He is young. He is strong. Shall we see . . . more?

Applause surrounded the courtyard and Zabin waved for one of the Turkish guards to step from alongside the podium; the guard moved in front of Billy and pulled off his loincloth. Applause greeted Billy's sudden nakedness.

Shoulders thrown back, Billy kept his eyes straight ahead of him.

The Spaniard shouted, '*Doscientos*!'

The woman called, 'I pay two hundred . . . twenty!'

'Two fifty,' bid the English voice.

Silence followed the last bid. Zabin waited for the next offer and when none came, he finally hit the podium with his gavel, calling 'Sold! For two hundred and fifty gold weight to . . . Sir Oliver Bull!'

The Turkish guards stepped forward; one guard picked up Billy's loincloth from the bricks, the other pulled him from the auction block. Both led him across the courtyard to a thunder of applause and wild shouts.

28

The Turkish guards led Billy from the courtyard, down narrow stone steps, along a damp underground passageway, until they reached a plank door. One guard opened the door with a large rusty key, the other guard shoved Billy inside and slammed the door behind him.

Alone in a low ceilinged room, lit only by a torch stuck into a wall-ring, Billy began pacing the floor, rubbing his shoulders to warm himself, wondering how long he would be left here, if this was the place he was to meet the man who had bought him, Sir Oliver Bull.

Hearing voices outside the door, Billy quickly backed against the far wall, standing alongside the torch, ready to grab and fling it as protection if necessary.

Hearing the key turn in the lock, Billy stood against the wall and watched the door slowly open.

The outline of a man appeared in the doorway, a broad-shouldered man wearing a short white jacket, red breeches hugging an athletic figure, and a pair of tall black leather boots.

He stepped cautiously into the small room, calling, 'Anybody here?'

Billy demanded, 'Who are you?'

The voice became more familiar, 'Old dog, is that . . . you?'

'Old dog?' Billy thought of the few people who knew his childhood nickname and blurted, 'Andrew?'

'Billy, old dog, that *was* you I bought off an auction block!'

Rushing forward, Billy cried, 'Andrew!'

Andrew Peake, a slim, solidly built young man a few inches taller than Billy, had wavy blond hair combed back from his face, a heavy brow, steely blue eyes, a straight nose and a strong, sculptured square jaw. He embraced Billy with both arms and laughed as he patted his back.

Billy hugged his older brother, repeating, 'Andrew, it's you . . . it's you . . .'

Andrew, holding one arm on Billy's bare shoulder, stepped back to appraise him, asking, 'What in the devil are you doing here, old dog? You're supposed to be sailing to China with Gabe Easton selling our silver.'

The mention of Easton, the Mexican silver ingots and China, instantly sobered Billy and he pulled back from Andrew, angrily warning, 'Don't speak to me about our silver, Andrew Peake, do you hear?'

Andrew stared at the sudden change in Billy's face, surprised by the indignation in his voice. 'Billy, what did I say? This is no time to get angry. I just paid a king's ransom to get you off a slave block!'

'Nobody forced you to part with your money, Andrew Peake! Nobody twisted your arm to buy me.'

'Billy, what's the matter with you?' Andrew reached for him.

Sloughing away Andrew's hand, Billy curtly said, 'If you're going to get me out of here, then do it. If not, go your own way and I'll find a way to survive. I have before, I will again.'

'Oh Billy, Billy, Billy, Billy! You're tired, you're under

great stress. You're probably starving for something decent to eat. I understand all that, Billy, my boy. But I do expect a little better reception from you than this. Old dog, we haven't seen one another for over three years. You suddenly pop up in a slave auction in the middle of the Indian Ocean. I pay two hundred and fifty–'

Billy irritably interrupted, 'If it's the money that's bothering you, Andrew Peake, you can take it out of my share of the silver and we'll call the score settled between us.'

Andrew was more baffled than ever. 'Billy, what's all this talk about money?'

'You tell me!'

'Then I *shall* tell you. I don't know how you found out about my present financial predicament. Perhaps you are merely guessing. But here's how it is–'

Taking a deep breath, Andrew appraised his younger brother's angry expression, again shook his head with concern and began his own story.

'Billy, the fact is I don't have a farthing to my name. I've had to submit a letter of worth on my arrival here. I can't even honour that. I'm here under false pretences–'

Billy irritably asked, 'And why did you come here in the first place?'

Andrew faltered, 'Why . . . I . . . I . . . I came for the slave auction.'

Billy demanded. 'When did you start buying slaves, Andrew Peake? Was it when you fell into making private arrangements and shady covenants with Gabriel Easton?'

'Billy, what's come over you? One minute you're laughing and hugging and greeting me like a long-lost brother, then the next minute you're sulking and glowering and talking about me making secret arrangements with Gabriel Easton.'

Andrew fixed his steely eyes on Billy, asking, 'Am I to worry about you, lad? Have they been mistreating you so miserably here? I know Turks can be cruel–'

Stubbornly Billy demanded, 'Where's Gabriel Easton?'

'Gabriel Easton?' Andrew was becoming impatient. 'I don't know a thing about Gabriel Easton. I went to Canton as we planned. There was no sign of you, no sign of Easton, no word from anybody waiting for me. So I became worried. Fortunately I found an old Irish captain who had passed six of Easton's ships rounding the Cape a month or so earlier. I truly did begin to worry when the Paddy told me he'd seen no sign of the *Lion's Lair* in the convoy.'

'And the reason for that, Andrew Peake, is because Gabriel Easton replaced the *Lion's Lair* with a schooner named the *Vandal Witch*. That's why. But then you know that, don't you? You're the one who signed that piece of paper with Easton, sent it to him in Boston and din't tell me–'

'Signed what piece of paper with Easton, Billy? What are you talking about?'

Billy paused as he studied his older brother. He asked timidly, 'You don't know about any new agreement?'

It was Andrew's turn to be angry. 'What damnable agreement?'

Billy's voice was weak, his face had softened. 'You didn't sign a new agreement with Gabriel Easton, giving him your written permission – signed and witnessed in Fort Marlborough – that he had authority to transport our silver to China on any ship of his choosing?'

'I certainly signed nothing of the kind, Billy Peake!'

Taking a deep breath, Billy shook his head, saying, 'Oh, Andrew, you don't know how glad, how very glad I am to hear that.'

'Glad? It sounds to me, little Billy, as if we have more troubles than even I suspected. It sounds to me as if Gabriel Easton – the swine – has been trying to cheat us, has perhaps already succeeded.'

Before Billy could speak, Andrew hit one fist against the palm of his other hand and turned around, cursing, 'Damn it! Why didn't I see this before now! It fits into what's written in that letter of yours.'

'What letter?'

Andrew began pacing the room, answering, 'When I couldn't find you in Canton, I sailed back home to Sumatra. There was a letter waiting for you at the Fort. I was worried so naturally I opened it.'

'Who was it from?'

'Somebody on the island of Jamaica called–' he looked at Billy, asking, '–could the name be "Rhinelander"?'

Billy nodded, 'Paris Rhinelander.'

'That's the name.' Andrew resumed walking, explaining, 'I couldn't make much sense out of the letter. But I did gather from it that you two had sailed together out of Boston. And that you had been put ashore in Africa at a slave station. This Rhinelander chap was kept aboard ship against his wishes by some reprobate named–'

'Kerr! Captain Stanley Kerr!' interrupted Billy.

'Kerr. That's the man.' Looking at Billy, Andrew asked, 'Was this Kerr a slave-runner?'

Billy nodded. 'Kerr's captain of the *Vandal Witch*, the schooner I told you about. Gabriel Easton hired Kerr to carry our silver. They had a scheme between them. Kerr broke away from the rest of the convoy on the third day out of Boston and made towards the west coast Africa. But he got his own ideas and is planning to double cross Easton.'

'A plan that didn't work.'

'What do you mean?'

'Your friend Paris Rhinelander writes from Jamaica that Kerr caught flux in the Atlantic crossing and died a few days after the *Vandal Witch* landed in Kingston. Rhinelander was set free from the hold but Kerr's schooner was impounded by the Crown's representative in Jamaica.'

Halting, Andrew turned to Billy and suddenly said, 'Wait a moment. I just thought of something. Was our silver aboard the *Vandal Witch* when Kerr sailed back across the Atlantic for the West Indies?'

Billy nodded. 'The ingots were there when Kerr abandoned me in Africa. I saw them with my own eyes. All neatly stacked on shelves to hold slaves. Kerr was greedy but not too adventurous. He didn't have the stomach to sail round Africa and carry out the plan we made of sailing to China.'

Considering the matter, Andrew asked, 'How much can you trust your friend, this Paris Rhinelander?'

'Fairly well, I think,' Billy looked at Andrew. 'Why?'

'Does this Rhinelander come from a rich family?'

'Sugar planters. They adopted him. Why? What are you thinking?'

'Rhinelander's family bought him the *Vandal Witch* when it was sold at a Crown auction.' Andrew looked at Billy, asking, 'Do you suppose the galley included all her cargo? Our silver?'

'How do you know his family bought him the *Witch*?'

'He wrote it in the letter. I'm just remembering it now.' Andrew looked at him. 'Would this Rhinelander consider sailing for China?'

'He's got nerve for it more than Captain Kerr. But I don't know if he'd do it.' Billy implored, 'Oh, Andrew, what else can you remember? Concentrate. Try to think.'

Andrew resumed pacing the room, running one hand through his long wavy hair, muttering, 'I wish I'd brought that damned letter with me. You could have read it and told me what everything means.'

'At least try to remember what it said, Andrew. Please, it's important.'

'I know, I know. Don't chivvy me.'

'The only thing we can do, Andrew, is get out of here. Go back to Fort Marlborough. Read the letter and start making new plans. There's got to be something we can salvage.'

'We can't leave.' Andrew stood in the middle of the room, staring at Billy, saying, 'Anyway, *you* can't leave. Not yet.'

'Me? Why not?'

Andrew looked down at the toes of his black leather boots. 'As I began telling you, Billy, I'm here under false pretences. I'm still under commission to the East India Company. But I'm here under the name of Oliver Bull, Sir

Oliver Bull. My letter of introduction to Hospodar is fraudulent. From a non-existent company – the China Merchant Company.

'Oh, a few names in the letter are real, like the name of the trading lord in Canton, Master Hu' An, who agreed a long time ago to buy our silver. I used his name in the letter, along with a few other names, claiming that they and this fictitious company, authorise me, Sir Oliver Bull, to buy slaves to develop a new plantation in a province in southern China.'

Billy stared at his brother. 'Why did you do a thing like that?'

'It's a plan I worked out with the East India Company.'

'Why would the East India Company want to involve themselves in a lie?'

Glancing at the plank door, Andrew lowered his voice, explaining, 'In the last three years, Billy, someone has been attacking our ships in waters north of here called the "Leather Triangle". The East India Company thinks the culprit is Hospodar, the Grand Master of Slave Island. Entire crews of ships have been captured, not only from our ships but from others as well. The crews never turn up in any slave markets – no Englishmen, no Irishmen, no colonials, nobody. That is, until today.'

Billy exclaimed, 'Because Hospodar sells them to private buyers, that's why! A Scotsman here told me.'

'But he sold you in a public auction, didn't he?'

'Only at the last moment. I have been working here in a quarry and building a wall. I worked right alongside a Scotsman named Macpherson who had been captured by Hospodar off a ship with the rest of the crew. Macpherson told me how no Englishman, no European, is ever sold at an auction here. That white slaves just disappear from Slave Island and more arrive to take their place.'

Andrew considered these facts, then asked, 'Would you feel threatened if you were left here a while longer?'

'How much longer? Where would you be going?'

'I must go to Mombasa to finish my work and then make

my report back to Fort Marlborough. I'd be away for maybe six to eight weeks.'

'What's going to happen to me here in that time? If you don't have money to pay for me now, how can you raise two hundred and fifty gold weight in Mombasa? Or do you plan to get it from the East India Company when you get back to Sumatra?'

'Give me time to think, Billy. Give me a little time to think about all this. As it so happens, Hospodar has invited me to an entertainment now. I'll try to talk to him and work out some plan.'

There was a knock on the door. Andrew lowered his voice, saying, 'We've been talking about our problems, Billy, but quickly, tell me something about Catherine. How is she? Does she miss me? Does she plan to come and join me soon at Fort Marlborough as my bride? Does the poor thing suspect her father's a cad and is trying to cheat us?'

Billy did not know what to say and finally asked, 'Did Paris Rhinelander write anything in his letter about Catherine?'

Andrew suspiciously eyed him. 'Why should he?'

'Andrew, get me out of here and then we'll talk about Catherine. Agreed?'

'You're right.' Andrew quickly embraced Billy before the door opened. He turned, calling back over his shoulder, 'I'll try to get back here as fast as possible, old dog.'

Then he was gone.

29

Beyond the main courtyard inside the fortress on Slave Island lay the Hall of the Corsairs, a cavernous chamber once used by Arab pirates for the storing of their booty. It now served as a reception area for guests during slave auctions.

Flags of many nations hung in neat succession from brass poles on both sides of the vast room. Sunlight poured through amber and ruby coloured glass set in tall windows gashed into the thick stonework, providing lush lighting for the chamber. The opulent atmosphere was further enriched by carpets layered on the stone floor and intricately worked panels of teakwood and ivory surrounding the room.

Tall spreading ceremonial umbrellas sewn from red, purple and yellow pennants, stood like giant mushrooms throughout the large hall, serving as interior oases where guests were served wine and food, and could recline on couches to smoke water pipes. Entertainers were also present in the Hall of the Corsairs, and the music from horns, lyres, mandolins and tambourines floated and jangled above the hum of many voices. People drifted along nooks and alcoves embedded in the walls, looking at the amusements provided for their entertainment – tumblers, puppeteers, fables enacted by strolling players, Arabian legends performed as living tableaux.

The variety of entertainments appealed to the many diverse guests.

Don Julio de Castenaldo, angry that the price for Billy Peake went higher than the two hundred gold weight allotted to him by the Sultan of Oman, found solace in a display of two Nubian wrestlers, as oiled and shiny as the black silken mat on which they fought. Their muscular bodies were naked except for silver-studded collars locked around their thick necks, and silver rings encircling the roots of their scotums and penises, making each man's organ remain erect as he hugged, gripped, flipped, pressed his opponent to the black silken mat.

The tall Algerian guest, Hamit Nizzan, also known as the Dey of Algiers, was fascinated by a combat between a man and a Ukrainian wolf, both the man and the snarling animal attached to the stone wall of their alcove by a chain, iron links long enough to allow them to dash at one another but not meet; the wolf lurched to sink his sharp teeth into the man; the man dodged, avoiding the bloodthirsty animal. Hamit Nizzan, the Dey of Algiers, remained transfixed by the behaviour of the wolf, watching to see if the animal would eventually grip the throat of the quickly-tiring man.

The Sultana Valideh, the Sultan's mother, surrounded by her court from the *Hamadan*, entertained Lady Iona inside a private enclosure of striped black-yellow-and-red silk erected at the far end of the hall; the Sultana's court slaves emerged from the ciborium, leaving Iona alone with the Sultan's mother.

Through all the activity, the music, the congestion of guests and entertainers, moved a variation on a Chinese dragon, a long length of red silk, stretched around a series of large wire hoops, a representation of an enormous phallus – complete with a head spurting fireworks – winding, twisting, spewing through the crowd assembled in the Hall of the Corsairs.

Andrew Peake stood with Hospodar at the foot of the wide black marble stairway at the entrance to the Hall of the Corsairs. He was impressed by the activity and the size of the room, but surprised that males and females moved so easily, so freely back and forth from the courtyard, disregarding any Eastern taboos of privacy and separation of women from men.

He remarked, 'This looks more like a bawdy European fair than a gathering of Muslims, your excellency.'

Hospodar held both hands behind his back as he studied his guests, visitors wearing towering feather headdresses, rich turbans, veils across their faces, jewelled swords dangling from sashes.

He pointed at a crowd gathering nearby and offered, 'Sir Oliver, a group of actors is portraying an old Moluccan legend. It's a very interesting story about a father seducing his son. Perhaps you'd like to see it?'

'Thank you, your excellency, but neither sodomy nor incest interest me.'

Hospodar gestured towards a pair of latticed doors. 'In that chamber, Sir Oliver, slave girls wait to please my guests.'

Andrew again declined, pleading, 'I've seen enough slaves for one day, Hospodar Pasha.'

'I do not mean slaves for you to buy, Sir Oliver. I am offering you a companion for the night. You tell me you weigh anchor tomorrow morning. You may want to enjoy a wench on your ship before setting sail.'

'Ah, now, that does tempt me, your excellency, but as I only have a short time left here on Slave Island before I depart, I think my time would be more wisely spent speaking to the slave I purchased from you.'

Andrew kept his eyes on the milling guests as he added, 'There is also a matter of business I would like to discuss with you, Hospodar Pasha.'

'You sound grave, Sir Oliver. Don't tell me you have changed your mind and want to withdraw your offer of two hundred and fifty gold weight.'

'Never. I am very pleased with the young man as well as the price.'

'Excuse me for saying this, Sir Oliver, but you must be a very rich man if you can spend so much money on a slave you have not even interviewed.'

'That is precisely what I want to discuss with you, Hospodar Pasha. You see, I am *not* a rich man. I only know rich men. Men such as the merchants who are my patrons in the China Trading Company.'

'I of course recognise all the names in the Company, I myself have been trying to do business with Master Hu'An in Canton. But politics in China have recently caused problems and the Chinese are closing their ports to foreign ships.'

'A revolution is imminent, I'm afraid. But Master Hu'An is a friend as well as a colleague of mine. Perhaps I can speak to him on your behalf. But before we discuss that matter, your excellency, can we review the matter of my letter of introduction to you? The China Trading Company generously gave me permission to buy men for a new plantation they are developing in the province of Kan Tai.'

'Yes, they authorise you to buy no less than twenty slaves, yet you only bought one . . . with the same amount of money you were to spend on the others.'

'As Grand Master of such an industrious place as Slave Island, you can appreciate the need for a responsible overseer, yes?'

'Certainly. But for two hundred and fifty gold weight? That is a great deal of money to spend on an overseer.'

Hospodar graciously smiled, adding, 'But I do not need to tell you how to conduct your business, Sir Oliver. I will only tend mine and, in doing so, I remind you that if you need to buy other workers, you will not be disappointed in the men I have for sale in the rest of the auction.'

'I understand you will be selling mostly Indonesians and Africans in the following two days. You see, Grand Master, I prefer Mediterranean, even European workers. As I said, China is in a volatile state at the moment and the China Trading Company prefers to have men completely alien to the present situation . . . if you can appreciate my meaning.'

Hospodar nodded, 'I still may be able to help you, Sir Oliver. There are men on Slave Island I never put into an auction sale.'

'European workers? Men coloured like the slave I bought today? Men who will not involve themselves in others' revolutions?'

Hospodar again smiled, adding, 'You decide how many slaves you need, Sir Oliver, how much money you can spend, then we will discuss what additional slaves I can produce for you.'

'I have an order to go to Mombasa and inspect slaves there. My orders demand me to sail tomorrow. I would like you to hold my letter of credit until I return. I think we will be able to arrive at some sort of bargain . . . as well as equipping you with a letter of introduction to my friend, Master Hu'An.'

'And when will you be returning to Slave Island, Sir Oliver?'

'No later than two months from today.'

Considering the proposition, Hospodar finally said, 'If I hold your letter of credit, I must also hold your slave.'

Andrew frowned. 'Your excellency, I would prefer not to leave the slave behind here. Master Hu'An is anxious–'

'To take a slave without paying for him, no, that is not possible, Sir Oliver. I also have my superiors.'

Andrew next argued, 'So if I leave my letter of credit, along with the slave, you will agree not to sell him to anyone in my absence?'

'I shall hold the slave for two months.' Hospodar turned away from Andrew, saying, 'Now, I believe that settles our business for the moment, Sir Oliver. So allow me to show you those slave girls.'

Andrew put out his hand to detain him. 'One last thing, excellency. I would like to speak to the slave I bought. If I am not taking him at least I would like to speak to him one last time, to tell him personally of my plan.'

'Impossible, Sir Oliver. The slave is not yet yours. You may choose a girl for the night and take her to your boat. But the slave –' Hospodar shook his head.

A voice called above the din in the vast room. 'Young Englishman! Young Englishman! *Ola!*'

Both Andrew and Hospodar turned at the sound of the piercing voice and saw Don Julio de Castenaldo, wearing a silk frockcoat with white lace ruffles at his throat and cuffs, walking with a tall silver-knobbed cane.

'How good to see you, young man,' said Don Julio in the lisping accent of proper Castilian Spanish. 'Is our gracious host filling your ears with stories about me?'

Andrew knew Don Julio and hoped he would not give away his true identity; he quickly said, 'Don Julio, you obviously do not remember my name. But we met in Madrid, at the Countess of Huenga. My name is Bull, Sir Oliver Bull.'

'Oh yes. I remember you distinctly . . . Sir Oliver.' Don Julio slyly added, 'And I intend to chastise you for buying the slave I so desperately wanted, that blond youth.'

Hospodar interjected, 'Don Julio, you still might be able to buy him.'

'What?' Don Julio looked from Hospodar to Andrew. 'You've changed your mind? Do you not want him?'

'Of course I want him. But I must sail to Mombasa to inspect more slaves. I am leaving my new acquisition behind for safe-keeping. And, mind you, I don't want you trying to steal him away from here, understand?'

'I would never dream of doing such a thing!' promised Don Julio. Then, looking back at Hospodar, he said, 'I'm not as evil as people say. You do know there are men who say I'm a pirate. And, I tell you, that if I ever find out who is spreading these rumours, they shall soon see that the Spanish temper is not to be taken lightly.'

Andrew bowed. 'We stand warned, Don Julio.'

Turning to Hospodar, Andrew said, 'Your excellency, you were telling me about some slave girls located nearby.'

'Oh, excuse me!' apologised Don Julio. 'I interrupt you gentlemen! How rude of me! Forgive me!'

Andrew breathed easier as he watched the Spanish nobleman disappear through the crowd, walking like a tall, wobbling stork. He wondered what work had brought him to Slave Island.

Don Julio de Castenaldo, looking back over his shoulder at Andrew and Hospodar, wondered, 'Andrew Peake! He obviously does not have the money to pay for his brother. But why is he sailing for Mombasa instead of back to his home on Sumatra? Is he also commissioned by the Sultan of Oman to find the young lover for the English girl? Is there any profit I can make by this sudden turn of events? Yes, I must go back to Mombasa.'

The slave girl whom Andrew chose from the Hall of Corsairs to accompany him aboard the *Roxanne* was a servant from Lady Iona's private apartments, the delicately boned Burmese girl named Mari who had been taught since childhood to be the servant to a man, not to be a mere passive object in love-making.

The Captain's cabin aboard the *Roxanne*, although comfortably furnished, had a compact, curtained bed built into a maghogany cupboard. Andrew Peake found difficulty in laying Mari on her back, pressing her legs in the air, crouching on his haunches between her open thighs to lower his mouth to her vagina, trying to practise his time-proven theory that once a female had enjoyed her first orgasm she would eagerly, anxiously continue making love throughout the night.

Mari, trained to be the adoring love partner and not an object of love herself, had at first resisted Andrew's actions, but Andrew, powerful and determined, persisted and soon Mari exploded her excitement. Forgetting about her schooling in the art of romance she allowed Andrew to make love throughout the night, pleased to have him assuming the leading role.

Finally, after seven passionate hours, when daylight was bleaching the sky grey outside the leaded porthole, Mari lay alongside Andrew, brushing his long wavy blond hair.

She said, 'You, Mister Sir, are man who buys the infidel slave.'

Andrew had been drifting to sleep, his mind moving between half-dreams and a jumble of thoughts about Billy, the silver ingots, Gabriel Easton, Catherine Easton, why Don Julio de Castenaldo was also on Slave Island.

He asked, 'How do you know English?'

'Sailors teach Mari as child.' She curled up against Andrew's naked body and repeated, 'Mister Sir, you are man who buys infidel slave?'

Turning his head on the white linen pillow to face her,

Andrew bluntly asked, 'Have you been to bed with him?'

'Mari?' she laughed. 'No, but Mari know the lady who love him.'

'*Who* loves him?'

Turning her head away, Mari confessed, 'It is bad for Mari to speak.'

Curling closer against her warm little body, Andrew cupped her small chin with one finger and said, 'Mari, whoever loves my slave, tell then to watch over him. I sail today, I'm leaving Slave Island. But I will come back here.'

'You leave?'

'But I am coming back. So do please find some way to provide care for the . . . slave.'

'I will try,' promised Mari. She lowered her eyes, asking, 'You see Mari when you come back?'

'I would like to.'

'So would I like to. Other girls, they go crazy and talk, talk, talk about infidel slave. But Mari like you better. No man good like you. No man make Mari feel all good inside like warm summer rain–' Pausing Mari smiled, repeating, 'Yes, Mari wait to see you when you come back, Mister Sir, yes?'

'Yes.' Andrew brushed her lips with his mouth, pulling her small body towards his penis hard between them.

30

'The Englishman is not taking the infidel slave with him.'

Iona stared at Hospodar standing in the doorway of her sleeping chamber. The first day of the auction had finished and caïques had taken the guests back to their ships. Iona was not sleepy, her mind too active with plans, considering the facts and information she had learnt throughout the day.

'Did you hear me?' Hospodar asked, walking further into her room lit by the glow from a pierced brass lamp hanging from the ceiling. 'The Englishman is not taking the infidel slave.'

'Why tell me?' Iona had dismissed her slave girls for the night and was looking out at the lights of the ships dotted in the bay, trying to discern which ship belonged to the Sultana Valideh.

'You showed interest in the infidel slave at the sale. I thought you would like to know he's still in the fortress.'

'Interest? I am interested in the gold he fetched,' she corrected, adding, 'as well as the fact that you might be risking war by putting him on the slave block. That is one reason I thought it was wise for me to spend more time with the Sultana. To be prepared if we need her to intercede on your behalf to Abdul Mohammed.'

'You two are getting on exceedingly well together, you and the Sultan's mother. If she were a man I might even be jealous.' Smiling, Hospodar stepped closer to Iona, saying, 'You do know that I am extremely jealous of you, Iona?'

Iona was not flattered. 'All men are jealous. It's a natural trait.'

'But you also tell me that you are jealous of me,' he reminded her.

Turning her head from the window, Iona impatiently asked, 'What is the meaning of this visit, Husband Pasha? Have you had too much to drink? Or is there something you want to talk about? I am tired. Please speak.'

Hospodar's bravado suddenly disappeared in the face of Iona's strong-mindedness. He had come here to carry out his plan but he could not act as he had hoped; his courage had abandoned him.

Falling to his knees in front of Iona, his voice softening, he pleaded, 'Oh, I love you so much, Iona. But I am so jealous of you. Sometimes the only way I can cope with my jealousy is to tell you that I am promiscuous. It makes me feel important, independent, more virile, to claim clandestine affairs. It makes me feel as if you care when you punish me.'

Iona looked at him, wondering what he now wanted her to do to him.

Hospodar, his masculinity quickly waning, continued, 'Iona, I heard rumours about you before I married you. Gossip about you and the Algerian named Hassan. But I felt myself lucky to be able to marry someone of your beauty, with your noble background. So I shut my ears to the gossip I heard and worked hard to overcome my jealousy.

'But now, Iona, now I want you to tell me with your own mouth. Not about your past, that is your secret. But I need you to tell me about your infidelities of the moment. Tell me so I can hear them with my own ears. So I don't have to listen to men like Zabin.

'Oh yes, your stories will deeply hurt me, Iona, hurt my heart, hurt my mind, hurt my soul. I hope they will hurt me. I can get enjoyment from them that way, enjoy my pain and hurt and learn to live with my jealousy.'

Iona, beginning to understand what Hospodar was trying to tell her, replied, 'In the past, Husband Pasha, you have asked me to punish you, to hold your cane bastinado in my hand, to inflict punishment on your body. But now you are asking me to hurt your . . . mind?'

He nodded, asking, 'Can you forgive me for that?'

'Hospodar Pasha, what if I have no stories, no confessions of infidelities to tell you?'

'Then make up one. Like the stories I invent for you about me sleeping with whores when I am away from Slave Island. Tell me stories, stories that will . . . excite me.'

'And how, Husband Pasha, do I know this is not a trap? Husbands punish, even execute their wives for infidelities.'

'Can you not see that your loving, jealous husband comes to you like a slave, begging you?'

'What if I refuse to play this game? And it is most certainly a game you are asking me to play, Husband Pasha.'

'Earlier I mentioned Zabin, Iona.' Hospodar now spoke in a more controlled voice. 'And, as you know, Zabin would tell me anything that happens on Slave Island for a pouch of papaver tar.'

Iona immediately understood; she said, 'You are blackmailing me. Threatening me to confess something which might not be true. You are saying you can bribe Zabin to attest to my infidelity, however false or untrue the charge may be.'

'I am.'

Iona began her story, beginning with events which had happened long ago, telling Hospodar in a low monotone how she had grown to love him since their marriage on the island of Kypros, but that their love-making had never satisfied her. In fact, their love-making had come to make her frustrated, then bitter, ever hungry for more abandoned sex.

As Iona could not longer trust Zabin, she also told Hospodar how Zabin brought slaves to her from the men's dormitory when Hospodar was away from the fortress. The slaves, though, had all been unsatisfactory lovers.

Waiting until she saw Hospodar beginning to masturbate to her words, Iona finally mentioned the subject of the infidel slave, Billy Peake, that they had made love, that he had satisfied her, but that now she did not even want to see Billy Peake again. Her infatuation with him was over, finished, ended.

'No more?' asked Hospodar, his hand pausing on his hard penis. 'You do not want to see the infidel any more?'

Iona shook her head. 'No more, Husband Pasha. I am tired of affairs with . . . men.'

Hospodar, kneeling in front of her, resumed moving his fist, gasping as he confessed, 'I am jealous . . . your words excite but hurt me . . . you have made love to men who please you more than I please you . . . I am worthless . . . no good to you as a man . . .'

Watching Hospodar kneeling on the floor, seeing him derive sexual enjoyment from humiliation, Iona wondered what he would do once he had reached his orgasm. Would he punish her for being unfaithful to him? Had he trapped her into making a confession and – if so – would he now try to punish her?

More than ever, Iona was thankful for the new friendship she had made with the Sultana Valideh. Perhaps the handsome woman was correct when she said that there was a special love between women which no man could supply.

Book Four

The Leather Triangle

31

To Billy's eye, Hospodar's ship, the *Cessina*, looked more like a work boat than a galley of war. Its mainmast supported a single beam flying a sail fronted by a bright scarlet foresail which billowed in the breeze and humorously reminded Billy of a tippler's big red nose. Despite his doubts – and amusement – about the ship, its performance impressed him, and he had come to respect the *Cessina*'s speed and manoeuvrability since they had left Slave Island.

Dressed in European clothing which Hospodar had given him at the outset of the surprise journey, Billy had not felt as comfortable, as relaxed since his days crossing Africa with Jenny.

Sea air, sharp and raw, was a welcome tonic after living in the damp room where he had been taken after the auction and kept isolated, with no further word from Andrew, until guards dragged him from the room, out to a small shoreboat, and aboard the *Cessina*.

That had been two weeks ago. Now, standing alone on the ship's high poop, Billy enjoyed its sharp pitch against the toss of persistent waves. He caught pinpoints of mist from spray breaking along the steeply raked hull. Eventually he heard Hospodar's heavy footfall on the main deck below him and saw him climbing a spiral staircase of teakwood.

Hospodar, dressed in his red turban, brown jerkin and pantaloons, and black leather boots, seemed to be more at ease aboard ship, too, than he had been on land at Slave Island.

In the past two weeks Billy had noticed something mysterious, almost vulnerable about the short, swarthy man. Hospodar was obviously ruthless, ambitious, determined to maintain order both aboard ship as well as in his fortress. But there was also an inexplicable quality to him, a trait which Billy could not comprehend.

Hospodar called as he approached Billy, 'Alone, infidel? You are like me, you enjoy being alone.'

Was Hospodar trying to be friendly, wanting to enjoy some conversation? Billy doubted it. A man who kept you prisoner, planned to force you into ignoble actions, was not a person who wanted to win your friendship. Hospodar had clearly and specifically announced to Billy the reason why he had taken him from Slave Island and dressed him in European clothes.

Billy answered, 'I'm standing here, watching the sun trying to break through those clouds over there, imagining what lands lie in the distance: the palm trees, the beaches of coral sand, the villages of grass houses, children poking sticks at crabs. I'm imagining all that, but then I remember the purpose of this voyage and I become sad, melancholy.'

'Melancholy? Infidel, are you a romantic? Do you enjoy thinking of life as being cheerful and happy all the time?'

'If cheer and happiness makes a romantic, yes, sir, I confess to being one.'

'You English, it's your religion and hymns that make you all so optimistic.'

Looking at the mist joining the sky and the horizon, Billy said, 'Hospodar Pasha, can you understand my confusion? You sell me on an auction block. The man who buys me disappears. Then you bring me aboard this ship, dress me in European clothes, tell me you are going to use me to lure helpless sailors–'

'You are squeamish about being a decoy. That is what's bothering you, infidel.'

Billy knew it was wise to show respect, even deference to Hospodar. But sometimes it was difficult to keep acting like an obedient slave.

He answered, 'Sir, back in England, down on the rocky coasts of Cornwall, men tie lanterns to donkeys for lost ships to mistake for lighthouses in storms. Those men are called "wreckers". And that's what I feel like, Hospodar Pasha. No better than some miserable, cursed . . . wrecker.'

'That makes you sad?'

'May I speak bluntly, sir?'

'Of course.'

'If I thought your plan would work, Hospodar Pasha, yes, my role in it would make me feel terrible, worse than sad. But we've been at sea for a fortnight and we've seen only one small fishing fleet. So I am hoping, Hospodar, actually praying to my god, that your plan is not going to work.'

Hospodar stood alongside Billy in the mist, staring out at the choppy sea. He said, 'Infidel, we sail a route called the Leather Triangle. It stretches from Java to Madagascar to Ceylon. One of the busiest parts of the Indian Ocean.'

Billy remembered every detail which Andrew had told him in their short meeting, facts ranging from the letter which Rhinelander had written from Jamaica to the mention of ships being captured in the waters called the Leather Triangle.

He asked, 'Hospodar Pasha, why do men call this part of the Indian Ocean the Leather Triangle?'

'Because of leather wrist straps holding galley slaves to their oars.'

'Do many Easterners still use slaves in their galleys?'

'Infidel, I had planned to ask you questions about the American colonies but here you are asking me questions about Asia!'

'Forgive me, Hospodar Pasha. You must ask me about America. I will tell you what I can. The Americas are a big land. I know only a few sections of it, the parts called New England and the Carolinas. But I once thought of making America my home.'

'What do you think now?'

'I do not think. I am a slave. I obey.'

'Infidel, you are clever. You will not always be a slave. Eastern slavery is not like the European enslavement of Africans. The Koran commands us to respect our slaves. Many slaves are freed. So tell me if – when – you are freed, infidel, where will you make your home?'

'As I said, I used to think America, but after seeing Africa, I don't know.'

'Africa? If you were enchanted, seduced by the mysteries of Africa, wait until you see the islands waiting for you in the East Indies. Islands like Ceylon, Bali, Sumatra, Malaya. Each one a paradise, each one a lush place topped with green mountains, decorated with long sandy beaches where birds of exotic plumage, trees with perfumed flowers . . .'

'Ship ho!' shouted a sailor hanging from high on the main mast.

Hospodar and Billy raised their eyes at the call, looking to see where the sailor was pointing.

'Ship ho!' shouted the man. 'Ship ho, Grand Master, to the east!'

Hospodar and Billy looked eastward, seeing a speck appear on the distant horizon.

Hospodar said, 'Infidel, you get your chance now to prove your worth to me.'

The sailors, a motley collection of rag-tag men from many Eastern countries and islands, ran with their muskets and flintlocks, scimitars and daggers, taking up positions behind sails, alongside the masts, kneeling by the covered railings.

Billy, looking at a three masted ship approaching them, momentarily hoped it was Andrew in a ship of the East India Company. But then he recognized the *Tricolore* of France.

'Hospodar, what if the ship sees your cannon? Opens fire on us?'

'Our cannons are concealed too well. And, also, infidel, no European ship fires on a distress flag.'

Hospodar motioned overhead at a white pennant now fluttering from the mainmast.

Billy asked, 'But Hospodar Pasha. Why do you trust me in the role you have given me? How do you know I won't shout out to them that this is a pirate ship? That cannons are trained on them?'

Hospodar tapped Billy's chest with his forefinger. 'Because, infidel, there shall also be a gun trained on you.'

The French frigate creaked and groaned in the lapping sea and a seaman lifted a megaphone to his mouth, shouting, *'Oay du bateau?'*

Billy held a brass spyglass to his eye and did not respond as he studied the ship, seeing she was marked the *Zephyrine* and that if not all, many hands were on deck.

The seaman next hailed in English through the megaphone, 'What troubles you, sir?'

Billy's first impulse was to shout a warning, to alert them that this was an ambush, a scurrilous trick to trap them. But glancing behind him, seeing the crew ready with their weapons, waiting with grappling hooks, cannons set in their catches, Billy knew it was too late to save anyone. He also saw the firearm pointed at him.

The sailor called, 'You fly the St John flag of distress.'

Billy, cupping his hands to his mouth, replied, 'We need medicine, fresh water.'

'Are your men sick with fever or wounds?'

Billy answered as he had been instructed by Hospodar. 'Wounds from attack.'

'Who attacked you?'

'A galleon, north to the Maldives.'

'Your ship shows no damage.'

'The galleon was awkward. We escaped in chase.'

'What flag did she fly?'

'Spain.' Billy lied as Hospodar had told him, continuing, 'It was the man known as the Spanish Pirate.'

The seaman turned to consult with the men surrounding him on deck. He soon ordered, 'Bring your wounded into view.'

Billy called, 'First answer a question for me. Tell me why you fly the flag of King Louis yet speak the tongue of King George.'

'Some aboard speak only French. But some of us are French citizens from an English ship, sailors and passengers rescued from shipwreck. We men help the good crew of the *Zephyrine*.'

'How many passengers do you carry?'

'Six women. Sailing for the missions of China. Good ladies schooled in medicine. Bring your wounded on deck and we will see if we can serve you.'

All the while the *Zephyrine* was drifting closer, finally scraping against the *Cessina*'s bulwark. When the two ships were side by side, Hospodar waved orders and his crew sprang into action.

Loud whoops filled the air, cries and shrill whistles. The raggedy-dressed sailors sprang from behind sails, jumping out from widths of hemp spread over them on deck, dashing with their grappling hooks towards the closing gap between the two ships.

Hospodar's attack was quick and neat: sudden shots boomed from cannons, sending back the *Zephyrine*'s crew. The cannons roared a second time, rocking the French vessel. Whiffs of blue smoke drifted between the two ships. The cannons roared a third time, masts toppled to the *Zephyrine*'s deck, splintering beams, ripping canvas, tearing rigging.

As the Turks swarmed like flies from the *Cessina* to the *Zephyrine*, Hospodar shouted, 'Take chains! Take irons! Bring slaves! Bring prisoners for . . . Slave Island!'

Fighting spread between the two ships, a loud clash of swords, a popping of flintlocks, deafening screams as scimitars stabbed, daggers slashed, garrottes drew quick lines of blood.

Billy's impulse was to run to help the *Zephyrine*'s crew. But he realized the futility of one hand against Hospodar's men, and he stood on the poop deck from where he could see not only the battle but also the women passengers being dragged from the hold.

Billy had never before seen a woman raped. He watched sailors overpowering the female passengers, ripping off their clothes, pushing them down on deck, fighting amongst themselves over them like dogs.

One fight broke out amidship between two men over a woman who quickly grabbed a club to defend herself. But another sailor hit her on the back of the head, pushed her to the deck, hoisted her full skirts, and began ramming his penis into her buttocks.

Two other pirates yanked a shrieking woman by the arms, while a third man ripped down the front of her dress, pulling his penis from his breeches. But a fourth man grabbed him by the neck, pushed him aside, and buried his face against the woman's naked breasts, not removing his mouth until blood flowed from the woman's bare skin.

A line of six ragged pirates formed in front of a woman lying motionless on deck, her legs open, all visible signs of life gone from her body; the men jeered and yelled as they impatiently waited to satisfy their lust on the corpse.

The body of yet another dead woman lay across the coaming, blood smearing her flesh, and limbs torn from her naked torso; a tall pirate stood above her, relieving himself with a long yellow arc of urine onto her body.

Billy, sinking to his knees, vomited aboard the *Cessina,* knowing that the Lord God Almighty would condemn him to everlasting hell fire for enabling such evil deeds to happen.

32

The Sultana Valideh, a broad-shouldered woman, her thin waist tightly clenched with a Berber's studded belt, enjoyed striding the halls of Slave Island in Hospodar's absence, wearing voluminous pantaloons, *chalvari*, a long width of cotton for a *dulbend* – a man's turban – tied not around her head but around her chest as a covering for her breasts. She ignored the Muslim edict that a female's face should be veiled in public places, or in the presence of strangers. Daily, Iona became more fascinated with the exotic, youthful-looking woman, a tall domineering, feline creature with flowing black hair, piercing blue eyes, skin smooth and the colour of rich tea.

The Sultana Valideh was equally obsessed with Iona and had lingered behind on Slave Island when the other guests had sailed away on their ships after the auction and Hospodar had headed northwards aboard the *Cessina.* Abandoning her court on the *Hamadan*, still anchored in the bay, the Sultana Valideh moved as a guest into Iona's apartments, inundating her with gifts – comfits, precious jewels, gold and silver boxes – and lavishing her with attention, telling her what a good time the two of them would enjoy together in the palace at Constantinople.

The Sultana Valideh – or Tyla Karazin, the Circassian name by which she preferred to be known – was determined to take Iona back to Constantinople with her aboard the *Hamadan.* She wanted them to live together as lovers in private apartments in the harem of her son's palace perched on Seraglio Point high above the River Bosphorus.

Iona was thrilled by the sudden prospect of going to Constantinople; but the newness, the forbidden excitement of enjoying another woman's love, both frightened and satisfied her. She had become quiet, a completely transformed woman, a docile and passive lover to the dominant ways of the Sultana Valideh, Tyla Karazin.

Before meeting Tyla Karazin, Iona had not enjoyed the social companionship of women, but, then, Tyla preferred to be thought of as a man rather than a woman. She attributed the reason for her masculine traits, her preference for women to men, to a life spent ulmost entirely inside a harem.

The two women lay together on cushions in Iona's apartments, Tyla explaining, 'It is because Abdul is my son as well as Sultan that I can speak so honestly about true happenings behind those latticed gates that deny entry to the outside world. A sultan's harem is no different from any Eastern seraglio and no harem is a soft, cosy den of cooing, swooning young females who are forever grooming themselves, making themselves attractive for men, pining for the moment when their lord and master will visit them.

'Oh, no! Women in harems are tigresses! Panthers! Vixens with little thought, or concern for a man. Oh, there are those ambitious women, of course, who vie for the Sultan's political favours. But few – if any – are interested in their lord for romantic reasons. Oh, no! Those sugary little confections are hungry for . . . power!

'My son has nine official wives, his *khadines*. He has more than four hundred concubines, *houris*, in his harem. I know for a fact that at least three of his wives sleep with knives beneath their head pillows – not only as protection from the six other *khadines*, or the many *houris* trying to murder them, but also from eunuchs hoping to make a place for some young, plotting darling who has bribed him to take her one step closer towards the Golden Throne of the True Empire!'

Time spent with Tyla flew quickly for Iona and she eagerly listened to stories about the powers of the Ottoman Empire; about duties allocated from the Sultan to the governor's palace, the *Dejnina*; how Tyla had been only fourteen years old when she had given birth to the Sultan, who now was not yet thirty; tales about court figures in the Sublime Porte and everyone – from the Chief Turban Winder to the Keeper of the Nightingale's Seed – trying to find a place for some daughter, niece or cousin in the Sultan's harem.

More than four hundred females living in a harem at one time created unique problems as Tyla explained. 'A houseful of odalisques is like a field of children. Leave them alone for a few hours and they divide themselves into groups. The weak-willed get trampled and pushed to one side. The strong are soon leading the pack, making up rules, organizing games. But a harem is as lawless, as dangerous as a field where little children play with sharp knives and poison. They invent their own cruel pastimes and more often than not the games involve love-making. There are strict rules to follow. Strong women act as the pashas, the husbands, but submissive, sweet little tulips like you, Iona, become wives. I beg you to come back with me to Constantinople to be my *khadine*.'

In the physical act of love-making with Iona, Tyla fondled Iona's breasts, working her rosy nipples into tautness, smiling pleasurably as Iona trembled in her arms, shaking like a girl.

Iona, sniffing the musk wafting from Tyla's golden skin, murmured, 'You make me feel as if I have shed . . . years.'

'Feeling young is one of the many rewards of love, my darling.'

'I feel like a lovesick girl. I have never before felt this youthful. Not even when I *was* young!'

'Because you have never before enjoyed another woman's love.'

'Never before have I felt so relaxed, so peaceful, so natural, so at ease in another person's company, male or female.'

Tyla smiled at the compliment. 'It is satisfying for me to see such changes in you, my little *khadine*. To see you becoming the person you are obviously meant to be. Men have made you hard, brittle, complex. You were ready to snap in two like a dry reed when I first saw you here. Yes, my darling, I arrived just in time to save you from some dreadful fate. I must take you away from this harsh, impersonal world of stone walls, of barren, constricting shores, of slaves. No, no, Iona, captives and prisoners of war are not the only ones held in bondage on this island. These rocks also enslave you.'

Iona devoured Tyla's soothing words, listening to her constant praise, responding to her promises, yearning for more of her love-making.

As days passed Iona obediently followed Tyla's orders: she washed the kohl from her eyes; she destroyed her many bottles and flasks of heady perfumes; she ripped and shredded a wardrobe of dramatically jewelled capes and billowing gowns. She began to dress simply, femininely, transforming herself into the woman Tyla wanted for a wife.

Iona's metamorphosis also included the destruction of her collection of phalluses. Tyla believed that a penis was vile and unclean and that it was sacrilegious for a woman even to have a facsimile of a male organ in her possession. She also contended that there was no need for a woman to use a phallic shape in love-making, not when she could be inventive and call upon her own vast range of physical attributes.

Iona kept no secrets from Tyla; she told her her life story, beginning with the early love affair she had with Hassan the Algerian, who years ago had unwittingly prepared her for a love affair with another woman; then, she progressed to details about how Hospodar enjoyed her beating him, torturing him, both physically and mentally, and she told about her recent assignation with the infidel slave, how the affair had originally thrilled her but had subsequently caused her torture, anguish and had only fuelled Hospodar's perverse demands on her.

Tyla already knew about the infidel slave. He had been the reason she and Iona had first spoken to one another. Tyla enjoyed reliving the moment when Iona had nervously asked her before the auction sale in the fortress courtyard if she would allow a woman in her entourage to bid on her behalf for the infidel slave. The risk Iona had taken in asking the Sultana Valideh to perform such an act had immediately attracted Tyla to Iona. She liked her courage.

Tyle's response had been what had awakened Iona to Tyla: Tyla had promised on the morning of the auction, 'I will allow a handmaiden to bid to the absolute limit of what I believe a man is worth to a woman. From then on, the value cannot compare with what you can get from another woman – and at a fraction of the price!'

Now, weeks later, when Tyla listened to Iona's history of

romance, hearing the story of the infidel slave being Iona's last male lover, Tyla said, 'Iona, my dove, what did you ever want with a young boy? A boy can only cause you worry and problems. The world is a cruel place, as you know, and people are unkind about love affairs between older women and young boys. They will call you a predator.

'My lovely Iona, it was past time for *you* to be the sexual object in a love affair; you and you alone to be the focus of *my* desires! Stop allowing yourself to be hurt by lascivious men, by young boys who know nothing of a woman's true needs. Escape with me into a paradise of women. That is the only answer – women for women. Forget about men. Be thankful you are making this discovery so early, while you are still capable of giving and receiving love. Consider the poor women in India, miserable wretches who are told to throw themselves onto burning pyres at the death of a husband! Is there anything more unnatural, more perverse than the act called *suttee*, when a woman must kill herself for a dead man?'

And women – or at least Tyla Karazin – were the answer to Iona's appetites. Their love-making was like nothing Iona had ever before experienced. Tyla laid Iona on cushions, running her darting tongue over Iona's body, working the palm of her hand against Iona's furry delta, pressing, kneading, inflaming Iona's vagina, fingering her clitoris, nibbling, one, then the other nipple. Next she kissed a path down the length of Iona's nakedness to her bare feet, nibbling each toe, making Iona writhe, squirm, toss with ecstasy, becoming weak with desire, frenzy and, above all, love.

Or, at other moments of passion, Tyla stood powerful, naked over Iona, mighty and conquering like an Amazon heroine, holding Iona's head between her strong hands, pressing Iona's face to the furry triangle between her legs, making Iona beg, cry, act the supplicant lover – her *khadine* – in front of her enacting the husband, the strong one.

Three weeks quickly passed and one night, after Iona

and Tyla had made love in bright moonlight pouring through the windows of Iona's private apartments, Tyla finally explained how she wanted Iona to speak to Hospodar when he returned home from his sea voyage.

Tyla said, 'You are to tell him – not ask, but tell him – that you are leaving on the *Hamadan* with me for Constantinople. If he asks how long you will be away, tell him to speak to me. But, believe me, Hospodar will ask me no questions. I have seen Hospodar. I have studied him. I know men like Hospodar and I am sorry to say this, my *khadine*, but your lawful husband is more interested in pleasing the Sultana Valideh than you. That is the way of life. Men obey power, listen to power, want to please powerful people. Men are all weak, my *khadine*. Why do you think so many women have to rely on each other to survive? Do you hear women complaining – whining – about living together in a harem? No! Certainly not! Women fight to get into harems! Their husbands, their fathers, their pashas put eunuchs in charge of them behind iron grilles. Men are so frightened that another man will ravish his *khadine* or *houri*. Silly creatures! The women are making love with each other! I even know eunuchs who make better lovers than men with both testicles hanging between their legs! Yes, it is a false rumour that a eunuch has no love life. Eunuchs use their mouths, their fingers, their lips. They have something more important than a penis. They still have their hearts! They can love, Iona! They can . . . love! That is what's important. Who needs a penis? Who needs a man! Who wants to live along with a man? Another stupid idea!

'Put a cat and dog together and see how they get along. They fight! They squabble! They bite and they scratch! No, men are stupid creatures, and too, too proud. They try to get as many women as they can and flaunt them like peacocks with peahens in a garden. Men collect *khadines* and *houris*, wives, concubines and mistresses only to flatter themselves. To make themselves look important. They see who can amass the largest harem. But women are the ones who benefit.

'So I assure you, in my vast knowledge of men, your husband won't stop you from sailing to Constantinople. Would he insult the mother of the Sultan? Never!'

Tyla, cradling Iona in her arms, added, 'Listen to me, my little turtle-dove, and I will take you away from this stone cage where you have been too long a slave. You think you have seen vast, awesome changes in yourself during the last three weeks. No my *khadine.* The soft, purring woman I see with my eyes has always been there. She's been covered with paint, driven with lust, a stranger to happiness only because men have made her that way. It took another woman to make you happy. And no man shall stop me from carrying you away from Slave Island!'

33

Billy stayed in the pungent smelling hold of the *Cessina* for the duration of the five-day voyage back from the Leather Triangle to Slave Island. He sat on a makeshift bed in the hold's prow, where pitch had been thickly applied in the Eastern maritime manner, a sticky protection of pitch and reeds against seepage.

Billy nibbled at hard white rice cakes given to him by a member of the crew with one eye, and he sipped at the coarse beverage, arrack, brought to him in a stubby earthenware jar. He spoke to no one, avoiding Hospodar, and he tried not to go on deck, frightened of seeing the *Zephyrine* sailing behind them, a skeleton of the frigate he had helped lure into captivity, now little more than a hull to be dismantled and its boards rebuilt into smaller craft by prisoners on Slave Island.

Back on Slave Island, Billy was given a room above the water-line in the fortress. A new slave girl visited him each day to serve as a companion but Billy turned away each potential concubine – rewards sent to him from Hospodar – and a different girl arrived at his door the next day. Rather than trophies or prizes for bold action, they were only grim reminders to Billy of butchery and enslavement of men, of rape of women.

Finally, on his sixth day back in the fortress, Billy reluctantly admitted a girl into the room, a delicately featured girl carrying a small basket of fresh figs which tempted his slowly improving appetite for food.

Tired and despondent, Billy peeled the purple skin from a ripe fig and began to realise he needed someone to talk to, that he was wallowing in guilt and self-persecution.

Refusing, though, to encourage the girl as a lover, he made her stand across the room from his pallet as he slowly, timidly began to speak to her. His words gained momentum and soon he was embarking on a full confession, unburdening all his troubles, all the guilt pent up inside him.

Pacing the stone floor, Billy told the girl how ashamed he was of himself, choking back the tears, saying, 'I did something so awful, so villainous and destructive. I betrayed men and, oh, those poor women! I shall never forget their screams, their mutilated and mangled bodies, how the Turks defiled them, even after they were dead . . .'

The slave girl, despite her few words of English, tried to console Billy.

She said, 'You no choice. You slave.'

Billy understood, but argued, 'I could at least have warned them! Somehow, some way. They were good people. They were going to give aid to . . . us! Give us medicine! Come to *our* rescue! That's the irony. Oh Lord, my good Lord, what have I done?'

'Slaves no choice.'

Sniffing back his tears, Billy said. 'Slavery is bad, yes. But being a slave is not the worst thing. The worst thing is seeing – actually helping – other men being *made* slaves. To take part in stripping another person of his freedom. Oh, if I ever get out of here, my work waits for me. My future will be spent making amends for the wrong I've committed.'

'People try to help slaves. But no good.'

Again, Billy understood the girl's pidgin English and he argued, speaking more to himself than to her.

'There must be ways to help slaves. What about those European societies? Charity groups? Mercy missions carrying ransoms? I've heard about such people – about families and friends – who send money and agents to rescue slaves from the Turks. But I don't want to help one or two slaves. I want to help hundreds, thousands of poor souls caught up in slavery. The world hears about African slaves in the New World, far across the Atlantic. But they forget about other helpless souls here in Asia.'

He continued pacing the room, his face twisted with anguish.

The slave girl tried to console him. 'You good person. You find way.'

Billy disagreed, 'No, a good person I am not! I am a coward, a weakling and a fool. But, oh yes, you can rest assured I will find a way to carry out my mission. I will find a way to make up for the hideous wrong I have committed . . .'

Stopping and turning to face the small-boned girl, Billy sniffed and said, 'See how selfish, how self-centred I am –' He forced a smile, confessing, 'I have not even asked you your name.'

The slave girl's small mouth turned into a grin and her elongated eyes became thinner as she smiled, answering, 'Mari.'

'Mari, isn't today the first day you've come here? Those were other girls who –' he motioned at the door.

Mari dipped her head, confessing, 'Mari do bad, too. Mari see other girls sent here. Mari give other girls silk to come you.'

'You . . . bribed them to come here? To see me?'

She nodded. 'Mari know Master Sir.'

'Master? Hospodar sent you?'

'No, no, not *Grand* Master,' she quickly corrected, '*New* master. New English Master Sir. Master in jacket white, legs red, hair gold like you.'

Billy understood the description and it fitted only one person he had seen on Slave Island.

He gasped, 'You know Andrew?'

Mari's soft brow wrinkled, 'And-rewww?'

Remembering that Andrew had assumed another name for his visit to Slave Island, Billy corrected, 'You know Sir Oliver Bull?'

Eagerly nodding her head, Mari said, 'English Master Sir.'

'How do you know *him*?'

'Master Sir chose Mari from slave girls for bed after party.' She smiled.

'Andrew made . . . love to you?'

'Andrewww? Why you say . . . And-rewww?'

'Sir Oliver made love to you?'

'Make you angry?'

Billy laughed. 'Angry? I am delighted!'

'Master Sir promises come back Slave Island very, very soon.'

'He's coming back? Oh, Mari, tell me everything that you know. If you saw him after Hospodar's party, you saw him since I did and know more than I do. What did he tell you? When is he coming back?'

Mari shrugged her small shoulders and raised the palms of her petite hands. 'Mari has no day. Master Sir tell Mari to see you good. But Hospodar take you away. Many changes happen on Slave Island. Lady Iona all time see Sultana Valideh . . .'

Stopping, Mari shook her head, saying, 'Mari talk no good.'

Billy, excited by this shred of information about Andrew, remembered how Jenny had asked him to put his arms around her on the morning when Captain Kerr and

Jack Razor had first dragged her into the palm hut with him at Razor Cove, how Jenny had apologised for wanting to feel the warmth of another body against her, but needed a brotherly, familiar reassuring touch.

Billy, looking fondly down at Mari, said, 'You are a very pretty girl and a good person, Mari. I intend you no harm. But I have been feeling so miserable, so lost, so lonely and unhappy lately, and you now come to me and tell me about . . . Sir Oliver and–'

Stepping forward, Billy pulled Mari towards him, enveloping her small frame in the warm embrace of his arms, closing his eyes, as he pressed her against his chest. He swayed back and forth, repeating, 'A little angel . . . just like a little angel . . .'

'Angel?' Mari did not understand.

Many fathoms below Billy's newly-assigned room in the fortress, Mustafa Zabin accompanied Hospodar along a dark, fetid passageway from the men's underground dormitory. Zabin hurried to keep pace with Hospodar's brisk steps, praising, 'This is the most prisoners you have brought back to Slave Island, Hospodar Pasha. I count no less than seventy men still alive, or not dying. They are strong and in good health mostly and the overseers report they already work long, hard hours in the quarry.'

Hospodar hurried along through the yellow torch light flickering at intervals in the dark passageway; the sound of dripping water echoed in the distance; rats scampered across the passageway, their long channelled tails rustling in the straw.

Carrying his cane bastinado behind his back, Hospodar said, 'Much of the credit is due to the infidel slave. He has a good honest face. His voice is loud, clear and trustworthy. Men believe him.'

'Ah, and I have noticed, Hospodar Pasha, that you have amply rewarded the infidel with a new room to sleep in as well as a wench.'

Hospodar looked quickly at Zabin. 'DId the infidel finally accept a slave girl in his pallet?'

Zabin smiled. 'I understand a girl from your wife's chambers is with him today.'

'About my wife,' Hospodar said, as he kept walking. 'Does she complain about anything these days?'

'Complain? Ah, Grand Master, Allah smiles on you! Lady Iona spends every day with the Sultana Valideh. Oh, what influence you will have in the Sublime Porte because of this friendship! Such a lucky husband you are, Grand Master Pasha!'

Hospodar frowned. He was pleased Iona had forgotten about the infidel slave, but he was baffled why the change had come about so quickly, so thoroughly. He knew he should also be pleased that his wife was friendly with someone as powerful as the Sultan's mother, the second most influential person in the Empire. But for some curious, inexplicable reason, Hospodar was uneasy. True, his disturbed state had much to do, he realised, with the fact that he had been celibate since returning to Slave Island, that he had been unable to pursue sexual fantasies with Iona, and there was no slave girl who pleased him.

The subject of Iona reminded Hospodar of another business matter he wanted to settle and, as he continued walking along the torchlit passageway with Zabin, he handed a leather pouch to Zabin, saying, 'Here, I want you to have this. It's a small reward.'

'Reward, Grand Master? What did I do for you?'

'You worked tirelessly at the auction and we made a good profit.' Hospodar lowered his voice, explaining, 'And you were also both my eyes and ears concerning my wife and the . . . infidel slave.'

Zabin, taking the pouch, said, 'Hospodar Pasha, this is truly a surprise.'

'I intend to reward you later with gold for your services at the auction. But this is just a small token of my gratitude. Inside the pouch you'll find some papaver tar for your enjoyment.'

'Papaver tar?' Zabin guardedly asked, 'Grand Master, who told you I indulged in . . . papaver tar?'

'If you do not, Zabin, then give it back!' Hospodar reached for the pouch. 'I will give it to someone I know who enjoys resin from the poppy.'

Greedily gripping the pouch, Zabin said, 'Oh no, Grand Master. Do you think I would be so ungrateful as to refuse a gift from you, my patron and master?'

'Good. I am pleased you accept my small token, Zabin, for the work you have done for me in the past and for the work I am sure you will continue doing for me in the future.'

Turning a corner in the maze of underground tunnels, Hospodar led the way up steep narrow stairs leading to the next landing. He said, 'Zabin, I plan to sail in two days' time.'

'You go on another trip so soon, Hospodar Pasha?'

'I may soon have the opportunity to sell infidel slaves in China. I must scour the Triangle while I have the young American slave still at my disposal. The Englishman, Sir Oliver Bull, comes back soon to claim him.'

Zabin, hurrying to keep up with Hospodar's rapid steps, suggested, 'Has your excellency considered "losing" the infidel slave? Sir Oliver Bull need never know what happened to the slave in his absence.'

'I considered that, of course, Zabin. But it is too risky. You see, Sir Oliver has a contact to sell slaves to in China whom I need. Sir Oliver promised to introduce me to a man in Canton named Master Hu'An. It is to Master Hu'An I mean to sell the slaves, perhaps two to three hundred white men before I am finished.'

Zabin promised, 'Then I shall keep a watchful eye on your new French and English slaves, Grand Master. They will be the basis for a new fortune.'

'But also relax when I'm away, Zabin. You have been working very hard.'

Zabin, pleased that Hospodar was appreciative of his dedication, bowed, touching his chest, forehead and turban. Yes, he knew he had made the correct choice siding with Hospodar rather than Iona, in betraying her adultery to Hospodar.

After leaving Hospodar, Zabin bolted the thick door of his room and sat down by the wooden table. He struck a flint to light his brazier on the table and began heating water to prepare the papaver tar which Hospodar had given to him.

Wondering what precious gift – how many coins – the Sultana Valideh would also bestow upon him when she eventually departed for Constantinople, Zabin anxiously waited for the water to boil.

Finally, seeing bubbles rising in the copper basin, Zabin reached for the leather pouch and removed two hard black chunks of resin. He crushed one piece in the palm of his hand and set it on the perforated disc placed over the boiling water.

Noticing a strange odour to the resin. Zabin held the second chunk to his nose and detected a pungency. Not recognising the smell and eager to enjoy the resin's soothing effect, he hurriedly crumbled the second chunk with his fingers and dropped the pieces onto the disc. He reached for the cloth to drape over his head to capture all the precious intoxicating fumes.

Leaning across the brazier with the square of cloth tented over his head, Zabin closed his eyes, took a deep breath and inhaled the first mesmerising draught.

Immediately, though, his eyes began to water; his nostrils burned as if he had breathed flames from the brazier. A sharp pain sped through his sinuses, down his throat, into his lungs, making his heart pound as if he were having an attack.

Gasping, his heart thudding inside his chest, his brain exploding like a succession of flintlocks, Zabin struggled to pull the cloth from his head. But in his panic he knocked over the burner, catching the cloth in the flames. The fire spread quickly to his turban and robe. Soon, jerking, kicking and burning like the torch on the wall, Zabin fell screaming to the stone floor of his locked room.

34

Hospodar sat in his cabin aboard the *Cessina*, studying Billy striding the main deck in his suit of European clothing. Hospodar noted that he appeared more relaxed and guessed that the slave girls had been the necessary antidote for his nerves.

Hospodar wished he himself felt as invigorated.

He could now count in weeks the time since he had last made love. In the eight days he had spent on Slave Island, he had only seen Iona twice and on both occasions it had been in the company of the Sultana Valideh. Iona had matter-of-factly announced that the Sultan's mother had invited her to Constantinople and, when Hospodar had inquired how long she planned to be away from Slave Island, Iona had told him to ask the Sultana Valideh for any details about departures, returns, the length of the visit.

Rather than jeopardise his career by questioning the Sultana Valideh, Hospodar had accepted Iona's announcement, wishing both her and the Sultana Valideh a good and safe voyage. He bade them carry his best wishes and salutations to the Shadow of Allah on Earth, His Supreme Highness and Most Wise of All Mortals, the Sultan Abdul Mohammed of the Sublime Porte.

Hospodar had left Slave Island on the morning after giving Zabin the pouch of papaver tar laced with antimony, silencing him forever about Iona's infidelities as a spouse. He had sealed the room and elevated an overseer from the quarry, Moman, to serve as deputy in his absence, to carry out the duties of the fortress until he could find a more adequate replacement.

As the sun sank below the horizon of the Indian Ocean, Hospodar remained in his cabin, reclining on the leather-weave hammock.

He had depleted his store of perverse memories about Iona and, in a desperate moment, he considered the possibility of bringing the infidel slave into his cabin, to demand that he tell him his side of the story, what it had been like to make love to his wife, to use an adulterer's tale as a spur for a masturbatory fantasy.

Hospodar quickly dispelled the idea. But his need for sexual fulfilment was becoming more intense and he did not know what form his next gratification was going to assume.

Hospodar's nervous state did not go unnoticed by Billy. On the sixth morning at sea, Hospodar's moodiness had become so severe that Billy saw him glowering at him from the doorway of his cabin.

Billy told himself he had his own problems to worry about, though, and continued concentrating on his plan, how he hoped to help people escape from slavery in the future.

Remembering how Hospodar had told him that many men did not remain slaves forever in Islam, Billy believed that if Andrew could not raise two-hundred-and-fifty gold weight to buy his freedom, he himself would find some way to escape slavery. And once a free man, he would dedicate himself to helping other men and women escape from shackles.

The Atlantic slave trade had its abolitionist champions, a growing number of spokesmen like Moses Brown, Quakers and other religious figures from England and the American colonies.

Who, though, dedicated themselves to freeing white people from slavery? Who brought the sufferings of 'infidel slaves' in the East to the public's eye? Those men whom Billy heard Arabs call '*N'zranis*'?

Billy remembered how people always accused him of talking too much and, as he paced the deck of the *Cessina*, he thought, 'Why not put my big mouth to some good advantage! Attract some attention to Eastern slavery?'

The first person Billy would help would, of course, be Jenny. He would earn who had bought her, track her down, raise money for her ransom, perhaps even use one of the mercenary figures which Macpherson had told him about, the people who found relatives of families in Europe.

A shout from the mast broke Billy's daydreams; he raised his eyes and saw one of Hospodar's sailors pointing eastward.

The sailor called, 'Ship, ho! Ship ho! Heave towards the sun!'

Hospodar and Billy stood side-by-side on the high poop deck of the *Cessina*; Hospodar held his brass spyglass to his eye, looking at a brig on the far horizon, the sun sparkling on the silver-capped waves stretching between the ship and the *Cessina*.

Billy knew that this time he must somehow warn the ship's crew and any passengers that the *Cessina* was a corsair ship, that pirates were aboard, ready to entrap them.

Studying the brig through the spyglass, Hospodar said, 'The ship sits low in the water. She's a merchant vessel.'

He handed the spyglass to Billy.

Billy took the spyglass, his hands shaking.

Noticing the tremble, Hospodar asked, 'What makes you nervous?'

Billy, raising the spyglass to his eye, replied, 'I still have trouble sleeping after your last . . . victory, sir.'

Hospodar grunted.

Fixing his sight on a three masted brig, Billy saw a smart, brightly-painted ship, glistening with gilt trim.

He next studied the flags on the mainmast. 'She's a colonial ship, sir.'

'Colonial? From where?'

'A British colony, sir.' Billy's first thought was of Andrew.

Reaching for the spyglass, Hospodar said, 'She's too small to be an Indiaman.'

Billy momentarily forgot his slave's deference to Hospodar and, keeping the spyglass, he studied the mast with growing fascination.

He said, 'She flies a . . . convoy flag.'

'What's that?'

Billy tried to remain calm as he explained, 'Below the red, white, and blue British colonial flag, I see a trade pennant, a double pointed banner showing she's part of a convoy.'

Hospodar scanned the horizon for other ships. 'A convoy from where? Where are the other convoy ships?'

The colonial brig had moved closer, the wind driving her topsails, filling the main course, sending the bowsprit across foamswept waves toward the *Cessina*, rapidly shortening the distance between the two vessels.

Cupping both hands to his mouth, Hospodar shouted to the sailor high on the mainmast. 'Do you sight other ships?'

The sailor hailed he saw no other vessels.

Billy, looking through the spyglass, now clearly and without doubt recognised the sharp colours on the convoy flag – an orange snake coiled on a blue field.

He said, 'Sir, I doubt if this particular ship sails with the rest of her convoy.'

Hospodar, anxious and impatient, irritably demanded, 'First you say she's a convoy ship, infidel! Now you say she sails alone! What do you mean? Damn it! What do you see?'

The convoy flag had surprised Billy. But he was quickly becoming more angry than nervous as he suspected to whom the ship belonged.

He handed the spyglass to Hospodar, saying, 'I see the name on the prow. She's called the *Lady Charlene*. The name means nothing to me, sir. But I do recognise the convoy flag. It belongs to a British trader I know in Boston.'

'Boston? The Americas?'

Hospodar, looking across the waves, studied the ship with renewed interest. And as he saw the ship trying to luff, to break with a gale, he suddenly spotted the sun's bright rays glint on cannons rolled into place.

'She's going to fire on us!' he called.

Turning to the main deck, he ordered, 'Raise the distress flag! Prepare cannons! Tighten sails!'

The wind caught the red foresail, spinning her into a quick eastern tack, and the *Cessina* gathered immediate distance on the colonial brig.

Hospodar, studying the brig's new behaviour through the spyglass, saw she was still fighting to change sail, to catch a new gust and flee, completely ignoring the flutter of a distress flag atop the *Cessina*.

Seeing that the heavy load made the brig sluggish in the water, Hospodar shouted to his gunners, 'Prepare to fire across her prow!'

Billy still remained silent but his mind was quickly working.

Hospodar next ordered, 'Men to fighting posts!'

The shabby pirate crew anxiously scurried around deck, crouching into position behind cannons checked into the dowelled railing; they knelt with prime flintlocks and gleaming scimitars behind the forecastle; they grouped by the stay-sails ready to throw grappling hooks when they came closer to their quarry.

Hospodar, turning to Billy, said, 'Quickly, tell me more about the convoy, infidel.'

Billy faltered. 'The convoy left Boston more than a year ago, bound for . . . China.'

'China? What happened to the other ships? Where are they?'

Billy remembered too well. 'There were seven ships at the outset. I sailed in this convoy, sir. I sailed aboard a schooner named the . . . *Vandal Witch*.'

'But you do not recognise this ship.' Hospodar pointed the spyglass across the water. 'The *Lady Charlene*?'

Billy shook his head. 'She's most likely a replacement for the *Vandal Witch.* Probably pressed into service in Jamaica.'

'Jamaica? Why do you say Jamaica? Jamaica is an island far south from your city called Boston.'

Billy did not immediately reply. He was remembering what Andrew had told him about a letter from Paris Rhinelander in Jamaica. He was remembering Andrew asking him if Rhinelander might bring the ingots to China himself.

Billy, silently standing alongside Hospodar, wondered if the brig was not only carrying his ingots but that Paris Rhinelander might also be aboard this strange ship called the *Lady Charlene*?

'Answer me, infidel!' Hospodar insisted. 'Why do you mention the island of Jamaica?'

Billy stammered. 'The *Vandal Witch* went back to Jamaica . . . from Africa instead of continuing to . . . China.'

'Is this the *Vandal Witch*? With a new name?'

'No, sir. I don't think so, sir. But the cargo might be the same, again bound for . . . China.

'China . . .' Hospodar savoured the word.

China, the name, the vast land, their sudden need for foreign slaves, everything about China tantalised Hospodar.

Looking again at the *Lady Charlene*, he mused, 'The convoy must belong to a very rich trader, a man rich enough to sail from the New World for China, to stay at sea for one year, to carry a load to make his ship sit so low in the water.'

Billy's stomach knotted with nerves when he thought that his silver might be the reason for the low ride in the waves.

Hospodar, turning back to the main deck, ordered his gunners, 'Fire across her prow. But do not sink her.'

The gunner bent into position and, with a flash of fire in the bright sunlight, the snubbed cannot boomed, shaking against the boltings, sending forth a volley, and a cloud of smoke rose over the deck and water.

As the smoke was clearing, though, a cannon exploded across the water, and the *Cessina* suddenly shuddered under the impact of a direct strike of a cannon ball from the colonial brig.

Hospodar shouted for a second cannon to be fired, but still insisted. 'Do not hit the brig! Do not strike her! She most likely has riches aboard!'

The gunner fired another warning signal.

The wind was bringing the *Lady Charlene* closer to Hospodar's ship, and the pirates began lining the deck, preparing their flintlocks, dirks, swords, grappling hooks to board the brig.

Billy, looking through the spyglass, recognized a figure standing on deck. He frantically shouted, 'Hospodar! Sir! Stop! Hold back attack!'

Hospodar was ordering his men into position, preparing them to carry a battering ram aboard so that they could break into the hatch and inspect the cargo.

Billy called louder, 'Hospodar! Sir! Hold back your men!'

Hospodar looked over his shoulder at Billy.

'It's Easton!' Billy shouted. 'Gabriel Easton's aboard that ship and he's not alone.'

'Easton?' The name meant nothing to Hospodar.

'Gabriel Easton. The Boston trader. The man who owns the convoy.'

Hospodar suddenly leered. 'Easton? He is rich? This . . . Easton?'

Billy, again looking through the spyglass, was thankful that he did not see Paris Rhinelander. But he did spot a small figure in a white dress standing next to Easton on the quarterdeck. And, on the far side of her stood a small man dressed in the gold-braided jacket of a sea captain.

'Infidel?' Hospodar inquired. 'Can I get a fine ransom for this Easton?'

Billy, lowering the spyglass, looked at Hospodar and

answered, 'Catherine Easton is with him.'

'Catherine Easton? Who is she? The trader's wife? Does he travel with his wife so far from home?' Hospodar shook his head at the conduct of infidels.

Billy, silent, was remembering what Hospodar's men had done to the missionary women aboard the *Zephyrine*, how they had raped them and defiled their bodies.

Next, Billy clearly recalled how Andrew had questioned him about Catherine Easton, asking him if Catherine still loved him, missed him, was coming to Sumatra to marry him.

He wondered, 'Is that what she's doing here so far from home? Going to Sumatra to marry . . . Andrew?'

A voice suddenly hailed across the waves from the *Lady Charlene*, a voice shouting through a megaphone, saying, 'This is Captain Henley. Your ship flounders . . . call off your men . . . or we sink you to the bottom of the ocean.'

The threat increased Hospodar.

Cupping both hands to his mouth, he roared, 'We'll board your ship and flay the white skin from every man, woman and child aboard.'

Captain Henley answered, 'Our cannons can blast you to Kingdom come, you unholy heathen!'

'Fire, and you will be destroyed, you damned infidels!'

Hospodar's crew was becoming more excited, moving restlessly on deck like dogs in a cage, waiting for Hospodar's orders to pour across the gap separating them from the colonial brig.

A second voice called from the *Lady Charlene*. 'Billy Paker? Is that you aboard that heathen barge, Billy Peake?'

Hospodar gaped at Billy. 'Infidel. You do *not* tell me lies! They do know you!'

Billy nodded, but kept studying the *Lady Charlene*. He could see that the brig was heavily armed, lined with cannons, ready with swivel guns to fight off any encroaching ships.

Unfortunately, though, the wind had abandoned the brig

and was bringing the deckful of armed pirates closer and closer to her.

Again, Billy thought of Andrew's betrothal to Catherine, about Hospodar's men eager to rape, about the atrocities which an entire crew of lascivious pirates would commit on one single female.

Hospodar demanded, 'Infidel, order them to surrender. I do not want to sink a rich cargo.'

'You heard them, Hospodar Pasha. They are determined to survive.'

'They are bluffing.'

Billy believed this too. Taking a deep breath, he said, 'Hosdopar Pasha, why don't you trade ships with them?'

'Trade . . . what?'

'Trade ships,' repeated Billy. 'Look around you. Consider your own chances. Your ship has been hit. It's badly damaged. So call off your men. Keep them at bay. Let the passengers and crew come aboard here. And you take their ship.'

'Infidel, what are you saying? Give up my ship? Lose the *Cessina*?' Hospodar laughed at the suggestion. 'I won't sink the colonial ship. I can easily win with hand-to-hand fighting.'

'You can fight, yes, sir. But they may not be bluffing. You are taking a big gamble. They are much better armed than you. Your men can rape and kill, yes. But those cannons are trained on us at this very moment. One move from your men and they will fire, sinking the *Cessina* and killing half your crew.'

'I will fire back!' Hospodar answered stubbornly. 'We are close! I will sink them!

'Then you both go down.' Billy shook his head, insisting, 'No, Hospodar. I do not mean to show you disrespect. But, please, sir, I implore you to promise them safe boarding aboard this ship in exchange for their ship and cargo.'

Hospodar suspiciously eyed Billy. 'And what is their cargo, infidel?'

Billy lowered his eyes.

Hospodar pressed, 'Infidel, you know what's in the hold of that ship, don't you? If it's so valuable, why would they abandon it?'

Billy said, 'I know Gabriel Easton. He's a coward. He'll do anything to save his own skin. Even forfeit that . . . cargo.'

'Infidel, what's in that hold? What is the cargo?'

'Silver.'

'Silver? What kind of silver?'

'Mexican silver ingots. Bound for . . . China.'

Below Hospodar and Billy on the main deck, the pirates were restlessly waiting for orders to start charging aboard the foreign ship; the two vessels were drifting closer and closer together; the men were beginning to shout, become angry.

Captain Henley hailed from the *Lady Charlene*, 'Our guns are trained on you. We have enough powder to explode you into damnation. One move and we sink you.'

Hospodar, ignoring the threat from the captain as well as the noises from his restless crew, studied Billy's ashen face.

He finally said, 'Infidel, I will leave you with the passengers and crew aboard this ship.'

Across the water, another voice hailed, 'Billy Peake, tell them to stay where they are or we sink all of you!'

The threat refuelled Hospodar's anger and he turned toward the *Lady Charlene*, shouting, 'Surrender to me! Or I'll hack you into pieces and throw you to the sharks!'

Captain Henley hailed, 'We'd rather sink than surrender to you.'

'That choice is yours!' Hospodar answered, and raised his hand, ready to wave his men into action.

'Wait!' shouted Easton from the *Lady Charlene*.

Hospodar roared, 'I wait only if you surrender your ship and come aboard bearing no arms.'

The announcement relieved Billy. He put his hand on Hospodar's forearm, saying, 'Thank you, Hospodar Pasha.'

Hospodar sloughed off his hand. 'Don't thank me,

infidel. You are right. We are sinking. But your friend is frightened by the threat of my men. I take advantage of his cowardice.'

As Hospodar turned back toward the *Lady Charlene*, continuing to shout across the gap closing between the two ships, quarrelling over terms of surrender, Billy turned away from the railing and descended the circular steps from the poop deck. He slumped across the main deck, through the crowd of restless pirates, dragging himself toward the hatch, not wanting to watch his fortune disappear again, this time in exchange for the safety of the woman his brother planned to marry.

Why at least could it not be for Jenny?

35

Make a decision, lad, and whether that decision be right or wrong, stand by it.

Those words of advice had been given to Billy Peake as a boy by his father, Anthony Roebuck Peake, and Billy kept reminding himself of that homely counsel as he worked in the hull of the *Cessina* with the few crew members from the *Lady Charlene* whom Hospodar had allowed to come aboard. Hospodar and his crew had disappeared on the *Lady Charlene* sailing north towards the China Sea.

Billy told himself to forget about the silver, that he had lost it before, but, worse, he had also once lost his dignity as a human being by betraying the *Zephyrine*. He at least had given Andrew what he wanted.

The *Cessina* was quickly taking in water and the colonial sailors from the *Lady Charlene* had never before seen caulking used in the Eastern manner, pitch smeared over canvas and strengthened by reeds and straw.

Billy, having spent many hours alone in the hull during the last voyage, as well as having laboured on the harbour wall on Slave Island, where straw and reeds had been used as a form of adhesive with lime for the stones, told the colonial sailors what he knew as well as finding containers of pitch and bundles of reeds in the ship. As Billy worked alongside them, he also explained ways in which the awkward ship sailed, luffed, pulled and strained with current and wind, all details necessary when reinforcing a temporary plug in a hole ripped by the cannot ball.

Four of the crew from the *Lady Charlene* were Scots sailors who had whaled in Nantucket; the stoutest and most red-faced of the group, Angus McFiddich, said, 'My daddy dabbed pitch on the roof of our wee corft back in the Highlands. So build me a fire, laddie, and watch me spread this golden pitch like a fine smear of butter fresh from Aunt Maggie's churn.'

Another sailor, Jocko Magnusson, found a heap of folded hemp in a dark recess of the hull and asked, 'Billy, are these put aside here for something of purpose or are they some queer Arabian sails?'

Billy recognised the hemp as coverings under which Hospodar's pirates had hidden before an attack. He answered abruptly, 'Use them. Use anything you find.'

Ezekiel Henley, the captain from the *Lady Charlene*, cautiously came step by step down the bamboo lader to the hold, ostensibly to inspect the crew's progress on plugging the hull. Eventually he pulled Billy aside, saying, 'My map shows we're lined south of this island called Ceylon. I am considering sailing north, hoping for help in these waters, Mr Peake . . .'

Billy had only briefly met and spoken a few words with Captain Henley after Hospodar had ordered the small party aboard the *Cessina.* He judged Henley to be an honest but unimaginative man and, remembering that Hospodar had kept south of Ceylon three days ago because of foul weather, he suggested, 'You would be wise, sir, to sail east, to my way of thinking.'

Captain Henley studied the map through wire spectacles perched on the bridge of his nose. He finally said, 'Such a route would take us to this long island here and, if I recognise these markings, there's a British fort on it called . . . yes, Fort Marlborough, where–'

'Fort Marlborough!' Billy was surprised they were sailing so close to Sumatra; he grabbed the map from Henley's hands.

Excited at seeing the marking of an elongated piece of land, Billy announced, 'My brother's stationed on Fort Marlborough, Captain! He's commissioned trade officer for the East India Company.

Captain Henley knew the name. 'Andrew Peake, of course. The Eastons both speak of Captain Peake and, if I'm not mistaken, your brother is betrothed to marry the young lady on deck.'

Billy tried not to grimace. 'Betrothed for over three years.'

'Then your brother's the man to help us organise a new ship to chase that heathen pirate in my *Lady*.'

'My brother's not on Sumatra at the moment, Captain. My brother is travelling to the mainland of Africa, visiting the native city of Mombasa on business for his employer, the East India Company.'

'No worry,' said Captain Henley, in a confident tone. 'The important thing now is that the wind's in our favour. We'll tack for Fort Marlborough with no further ado.'

Turning towards the bamboo ladder, Captain Henley paused and said, 'Mr Peake, I know you've been under great strain. Being held captive by those heathens and probably worse. But could you perhaps find time to come up on deck to speak to Mr Easton? He, as well as Miss Easton, are both understandably disturbed by recent developments and are both under great strain . . .'

Billy had not seen Gabriel Easton since Easton and Catherine had boarded the *Cessina*. He had no intention of seeing them now. He replied, 'Captain Henley, I have nothing to say to either Mr or Miss Easton. Not at the moment.'

'If there is contention between you, I respect it. Forgive me for saying, sir, but a few hospitable words might prove to be the best for the entire –' Henley gestured at the shadowy, questionable state of the hull, ' – ship.'

Billy disagreed. 'The best thing for this "ship", Captain Henley, is for me to stay down here working alongside your crew plugging that hole.'

Angus McFiddich, overhearing the conversation between Billy and Captain Henley, called, 'Go up, laddie. Go up. Me, Jocko and the lads here have the work all in hand.'

Billy frowned, but Captain Henley was already mounting the rungs of the ladder, calling to Gabriel Easton that Billy Peake was coming on deck to speak to him.

Gabriel Easton, looking tired, his face burned both by the sun and the wind, dishevelled in a tattered linen frock coat and breeches, nevertheless exuded more than a modicum of his old confidence. He generally appeared little different from the last time Billy had seen him on the stormy morning in his office high above Boston's harbour.

Easton, fingering the jagged, lightning-shaped scar on his cheek, said, 'Captain Henley tells me your advice is to sail east, that such a course would land us on Sumatra. I approve. We can obtain a ship there and chase those godless pirates who absconded in the *Lady Charlene*. He, Captain Henley, a good man, furthermore explained that your brother, Andrew, is presently not ensconced at Fort Marlborough. Sad. For I *do* want to see Andrew as, of course, does dear Catherine, and soon. But let us regain the *Lady Charlene* and then sail back to Fort Marlborough, celebrate and make plans for the wedding and enjoy –'

'Mr Easton, hopefully you're going nowhere but back to Boston.'

Easton stared at Billy.

Billy was tired and in no mood for argument, nor for

making plans for a marriage he did not approve of but which did not concern him. He continued, 'I cannot speak for my brother, but as far as I'm concerned, Mr Easton, you and your daughter will stay on Sumatra as long as it takes to find a ship to carry you back down around Africa's Cape, up the Atlantic to England or Boston.'

'Why . . . why . . . why, I don't understand? We're soon to be related. We're all in this together.'

'The only thing we're in together, Mr Easton, is a ship fastly taking in water.'

'But Andrew . . . my daughter . . .'

'Mr Easton, your daughter is betrothed to marry my brother, true. And I made a decision – rightly or wrongly – to put her life, her safety, her importance to Andrew, above the value of our silver. But that decision does not bind me from telling at long last my opinion both of you and your daughter.'

Billy eyed Easton, asking, 'And it was our silver ingots in the hold of the *Lady Charlene* which made her ride so low in the water, wasn't it?'

Easton reached for the scar, fingering it, nervously admitting, 'Of course. I never once denied it. But I suspected –'

Billy interrupted, 'Mr Easton, I won't tell you what *I* suspect about you or your daughter. But I will say –'

Billy, seeing Catherine approaching them across the deck, stopped.

Catherine Easton, trying to protect herself from the tropical sun, wore a large straw hat tied to her head by a ragged silken sash. She looked strained, tired from travel. She made no effort to speak to Billy, to thank him, to chastise him, nothing, not even to greet him.

Billy, knowing that he and Catherine Easton shared no fondness for one another, turned back to Easton, saying, 'I think it's best for us not to speak until we reach Sumatra. Our present situation here at sea is grave enough without us quarrelling, making accusations –'

'Easton stuttered, 'But . . . but, Billy, please –'

'I will tell you this much, Mr Easton. I believe you lied to me in Boston, that you tried to swindle both Andrew and me. I contend that you allowed me to sail aboard a slave ship giving Captain Kerr orders to abandon me at Razor Cove on Africa's Slave Coast. I can readily expand my list of accusations and I will in due time – but for the moment, I maintain we should have as little as possible, if anything, to do with or say to one another.'

Billy turned towards the hatch, starting to descend the bamboo ladder to the hull.

Easton grabbed for his arm. 'Kerr! He's the blackguard! It was Captain Kerr who broke away from the convoy! You know that fact for yourself. Kerr broke away three days out of Boston! But what you don't know is what happened to Kerr after he left you in Africa!'

Billy stared at Easton. He looked at Catherine idly standing nearby. He asked, 'Do we truly – *truly* – Mr Easton, want to discuss this now? In front of your daughter?'

'Is it not best always to air the truth?' asked Easton, his eyes bloodshot.'

'Truth about Jamaica?' asked Billy. 'Truth about Paris Rhinelander? Truth about you sending Rhinelander to Africa aboard the *Vandal Witch* and not to England as you had promised him?'

Catherine, tugging on her father's sleeve, asked, 'Did you tell Billy that Paris Rhinelander's father was rich enough to buy him the *Vandal Witch* in Jamaica?'

Easton muttered, 'Be quiet, Catherine. Not now.'

Billy looked at Catherine. 'Your father told me nothing about any recent occurrences in Jamaica. I would know nothing about them if Paris Rhinelander himself had not written a letter to me.'

Catherine quickly glanced at her father.

Easton scoffed, 'He's bluffing, Catherine. Ignore him. There's no letter.'

Billy nodded, 'Yes, I'm bluffing, Mr Easton. I'm bluffing by saying that Paris Rhinelander wrote me a letter and sent it by convoy to Sumatra. I'm also bluffing when I say that my brother, Andrew, read the letter and personally related its contents to me.'

Easton jeered, 'And when, pray, did you last see your precious brother, Billy Peake?'

Interrupting, Catherine shrilled, 'What did Andrew read in a letter written to you by Paris Rhinelander? That's what I demand to know – what did Andrew read in a letter? Some lies about *me*, I suppose! Some awful, dreadful lies!'

Turning to Catherine, Easton again insisted, 'Child be quiet! He's bluffing, I tell you. Or he's been exposed too long to the tropical elements and his brain is demented.'

Billy asked, 'Miss Easton, are you worried that Andrew has discovered your father procures lovers for you? That there is no man in Boston who can satisfy your . . . needs?'

'That's not true!' screamed Catherine, the sun bonnet tumbling from her head.

'What's not true?' asked Billy. 'That your father did not procure Paris Rhinelander for you, did not entice him to move to Boston from Port Royal? Or is it not true that you can find no man in Boston to please you?'

Frustrated, tired with the heat, exhausted from life aboard ship, Catherine turned to her father, scolding, 'Papa, you told me you paid Paris Rhinelander to hold his silence about me.'

'I said, child, silence your tongue.'

Easton turned back to Billy, snidely asking, 'And what else did you supposedly learn from this letter written to you by Paris Rhinelander – a man of dubious character and shady origins, I must add?'

Billy controlled his anger, saying, 'The letter sits on a desk in Sumatra. Why don't we all wait until we can read it very carefully, study it like a book, line by line, when we get there?'

Easton glanced quickly towards the poop deck, to Captain Henley standing alongside the tall rudder.

As if reading Easton's thoughts, Billy said, 'No, it will do no good to try and sail to another port, Mr Easton. It's either Sumatra or . . . drown.'

Catherine began to sob, asking 'Oh Papa, why did you take me from Boston? Why did we have to sail to Jamaica to get that silver from that old *Vandal Witch*?'

Billy had heard enough. He turned to descend the bamboo ladder, preferring not to witness an Easton family row. He had definitely noticed that Catherine Easton looked more than tired; she appeared disturbed, her eyes shining like a mad woman's. If an argument ensued between the Eastons, Billy was certain it would be unsavoury, not an event he wanted to witness.

'There's a curse on it, I swear,' sobbed Catherine Easton, leaning her head against her father's shoulder. 'There's a curse on that silver and I'm the one who has to suffer.'

'Shhh, dolly. Try to be brave.'

'But it's not fair,' Catherine hysterically sobbed. 'We don't know where your other convoy ships are. That dreadful Paris Rhinelander wrote some awful letter about me. Andrew will probably never marry me now. And, on top of everything, we're poor, oh, we're so poor!'

'No, we aren't poor, Catherine. We just don't have any money. Not at the moment. But I still have the trading company in Boston. We'll go back there. Some way, we'll start afresh.'

'Boston? Whatever happened to our plans to go back to London? The opera? A house in Mayfair or Belgravia? And shopping! I want to go shopping!'

'I told you, Catherine. We can't go to London, not for a while yet.'

'Oh, Papa, Papa! How can you do this to me?'

'I'm not trying to hurt you, Catherine. We haven't even arrived on Sumatra yet. Let's wait to see what happens there.'

Andrew will abuse me, that's what! And I won't like it.'

'It's our word against Paris Rhinelander's, isn't it?'

'Not any more. Paris Rhinelander and Billy Peake were on the same ship. So it's our words against Paris *and* Billy. Oh, none of this horridness would have happened, Papa, if you had been more clever than to put them on the same ship!'

'Catherine, never say your Papa's not clever.'

'Well, you're not! Sometimes you are stupid!'

'Be silent.'

She glared at him, her eyes ablaze in their sockets, as she demanded, 'We would not be here if you were clever, would we? If you were a clever business man?'

Easton's jagged scar twitched on the side of his face. 'What did you say?'

'I said you're not even a good business man. You're hopeless.'

'Catherine, I wish you had not said that.'

'Why not? It's the truth. You never were a good business man. If you had been, we wouldn't be poor now. You wouldn't have gone bankrupt in England. We'd still be living in London. No, you are stupid and dumb and –'

Easton slapped her.

Catherine held the side of her face, staring disbelievingly at him, glaring at him, hating him. Her eyes showed loathing, bitterness, the flare of madness.

Easton warned, 'Don't you ever say that to me again, you hear, Catherine?'

'You stupid, mean old man.'

He slapped her again.

Catherine, holding up both hands as protection, shouted, 'You stupid, mean, cruel . . . *dumb* man!'

Easton, jerking away Catherine's hands from her face, slapped her harder, ignoring her screams. He knocked her down to the deck, kicking her, hitting her until Captain Henley ran from the poop deck to pull him off her body.

Catherine lay curled on the deck, sobbing, screaming about the curse of Mexican silver ingots.

36

The wind dropped by sundown, gusting only enough to give a limp shape to the *Cessina*'s scarlet foresail; the snubbed prow pushed southeasterly through the slightly ruffled water. A current more than wind carried the ship through the inky darkness which had quickly enveloped the water at nightfall, now making vision impossible from deck.

Overhead, thick black clouds lay low in the sky, pieces of night's cotton muffling the sound. The air was heavy, humid, as if perfumed by the sweet scent of an approaching tropical storm.

All activity had ceased on deck. The atmosphere was almost religious. The Scottish sailors, having temporarily stanched the flow of water in the hull, had come up from the hold and waited quietly like mourners vigilant at a wake.

Captain Henley, still shocked by Easton's conduct, by a father physically attacking his own daughter, stood silently on the high poopdeck, stationed alongside the long-handled rudder, like a censorious parson inside his pulpit.

Gabriel Easton crouched miserably like a lost sinner in a far corner of the main deck, his head slumped between his knees.

Catherine Easton lay curled in a nest of hemp rope in the opposite corner of the main deck, mumbling to herself, occasionally sobbing, then giggling; she was speaking to an imaginary person, carrying on a conversation with a former servant, Nurse Bingey, who had tended her long ago in the nursery of their grand London home.

Billy Peake, standing at the foot of the main mast, studied all these people, watching how they each coped with the uncertainty of the situation, with overwhelming darkness. He occasionally glanced up at the distress flag, still hanging from the top mast, waiting, praying for the white pennant to snap in the wind, to announce that a wind would soon catch the main sail. But the only sounds he heard were the gentle lapping of surf against the hull, the occasional crack of the slackened foresail, the creak of the rudder, and Catherine Easton's disturbed voice, a sound caused by a mind snapped under strain, of someone who had perhaps always been unbalanced, troubled, but protected by the advantages, comforts, privileges provided by money.

'Ahoy! Identify yourself!'

The sudden call in the blackness startled Billy; he stiffened against the mainmast, looking around him in the thick darkness. The Scotsmen stood to immediate attention; Captain Henley stepped forward, trying to see through the murky darkness who had hailed them.

Through the night's blackness a voice again shouted, 'Identify yourself or we *sink* you!'

Billy raised his eyes, not to the distress flag, but high, high above him, for the voice seemed to be coming from above him, from a great height, as if from the sky, yes, the very heavens.

Wondering if he had gone as mad as Catherine Easton, Billy raised his head and timorously called, 'We're abandoned on ship . . . hoping to reach Fort Marlborough . . .'

The voice – with a heavy East London accent – boomed back heartily through the sooty night, 'Stop hoping, sailor, or you'll ram the hull of the *Devil's Dragoon* and then you'll have to answer to Commander Andrew Peake, who's in a bad enough mood without having drifters ram his ship in the middle of Marlborough harbour!'

'This is . . . Fort Marlborough?'

'It ain't The Nag's Head in Whitechapel!' roared back the voice. 'And more's the pity, sailor, because a shot of malt whisky in a pint of ale would be better to swill down than this soup!'

At the mention of malt whisky and ale in faraway pubs, a cheer went up from the Scotsmen aboard the *Cessina*.

At that same moment, a sudden gust puffed at the dark clouds, allowing a ray of strong moonlight to pierce through the blackness. It illuminated a gargantuan ship, a fabled East Indiaman, behind which lay a wharf edged by a long sandy beach.

The wind came stronger; clouds scudded, separating farther apart for the moon's bright beacon to shine on lush mountains, to light a range of dormant volcanoes, rich with tropical vegetation, to glow on a settlement of small grass cottages, palisades, larger houses with thatched roofs turned up at either end.

The accommodating breeze carried the rich scent of jasmine and sandalwood across the bay, and soon there was a twinkle of one light here, the glitter of another light there – a settlement welcoming in the night. The surf lazily licked a sandy beach lined with fishnets, catamarans, palm trees: a shoreline of the East Indian island of Sumatra.

Book Five
Pirate Masters

37

Andrew Peake, dressed in white breeches and a blue cutaway coat, lounged alongside Billy in a pair of deep buttoned-back leather chairs flanking a round oak table placed below tall mullioned windows in the stern cabin of the *Devil's Dragoon*, the Indiaman under Andrew's command, weighing eight hundred tons, stretching one hundred-and-fifty feet in length, and thirty-five feet across.

'There'll be plenty of time to show you Sumatra, old dog, and tell you about native life there when we return with Hospodar in chains.' Andrew sat with black leather boots crossed in front of him, hands casually gripped behind his head of wavy yellow hair.

Billy had not slept in the fourteen hours since he had arrived last night at Fort Marlborough aboard the crippled *Cessina*. The realisation that he was once again a free man, and sailing so quickly with Andrew aboard the *Devil's Dragoon* in pursuit of Hospodar and the silver, had quickly revived his energy.

Andrew had allocated his private living-quarters on Sumatra to Gabriel and Catherine Easton, moving for the night with Billy into his offices at the East India Company; there had been little time to find new clothes, so Billy had replaced his ragged garments with the clothes of a hearty young midshipman from one of the two marine ships escorting the *Devil's Dragoon*.

Dressed as an East India marine, Billy had a lot to bring Andrew up to date with – all that had happened to him since they had parted company on Slave Island. His role in the capture of the *Zephyrine*, how Hospodar had rewarded him with a new room in the fortress and a steady stream of concubines at his door. Billy confessed, 'I turned away all the girls except one who brought me a basket of figs, a sweet little thing bribing her way into the room to talk about . . . you.'

Andrew laughed. 'About me?'

'You haven't forgotten Mari?'

'Ah, Mari!' Andrew's grin widened as he remembered the slight Burmese girl and how she had resisted him trying to prime her for night-long love-making in his ship's cabin. He said, 'Mari indeed was a "sweet little thing". I would have liked to have taken her with me to Mombasa.'

Billy said, 'You still haven't had time to tell me what happened in Mombasa. But I didn't expect you to find the money for me there.'

Andrew was grateful for Billy's cheerfulness. 'I failed to raise the two-hundred-and-fifty gold weight both in Mombasa and from my Board of Governors back on Sumatra. I'll tell you all about that fiasco after I make one small complaint to you, old dog.'

'"An older brother's prerogative is to complain" – isn't that what you always used to tell me?'

Andrew laughed, nodding at his bullying ways, then proceeded, 'Old dog, why haven't you told me a little something about – what's that girl's name? Jennifer Brett?'

Billy sat forward in his chair – instantly his good spirits disappeared.

He demanded, 'How do you know about Jenny?'

Billy's sudden change of mood surprised Andrew.

'Andrew, where did you see or hear about Jenny?'

Andrew, began to stammer. 'A Spaniard . . . you remember a Spaniard bidding on you at the auction?'

Billy nodded. 'Hospodar often spoke of that Spaniard. In fact, Hospodar used him as a scapegoat when we lured ships into our trap. He called him "the Spanish Pirate".'

Andrew shook his head. 'I've heard that nickname for him. But no, Don Julio de Castenaldo is no more a pirate than you or I am, Billy. Perhaps not as much.'

Billy remained serious. 'Andrew, tell me about Jenny.'

'Jenny sent Don Julio to Slave Island to buy you, Billy.'

'Jenny sent Don Julio to buy . . . me?'

'Jenny and the man who bought her in Khartoum, the Sultan of Oman.'

'Jenny was bought? She's a slave?' Billy grew more anxious, demanding, 'Where is she, Andrew? You must tell me everything you know. Tell me immediately!'

'Calm down, old dog. Calm down.'

'But Andrew, I love her! I love Jenny!'

'You are convincing me of that fact very well, Billy. I read it in your face. I hear it in your voice. Believe me, I would not have hesitated to tell you about Jenny before now had I known–'

Billy anxiously interrupted, 'How did Don Julio find Jenny? Where is she? Who is this Sultan?'

'The Sultan of Oman, Billy,' Andrew said. 'He is a very humane person. Somewhat of an eccentric but very much of a gentleman. He purchased Jenny in Khartoum. Brought her south in a caravan. At this very moment, he and Jenny are in a palace outside Mombasa. Jenny is fine. And if you will sit there quietly in your chair, Billy, I will tell you everything I know.'

'I love her, Andrew! Do you know what I'm saying. I . . . *love . . . her . . .*'

Andrew stared at Billy, waiting for him to settle back into the chair so he could begin his story.

Billy listened to Andrew's story of Jenny and the Sultan of Oman, how the Sultan had given Don Julio a limit of two-hundred gold weight to buy Billy's freedom at the auction, how Don Julio had met Andrew in the Hall of the Corsairs, but did not divulge Andrew's true identity to Hospodar, and how Andrew had met Don Julio again in Mombasa.

Finally, unable any longer to hold his silence, Billy demanded, 'Did Don Julio take you to see Jenny when you met him in Mombasa after you left Slave Island?'

Andrew shrugged helplessly. 'I offered Don Julio bribes. Money. Favours. Everything. But he insisted that the Sultan would not let me – or anyone else – see Jenny. Not for the moment.'

'Why not?'

'Because of her condition.'

'What condition?'

'Her pregnancy. Arabs will not allow pregnant women–'

Andrew stopped, asking, 'You did know Jenny was pregnant, didn't you?'

Billy lowered his eyes, 'I suspected she might be.'

Andrew held his eyes on Billy slumped in his chair; he finally proceeded, 'To be brutally frank, Billy, I wondered if Don Julio might be trying to use Jenny's pregnancy to his advantage. To double-deal us against the Sultan of Oman. To get us to buy Jenny and your child.'

'He would do such a thing?'

'Don Julio is a professional mediator, Billy. What the Arabs call a *fakkak*. That's how he makes a living. But when I met him in Mombasa he was less interested in Jenny and more eager to know about white prisoners on Slave Island. I repeated your story to him about the European slaves Hospodar never puts on an auction block but sells by private treaty. Don Julio plans on going back to Slave Island and that's when–'

Andrew stopped.

'That's when what?'

'I shouldn't be telling you this, Billy. I don't want to raise your hopes.'

'Andrew, tell me.'

'Don Julio will try to bring Jenny with him to Slave Island. To meet you there.'

'Try! He bloody well do better than *try*!'

'Jenny might not be able to make the voyage, Billy. Also, there's ourselves to consider.'

'What about us?'

Andrew reminded him, 'We are on a chase after Hospodar. Or have you forgotten?'

Billy, gripping both fists in frustration, said, 'Everything is so close yet so far!'

'Have faith, old dog. Have faith.'

Raising his eyes and staring at Andrew, Billy said, 'Can I ask you a question?'

Andrew nodded.

'Do you think Catherine Easton could possibly be right? That the silver ingots might very well be cursed?'

'Cursed? No, Billy. If it had not been for the silver, you would not have been on the *Vandal Witch* and met Jenny. Curses do not bring love, Billy.'

'But if it had not been for the silver, Andrew, you might not have lost Catherine.'

Taking a deep breath, Andrew said, 'Fine. Let's talk about me for a moment. To be truthful, I reread your friend's letter after returning to Sumatra from Mombasa. And knowing more facts after I had spoken to you in the fortress, I realized from the letter how lucky I was – or am – to have escaped marrying Catherine Easton.' He tapped the breast pocket of his jacket.

Billy looked at the jacket. 'What do you have there?'

'The letter from Paris Rhinelander.'

'But you gave Rhinelander's letter to Gabriel Easton this morning. When he came from your rooms to the pier to bid us farewell. I saw you do it.'

'I most certainly did no such thing.'

'But I saw you hand him an envelope before we stepped into the shoreboat to bring us to the *Dragoon*.'

'Perhaps so. But the envelope most certainly did not contain your friend's letter. Why would I ever do a thing like that?'

'But Easton demanded the letter. He said he understood it contained slanderous material about his daughter, and that he would take us both to a court of law to obtain it.'

'Exactly! How dare a man who tried to cheat us – rob us of our inheritance – make such demands!'

'But you remained so calm when he was making those outrageous demands.'

'Is it wise to become as foolish as fools?'

'What did you give him?'

Andrew shrugged.

'Andrew Reynolds Peake, what did you give Gabriel

Easton in that envelope this morning when we left Sumatra?'

Andrew turned away from Billy. 'I earn a decent amount of money as Commander for the East India Company. And last night, after seeing the Eastons sitting like a pair of ragtag gypsies in my quarters, I decided to give them money for a comfortable journey back to the Colonies, as well as a bank draft redeemable in Boston.'

'You gave them money?'

Andrew nodded.

'That was very generous of you.'

Andrew shrugged. 'It's plain to see that Catherine's going to need a long, recuperative rest. Medical attention requires money, Billy, money which the Eastons might not have in the immediate future.'

Andrew, withdrawing a thick packet from inside his jacket, flippantly reminded Billy, 'And do not forget, old dog, that I had a nickname, too.'

Billy nodded, smiling. 'I remember . . . Robin Hood.'

Andrew handed the envelope to Billy and left the cabin.

Billy, alone in the cabin, sat in the chair, staring at the envelope in his lap.

Did he want to open and read the letter? Dredge up memories from the past? Learn how Paris Rhinelander had sailed back to Jamaica aboard the *Vandal Witch*? How the miserable slave cargo and Captain Kerr had died a wretched death from the flux? Catch a glimpse of the far distant past? Or would he rather sit here, trying to solve some problems of the future?

Billy chose the future. And tucking the letter into the pocket of his midshipman's jacket, he immediately began touching the tips of his fingers, counting months backwards to see if he could indeed already be a father.

38

Andrew estimated that Hospodar had four days' gain on them and, allowing for Hospodar's cargo to diminish his speed, Andrew considered the *Devil's Dragoon*'s chances to be fair for overtaking the *Lady Charlene*.

In his judgement of the possible distance between the two ships, Andrew hoped to increase his advantages by sending ahead two Marine ships which the East India Company had allotted him in his attempt to catch the pirate, the two ships ordered to leave despatches at prearranged stations dotted along the China Sea, or to return to Andrew with reports.

Eight, nine, ten, eleven, then a dozen days passed. But no report arrived from the Marines, and no despatches appeared at any station.

Becoming vexed as days passed as quickly as leagues, Andrew began to doubt the wisdom of choosing a route along the Philippine Islands, of following Hospodar into the great China Sea.

When neither of the Marine ships appeared after the third week out of Fort Marlborough, and after Andrew still found no sign waiting for him at the next station, the Paracel Islands located three-quarters of the way across the South China Sea, he began to wonder if Hospodar in fact had not sailed to Canton as he had suspected but, instead, had taken the silver ingots back to Slave Island – or to some other port.

Andrew and Billy sat at supper in the stern cabin of the *Devil's Dragoon*, over a meal of roast fowl, rice, and a root vegetable called *kiline*.

'Billy, tell me about this Grand Master of Slave Island,' Andrew said, ignoring his portion of food tastefully arranged on a white porcelain plate banded with blue and gold. 'Is Hospodar the kind of man to risk meddling in foreign revolutions? Is he brave enough to go to China at this moment?'

The food aboard the *Devil's Dragoon* was always delicious as well as being plentiful, and Billy gobbled more than his share at every sitting, pleased to have left his days of dried fish and a calabash of gruel in the past.

Wiping a dab of grease from his chin, Billy sipped at his crystal glass of claret, answering, 'Hospodar is cautious, a man who worries about the opinions of his superiors.'

'He wasn't too worried to sell white slaves to the Chinese!' Andrew was not even enjoying the decanter of rich claret. 'What else do you know about Hospodar? What do you think of him?'

'Hospodar is a man who likes to be alone. He broods. He ponders. But I suspect he's also impulsive, a bit of a renegade.'

'Does he have a dread of making calamitous mistakes? Is he fearful of taking a wrong turn?'

Billy pondered the question, chewing a mouthful of the root vegetable, deciding he liked its celeriac taste.

Finally, he replied, 'I often heard Hospodar complain about men telling lies about him to the Grand Sultan in Constantinople. He's worried about his reputation in the Sublime Porte.'

'That would be natural for a man in his position. And no clue to me about his true character.' Andrew rose from the table and began to stride the length of the panelled cabin. He vexed, 'Am I wasting everybody's time on some wild goose chase? Is Hospodar not going to China with our silver?'

Billy reminded his brother, 'Hospodar sailed north-east when he left on the *Lady Charlene*. There was no reason for him to deceive Captain Henley and us poor wretches abandoned on the *Cessina*. We were sinking and how could we follow him?'

'True. He would not be nervous of you following him. Probably not even escaping that ship.' Andrew remained agitated as he continued pacing, saying, 'Who is he frightened of, Billy? Is he frightened, is he cautious of anybody?'

Billy, leaning across the round table to fork a fowl's leg from Andrew's unfinished plate, asked, 'He worries about somebody called the Dey of Algiers.'

Andrew stopped; he turned around to look at Billy. 'The Dey of Algiers?'

'Ummm.' Billy was thoroughly enjoying the drumstick.

Andrew said, 'Yes, I saw the Dey of Algiers at the auction sale on Slave Island. I noticed that he and Hospodar did not speak. Of course. Why did I not think of that before?'

'Think of what?' Billy dropped the bone to his plate.

'The Dey of Algiers!' Andrew grew more excited, clasping his hands behind his back, pacing more quickly up and down the cabin. 'Algiers is in North Africa. The cornerstone of the old Barbary Empire. An age-old trader with – and enemy of – Spain. Spain is rich with minerals from the New World and geographically very close to North Africa. Algiers is the market-place for all minerals in the Ottoman Empire. But, if Hospodar and the Dey of Algiers are enemies . . . and if Hospodar does not want the Sublime Porte to know he's amassing a private fortune, then–'

'Then what?'

Andrew pounded the fist of one hand into the palm of the other. 'Yes! Hospodar is indeed sailing to China! But where is he? *Where is he*? Where is the bloody bastard?'

39

Gabriel Easton wished he had never conceived the idea of bringing his daughter with him from Boston on an arduous long sea voyage to the East. The risk of scandal in New England did not match the calamities they were encountering here in the Indian Ocean.

All hope of marrying Catherine to Andrew Peake had disappeared, was gone. The envelope of bank notes, and the letter of credit for the Boston bank which Andrew had given him, answered that question, along with Andrew's instructions about the next ship sailing from Sumatra. Andrew was telling him to leave Fort Marlborough with Catherine before he and Billy returned.

Easton, sitting in a cool evening breeze on the wooden verandah of Andrew's quarters in the settlement of Fort Marlborough, fleetingly considered keeping the money and remaining here on Sumatra. What did he have to leave for? He had heard no word about his convoy and, even if six of the seven ships reached China, what profit would there be in it for him? His English creditors would quickly grasp any financial rewards. His hope for riches had been the silver.

Such a notion, though, was folly. The idea of remaining here in Fort Marlborough and trying to reinstate Catherine – and himself – would not only be foiled by Billy's testimony against him, but also by Captain Henley's change of attitude. The sea captain, although still suffering from being adrift aboard the *Cessina*, said vile things against Easton for physically attacking his own daughter.

Catherine. Yes, the root of all Easton's problems was his daughter, he realised, and now she was oscillating between madness and a worrisome lucidity, between being a child and a brazen-mouthed whore.

None of Catherine's foul words, though, were as hurtful to Easton as her harangue against him for being an unsuccessful businessman, a failure in life. That accusation had stung the worse because secretly Easton knew it was true.

A sudden noise in the bedroom adjoining the verandah disturbed him and, rising from his rattan chair, he called, 'Catherine, have you awakened from your nap?'

Receiving no answer, he called again, and still hearing

nothing, he went into the white-washed room where he saw the empty bed where she had only moments ago been resting.

Looking around the room, he called, 'Catherine?'

The room was furnished simply, in cane and mahogany furniture, a man's room, spartan and tidy, with only a few decorations on the walls – crossed sabres, a pair of flintlocks, and a large pastel drawing of Catherine in a gold oval frame.

Looking at the portrait, Easton thought, 'How Andrew cherished that girl. But she went and ruined everything, everything, for me as well as herself.'

Moving toward the archway separating the bedroom from the small sitting-room where he slept, Easton again called, 'Catherine, are you in there?'

Alarmed when he did not find her in the second room, Easton moved to the door and saw a fat Eastern woman – Andrew's housekeeper – waddling down the hallway.

He called, 'Good woman, did you see my daughter leave?'

The woman, speaking the pidgin English which the natives of Fort Marlborough had learnt from the British, answered, 'Your girl say go meet you, sir.'

'Meet me?'

Smiling a mouth of toothless gums, the native woman answered, 'Down below, sir. Down below in square.'

'But I was on the verandah, you fool!'

The woman's round face fell.

'Never mind,' Easton said, quickly, 'Which way did she go?'

The woman pointed down the long hallway, toward the narrow stairway leading to the square.

Breathless by the time he reached the foot of the steep wooden staircase, Easton saw that the cobbled square was already filling with people beginning their evening promenade around the rain trees. He wondered if he should go upstairs to put on his coat, so as not to risk ruining his reputation by running around the small settlement in his shirtsleeves.

Spotting a stabler to whom Andrew had introduced him,

Easton forgot about etiquette and hurried across the corner of the square.

'Young man,' he called to the dusky-skinned youth. 'Did you perchance see my daughter pass?'

'Daughter?'

'A young girl. White dress. Blonde hair.' Easton held out his hand, saying, 'This tall.'

Nodding, the stabler said, 'Yes, yes. She go look for brother.'

Easton now was totally confused. 'Brother?'

'Brother who sail tonight to Cape. Sail on big ship in harbour. But I tell her sailor doss hall no place for young lady to go. But she go there.'

'A doss . . . house?'

The stabler nodded, saying, 'Big hall where all sailors sleep when they come on island.'

Easton already feared the worst. 'And where is this sailors' . . . doss house?'

The stabler pointed to the bottom of the square. 'Very close.'

Gabriel Easton realized he had better go back upstairs to the room, not only for his frock coat, but for the brace of flintlocks he had seen on the wall.

His clothing soaked with perspiration by the time he returned to the square, Gabriel Easton kept to the building's edge, carefully moving along the rain gutters which edged the cobblestones, moving stealthily in the growing shadows toward the large, barn-like structure clearly marked 'Sailors Rest and Haven'.

Easton's heart quickened as he heard a man slur, 'She's a right drab, fair enough. A right strumpet straight from old London.'

'Me? I haven't seen such a molly since I left home,' added another man. 'I ain't seen such an eager whore since leaving Liverpool.'

Easton slipped through the door, both hands inside his frockcoat, resting on the butts of the flintlocks tucked into his waistband; his eyes became accustomed to the light inside the sleeping hall and, as he surveyed the field of bedrolls spread across the straw-covered floor, he saw a group of men gathered in a corner, men talking amongst themselves.

Moving towards the group, Easton next heard a woman's voice, a voice he barely recognized, saying, 'Come on! You say you're all men. Let's see some proof of it!'

Catherine lay inside the circle of men, her legs spread as a red-haired young man drove his penis into her vagina and she propped herself up on her elbows looking at the other men.

Her hair hanging in dirty shanks around her dirt-smeared face, she goaded, 'Men you call yourselves – don't make me laugh! I'm saying I want two pricks inside me together. But it's going to take a longer prick to fit in alongside this piece of meat!'

Catherine's words, her appearance, momentarily stunned Easton. This was worse than anything he had ever before seen or heard, even from her.

A black-haired sailor stepped forward, a young man who dropped his trousers to his knees and, holding a long penis in one fist, he asked, 'How's this, my beauty?'

Catherine was not impressed. 'Let's see what it can do before we start pinning blue ribbons on you!'

The sailors roared with laughter in the circle they had formed around Catherine and her temporary lover.

Waving the black-haired sailor to step forward, she said, 'So let me teach you how to screw with two pricks together.'

Pushing at the red-head still lying on top of her, she ordered, 'You rise to your knees, Red, and fall on your back, but don't take your willy out of me, hear?'

Waving again at the other sailor, she prompted, 'Now, boy, you come and squat in front of your friend. Squat facing me. And poke down that big willy of yours, driving it in alongside the small sausage your friend's jabbing me with. Here. You might need some greasing–'

Catherine raised one hand to her mouth and spat on her

palm, then handed the saliva to the sailor for lubrication.

The gesture made Easton stumble back, shaking his head with disbelief, unable to comprehend that this coarse looking, foul-speaking young woman was his very own daughter. But there was no doubt about it. She was! She was his . . . baby girl!

Catherine, lowering her back to the straw as the two sailors worked to obey her instructions, beckoned with both hands to the other sailors, coaxing, 'What's the matter, men? Don't you have pricks between your legs? Let me see them? Let me see how big they can get!'

Suddenly, a loud boom echoed inside the sleeping hall; the sailors pulled back in horror from Catherine, as a fountain of blood sprang from the centre of her forehead in a rich scarlet stream.

Gabriel Easton, standing over his daughter, dropped one flintlock on her lifeless body, and then raise the other weapon, put it toward his own head, and pressed his finger on the trigger to take his own life as well.

40

The sign finally appeared, a towering white pyramid on the western horizon, great canvas sails of a Marine frigate slanting across silver-capped waves towards the *Devil's Dragoon*, bringing Andrew word of Hospodar's whereabouts.

Captain Rodney Coalport, Commander Adjutant of the frigate, crossed between the two ships in a deck boat, greeting Andrew with military salutations, then with a gentleman's handshake, reporting, 'The Turk has been found. Along the Chinese coastline of Tongkin.'

Andrew anxiously asked, 'Did he fire on you or try to take flight?'

Coalport, distinguished by severe aquiline features, replied, 'It was eventide, sir. We were preparing to send a party ashore to fetch fresh drinking water when we recognised our prey in a cove. We followed your orders, sir, and gave an immediate two flag salute. Obviously, sir, we cancelled our foray ashore and resumed sailing along the coastline, conducting our departure slowly, as if the Turk was a friendly ship.'

'What flag does he fly?'

'British colonial, sir.' Coalport's face was immobile, his voice without expression. 'As well as a convoy pennant, sir.'

Andrew was not surprised that Hospodar still manned the American ship as part of Easton's convoy.

He asked, 'Does our other ship remain at chase?'

'From a distance, sir. Preparing to wait near the Gulf of Tongkin.'

'Tongkin?' Andrew knew the section of Chinese coastline. 'Hospodar's headed for Canton, there's no doubt of that.'

He then dismissed Captain Coalport, sending him back to Fort Marlborough with the report as he himself sailed to rendezvous with the other East India frigate.

It was late afternoon, three days later, when Andrew located the second Marine frigate: he liaised with the commanding officer, Cedric Buckingham, and preceded the frigate to a cove where Hospodar was spending the night.

Fog enshrouded the rippling water and lightly-timbered coastline; Andrew and Buckingham agreed that Hospodar would undoubtedly weigh anchor when the fog lifted and set sail on the last leg of the voyage to Canton.

Andrew said, 'We must attack in the fog.'

Buckingham, a ruddy-faced man with a large stomach, considered the fog, saying, 'Excuse me, sir, but you must have a damn good plan if you plan to attack in this porridge.'

'I have an excellent plan, Mr Buckingham,' Andrew answered. 'And it involves you being prepared to back me at precisely the correct moment.'

Andrew proceeded to explain his plan, dismissed the officer, then met with Billy to inform him that they would go in long boats to surprise Hospodar and his pirate crew sleeping aboard the *Lady Charlene*.

A few hours later, the fog thicker than it had been before midnight, but with daybreak now gently breaking through the grey haze, Billy and Andrew sat in the prow of the first of three long boats. The oarsmen quickly, steadily cut the oaken blades into the still morning water, the three boats moving closer towards the *Lady Charlene*.

Billy, hunched forward in the prow, eyes alert to every shadow in the greyness, whispered, 'This dark may be morning, Andrew, but hell itself can't be so black.'

Andrew sat upright, his tricorne placed forward on his brow. 'Billy, when night falls in these waters, it spreads like ink from an octopus.'

Billy, remembering sailing into Marlborough Bay in similar murkiness, whispered, 'Men hereabouts must have eyes like cats.'

As the oars cut into the smooth pewter water, pulling the three craft through the fog, Billy went on, 'Andrew, will the gunman be able to strike through this with a cannon?'

Andrew had not yet told Billy all his plan; he glanced back over his shoulder at the other two long boats, seeing them following slowly in the wake; he then strained to see the vague outline of Buckingham's frigate in the near distance.

He answered, 'Worry more about timing than visibility, old dog.'

'From the Marines?'

Andrew nodded. 'But don't worry when they fire. It'll only be a smudge ball.'

'And what's that?'

'A cannon ball Lord Kierhan used in India. More sulphur than powder.'

Billy tapped his shoulder.

Andrew turned and, looking, he saw the full shape of the *Lady Charlene* rising only a few yards in front of them.

Now, noises could be heard floating across the water: the hack of a cough, the clank of a tin kettle, the creak of the rigging. . .

Andrew motioned to his oarsmen; all movement ceased on the long boats, except for one sailor in each boat who gently, quickly, stealthily paddled them around the stern of the *Lady Charlene.*

The three small craft then waited in the darkness, rocking gently in the rippled surf, waiting for–

Boom! A cannon thundered behind them; a whistling sound sped across the water and, in one loud explosion, the *Lady Charlene* flashed in the early morning's faint light.

As an instant cloud of white smoke spread across its deck, up the masts, from poop to jib, Andrew jumped to his feet, shouting, 'Now! Aboard!'

Springing towards the nettings, Andrew and Billy led the men up to the taffrail; the crews from the other two long boats following, their sabres and flintlocks drawn and primed.

Hospodar's pirates poured from the ship's hold, the air filled with loud shouts and screams.

Despite the fog, and smoke from the sulphur ball, a confrontation began with clash of steel and pop, pop, pop of firelocks.

Andrew and Billy, holding handkerchiefs to their faces as protection against the sulphur, moved quickly toward the main cabin; Billy carried a brace of pistols; Andrew was armed with a sabre in one hand, a flintlock in the other.

As the fighting grew louder behind them, the clatter of sabres, explosions of pistols, the ripping of sails, Andrew and Billy halted in front of the main cabin's door.

Andrew, leaning his head forward to hear voices, beckoned Billy to listen, asking, 'Is that . . . Hospodar?'

Billy listened, shrugged.

Inside the cabin, shouting now thundered, but Billy still shook his head – he did not recognize the voice.

Andrew raised his leg, pulled back his foot, and kicked open the door; he and Billy dashed inside, positioning themselves on either side of the door jamb, standing ready with flintlocks and sabre in hand as smoke from the deck spread quickly into the cabin.

When the sulphurous haze began to lift, they saw the shape of a dusky-skinned man standing in the middle of the small cabin, naked to the waist, grasping a cane bastinado in one hand, holding the other hand across his chest as he coughed from the fumes.

Then they saw a man lying on the floor, a naked man whose hands and ankles were trussed with leather thongs, his buttocks red from being caned with the bastinado.

'Hospodar!' gasped Billy.

Andrew held the tip of his sabre to the throat of the dusky man whilst he grabbed a robe from a chair and threw it at Hospodar.

He said, 'My men cannot take you naked to Fort Marlborough!'

Then, pushing the dusky prisoner out of the door, Andrew disappeared from the cabin.

But Billy remained, staring at Hospodar, gaping at the ladder of red welts on his back, his bare buttocks.

In a weak voice, Hospodar gasped, '. . . infidel.'

The sound surprised Billy and he backed toward the door.

'Infidel . . . answer me one question . . . only one question . . .'

Billy hesitated by the door, saying, 'Sir?'

'Infidel . . . tell me . . .'

'Tell you what . . . sir?'

'Tell me what it was like . . . making love . . . to my wife?'

Billy, feeling a rush of pity for this wretched creature

bound on the floor like a hare, answered with a sudden inspiration.

'Sir, your wife . . . your wife made me pretend I was you, Hospodar . . . Pasha.'

Turning, Billy fled from the cabin.

41

Pleased to have Hospodar captured but dissatisfied that a job was still incomplete, Andrew despatched his Indiaman along with the Marine frigate, back to Sumatra, giving Captain Buckingham orders to take Hospodar prisoner, keeping him – along with the pirates – in bilboes, to be held for trial at Fort Marlborough. He then embarked to sail with Billy, accompanied by a skeleton crew, aboard the colonial brig, the *Lady Charlene*, taking the silver to Canton.

Enjoying the lee wind speeding them along the China Coast, Billy stood with Andrew in the forecastle, his hair yellow as cornsilk and his face deeply bronzed; he said, 'You told your colleagues we sail for Canton. But you didn't tell them we plan to sail down to Slave Island from there.'

Andrew sniffed the sweet breeze wafting from a coastline dotted with windswept pine. 'The less Fort Marlborough knows about my activities, the better.'

'Will the Company punish you for evacuating your ship?'

'But the *Devil Dragoon*'s mine, Billy. I'm lord of the castle. You know that. I own the bottom.'

'Bottom?'

'That's East India Company language. When a commander owns a ship as I do, he owns the "bottom", what's left on an old ship, a keel. The "bottom" rights are passed from one owner to another. It's a strange law, a queer saying, and I don't truly understand it myself or how it got started.'

'If you don't understand, then how's a noddy like me to grasp it?'

'Stick around, old dog, and you'll learn the mysteries of the East India Company. There may be a lot of headaches and problems. But there's adventure waiting for a man in the good old Company, too.'

'You like working with . . . the Company, don't you?'

'It's like being part of an institution, old dog. The Company was originally chartered back in sixteen hundred by Good Queen Bess, founded by one-hundred-and-one English bankers and merchants, seeking the Crown's permission to trade beyond the Straits of Magellan and the Cape of Good Hope.'

'They must have done a good job of it. That was over a hundred-and-fifty years ago.'

'The spice trade was new then, and so good a job did the Company do that they quickly outflanked the Dutch and the Portuguese who'd been controlling the East Indies up until then. They began bringing everything back to the London docks – silks, cottons, teas, peppers.'

'Judging from your contentment, Andrew, you prefer adventure to trade.'

Andrew playfully slugged Billy. 'Am I too different from you, old dog?'

Time passed quickly, jubilantly, for Andrew and Billy as they skirted the southern China coast; they passed from the subject of the East India Company to stories about the volcanic islands of Sumatra and Java, to theories about Gabriel and Catherine Easton's future.

The early morning sun glimmered across the water; Andrew and Billy were on deck debating how they could find a cargo for Captain Henley to take back to the New World, when, suddenly, a cannon fired from the shore across their prow.

Billy looked toward the scrub pines. 'What was that?'

Andrew studied the craggy granite boulders. 'A warning

salvo. We are foreigners in Chinese waters. Also, a revolution's going on–'

He stopped; he was listening to a new sound.

From beyond their prow came the beating of drums, a rapid sound rising from low, long narrow boats quickly approaching them from the distance.

Oriental oarsmen with shaved heads rowed in unison to the steady rhythm of the deep drumbeat, red oars rising and dipping like the multiple wings of a dragonfly, making the long vessels skim over the water along the coastline.

The boats surrounded the *Lady Charlene* and, soon, Chinese soldiers climbed aboard, armed with long sabres, moving quickly in a search around deck in their bare feet.

Satisfied, they shouted over the portside and a short Oriental man – dressed in loose-fitting red-and-black striped pantaloons and robe – quickly climbed up the ladder and walked directly to Andrew and Billy.

Andrew bowed to the short man, elbowing Billy to do likewise; he produced a brass cartouche from his jacket pocket, extracted a piece of vellum, and handed it to the Oriental.

The Oriental studied the document, motioned for his men to search the boat and remained standing with Andrew and Billy, silent and unsmiling, until the soldiers returned to report to him in a dialect neither Andrew nor Billy understood.

The Oriental bowed, returned the document to Andrew, and waved his men towards the ladder.

The drums resumed, striking a pace for the long scarlet oars, and the narrow boats began escorting the *Lady Charlene* along the craggy coastline.

The land quickly became covered with signs of habitation, of grass huts, black tents, people living in caves and stone shelters.

Soon, they were moving into a wide bay, then a harbour crowded with boats of many styles and sizes, with canvas and rattan and brown leather sails.

As the long narrow boats now towed the *Lady Charlene* through the harbour congestion, Billy stared at the odd collection of vessels, and at a city rising like a squat jungle on a hill.

He asked, 'Canton?'

Andrew nodded and pointed toward a junk built with a high poop deck and black battened sails.

He announced, 'And there, old dog, is Master Hu'An.'

Master Hu'An, an obese man with a small black silk hat perched atop his round shaven head, rested on a teakwood bench in the poop of his junk. Attendants flurried around him, beating silk fans, shading him with umbrellas fringed with pearls, waving porcelain jars of incense in the air, holding wicker cages of warbling canaries, making notations on clay tablets, bringing, removing cups of drink, food, powders.

Billy and Andrew, sitting below Master Hu'An on the junk's main deck like visitors to a royal court, accepted the trading lord's hospitality of rice wine, nut cakes and delicate pastries, but they spoke neither to him nor to one another, as they watched the harbour activity, waiting for scriveners to count and appraise the ingots in the hold of the *Lady Charlene* anchored alongside the junk.

By midday, Billy and Andrew had grown accustomed to the harbour stench, and to the cacophony of shrill voices, clanging bells, chattering stewards, the movements of servants, soldiers, guards.

The sun passed its midday zenith, and was sinking down the western sky, when Master Hu'An finally raised his right hand, pressing together the cluster of long lacquered fingernails, beckoning Andrew and Billy to rise and approach him.

They mounted the steps to the poop, feeling like commoners being commanded to appear before royalty.

'English sirs.' Master Hu'An bowed, speaking in slow, perfectly enunciated English. 'My stewards conform they count five hundred thousand gold weight of silver bricks in your ship, that the brocks are of pure silver, and are now in my storehouses.'

Andrew nodded his consent.

Master Hu'An, pointing his long fingernails towards the *Lady Charlene*, continued, 'My stewards also tell me bricks of gold equalling the same value have been carried to your ship. You may now count them.'

Andrew and Billy looked toward the brig, seeing a formidable line of soldiers staring at them, men resting swords on their shoulders, their faces set like plaster masks.

Andrew bowed to Master Hu'An. 'We accept your word, Master Hu'An.'

'You are most gracious, English Sirs.'

'And you, Master Hu'An, are honourable.'

'I respect your courtesy and ask you, English Sirs, to respect the present situation in China.' Master Hu'An explained. 'You arrived in Canton only this morning. Please do not think us unhospitable by not extending you more kindness. Our land is not prepared in these troubled days to greet visitors as we have done in the past. We can only serve you by giving quick and safe passage in and out of our waters.'

Andrew began to speak but Billy stepped forward.

He said, 'Master Hu'An, may I ask a question?'

Andrew whispered, 'No, Billy . . .'

Billy proceeded, 'Sir, did a convoy from the Americas, six ships sent by Gabriel Easton, arrive in Canton?'

Master Hu'An nodded. 'Six ships arrived here from the Americas. Six ships bringing furs, tobacco, ironware. They unloaded their cargo. But departed with less, far less than you, English Sirs.'

Andrew stepped alongside Billy, saying quickly, 'We are grateful for your generosity.'

'We want to give more.' Master Hu'An shook his head, adding, 'We regret these are sleeping days for the traders of China.'

Andrew praised, 'But with wise men like you, Master Hu'An, prosperity is not far ahead for your land.'

'There are kings from many provinces in China who want to eat from the same bowl of power. We merchants of Canton can only be their servants.'

Master Hu'An bade Andrew and Billy a safe voyage out of China, ordering his guards to escort them from the harbour and, as the drums resumed their heavy tattoo, a path broke through the tangle of junks, sampans and dhows, and the *Lady Charlene* moved back toward the coastline.

A bright silver crescent hung in the dark China sky, the drums having disappeared into the night, when Andrew and Billy finally threw their arms around one another, dancing on the deck of the *Lady Charlene*, then broke open a keg of brandy to treat the crew to a celebration.

Billy, raising his cup, hailed, 'And here's to my brother! The lad who first realized that one man's silver is another man's . . . *gold*!'

Andrew, laughingly accepting the toast, rejoindered, 'And here's to my baby brother who never once harboured doubt, nor lost faith, in my integrity and loyalty to him!'

Billy gave him two fingers up. And, again, the crew laughed, although knowing noting of the history which had led to this floating celebration in the South China Sea.

42

'I was listening to you talk to that fat Chinaman in Canton, Andrew, and you sounded like a fine lord in Parliament, giving speeches. I could never do that, talk like you, all manners and graces.'

'It comes from practice, old dog. There's no art to talking. If the Irish can do it, anybody can.'

'No, you've got the knack, Andrew. My tongue gets tied and I trip over words as if they were stones in my path. Except when I get angry, and what good does it do me then? I don't like to be angry.'

'Billy, while you've been listening to me in these days sailing down from China, I've been looking at you. And do you know what I've been seeing?'

Billy shook his head.

'Seeing you dressed in those midshipman's clothes, Billy, I've been seeing a new recruit for the Company.'

'The East India Company?' Billy scoffed. 'You're joking.'

'Not necessarily like me. I don't think you have the patience for the politics needed for a trading commander. I was thinking more about the possibility of you joining the Marines.'

'Me? In a navy?'

'I could get you a place as midshipman. It might be worthy of your consideration. The pay's not much. But you don't need the money, do you? You're a very rich young man.'

Billy considered the proposal, then said as he leaned against the starboard railing, staring out at the blue-green churn of the sea, 'Andrew, I made a promise to myself after I betrayed those poor people aboard the *Zephyrine*. I promised myself I would help people escape from slavery. Not one or two people. But as many as I could. Like a job.'

'A good and noble decision,' Andrew said. 'And who knows? You might be able to do that very thing in service to the Company.'

Billy realized that Andrew was not joking about the possibility of him remaining in the East Indies.

Andrew added, 'I know you've talked about buying farmland in the Virginias, and you now can afford to purchase a fine Crown lease in America.'

Billy stared out at sea. He had been putting off making any decision about the future, about what he planned to do after the Chinese adventure.

He confessed, 'To be honest, Andrew, I don't know what I'm going to do until I find . . . Jenny.'

Andrew repeated the promise he had made to Billy, 'If there's no sign of Jenny at Slave Island, then we'll head straight to the African mainland to see the Sultan of Oman himself. Whether he be in Mombasa or Madagascar or wherever.'

'I appreciate you taking this time, Andrew. And although you may own the bottom – or top – or whatever you own of the *Devil's Dragoon*, you're still a Commander, and I know you can't go sailing around the seas with me trying to find my Jenny lass.'

'Don't forget, old dog. I'm as rich as you are now. And if the Board of Governors raises hell, I'll make an offer on all their . . . bottoms!'

Billy laughed; but, somehow, his laughter did not ring true; he was troubled, anxious to reach Slave Island, to see or receive word from Jenny.

Billy spent less and less time with Andrew, working more and more with the crew, or merely standing alone by the railing, feeling the sea spray, considering what Andrew had said to him about joining the East India Company, becoming a midshipman, to stay in the East.

The East Indies. Southeast Asia and the Orient. The Indian Ocean. The gateway to the challenging Pacific Ocean. Billy like this part of the world. The exotic sights. Sweet smells intermixed with foul. Coral reefs and thorn trees and waxy white flowers and people with gold yellow skin. The Arabs. The Africans. The Indians. The Orientals. The intrigue which kept a man's mind sharp, alert, forever working. A feeling of challenges, of ancient civilizations, but also the adventure of a fresh, new spirit.

Thinking about remaining here, fulfilling a promise he had made to himself, Billy reconsidered the notion of sailing back to America, perhaps even to buy rich farmland in England, in Dorset, Somerset, even down in Cornwall. But everything depended on how quickly he found Jenny.

Billy's emotions – desires – became more confused the farther they sailed south, the closer they moved toward the fortress, and the possibility of finding – or not finding – Jenny.

Andrew called from the forecastle. 'Old dog, look to the south.'

Billy looked in the afternoon's misty light.

'Isn't that smoke?'

Billy saw what at first appeared to be storm clouds, but the more he studied them, the more he realized they were not clouds, not a tempest, not a twisting hurricane.

'Smoke,' he answered. 'And it's rising from . . . Slave Island.'

The bay and harbour fronting the stone fortress on Slave Island was filled with boats, ships, feluccas, dhows, vessels as varied and crowded as they had been in Canton's busy harbour.

Signs of plunder were everywhere. Smoke billowed from the open gates, doors, windows. Slaves rushed back and forth from the fortress to the harbour yard, men and women shouting, crying, laughing, carrying furniture, bundles of cloth, spears, kettles, piling their booty in the yard, making heaps in small boats which would carry them to ships waiting in the harbour, or tossing objects haphazardly into the lapping surf.

The fortress was being ransacked, emptied and pillaged, by the slaves, and the sight shocked Billy and Andrew as they stepped ashore from their skiff.

Don Julio de Castenaldo, his foppish velvet clothing untouched by the rampage, wobbled towards them from down the rocky shoreline, waving his lace handkerchief, calling, 'Captain Peake! Captain Peake! See what I've done!'

Andrew angrily called, 'You did this?'

'*Si*' he jubilantly answered. 'I sailed back here immediately after you told me in Mombasa about white men held prisoner down in the dungeons. But there was nobody guarding this place! Hospodar was gone! His deputy was gone! Even Lady Iona was nowhere to be found! The only man left with any authority was some idiot Turk who stupidly opened the gates for me, and my *meteodores* – the Arab slave-runners who help me.'

Andrew, staring in bewilderment at the ragged, shouting stream of men and women, said. 'But this is total . . . confusion!'

'This is freedom, Captain Peake! Freedom for hundreds of men! Many slaves, of course, are nothing but common, filthy pigs. But I found men from the finest families in Naples . . . Seville . . . Barcelona . . . Venice . . .'

Andrew fumed, 'But many of these slaves are also Arab and Indian and African. They have no homes to go to. What will happen to them?'

Don Julio was unconcerned. 'If they are strong, they will survive.'

'Don't you realize, Don Julio,' Andrew shouted, 'that a free man is as wretched as a slave if he has no home to go to, no work, no food, no shelter?'

Don Julio motioned to the many different ships in the bay, saying, 'But there are boats sailing to many islands. The people will be spread out along the mainlaind and all the many islands, Captain Peake.'

'Cities and towns will turn them away!' Andrew looked at the men and women running with their newly found freedom, lamenting. 'But it is too late to do anything. Look. You have unleashed havoc for your own rewards.'

Billy stepped forward, saying, 'Enough about you freeing these slaves. What have you done with Jenny?'

Don Julio looked from Billy to Andrew. 'Jenny?'

Andrew explained, 'The English girl we discussed in Mombasa! The girl who sent you here to buy my brother!'

'Ah, yes! The English girl! The girl with red hair!'

Billy, glancing at the smoke pouring from the fortress, said, 'I hope for your sake she's not inside there.'

Don Julio looked nervously at Andrew, saying, 'Captain Peake, may I have a word with you?'

Billy shouted. 'No, Andrew! Don't give him another penny! He deserves nothing but a sound . . . flogging!'

Haughtily, Don Julio said, 'I do not want to speak about money!'

A voice called from behind Billy. 'Laddie boy!'

Billy turned and saw Brian Macpherson running across the rocky incline towards him.

'Laddie boy, there's been a revolt inside the castle!' We're all free! Free! It didn't take no musket to ransome me from slavery after all! This old man got out for . . . free!'

Macpherson, waving to his companions that he would soon catch up with them, reported, 'Laddie boy, those ships you see there in the harbour will be taking us where we want to go. I chose the island of Java. I hope to catch a boat rounding the Horn.'

Billy suggested, 'No, Macpherson. Go to the island next to Java. Go to Sumatra. There are other Scotsmen waiting there at Fort Marlborough. Tell them I sent you and they'll see you get in a crew sailing to America. Now, run!'

'Good luck to you and yours, laddie!' Macpherson called as he was swept along with the crowd. 'May the Good Lord bless and keep you!'

Turning back to Andrew, Billy saw that Don Julio was gone, that Andrew was standing alone on the rocky shore.

Andrew held a black string in his hand, staring down at a single black bead hanging from it.

Billy instantly recognized the bead, remembering what it had once meant, and instantly realized what the lone obsidian bead now was telling him.

He said, 'She's dead.'

Andrew nodded. 'I'm afraid so, old dog.'

The wind was rising, the smoke blowing thicker, more strongly from the fortress, across the harbour, out to sea, encircling the many ships and boats crammed with people, their voices, their happiness, their hopes carrying across the water.

Andrew and Billy remained sitting on the shore, Andrew repeating the story which Don Julio had told him, the story of how Jenny had given birth to a child in the Mombasa palace of the Sultan of Oman, how the Sultan had summoned an endless string of doctors, surgeons, even magicians, and witch-doctors called *hogans*, to help save her life. But when Jenny had finally died, the Sultan wept and promised Allah to give her child – a boy – a home forever in his palaces, to raise him as his own son.

Andrew tried to console Billy. 'Your Jenny died for a good reason, Billy. She died to give . . . life.'

Billy's shoulders were hunched forward; his voice, low and effortless. 'I wish you could have seen her, Andrew. She was just a tiny little thing. Like a sparrow.'

'Billy, I'll see your son.'

'Andrew, will you go back to Mombasa with me? To that palace? Now? I can't let that Sultan raise my son. The babe's mine. I want him. He's the only thing I've got of Jenny's in the world. He's ours. Hers and mine. Will you come with me, Andrew? Now? Please?'

Billy moved to stand, to leave immediately.

Andrew put his hand on Billy's shoulder. 'Hold on, old dog.'

Billy rested on the heels of his boots.

Andrew said, 'You know I'd go to the end of the world for you.'

Billy nodded. 'I know that.'

'And I'll go to Mombasa. But only on one condition.'

'What's that?'

That you bring your son back to Sumatra. At least temporarily. That you make Fort Marlborough your home. Till you get settled.'

Billy considered his older brother's stipulation, then asked, 'Does your other offer still hold? About trying to get me into your Navy?'

'Of course it does.'

'Do you think my little . . . mite will be embarrassed if

his pa, if his big lump of a pa is nothing but a . . . midshipman?'

Andrew tried to be cheerful, answering, ' "Little mite" would probably be very proud of "pa". Espcially if "pa" started to think of a better name for "little mite".'

Billy hung his head. 'I've already got one.'

'You have?'

He nodded. 'When Jenny and I were crossing Africa, she used to say she'd start worrying about me when she didn't hear me tramping behind her and singing . . . singing like some blue jay . . . I know Jenny would want our lad always to be happy and singing, too, and so I think . . . I think he should be called . . . Jay . . . little Jay Peake . . . son of Mr and Mrs . . .'

Billy faltered.

Andrew put his arm around him. 'Old dog, now–'

Billy shook his head. He could no longer speak.

'Steady now, old dog–'

Billy, clenching his stomach with both hands, bent forward, his chest heaving with deep gulps, torturous sound coming from deep within his body.

'Old dog. Please, don't–'

But Billy could not stop. He cried, gulping, twisting with the tears, feeling a pain jab through his chest. And in a rush, he felt innocence disappear from his heart, vanish like the whorls of smoke pouring from the stone fortress, being swept out to sea from Slave Island.

Fiction

☐	**Options**	Freda Bright	£1.50p
☐	**The Thirty-nine Steps**	John Buchan	£1.50p
☐	**Secret of Blackoaks**	Ashley Carter	£1.50p
☐	**Hercule Poirot's Christmas**	Agatha Christie	£1.50p
☐	**Dupe**	Liza Cody	£1.25p
☐	**Lovers and Gamblers**	Jackie Collins	£2.50p
☐	**Sphinx**	Robin Cook	£1.25p
☐	**Ragtime**	E. L. Doctorow	£1.50p
☐	**My Cousin Rachel**	Daphne du Maurier	£1.95p
☐	**Mr American**	George Macdonald Fraser	£2.25p
☐	**The Moneychangers**	Arthur Hailey	£2.50p
☐	**Secrets**	Unity Hall	£1.75p
☐	**Black Sheep**	Georgette Heyer	£1.75p
☐	**The Eagle Has Landed**	Jack Higgins	£1.95p
☐	**Sins of the Fathers**	Susan Howatch	£3.50p
☐	**The Master Sniper**	Stephen Hunter	£1.50p
☐	**Smiley's People**	John le Carré	£1.95p
☐	**To Kill a Mockingbird**	Harper Lee	£1.95p
☐	**Ghosts**	Ed McBain	£1.75p
☐	**Gone with the Wind**	Margaret Mitchell	£3.50p
☐	**Blood Oath**	David Morrell	£1.75p
☐	**Platinum Logic**	Tony Parsons	£1.75p
☐	**Wilt**	Tom Sharpe	£1.75p
☐	**Rage of Angels**	Sidney Sheldon	£1.95p
☐	**The Unborn**	David Shobin	£1.50p
☐	**A Town Like Alice**	Nevile Shute	£1.75p
☐	**A Falcon Flies**	Wilbur Smith	£2.50p
☐	**The Deep Well at Noon**	Jessica Stirling	£2.50p
☐	**The Ironmaster**	Jean Stubbs	£1.75p
☐	**The Music Makers**	E. V. Thompson	£1.95p

Non-fiction

☐	**Extraterrestrial Civilizations**	Isaac Asimov	£1.50p
☐	**Pregnancy**	Gordon Bourne	£3.50p
☐	**Jogging From Memory**	Rob Buckman	£1.25p
☐	**The 35mm Photographer's Handbook**	Julian Calder and John Garrett	£5.95p
☐	**Travellers' Britain**	Arthur Eperon	£2.95p
☐	**Travellers' Italy**	Arthur Eperon	£2.50p
☐	**The Complete Calorie Counter**	Eileen Fowler	80p